NO ONE
LEFT
TO TELL

By Jordan Dane

No One Left to Tell
No One Heard Her Scream

Coming Soon

No One Lives Forever

JORDAN DANE

NO ONE LEFT TO TELL

AVON

An Imprint of HarperCollinsPublishers

This is a work of fiction. Names, characters, places, and incidents are products of the author's imagination or are used fictitiously and are not to be construed as real. Any resemblance to actual events, locales, organizations, or persons, living or dead, is entirely coincidental.

AVON BOOKS
An Imprint of HarperCollins*Publishers*
10 East 53rd Street
New York, New York 10022-5299

To my grandparents—
Cosas Finas and Póg Mo Thóin—
In any language, these phrases
translate to love in my family.

Acknowledgments

For me, this book focused on family—a foundation we all share in one fashion or another. My grandfather Ignacio was the historian and writer in my family. I sometimes feel him with me guiding my hand, particularly with this story. But I feel others too. My grandmothers, Pearl and Hortense, both had green eyes like mine that sparkled with good humor. And according to my dad, he will always love me more than I love him. To him, home is wherever he's at. Can't argue with that. The latest news is that my mom has her own version of e-mail that's faster than bandwidth. It's called t-mail. She invented it. We're still working out the bugs. It seems that whatever news goes in, turns into something else by the time it's delivered via a quick phone call from her, but at least it happens fast. And don't get me started about the rest of my fam-damily. My zany relatives up north have taught me there's no subject matter off limits when it comes to poking fun. Believe me, we have tested the boundaries of good taste. And my sibs—Ed, Ignacio, Debbie, and Denise—had shaped my world growing up. One thing I can say with certainty: If I was bad, it was always their fault. If they think otherwise, let them write their own book. Simply put, we are all products of our life's experiences and those who have come before. Our own piece of immortality—or justification. And despite what I have previously stated, I feel blessed in that regard. You can quote me.

To the joy of my life, my husband and best friend John, words can't express how I feel. Surprising for an author, huh? Oftentimes, I don't know where I leave off and you begin. You are truly my better half.

Special thanks to Dana Taylor, who has always been a believer, even when I had my doubts. And to my dear friend Katie Kuhne, who always has my back. One day, Kates, we're gonna have to meet. And with every story comes plenty of research. For things I enhanced for the sake of fiction, no one is accountable except me. But for everything I got right, special gratitude to the police department of the City of Edmond, Oklahoma, for the training I received as part of the Citizen's Police Academy, a wonderful program conducted by Lieutenant Cleo Land, a role model and real life hero. (When he reads this, he'll blush as red as his hair.)

Last, but certainly not least, I'd like to express special thanks to my agent, Meredith Bernstein, for believing in my talent. And I'd also like to extend my heartfelt gratitude to my discerning editor, Lucia Macro, who took a chance on an unknown and still has a sense of humor about it.

CHAPTER 1

WAREHOUSE DISTRICT
SOUTH CHICAGO

On the trail of money, Mickey Blair sniffed out opportunity like most men chased skirts—one led to the other, but cash never got a headache. The piece of paper fluttered in his hand as a brisk wind caught its frayed edge. He scrolled it with spread fingers to read his own scribbling and looked up, squinting against the cold to verify the warehouse number. The place was a pit. He stuffed the crumpled paper into his overcoat. He'd hoped for better arrangements from his potential new client. The e-mail he'd received late yesterday had been cryptic, but he was confident the job would be simple and the money irresistible. The best kind of incentive. A glance at his Rolex assured him he wasn't late.

With the sun fading into the layers of dark clouds along the horizon, the bite in the air stung his cheeks. Large, wet flakes accumulated on the ground, defying the swirling gusts. With a sideways glance, he caught sight of his black Mercedes parked to the left. His latest toy. He'd soon have it stored for winter. Time to break out his SUV. His work provided a nice little nest egg. Images of white sand beaches filtered through the cold. The imagined scent of coconut teased his senses. He pictured grains of sand clinging to his dark skin slick from tropical oils. Before long, he'd be set for life.

Killing was a lucrative business.

Safely locked away until he needed it for a job, his custom-made Heckler & Koch sniper rifle had been a good investment. At his age, he had cultivated a dependable, discreet reputation over the years. Mickey enjoyed the best of both worlds—flying below the radar of law enforcement while reaping all the benefits of his deserved notoriety. The art of assassination provided him a life worth living. He loved irony, when it suited him. A smile influenced his swagger as he approached the side entrance to the building. His unfastened overcoat buffeted in the breeze. Instinctively, he felt for his gun, a SIG Sauer secured in its leather holster under his suit jacket.

After a tug at the metal door, he rubbed his palms together to wipe away the rust and dirt, careful not to soil his coat or Armani suit. Once inside, he shortened his breaths to lessen the intake of stale air and surveyed the carcass of the old deserted warehouse. But his next breath morphed into an instinctive gasp when the door slammed shut behind him. He turned and heard a key slip into the lock. The dead bolt slid into place. And he caught the distinct sound of someone running away. He yanked at the door, the filth of the cement floor crunching underfoot. Locked.

"What the hell?" he muttered under his breath, then called out, "This isn't funny, you sick bastard."

Slowly, he gaped over his shoulder into the cavernous space. In the split second his eyes oriented to the murky and cluttered interior, the lights went out. Complete darkness. His equilibrium distorted, he couldn't see his damned hand in front of his face. He raised his weapon, fingers tensed against the grip.

"If this is some kind of joke, someone's gonna get shot!" He raised his voice, covering his tension with attitude. "I don't have time for this."

"Make time." A low voice assumed familiarity. An echo disguised its origin. "I made time for you."

The sound mutated to a whisper, prickling his skin.

"Do I know you?" Mickey swallowed hard. His eyes searched the dark for anything at all. No answer. The man wasn't giving him a chance to locate his hiding spot, offering a target for his SIG Sauer.

A glimmer drew his attention. Heading toward the flicker of light, he felt his way along a barrier of varying height, stubbing the tips of his shoes. In no time, he lost his way. He couldn't tell where he had entered the old building.

Thud! Thwack! Two rounds hit his chest. A burst of liquid burned his nostrils. Vapor stung his eyes. Silenced gunfire? His hands reached for the sore spots under his suit, rubbing the welts. Anger got the better of him. He returned fire. Pointing his gun into the dark, he shot twice before thinking. Muzzle flash blinded him. Fingers pressed against his eyelids, he squeezed his eyes shut and listened to the ricochet.

"Who are you?" he shrieked. Spittle ran down his chin. Feeling like a cat with nine lives, he bristled with hostility. If the pellets had been real bullets, he would've been dead. "What kind of game are you playing here?"

The air was stagnating and thick. Sweat trickled from his brow, nearly blinding him with its sting. He leaned against something firm. All he needed was time to think. *God, think!*

"Who the hell are you people?" he shouted. More than one person hid in the dark. Strange animal noises erupted overhead. The muffled sound of laughter mocked his torment, his only reply.

Although he couldn't be certain, it appeared they were herding him through a maze of obstacles. They pounded him with pellets of some kind. The animal calls only got worse—clamoring all around him. Primal instinct kicked in and panic gripped him hard, squeezing his chest. Remembering to close his eyes, Mickey fired two shots, reminding them he would be dangerous up close.

"There's been a mistake. I was asked to come here. Some guy had a job for me," he cried, trying to reason with his faceless attackers.

What the hell had he done? The irony wasn't missed on him. Now the tables were turned. Normally the predator, this time he would be the hunted.

Blood boiled under the surface of his skin. He shrugged out of his overcoat and kicked it aside. Tugging at his tie, he pulled it over his head and hurled it into the dark, not caring where it landed. Only a week ago, he'd bought the designer tie, more impressed by its price tag. Now, he didn't give a rat's ass about any of it. His fingers slick with sweat, he yanked at the collar of his shirt. Buttons popped off onto the warehouse floor.

He squinted in every direction. Nothing but blackness. Emptiness magnified the sound of his heart. Another blast from above. Something slapped him hard. It burned the skin of his neck. He winced and shrugged a shoulder. An object stuck to his body, then slid under his collar and down the inside of his shirt. His fingers followed the path, but he gave up trying to find it.

"What the hell—? Jesus. What's *wrong* with you people?"

With these bastards tracking him in the dark, it meant only one thing. He had to find a hole to hide, unsure where that might be. Feeling his way on all fours, Mickey crawled to change positions. His fingers felt along a wall. But he didn't know if he'd be heading for the door or deeper into the maze. One way might be his salvation. The other would be certain death.

Thwack! A round hit above him. On instinct, he covered his head with an arm. *A damned sitting duck!*

No time for doubt. He had to move. Slowly, he stood and picked a direction to run, a hand out in front. He had trusted his luck for a lifetime. Surely, it wouldn't fail him now.

Thud! An explosion against the side of his temple sent swirls of blinding light through his head. His eyes on fire, they burned like acid. Chills of shock ran through him. When he slumped to the floor, his gun skittered across the cement, lost in the darkness.

Stunned, he needed only a moment to catch his breath. Only a moment. He pushed against the wall behind him, struggling clumsily to his feet. But a deathlike stillness seized him. A presence eased closer. Slowly, he turned his head, tears rolling down his cheeks. Someone was . . .

An arm gripped his chest, cradling him in the grasp of someone standing behind him. He smelled alcohol on the man's breath.

"You're mine now." The intimate whisper brushed by his ear. It shocked him. The familiarity sounded like it came from the lips of a lover. "Don't fight me."

For an instant, Mickey relaxed long enough to hope—maybe all this had been a mistake. Then he felt a sudden jerk.

Pain . . . searing pain!

Icy steel plunged into his throat, severing cartilage in its wake. A metallic taste filled his mouth. Its warmth sucked into his lungs, drowning him. Powerless to free himself, Mickey resisted the blackness with the only redemption possible. He imagined high tide with him adrift. He struggled for air, bobbing just beneath the ocean surface. The sun and blue sky warped with a swirling eddy. Mercifully, sounds of surf rolling to shore clouded the fear when his body began to convulse. Dizziness and a numbing chill finally seized him. And the pounding of his heart drained his ability to move at all.

Then a muffled gurgle dominated his senses—until there was nothing.

Euphoria swept through him with Blair's last breath. The man's body now hung limp in his arms. With a gloved hand, he reached for the night-vision goggles and tossed them to the floor. He filled his lungs with the coppery aroma of fresh blood. Closing his eyes, he released the body to fall hard to the cement. He'd used the ego of his prey as a weapon against him. His plan had worked. As he thought of Mickey Blair lying dead at his feet, only one thing came to mind.

"Death humbles you when nothing else can."

The sound of laughter dotted the dark landscape. His men rose from their positions, one by one. It had been a successful hunt. The contractor on this job would be pleased. With the overhead light crackling to life, shadows ebbed from the grisly tableau.

"Job well done, men." He raised his voice, relishing the attention. He stood amidst his men. Their applause and shouts fueled his adrenaline. "But it ain't over. Let's get this place cleaned up. We got a delivery to make. And we're on a tight schedule."

St. Sebastian's Chapel
Downtown Chicago

Father Antonio's footsteps echoed along the dimly lit corridor between the rectory and the chapel, accompanied by the soft rustle of his cassock. The nip of an early freeze bored through mortar and stone, intensifying the musty, dank smell of the old church. The change in season always challenged his patience.

"Holy Father, why do you torment me so? Have I not been a good servant?" The young cleric smiled. His feelings toward the first cold front had been cultivated from childhood. It had nothing to do with his vocation or his faith.

Arched windows lined the hall, offering a secluded view of the church cemetery. His heart sank at the sight of a dusting of snow that outlined headstones and crypts. Images of death, covered by an early winter, encouraged his reflective nature. And sparse lighting along the perimeter of the graveyard only marginally repelled the decaying gloom. He identified with the daunting struggle of light against dark—a symbolic reflection of his life's work. Without slowing his pace, he let his eyes drift from one window to the next as he walked through the dim passageway.

But tonight, a lone man caught his attention. Father Antonio stopped. His breath fogged the small glass pane.

"There you are, my friend. What demons have drawn you out on such a cold night?"

Bundled in a long dark coat, a man hunched against the cold under a pale light, his back turned toward the priest. His body cast a faint shadow in the mantle of snow. A gust of wind swirled white crystals at the man's feet, clinging to the hem of his overcoat. Despite having only a scant glimpse of him, Father Antonio knew his identity by the family tombstone.

Years ago, he'd investigated the gravesite to learn his name. With the man so reticent to talk, the cleric had succumbed to his mortal weakness of curiosity. He'd invaded the stranger's privacy by searching cemetery records and old newspaper stories at the library—a result of another long winter season with too much time on his hands.

"Come inside, where it's warm, my friend. Or do you relish the weather's punishment?" He understood the need for penitence.

It was the man's ritual to stand by the grave before he'd wander into the smaller chapel to sit in the last pew on the left. Always, the man would be rapt in his own contrition. But tonight, his observance changed. He turned to look directly at Father Antonio from across the burial ground. The man peered up through the murkiness of dusk. His eyes locked on to the priest.

Father Antonio gasped. He stepped back from the window, his reaction purely instinctive. With his heart battering his chest, he closed his eyes and filled his lungs. After a moment, he exhaled with deliberation to calm his panic.

"Not very charitable, Antonio," he muttered, shaking his head. Why would he react so strongly? But he knew the answer to that question the instant he examined his recoil.

The eyes of the man were haunting. Beyond the sadness the cleric expected to find, death shadowed the stranger. That fact tempered any further interest the priest had in him. Chastising himself for his weakness, Father Antonio forced his gaze into the graveyard once again. He wanted to redeem himself as a compassionate man. But the stranger had gone.

In that brief instant he'd ducked for cover, the man had vanished, leaving only faint impressions in the snow that he'd been there at all.

"Holy Father, give me strength," he pleaded, whispering for his own benefit. Glancing at his watch, he noticed it was after seven. Already late by his usual schedule. Now, he'd have to rush through prayer after this little delay.

Resuming his duties, he headed for the entrance to the auxiliary chapel. With the larger cathedral closed for restoration work, the smaller facility remained open to the public at this hour. Unlocking the breezeway door into the church, he was surprised to find the chamber dark. Light from the street filtered through the ornate stained-glass windows. Eerie hues of blue and red spilled across the floor, eclipsed by shadows of tree limbs tossed in the brisk winds off Lake Michigan. The stone walls of St. Sebastian's muffled the howl of the winter blast.

He expected the stranger to be seated in his usual spot at the back of the church, not sure how he'd handle the awkwardness of seeing him. A sense of relief came when he found the place dark and empty.

Allowing his eyes to get accustomed to the dark, he remained at the door. He listened to the sounds of a room he knew well. With the stillness, he presumed he was alone. But who had turned out the lights? Feeling his way in the dark, he found the control panel for the interior lighting.

"Let there be light," he commanded. Slowly, he turned the knobs for the fixtures along the walls. It would be all the light he'd need.

With barely a glance through the church, he set about his routine. Late-night confessions in this urban setting brought a variety of sinners to God's door. Over the years, Father Antonio had grown familiar with many of their faces, people who'd be invisible to others in the light of day.

Kneeling at the base of the crucifix, he closed his eyes to pray for his flock. It had become his nightly ritual before he'd slip into his confessional at the first sight of a sinner seeking absolution. The hush of the church graced his prayer, making it easy to lapse into the familiar. But a faint repetitive noise beckoned his awareness, detracting from his purpose.

A rhythmic patter summoned his consciousness.

A measured, tedious sound.

Being a resident of St. Sebastian's, he'd grown accustomed to rain finding its way through the worn roof of the rectory. But the chapel and its sacristy were another story. Opening his eyes, he caught sight of motion to his left. He spied the offending puddle. A dark, slick pool collected at the base of the crucifix. It bled through the spacing between the patterned tiles. Now, a metallic odor invaded his senses, mingling with the sweet aroma of incense. Nearly choking on his next breath, Father Antonio felt the chill of the empty chamber crawl along his flesh.

Inch by agonizing inch, his eyes trailed up the wall.

The beautiful porcelain face of Jesus Christ, forever frozen in his sacrifice upon the crucifix, had been replaced. Lifeless eyes stared down at him. Grotesquely twisted in death, a man's head dangled at an odd slant, contorted by a gaping wound across the throat. The body reflected the pale light of the church in its thin furrows of blood.

A muffled scream gained momentum, reverberating through the chapel. For a long while, Father Antonio hadn't realized the cry was his own.

Detective Raven Mackenzie spotted her partner, Tony Rodriguez, on the sidewalk outside St. Sebastian's on Erie Street. His silhouette was backlit by rotating beacons of red and blue from the police cars parked behind him. Captured by the streetlamps overhead, plumes of exhaust fumes drifted in vaporous clouds.

The flashing color should have been a deterrent to spectators, warning of police activity in the area. But every nutcase in the vicinity came to watch the show despite the weather, like there wasn't enough murder and mayhem conveniently available by clicking the TV remote at home. And the purveyors of bad news gathered like vultures. Huddled en masse, the media stood along the street, voices raised with questions, vying for attention. She studied the rank and file of expectant faces, well aware how cynical she'd become in the last two years since her assignment to Homicide as a new detective.

"Hell, you live closest. What took you so long, Mackenzie?" Rodriguez grinned, his words fogging the air.

Being on call, she had her evening interrupted by the chirp of her cell phone, the jaded voice of her partner on the other end of the line. She'd just popped in her

latest DVD acquisition and was chowing down on a
mega bowl of cereal. Nothing that couldn't be interrupted.

"Quit your whining, Rodriguez. Your wife would
probably love to get a whole five minutes out of you."

Irregular gusts whipped between the buildings,
gaining momentum. She walked beside him down the
sidewalk next to the main cathedral, heading for the
smaller church. The darkened stained glass encased in
stone brought back memories of an untainted childhood. But she hadn't seen the inside of a church in a
very long while. Somewhere along the way, real life had
severed the link.

"Yeah, yeah, yeah. I don't get any complaints in that
department, thank you very much." Raising an eyebrow, he badgered her. "At least I got a life, such as it
is."

"What are you talkin' about? I've got a life. I was
spending some quality time with Walt. Just started
the Platinum Edition of *The Lion King* before I was so
rudely interrupted."

Normally her penchant for classic animated Disney
had been a secret she kept all to herself. A ritual lovingly instigated between a father and daughter. But
Tony had found her *Cinderella* DVD on her coffee table
once, before she'd tidied up and shelved it in her small
media room, another eccentricity. Without the excuse
of having kids, or even a husband for that matter, she'd
been busted and had to fess up. So she'd been forced to
contend with his incessant ribbing ever since.

"Sorry. What can I say? It's all about the circle of life,
Raven." He shook his head and shrugged, gently bringing her back to the reality of their situation in Disney
lingo.

"*Hakuna matata*, my friend." She grimaced against the chill. "No worries."

The idle chitchat allowed her to prolong her sense of normality—in denial that she'd soon look into the glazed eyes of another victim, sharing the intimacy of death. But casual conversation at the scene hadn't always been a part of her demeanor. In her first few investigations, she had remained stone quiet when she crossed the yellow tape, the pit of her stomach wrenching with anxiety. Now, she and Tony talked about nothing, their humor masking something neither of them wanted to discuss. But she'd never learned how to rid herself of the twist in her gut. It came with the territory.

Out of habit, she felt for the CPD badge clipped to her jeans belt loop under her sweatshirt. She moved it to an outside pocket of her leather jacket. It would give her clearance through the yellow tape and beyond the line of uniformed police officers protecting the integrity of the crime scene.

"What do we have, Tony?" She pulled a small notepad and pen from her jacket, making a note of the date and time. Tugging at the bill of her ball cap, she continued toward the front steps of the chapel. "DB in a church? What a world, huh?"

"I don't know. Maybe dying in a church is like getting sick in a hospital. Could be worse, I guess."

A young officer held his hand up, but let them pass when she tapped her detective's badge and muttered in reflex, "Homicide." Then she indulged in the twisted banter only another cop would appreciate.

"Dead is dead, Tony. No matter how you slice it."

"Don't say slice, Mac. Trust me on that one."

Donning her game face, she walked through the main door, snapping on her latex gloves. Down the main aisle and to the left of the altar, lights were ablaze. Crime-scene investigators were already hard at work taking photos, dusting for prints, and bagging and tagging evidence. Staring at the wall to her left, she caught the macabre sight, barely aware she held her breath.

Flash. The split-second flare of a camera cast a sickly pallor onto the face of the dead man. *Flash . . . Flash.*

A man in a rumpled suit hung from a crucifix. His body covered the porcelain likeness of Jesus Christ, strapped in front of it with rope. As she looked at his suit, an odd thought found fertile ground in her mind. Dressing for work this morning, did the man deliberate on his choice of suit or contemplate his shirt color? *All of it . . . so pointless.* Raven's world had grown colorless, accented by varying shades of mortuary black. This same theme had infringed on her peace of mind more than once lately.

"You all right?" Tony reached for her elbow. His dark eyes centered on her, blocking out everyone else in the room.

"Yeah." She waved him off. "Just thinking about something else. It doesn't matter."

"There is nothing else, Mackenzie. For people in our line of work, it all begins when we cross the line. Remember that." He smiled faintly, falling into the role of her training officer once again. After she nodded, he turned and blended in with the others.

"It all begins when we cross the line," she repeated one of Tony's favorite sayings to reinforce the thought—getting her head back in the game.

But crossing the line for Tony meant the crime-scene barrier set in yellow tape. For Raven, it took on a more symbolic meaning. Crossing a line meant risk. And in taking that risk, change would be inevitable. Was she prepared for a change in her life? When she gazed around the room, a familiar thought gripped her.

"There's gotta be something else, Tony. At least, I hope so," she whispered as if in prayer. And St. Sebastian's was a good place for that.

Raven drew closer to her partner. She heard him give a directive to one of the beat cops. "Canvass the neighborhood. See if we can catch a break, find someone who caught some suspicious activity outside the chapel. You know this neighborhood best. Grab yourself a team."

The senior CSI, Scott Farrell, jutted his chin in greeting. "Hey, Raven."

"Hey, Scott. You just about ready to bring him down?" she asked as Tony joined them. Her gaze traveled up the wall following the rope that suspended the cross and the body. "Looks like a job for more than one person. What do you think, Tony?"

"Yeah, looks that way. Our priest over there says they haul the cross down for cleaning. That's the only reason it's not permanently attached to the wall. Without the DB, one person can break a sweat just with the crucifix. But with the added weight? Yeah, it's at least a two-person job," Tony replied, watching as two CSI techs strained to lower the body. "So we're looking for more than one suspect with no respect for the church. Two to hoist, but only one to do the carving."

Raven scribbled a note, then focused on the sign pinned to the dead man's shirt. The words were printed in ink. Safety pins fastened the scrolled message.

Seek the truth, Christian!

"No respect for the church, but what do you make of the sign?" she countered. "Religious fanatic?"

"Could be." Her partner sighed. "Zealots are the

worst to figure. Maybe digging into the vic's background will tell us something."

Looking over her shoulder to the priest sitting in a pew three rows back, she asked, "We got a witness?" Even from this distance, she saw the man shaking, his eyes avoiding the gruesome sight of the body being lowered.

"No. No such luck. That'd be way too easy," Tony replied, a look of compassion on his face. "That's Father Antonio. He found our DB and called in the nine-one-one. No sign of forced entry. The chapel is usually open at this hour."

Lowering his voice, he added, "The good father is pretty shook up. Once we get the body bagged and off the premises, we'll talk to him. See if he remembers anything new."

She studied the priest. Short, dark hair framed a full face with childlike eyes. Yet after what he'd seen tonight, she felt certain he'd be irreparably marred by his experience. When she started to turn away, he caught her eye for an instant. Raven understood the pain conveyed in that look. She wanted to smile, but couldn't bring herself to do it. A slow nod was all she managed, but it had an impact. The priest returned her gesture, then closed his eyes briefly before sinking into the pew.

"Easy now. Lay him down easy," Tony directed.

With the cross and body lying flat on the floor, a CSI team member snapped countless photos. Raven felt like an interloper into the dead man's final moments. The horrified expression on his face was frozen in time, immortalized as evidence by the camera.

Raven scrutinized the body and noticed something peculiar. "Where's his coat? On a night like this, he should've had a coat." Tilting her head, she tried to get a better look. "And his tie is missing. Expensive suit like that would have a tie."

"Good eye, Mackenzie." Tony nodded. "And the slice and dice with a knife might make it personal."

Once the cameraman left, Raven stepped closer to the body and directed her question to Farrell. "Shouldn't there be more blood? I mean, a wound like that?" Kneeling, she stared dispassionately into the mutilated face of the victim. Her training helped to obscure the horror, but she knew this would be one more image to keep her up nights. "There's no arterial spray, either."

"We'll know more after the autopsy, but yeah, it looks like this isn't the kill site. There'd be more splatter in the church if the cut were made here. And check this out, fresh drain over dried." Scott knelt by her, holding a pencil in his gloved hand. He pointed to the dried stains on the man's suit. "The minimal pooling we see at the base of the cross was probably only made when the body was first hoisted up. What little blood was left at that point. That'd be my guess for now. With the temp in the room, won't have anything definitive on time of death until the ME does the postmortem. But my best guess at this point is two to three hours."

Her partner narrowed his eyes and stared at the face of the dead man, pointing a gloved finger at his temple. "What's this? Looks like some kind of bruise."

The CSI man leaned closer. "'Bout the size of a nickel." Pulling back the shirt collar of the victim, he pointed out, "Looks like there's another contusion here, on his neck. Not prepared to give you an answer on that one. We'll know more from the ME."

"And what's that smell?" Tony asked, sniffing the air near the vic's face and clothes. "Something medicinal or chemical?"

Raven closed her eyes and inhaled, sensing the first thing out of order. "Alcohol. I smell rubbing alcohol." With another whiff, she added, "It's all over his suit."

"I'll run an analysis on that, skin and clothes," the CSI man offered. He gave direction to one of his techs. "No sign of defensive wounds, but let's get those hands bagged. We may get some trace under his nails."

"Robbery's not the motive. Check out his Rolex." Feeling for the man's wallet, Tony found it tucked in his breast pocket. "And he's still got his money and credit cards, but no gun in his holster. Guy might've used it, though." Directing his next comment to the CSI man, he asked, "What about gunshot residue? We'd better check for GSR on his hands. See if he fired it recently."

With the dead man's jacket open, her partner found an ID badge with photo clipped to his belt. "Our vic is Mickey Blair." Concern registered on his face when he looked at Raven. "And it looks like things just got more complicated."

Tony held the badge for her to see, and Raven sighed. "Well, how'd we get so lucky? We'd better let the chief know."

"Let me know what?" The booming voice of Chief Sanford Markham echoed down the aisle. With the press out front, the man never failed to take full advantage of a good photo op.

The tall, elegant black man walked toward them, dressed in a tux with a long wool coat and scarf buffeting in his wake. Raven always suspected the man had been born on Krypton, a distant relation to Superman with his x-ray vision and supernatural hearing. And now it would appear Chief Markham had a life outside the office, something she couldn't claim. In reflex, she stood at attention when he neared.

Tony had been slower to react, but quicker on his reply. "The man worked for Dunhill Corporation as security. Nothing like a high-profile murder investigation."

"This man might only be a foot soldier. Maybe it doesn't have to be high profile," Chief Markham contended, his eyes taking in every detail of the scene. "In fact, I insist on it. This type of case can get ugly fast. I want low profile with every *i* dotted and every *t* crossed."

"Everything by the book, yes, sir," Tony replied, with a glance toward Raven. "Like always."

"Not just 'by the book,' Detective. I know Fiona Dunhill. She can be a tough woman if she chooses to be, and politically well-connected."

"What are you suggesting, sir?" Tony's body stiffened.

"I'm not suggesting anything except to get the job done quickly, and with a little finesse, Detective Rodriguez. Make sure you cooperate with Mrs. Dunhill to the extent possible, without compromising the case. Do I make myself clear?"

"Yes, sir. Crystal." Tony waited for the man to turn and head toward the exit before he muttered, "Clear as mud."

"I heard that." Without missing a step, Chief Markham lifted his hand and shook a finger in admonishment. He kept walking, but bellowed over his shoulder, "And can you two dress a little more professionally when you talk to Fiona Dunhill? Quit taking fashion tips from Vice and Narcotics."

Raven's jaw dropped. She glared at the back of the chief's head as he left the chapel. Very uncharacteristic for a murder scene, a low rumble of laughter echoed through the room. It ended when she tried to catch the offenders. Even Father Antonio had been distracted enough to break his solemn expression with a faltering smile.

Tony only shrugged, checking out her attire. "Personally? I've always liked your taste in sweatshirts." With a grin, he tugged at the brim of her cap. "And your Cubs cap is way cool. A sure sign of a bleeding heart, always rooting for the underdog."

Her father's Cubs ball cap and her family home, a small bungalow on the fringes of the northern suburbs near Lincolnwood, northwest of Wrigley Field, had been part of her inheritance. Sergeant John Mackenzie had died in the line of duty fifteen years ago when she was nearly seventeen. With her mother dead just after her birth, she'd been practically raised by the Central Station House, without a female influence in her life. Coming from a long line of police officers, Raven had little choice but to pursue law enforcement as a career. It was a connection to her father—a bond they shared that transcended his death.

"You're not exactly Mr. GQ, Tony. Look at you." She fought to hide a smile. His Menudo concert T-shirt was his prized possession. She didn't have the heart to make fun of it. "I guess between the two of us, we're walking billboards."

"Don't be slammin' my tee. I love Menudo," he mumbled under his breath, hand over his heart in mock sincerity.

"I know, Tony." She indulged the man with a pat on his shoulder.

"Ricky Martin was in Menudo. Did you know that, Raven?" he whispered, adding a conspiratorial wink.

"Yes, Tony. And I'm livin' '*La Vida Loca*.'" She

nodded, humoring him. She made some final notes in her book, but couldn't resist a quick glance down at her attire.

She had to admit she'd been influenced by Tony's usual fashion choices. The man worked undercover and came from the ranks of Narcotics. And being called at all hours, Raven paid little attention to her work clothes. She usually pulled her dark hair into a quick ponytail and poked it through the back of a ball cap. If she needed to deliberate over a case, she'd usually turn the cap around, rally style. Her good-luck ritual. It helped her think more clearly.

Over the years, she'd sacrificed fashion for function, working in a male-dominated career. Wearing makeup and donning anything remotely feminine always drew unwanted attention. These days, her fashion accessories included her badge, handcuffs, cell phone, a nine-millimeter Glock tucked into her shoulder holster, and a .38 strapped to her ankle. Being a gear freak, like most cops, she ordered more equipment and clothing from Galls law enforcement Web site than she did from any hoity-toity fashion catalog.

"Come on. Back to work." Tony's voice summoned her. "You done here, Raven?" After a quick nod from her, he gave the order, "Go ahead. Bag him."

When the gurney rolled down the center aisle, with her partner following, Raven wandered toward Father Antonio and sat beside him. Someone had given him a cup of coffee. The Styrofoam cup shook in his hands every time he sipped.

"The caffeine will probably keep me up tonight, among other things." He raised the cup, but stopped and lowered it again, avoiding her eyes. "Sorry. I don't know what I'm saying anymore."

"It's okay, Father. I understand. I'm Detective Raven Mackenzie. And that's my partner, Detective Tony Rodriguez." She shook the hand he offered. Tony waved from a distance, then joined them. He sat in the pew in front.

"Tell me what happened, Father Antonio," she began.

"Not much to tell. I came here to take confession. Got to the chapel just after dusk, maybe a quarter after seven. I was running a little behind my schedule, so I wasn't paying much attention, I'm afraid. That's when I found . . ." His voice trailed off. He took another sip of coffee. The dark, steaming liquid quaked in his grip. With the cup now held in his lap, Raven stared down into the dark ripples of his coffee when he spoke.

"I was praying when I heard the dripping sound. I thought we had a roof leak in the chapel." He tried to find humor in his assumption, but his laughter sounded more like a choked sob.

With the priest's last remark, Raven found the eyes of her partner, to see if he'd caught the same thing. But his face was unreadable.

She persisted, "Did you see or hear anything out of the ordinary, Father?"

"It was dark," the priest replied. His eyes stared straight ahead, as if he were reliving the moment. "The chapel lights are usually on, but they weren't when I came in."

"And did you know the deceased, Father? Did he come to church here?" she asked.

"No. But I didn't—I couldn't look at him." The priest shook his head, struggling to block the memory.

"Can you think of anything else?" she prompted.

The young cleric shook his head, staring into his coffee cup.

"Well, if something comes to you, anything at all, call me. Even the smallest detail might help." Raven handed him her business card. Touching his arm, she got him to look her in the eye. "Be sure to get some help in dealing with this, Father. Don't try and do it on your own. Call me if you need a referral."

"Thank you, Detective. I appreciate your concern. I'll call if I think of anything."

Father Antonio stood and shook their hands. Two other priests escorted the young man back to the rectory. She and Tony watched him walk away.

"You thinkin' what I'm thinkin'?" She glanced toward her partner.

"Depends on if you're thinking Starbucks and a Krispy Kreme would taste pretty good right now and that you'd like to get home before midnight. But if you're thinking that, I'd say we been partners too long," he bantered. When she narrowed her eyes, giving her best sarcastic look, he asked for clarification. "Enlighten me."

"I was just thinking about that whole blood-dripping thing, and how he heard that. I think our good father had someone watching over him tonight." When Tony looked puzzled, she explained. "The vic's blood was still dripping. That means Father Antonio barely missed the killers making their renovation to St. Sebastian. I think that whatever made him late probably saved his life."

Raising his eyebrows in agreement, he pursed his lips and nodded. "Interesting observation, Mackenzie. Well, you know what they say? He works in mysterious ways."

"Maybe Father Antonio's guardian angel will bring us good luck." She punched Tony's arm affectionately. "Now let's go tackle some paperwork. With us talking to Fiona Dunhill tomorrow, I got a feeling a mountain of paper, stale coffee, and secondhand smoke from the bullpen is gonna seem like heaven."

Even though false bravado tempered her voice, she knew enough to worry. Money and power were a deadly combination in the wrong hands.

And Fiona Dunhill had both.

CHAPTER 2

DUNHILL ESTATE
SHOREVIEW HISTORIC DISTRICT

"Get a load of this place!" Tony gawked at the acres of pristine countryside. "They must have a riding mower."

"People like this don't get their kicks from wrangling the trusty Toro. They hire it done," Raven teased.

Her eyes on the rearview mirror, she made note of all the firepower carried by the armed guards at the imposing fortress at the front gate. Security personnel dressed in black uniforms commanded the precision of the military. Maybe more like well-paid mercenaries. But mission accomplished, the entrance to the Dunhill Estate was a battlement.

Yet once inside the grounds, she found the view spectacular, despite the cold gray morning. Age-old oaks were rooted to the fertile soil, the expanse of their branches giving an air of timelessness. Slowly negotiating the curves of the asphalt drive in her police-issue burgundy Crown Vic, Raven marveled at the grand estate looming on the horizon—a white colonnade of southern charm with the backdrop of Lake Michigan.

"This place is like a throwback to the late eighteen hundreds—and so close to the heart of Chicago. Amazing!" She widened her eyes in awe.

They pulled up to the front tiled steps. Raven suddenly felt intimidated by the size and opulence of the manor. Tony must have felt it, too. He squirmed in his seat, crooking a finger between his neck and shirt collar.

"I thought this clip-on tie wouldn't feel so tight around my neck, but my damned shirt collar is choking me."

Raven fought to hide her amusement. Apparently, there were no secrets between her and Tony if he admitted owning a clip-on tie, much less had the nerve to actually wear it.

"I know you're not comfortable, but you still look nice, partner." She grinned.

When he stopped his fidgeting and returned a smile, his dark eyes softened. She knew his pale blue oxford button-down didn't fit anymore. And admittedly, his brown herringbone sport jacket, with its dated elbow patches, should have remained hidden in the back of his closet. But Tony was her partner, for better or worse. Today just happened to tip the scales on the side of worse.

"You clean up good. But I miss your old man's Cubs hat." He winked.

Most of last night, she'd debated what she'd wear to the Dunhill mansion. Her navy pantsuit hid all her usual accessories of gun, badge, and handcuffs. So function won out. For fashion's sake, she left the ankle-strapped .38 in her locker at work. This hour of the morning, a massive shoot-out seemed unlikely at the posh estate. And with the welcoming committee out front, she'd be severely outgunned.

"Before we get in there, let's talk game plan, Raven. What did you find out about Fiona Dunhill?"

She shifted her weight in the front seat and turned to her partner. "From what I've researched, Dunhill Corporation doesn't fund all this grandeur. That's just a smokescreen. The real money came from the illegal arms trading of Charles Dunhill, the late husband of Fiona."

"Yeah, kinda remember him from the old days. To tell you the truth, I was kinda surprised a socialite like Fiona Dunhill would've taken over the business after her old man's murder. Crime families run by women are so rare, but I guess it's not unheard of," Tony reflected. He turned his gaze toward the front door. "And she's evidently doing a damned fine job of it."

"But she's still involved with that dirty little business, Tony. Or maybe she's just turned a blind eye to it." Furrowing her brow, she corrected herself. "Actually, from what I've read, she took that side of the business and went underground, laundering the dirty money with the legitimate end of her investments."

Raven's life had been about order and the law. So a woman like Fiona Dunhill didn't add up in her book. But she knew her partner would temper her strong tendency toward black and white. Tony was far more pragmatic, better able to tolerate the gray in their world.

"I'll give her this, the woman's a total contradiction. And she's pretty shrewd, not being caught and all. Hard to track that kind of money trail." He shook his head.

"So, what else do we want out of this visit?" Raven prompted.

"You heard the chief—quick and by the book. Kind of pie in the sky to think we can bring her down on all her illegal activities, no matter how tempting that might be. But we've got a murder to solve." Reaching for the door handle, Tony looked concerned. "I just hope she doesn't erect any major roadblocks."

Raven stepped from the car and slammed the door. She felt the thrill of the chase as she caught Tony's eye, but butterflies the size of vultures were cavorting in the pit of her stomach.

"Come on, partner. Game face on. We're crossing the line."

In the hallway of the second floor, Fiona gazed at her reflection in the ornate gold-framed mirror. The same dark green eyes stared back, but the intensity of youth was long gone. Or maybe her tired expression had more to do with the news she'd heard from the guards at the front gate. Two police detectives were now in the parlor, waiting for her.

"We are not punished for our sins, but by them," she muttered.

Short, auburn hair streaked with gray framed her face. Mindlessly, she tugged at its strands. Her once-flawless complexion looked pale in this light, without the blush of youth. She'd grown accustomed to the deepening lines on her face. But this morning, they were more pronounced and showed every one of her fifty-four years. While her socialite friends were being jabbed with syringes of Botox or scheduling discreet facelifts, she had been determined to live with every crease. She would accept her penance with grace.

"Time to face the music."

With her hand sliding along the banister, Fiona took her time coming down the steps. Her pale blue silk ensemble clung to her body. The fitted material made her feel manacled. She kept her eyes on the open door to the parlor, near the front entry. A young woman sat on the divan by the hearth. Her shoulder-length, jet-black hair reflected an aura of crimson with the fire crackling behind her. Even in profile, the young detective was most attractive. A dark-skinned man in khaki pants and brown sport coat paced in front of her, adjusting his tie and collar with a finger. At the base of the staircase, she raised her chin and drew back her shoulders, donning the persona of her public life.

"To what do I owe this pleasure, Detectives?" Fiona breezed into the room.

"Good morning, Mrs. Dunhill. I'm Detective Tony Rodriguez and this is Detective Raven Mackenzie." Both held their badges for her inspection. "We're investigating—"

"Before we get started, may I offer you coffee or tea?" she interrupted, with a casual smile. Without waiting for a reply, she turned toward her attendant standing inside the door. "Benjamin. Please bring in a coffee service and some pastry for our guests. I'll have my usual Earl Grey tea. Thank you."

When the manservant left the room, Fiona seated herself in a brocade wingback chair and adjusted her dress hem over her knees. Detective Rodriguez relaxed enough to sit next to his partner on the davenport. The warm glow of the fire flickered on their expectant faces.

"Sorry to interrupt. Please continue."

The male detective spoke. "I'm afraid I've got some

disturbing news. We're investigating a murder. And the victim was one of your security people, Mickey Blair. His body was found last night at St. Sebastian's, a local church in downtown Chicago."

She fought to keep the look of shock from her face, but she was certain she failed. She would have to do better.

"Mickey Blair, you say? In security?" Her voice cracked. She cleared her throat to disguise her mistake. "I'm not sure I recall the name, but I have a large number of people under my employ at Dunhill Corporation." As she suspected, her past had come calling, not a welcome visitor.

"We'll need access to Mr. Blair's duties and his personnel records, anything to give us a clear picture of him. Who can help with that type of information?" he asked, flipping open a notepad.

Detective Rodriguez commandeered the conversation, but the young female detective captured her interest. Raven Mackenzie sat, her eyes fixed on Fiona's every move. Even returning her stare, she couldn't shake the young woman's dark eyes. They hadn't faltered for an instant—unnerving. But intimidation would turn the tables.

"Dunhill records are confidential, and as for his duties, that is certainly off-limits."

For the first time, the young female detective spoke. "Why would you fight us on a murder investigation of one of your employees? Especially if you aren't familiar with the man or his duties, as you say."

Detective Mackenzie was too clever for her own good. Rigid in her chair, Fiona clenched her jaw and took a breath before speaking. A potential solution came to mind.

"Perhaps I didn't make myself clear. Certainly I would like to get to the bottom of this. But unless I can be assured you're working with one of my own people in this investigation, without limitation, then my full cooperation shall never be granted."

Turning two detectives loose to pry into her dealings with Mickey Blair was unthinkable. Without question, she trusted only one person to look out for her interests. Yet she couldn't picture him working with the police, under *any* circumstances. She'd have to do some pretty fast talking to convince him to do her bidding. And he'd have to set aside his animosity for law enforcement. But she knew he would be her only hope.

"A court order would be required, making your efforts an uphill battle. And the head of my security would conduct his own private investigation, completely autonomous to your endeavor." She kept her face stoic, a payoff from living a life in charge. "And I may not be in the mood to share."

An awkward void in conversation filled the room. Only the steady crackle of the blaze persisted. Fiona pressed, "Now that I've conveyed my meaning adequately, I assure you, it is far better to work in concert with me than against my wishes. So do we have ourselves a bargain?"

"Do we have a choice?" Detective Mackenzie's resentment was unmistakable.

"None, actually. I'm glad you've seen the light. I'm sure your delightful Chief Markham will be most happy. He and I have known one another for years." She reminded them of the political pressure she wielded.

Breaking the stalemate, Benjamin entered the room with a silver tray, setting down the coffee and tea service on the table in front of the detectives. "Is there anything else, madam?"

"Everything looks lovely, Benjamin. Thank you. Detectives, please. Join me." In a peace offering, Fiona extended her hand, then reached for her cup of tea. Detective Rodriguez poured some coffee, with his partner eventually following his lead.

"So who is our new comrade in arms?" Detective Mackenzie asked, stirring a spot of cream into her coffee. "And he'd better like long hours and lousy coffee. We can't use an eight-to-fiver."

"Christian Delacorte is head of Dunhill Security, and I can assure you he is strictly twenty-four/seven. I wouldn't have it any other way. He's more like family. And as for his cultivated taste in coffee, I'm sure you'll find he doesn't compromise."

"Great! Nothing like breaking in a rookie. So where can we find Juan Valdez, connoisseur of java?" The young woman's wit amused her partner. The man nearly choked on his coffee. But Fiona suspected her security head would find difficulty tolerating it. Especially given the fact Raven Mackenzie carried a badge.

"I am certain at this hour, Christian is working off some steam with his men. He won't be pleased with his new assignment. So I'll have to finesse his cooperation. Maybe even order him to work with you, if it comes to it."

Seeing a spark of hope in Detective Mackenzie's eye, Fiona interceded, "Before you ask the obvious, Detective. Let me clarify. If Christian chooses not to take this assignment, I won't force him. But you won't get my cooperation, either."

"But you're his boss. Ordering is what bosses do. Only they call it delegating or a paradigm shift in responsibility—whatever the new corporate buzzword," Raven asserted.

"Let's just say that Christian is his own man. And I trust him implicitly. He always has my best interest at heart. He's been a part of this family since he was a boy of ten. But you should be aware he has a past where law enforcement is concerned, I'm afraid."

"A criminal record?" The young woman's eyes flared.

"No, Detective, nothing so mundane. And I won't be talking out of school. Not about that. He is a deeply private man." Images of Christian emerged in Fiona's mind, flashes of him as a child and the man he'd grown to be. "You'll discover his nature soon enough. I've had the pleasure of getting to know him better over the past twenty-five years, and he's still a fascinating puzzle."

"You said he was blowing off steam. Where is he? The spa? The tennis court, maybe?"

Taking a sip of her tea, Fiona hid her enjoyment of Detective Mackenzie's assumption. She ignored the implication that Christian was a *kept man*.

"I shall escort you to the war room, so you can see how he amuses himself with a few of his men. Christian constructed it for his use, and named it appropriately. I have to warn you. He's not expecting you. I'll have to convince him to do my bidding. But I can be most persuasive."

"Yes, ma'am, we can attest to that." Detective Rodriguez nodded.

"Persevere, Detectives, and he'll cooperate when he's ready." Fiona stood, allowing them to set down their coffee cups. "Follow me."

"This way, Detectives." Mrs. Dunhill directed them with a wave of a hand. Her genteel voice echoed down the long corridor.

Oversized tapestries and ornately framed oil paintings adorned paneled walls on the second floor. Raven hadn't seen anything like it. The extravagance took her breath away, but the theme displayed in each piece disturbed her. Ancient battles and death were forever frozen in time. The art of warfare commemorated in exquisite colors and gilded frames, as in a museum.

"Charming. Who did the art selection? Attila the Hun?" Raven muttered to her partner, but her hostess must have heard.

"Christian selected each piece. Once you see the war room, you will understand completely. He has a sense of humor, albeit black as coal." Mrs. Dunhill had been reserved until now. But when the woman raised a corner of her lip into a quick show of cordiality, Raven got the distinct impression Christian Delacorte had earned her respect.

"After you." Their escort smiled and held a small door open to usher them inside. Built into the wall at the end of the hallway, the door's dimensions were dwarfed in comparison to the grandeur of the rest of the manor.

"Why do I feel like Alice looking down a rabbit hole?" Raven whispered as she stepped across the isolated portal.

"And Fiona Dunhill is beginning to look an awful lot like the Cheshire cat," Tony mused. "Minus the furry striped tail. I hope."

Once inside the strange room, Raven's eyes adjusted to the murkiness of dimmed recessed lighting. Steps descended along four rows of stadium-style seats. A focal point of the room was the wide window down front. And a cavernous antechamber lay below, just beyond the glass. A door on the left connected to stairs leading to the floor of the gymnasiumlike chamber. Raven saw the interior of the larger room strewn with barricades, hulls of old cars, and walls of sandbags, looking like a war-ravaged village.

"This is our observation room. Please take a seat in the front row, Detectives. It looks like we haven't missed much." Mrs. Dunhill's voice was mixed with pride and fascination.

Faint voices sounded on the overhead speakers within the confined space. Drawing her attention to the floor below, a group of uniformed men circled a shirtless man, clad only in his black uniform pants and military-style boots. The group seemed oblivious to their presence. One of the five men blindfolded the man in the center. With a hood placed over his head, he looked like he would face a firing squad, minus the last smoke. His tanned muscular torso glistened with sweat, but the others looked well-rested. Their uniforms were impeccably creased. What had this poor man been put through before she'd entered the room? He must have drawn the short straw and would pay for his bad luck.

Transmitted over the speakers above, a guard's voice penetrated the quiet space of the observation deck. "If you're ready, lights out."

After a nod from the hooded man, the overhead light extinguished. Blackness filled the large chamber. Raven couldn't see a thing below. Her hands tightened on the armrest. Edging forward, she peered through the dark.

"I'm turning out the lights here as well, but the glass is equipped for night vision. You'll be able to see everything, just like the guards. Only they'll be wearing night-vision goggles," Mrs. Dunhill explained. "The window is a mirror into the chamber. They can't see us, but we can see them."

The small space went pitch-black for only a second until the viewing window activated. Raven's eyes adjusted to the crimson glow cast into the room.

"Speaking of Disney, our new partner must be Goofy," Tony whispered for her alone. "The man's gotta be twisted. What sort of guy orders his men to go through this kind of abuse and calls it training?" He shook his head. "That poor hooded bastard is like a lamb bein' led to slaughter."

In awe, Raven's jaw dropped. Realizing what was about to happen, she spoke aloud, "What the hell is going on down there? Is he insane?"

"Most probably." Fiona spoke in a hushed tone. The pale red glow cast an eerie shadow on her face. "But watch. This is remarkable."

Equipped with night-vision headgear, the small army of five waged war against the hooded man. To Raven's utter astonishment, the guy going solo was the aggressor. Before any of the guards moved, one had been incapacitated by a spin kick to the gut. A quick jab followed, directed at the man's head. But the blow had been pulled up short to avoid injury. The guard doubled over. Gasping for air, he'd been taken out of play. The count was four to one. The fox eluded the hounds for now.

In their dark uniforms, the four remaining men nearly blended into the blackness. And the hooded man with dark pants looked headless—a fierce torso suspended in the gloom. Radiating the crimson of night vision, his body reflected a strange aura.

Being one to root for the underdog, Raven found herself pulling for the guy who should've been at a disadvantage. Edging closer to the window, she felt Tony doing the same.

The hounds circled the fox, coming in for the kill. Raven tensed, holding her breath. One man raised an odd-looking rifle to his shoulder and fired a round at the prey, narrowly missing his chest. A streak of color dribbled down the wall where he'd been standing. Anticipating the shot, the fox had rolled to his right and ducked for cover behind sandbags. But just as quickly, he prowled again, going after the man who fired the shot. The very weapon used on the offense gave away the guard's position—a deadly game of Marco Polo. Raven reminded herself that the guy was blindfolded. *How extraordinary!*

"Is this paintball?" she asked, keeping her eyes fixed below. "In the dark?"

"Christian adapted a variation of the game, adding the hood and blindfold." Fiona's voice was monotone, barely a whisper. The war game captivated the woman.

A loud groan erupted over the speaker. The fox took out another hound.

"And where is Christian? Watching from somewhere while this poor schlub gets nailed?" Tony scoffed.

"That poor schlub *is* Christian, Detective Rodriguez. Didn't I make that clear?" Raven heard the smile in the woman's voice. "He'd never expect this from his men. All he wants is for them to do their damnedest to take him out of the game."

Silence. Her partner caught her eye with a puzzled look.

"Anyone ever do that?" Tony's voice filled with admiration. He scooted forward to check out the action below.

"No. Not to my knowledge."

Mrs. Dunhill was proud of her head of security—a man who'd just used one of his guards as a shield for a paintball blast. With his forearm around the guard's throat, and a hand grappling the man's head, he could have easily broken his neck. But this was a training game and not about killing. The guard held up his hands in surrender. Delacorte had taken out three of the five hounds.

Raven narrowed her eyes into the blackness. *This was their new partner?* So much for treating him like a rookie on a murder investigation. This man wouldn't be fetching coffee or allowing them to fill his days with busywork. Yet the prospect of working with him intrigued her.

A marvel to watch in the dark, he felt his way without benefit of eyesight. The man reacted like a bat using sonar to navigate. His controlled and powerful movements were efficient, a predator on the prowl. Narrowly escaping one paintball round after another, Delacorte reacted on pure instinct.

"I got a feeling about our new partner," she whispered to Tony. "I think we just invited the fox to our henhouse. And his name is Colonel Sanders."

"I hear ya." Tony nodded. "Old-fashioned or extra crispy? Either way, we're fried."

Mrs. Dunhill's voice broke the eerie calm of the room. "I hate to interrupt his sport, but I'm sure you have work to do, a murder to solve."

The floor below grew quiet. On the hunt again, the fox searched for his next victim. Fiona Dunhill stepped forward, speaking into the intercom. Her voice echoed into the cavern. "Christian? We have guests. And I need to speak to you, please."

Slowly, the men stood and removed their headgear, but only after Christian capitulated by raising his hands. Lights gradually brightened and the guards dispersed. The war games were over.

After a furtive glance, she turned off the intercom to give Christian and her some privacy. "If you'll excuse me. I'll only be a moment." The older woman left the room and descended the stairs, looking unsettled for the first time today.

"Something we said?" Tony chided.

Yet Raven felt uneasy, strangely disappointed the match was at an end. Drawing closer to the viewing window, she nibbled at the inside of her lip, waiting. When Mrs. Dunhill approached the man left standing, he tugged at his black hood. Raven found herself eager to put a face to the name of Christian Delacorte.

Barely winded, Christian pulled off the black hood, then yanked the underlying blindfold to hang around his neck. His dark hair tousled, he ran fingers through the waves to straighten it. With a questioning look, he asked, "What's up, Fiona? What's so important?" Concern softened his usually solemn expression.

"Sorry to have interrupted you, Christian. But something has happened. I need your help." She watched his reaction.

"Anything. Just ask." Tossing the hood aside, he reached for a black T-shirt lying across a sandbag barricade. Ready to pull it over his head, he stopped when she reached for his arm.

"Don't be so quick to volunteer." She felt the warmth of his skin, slick with sweat. "I'll understand if you can't do as I ask. But I don't trust anyone else."

"That sounds ominous," he replied. His rich voice echoed in the war room. "Guess you better fill me in. Come on. I'll follow you upstairs."

"No. We can't go up just yet. I need to talk to you here, now."

Without pushing, he waited for her to speak. Christian's penetrating stare caught her by surprise. His gaze acted like a truth detector. Even in childhood, his eyes best captured his guarded nature. It hadn't always been so, but tragedy changed a person. She knew that from experience.

"Two homicide detectives are in the observation room. Mickey Blair got himself killed last night." Saying it aloud made her stomach twist. "His particular skills earned him business apart from his security work at Dunhill. And I'm afraid this work may have contributed to his death."

Christian narrowed his eyes, the sternness back in his expression. "What are you leaving out?"

At first, Fiona didn't know what to make of Mickey Blair's death. The man had seen the dark side of her nature and had kept her secret, true enough. But with him dead, there was no one left to tell. She might have felt a weight lifted off her shoulders, except for one thing. Someone else had pointed an accusing finger by stepping in the middle and killing Blair in the process. And that scared the hell out of her.

Christian waited for her answer. Revealing everything to him might cost her his devotion, so she tempered her candor with a gnarled fraction of the truth.

"In a past life, I did some things I'm not proud of. And Mickey was part of that life." Her throat clenched. A tear slid down her cheek. She turned her head, avoiding his stare.

"Did you have anything to do with—" He stopped. As he stepped closer, she heard his whisper. "Just tell me what to do. I'll protect you." His hand gently squeezed her shoulder.

His willingness to safeguard her interests, without

fully understanding the truth, touched her deeply. It re-assured her she'd chosen the right man to trust with her life. Turning, she looked him in the eye, speaking in a hushed tone.

"No. I didn't have him killed. At least, not in the way you might imagine."

"You're being so damned cryptic. How can I help if I don't understand."

"I need you to work with the police on their investi-gation. They've already agreed to—" She never got the chance to finish before he shot back.

"What? Why the hell would I—" Anger brought color to his cheeks. He pulled away from her, throwing his shirt to the floor. "You know how I feel about the damned police."

"And I wouldn't ask you to do this if it weren't my last option, Christian." She hated seeing his pain revis-ited. Every muscle in his body tensed with her cry for help. "I don't trust anyone else. Please."

"Damn it, Fiona!" He crossed his arms over his bare chest, his face tight with a grimace. After a long moment, he dropped his head and eased the tension in his muscles. "Damn it," he whispered. "What do you need me to do?"

Raven spotted another security camera following her every move in the observation room. The whole estate was overrun with red blinking eyes of the high-tech va-riety. Nudging her head in the direction of the surveil-lance equipment, she informed her partner.

"Looks like Big Brother is watching. They probably got cameras in the john. What do you think?"

"God, I hope not. I gotta use the facilities before we leave. If they got cameras in there, then my big secret will be out. Every woman in the greater Chicago area will be lookin' for some lovin' from Don Juan Rodriguez." He smirked, raising an eyebrow.

"Probably more like Speedy Gonzales. And it's amazing your ego fits in this room." She rolled her eyes, then turned to watch the drama unfolding in the war room. From this distance, she couldn't tell much about his looks, not having a clear view of his face. But it would appear java boy didn't like his new assignment, gauging by his anger. This was just fine by her. She didn't need a new partner. "Would love to be a fly on the wall down there."

"With your luck, you'd get swatted once the lights went out. The guy's deadly in the dark."

"Story of my life, partner." She shrugged.

Before Tony asked what she meant by that, her cell phone rang. Saved by the bell. She answered the call, "Mackenzie."

"Detective Mackenzie?" a soft voice called her name amidst the static of a bad connection.

"Father Antonio? Is that you?" Knitting her brow, she pressed a finger to her other ear. "I can barely hear you."

"Yes, it's me. You said to call if I remembered anything." The priest raised his voice.

Raven paced the floor trying to get better reception, but nothing helped. "Yeah, I did. Do you have something to add?"

Leaning against the viewing window, she plugged her ear tighter. From the corner of her eye, she caught movement down below. Mrs. Dunhill and Christian Delacorte were headed upstairs, with Mr. Security slipping a T-shirt over his head. With her so close to the glass, she was pleased she couldn't be seen from their side of the two-way mirror. But soon, her privacy would be gone.

"There was a man in the cemetery last night."

"You saw someone?" Hunching her shoulders, she tried to find a spot that gave her the least amount of static. Had she heard the priest right? Tony stepped closer, nearer the viewing window.

"Yes, well, sort of. But he didn't come to the chapel that night. He broke the pattern."

"What are you saying, Father?"

"I'm sorry, I'm not making any sense. Let me start over. I saw a man in the cemetery last night, just before I went to the chapel. Probably why I was late."

"Did you recognize the man, Father Antonio?" She heard hope in her voice. But the sound of footsteps on the stairs, outside the room, made her heart beat faster. "What did you see?"

"I didn't really see his face clearly, but I know who he is from researching his family's gravesite. I've got newspaper clippings, articles from when they died. I know who he is."

A shadow fell over her shoulder, eclipsing the light from the war room chamber. Slowly, she turned, coming face-to-face with—

Christian Delacorte stood on the stair landing outside the observation deck. His eyes lined directly with hers, as if he knew exactly where she stood on the other side of the two-way mirror. With only thin glass between them, his stare stole her breath like a thief.

Most women would find him strikingly handsome with his dark green eyes, strong jawline, and full lips. Raw sensuality. His physical size surprised her. Up close, his broad chest, muscular arms, and narrow hips dominated her. With his skin still flush from exertion, it seemed to radiate the same heat to her face, warming her cheeks. On a cold night in Chicago, the man could replace her space heater, hands down.

Yet a glacial hardness to his eyes shot chills down her spine—an electrifying sensation that closely resembled desire, in her book. The word "intimidating" came to mind. Dangerous. Yet it was more than that. His masculinity commanded her senses in every way. No doubt, this man could push all her buttons—even ones not in the instruction manual. But he wasn't a man to trifle with.

Nearly dropping the phone, she cleared her throat and finished her call. "That's good, Father. We'll be right over." Fumbling with her phone to disconnect the call, she couldn't take her eyes from Delacorte. His glare never wavered.

She whispered, "Can he see me, Tony? How the hell can he see me?"

"'Cause he ain't human, that's why. I think I seen this on *Buffy the Vampire Slayer.*"

Fiona Dunhill touched Christian on the arm in an apparent effort to stop him from playing his intimidation game. But before Cruella De Vil and Count Dracula joined her and Tony, Raven let her partner know what was going on.

"We've got a stop to make before we head back to the station house, Tony. Our priest may be a witness after all."

Fiona stepped into the observation room before him. His eyes adjusted to the dim lighting. Christian squinted, searching the room for—

"Detective Raven Mackenzie." A woman with dark hair stepped forward, extending her hand. Her dark eyes never flinched, even when he returned a glare. She spoke again, "And this is my partner, Detective Tony Rodriguez."

With only a brief glance down to her hand, he ignored the gesture and walked by her, totally neglecting the other man. He winced at the pain of a burgeoning headache. Today would be bad. He pressed a finger to his temple, hiding his discomfort.

"Sorry. I need to wash up." He knew that sounded lame, but he didn't give a damn.

His sweat gave him a pathetic excuse not to be more civil. Normally, he wouldn't care what they thought, but Fiona might. It was the best he could do with the war still raging in his head. His war games took a toll every time he indulged in them. But they were a compulsion he couldn't ignore. They had been his salvation—and his curse.

"Yeah, well—" The woman pointed a finger at him. "Nice meeting you, too."

Fiona broke the tension in the room. "Christian agreed to work with you. As we discussed, he's to be part of your investigative team, with all privileges. That's the only way you'll get my full cooperation. Do we have an understanding? Or shall I call Chief Markham and have him settle this?"

Christian turned back and eyed the female detective. He let his gaze take liberties. The rude behavior had been intended to intimidate the cop. But once he got started, the maneuver backfired. He liked what he saw. *Liked it a lot.*

Her shapely legs and the hint of an athletic build under her suit only conjured up distracting images of the bare skin underneath. And her jacket did little to disguise her full breasts. When she caught him staring, the woman crossed her arms and returned the gesture. He cocked an eyebrow.

Interesting . . . and gutsy.

Her piercing eyes nailed him, strafing his body with greedy interest. And apparently, she had no intention of backing down. She refused to be intimidated. *Yet another seductive quality.*

Her partner's voice interrupted their restrained skirmish.

"No, no need for that, Mrs. Dunhill. I think we understand one another." Detective Rodriguez stepped forward, placing himself in front of Raven to break the growing tension. Directing his next question, the detective sent a clear message for him to back off. "I'd say our next step is to set up a game plan. If you're free later this afternoon, say around three, I'd like to have you come to Central Station on South State Street to catch up on what we have so far. Does that work for you, Chris?"

With his deliberate and pointed use of the familiar nickname, Detective Rodriguez got the desired results. Slowly shifting his eyes, Christian refocused his attention toward the man. "The name's Delacorte. And if you'll give me some time to freshen up, I can come with you now."

Abruptly, the female detective interceded, "No, that won't be necessary. And like you said earlier, you need to wash up. An excellent idea." Her dark eyes full of attitude, she tilted her head. "Take your time. We have an errand to run. Three will be soon enough."

He ignored the obvious bum's rush she gave him, curious about the woman. But dark memories had already started to rise to the surface of his consciousness—a white noise that would escalate. He didn't have much time before the onslaught began.

"Raven. That's an unusual name."

"If you ask Tony here, he thinks it's because I come from a long line of Raven lunatics."

"I can see the family resemblance." He hurled the first volley across her bow, but didn't stick around to see the indignation he knew would be in her eyes. "See you at three."

Christian had to get out, unable to wait any longer. Leaving Fiona to deal with them, he stepped through the door into the second-floor hallway. His footsteps echoed in the corridor, then down the staircase. He headed for his quarters, a small cottage near the pool that had been closed for the season. All the while, his mind was adrift in the past. With war games fresh in his memory, the images blurred with his childhood terror, as they always did.

Not like always, Delacorte! This time is worse.

The flashes of memory came—wave after wave. Fiona's request must have instigated the intensity of his reaction. But he couldn't stop it. The violent images intruded on everything. Even in broad daylight, their assault clouded the familiar sight of his cottage.

Unending darkness escalated into suffocating fear. Torturous screams stabbed his memory, only drowned out by incessant gunfire and a painful ringing in his ears. And the feeling of being completely defenseless unleashed debilitating despair.

God, please. Not now!

Catching sight of the cottage, he quickened his steps and distracted himself with a recollection. As a boy, he'd been terrified of the dark after that night, when his life had been changed forever. But now, he found an odd sense of relief with the anonymity of it. It took him years to cultivate the feeling. But in doing so, he'd paid a price—isolating himself in his obsession.

Get a grip, Delacorte!

Closing his front door behind him, he shut his eyes and slowed his breathing. Clammy skin scurried chills across his chest. His demons were never far from the surface.

"God, Fiona. This time, you've asked too much."

Gray slush glistened on the road, plastering Raven's wheel wells with melted snow, dirt, and salt. The sun fought a losing battle, eventually covered by the on-slaught of dingy clouds. When she drove by the chapel, Raven caught sight of the yellow police tape whipping in the breeze. In the stark daylight, it served as a cruel reminder of what had taken place only last night. Children played on the sidewalk, yards from the barrier. The murder investigation, coupled with the renovations to the cathedral, left this neighborhood without its shining spiritual beacon. Another obligation tugged at her. She had to find the killer and restore balance to this community. Pulling into a parking spot in front of the rectory, she listened halfheartedly to Tony's advice.

"All I'm saying is, you better not push this guy too hard. He doesn't look like the kind of guy who'd take it well. He's dangerous, Raven."

"Yeah, I hear ya, partner." Killing the engine, she turned to him. "It's just that he got under my skin. And when people do that, I push."

"Don't I know that." He chuckled. After sliding out of the car, he slammed the door. "Hey, before we go in there, just wanted you to know I have no intention of sharing everything with our new partner from Transyl-vania. You and I are gonna sanitize that file. He's only gonna see what we want him to see. It's still our case."

"Glad to hear you say that, partner." She grinned and

tapped her fist to the top of her gray-splattered Crown Vic. "Now let's see what the priest has to say."

On the stoop, Raven pushed the doorbell, hearing the buzzer muffled behind the door. Father Antonio answered the chime. Eyes puffy from lack of sleep, the young priest looked older.

"Thank you for coming so quickly. Can I get you any hot tea or coffee? It's such a chilly day."

"I could use some coffee if it's made," Raven replied. Tony followed them, letting her establish rapport with the priest once again. A practiced maneuver. "You didn't get much sleep, huh?"

A fleeting smile flashed across the cleric's face. "No, not much. But it helped to pray. I didn't feel alone."

Knitting her brow, Raven wondered if it would be that easy. Could she erase the images of death with prayer? Or would her petition fall on deaf ears? A part of her didn't want to know the answer to that question.

"I brought the file from my room. It's on the table," he offered. He gestured around the small kitchen and break room. "Please, fix whatever you would like."

Raven quickly filled a mug with black coffee, forgoing her usual cream. She couldn't take her eyes from the manila folder on the table. Once at the table, she pulled out a chair and sat near the priest.

"So, tell me about what you saw last night, Father."

"When I was on my way to the chapel, I saw him at his family's gravesite. He comes here often."

"You said before that the man didn't follow the pattern. What did you mean by that?" she asked.

"I think he saw me watching him. That's probably why he didn't stay. The man's eyes. I have to admit it. He scares me." Father Antonio met her gaze, then clarified, "He usually goes to the cemetery, then comes into the smaller chapel. He never talks to anyone, just sits in the back pew. But last night, he—"

"He what, Father?" Tony edged closer. "What did he do?"

"He just—vanished."

Tony tilted his head, then smiled. "People don't just vanish, Father. With all due respect, were you nipping at the sacred chalice?" *Humor*—the great equalizer in Tony's book.

Father Antonio chuckled. "No, I can assure you I was not imbibing in wine, Detective. But the man didn't come into the chapel. He just left, I suppose. Like I said, the chapel was dark when I got there. Someone turned the lights out. All I know is that I saw this man in the cemetery before I found—"

Raven's gaze dropped to the manila folder placed before her. "And you said you know who this man is? You did research on him?"

"Yes. I hate to even admit it now, but I was curious about him. He was always so reticent to speak to me, so I . . ." His voice faded. Pushing the folder toward her, the priest added, "Take a look for yourself."

Raven opened the folder, finding countless newspaper clippings and other documents in the file. But one name she recognized.

"Are you sure about this, Father?" After Father Antonio nodded, she looked across at her partner. "You're not gonna believe this, Tony."

CHAPTER 3

Raven pulled at the collar of her coat to fend off the chill. She still held the file Father Antonio had given her. With Tony at her side, she stood within the wrought-iron gates of St. Sebastian's cemetery—her eyes upon the headstone marked *Delacorte*. Roses wilted by the freeze lay abandoned at the base of the stone jutting from the ground. And the floral offering eclipsed a marker for a child. A tribute of a weathered cloth doll lay against the monument. Christian Delacorte's parents and younger sister had been killed on the same date, according to the headstone.

And the newspaper clippings in Father Antonio's file told little of how a ten-year-old boy had escaped the same fate.

"You know how I feel about coincidences, Raven." Tony's voice drew her back. "Delacorte was here last night."

"Not to play devil's advocate, partner, but the priest didn't exactly get a good look at him." Looking back over her shoulder, she turned toward the breezeway windows to the right. "Not from this distance—and in the dark with snow falling? He won't make a credible witness."

"Maybe we just see what Delacorte says about it. We'll get a shot at him this afternoon at three. We pretend to catch him up on the case, then turn it into a subtle interrogation. You up for the challenge of one-on-one with Mr. Freeze?"

"I don't want to hog all the fun. Why one-on-one?"

"Just seeing the way you got to him at the Dunhills'. If anyone can get Delacorte to talk, it'll be you." With caution in his voice, he added, "Be careful with this guy. If he's dirty and you push the wrong button, he could be real dangerous. But I'll be in the next room, watching his every move."

Raven wasn't sure if Tony didn't have that backward. Christian Delacorte slipped his way under her skin without effort. She would've preferred to pass on round two with him, especially with her shrewd partner watching behind a two-way mirror.

"Not sure I agree with your take on it. But if we're gonna do this thing, we'd better run a background check on Delacorte. I gotta have more ammunition on this guy."

"Agreed," he replied. Her partner turned to head back to the car, then glanced over his shoulder. "Let's get out of here. Place gives me the creeps." He wandered away, muttering, "Which is ironic considering what I do."

But Raven found herself rooted at the grave, wondering what drew Delacorte back here, time after time. Images of her father's funeral flashed in her mind. Even though he'd been taken from her by an act of violence, she hadn't witnessed his death. Her memories were grounded by a father's love. Yet in contrast, what monsters lurked in Delacorte's past? Only a young boy, he'd seen everything, according to the newspapers. She couldn't imagine such horror. Some of the articles in the priest's file alluded to a bungled police raid by crooked cops. Nothing proven.

She now understood Christian's resentment toward law enforcement—even if it did hit close to home. And to compound the outrage, his desire for retribution couldn't be directed at anyone in particular. Charges were never filed. She had no doubt he believed a massive cover-up had robbed him of justice. No wonder he bristled with hostility to the badge.

Despite feeling a connection to this man, she had to remain objective in her investigation. If he had killed Mickey Blair for a reason they'd yet to uncover, she must be able to see it and act upon the evidence. Her sense of duty bound her to that pledge.

But something gnawed at her gut. Nothing about this case looked simple. And with Christian Delacorte involved, she had the feeling things were going to get complicated.

The smell of fast food came from her wastepaper basket, providing a necessary alternative to the ever-present odors of cigarette smoke and stale afternoon coffee that permeated the bullpen of desks across the homicide department. Someone had left a nearly empty coffeepot on the burner. The stench lingered heavy in the air, challenging her ability to block it out.

Reading over the file on Delacorte, she was lulled by the usual background noise. Ringing phones, the never-ending sounds a metal desk makes, and idle sports diatribes in low male voices. From various searches, she uncovered that Delacorte had graduated with honors from the business school of the University of Chicago with an MBA and a minor in computer sciences. He had also received training from the FBI SWAT school in Denver and had achieved expertise in hand-to-hand combat, handguns, executive protection, and high-speed driving—all the credentials of a security specialist.

But his unique training method in the dark seemed highly unusual, almost a personal fixation. Raven made a note in the margin of a page. The thought steeped in her brain as she tapped the eraser of her pencil against the file.

Overall, he was squeaky clean. Certainly, nothing implicated him as a killer. The chief wanted a briefing on the investigation by the end of the day. And they didn't have much to report.

"You know, after we checked out Blair's apartment, I kept thinking we missed something," she muttered, looking up from the manila folder. "We found an SUV in his garage, but the man struck me as a guy with more extravagant taste in vehicles, so I checked DMV. His Mercedes was AWOL. I issued an APB on it. Maybe something will turn up."

"Yeah, good idea. It's shaping up to be a long day. After Delacorte, we talk to the ME, then update the chief. He'll wanna know about the autopsy report before his press conference at six." He knitted his brow. "Want a cup of coffee? I'm buying."

"Very generous of you, Rodriguez, considering this swill is closely related to toxic waste. They wouldn't dare charge for it. Maybe we should analyze the stuff in the forensics lab." She shook her head, declining his offer.

"Not a good idea, Mac. In this case, I'm a firm believer that ignorance is bliss."

Before making the trip to the break room, Tony called home to let his wife, Yolanda, know he'd be late. The sound of Spanish spoken softly into the phone had grown familiar. She'd even begun to pick up a word or two. After hanging up the phone, he reached for his wallet.

"Five bucks says he's late. You gonna take that bet?" Tony taunted her with money. He waved it under her nose and dropped it on her desk as he walked by. "Guy's got a lot of attitude."

When he returned, sipping his coffee, Raven replied, "Yeah, I'm gonna take that bet. I got five that says he won't be late. Let's synchronize our watches. Six till three."

"No, nothing doing. We use the bullpen clock, and according to that, he's got three minutes to—"

Before Tony finished, the desk sergeant stuck his head through an open door. "Hey, Mackenzie and Rodriguez. Got a man by the name of Delacorte asking for you two. What shall I do with him?"

"We'll come get him." She smiled, then stood and pocketed Tony's five-dollar bill. "Aha! You shouldn't be placing any bets today. That clip-on tie is bad luck."

"I think you're right. Wish I'd thought of that." He yanked the tie from his shirt collar and tossed it onto his desktop, then unbuttoned his shirt. "Not sure I've ever heard when a clip-on tie brought any other kind of luck."

With a sly look, Tony asked, "Hey, wanna bet the vampire Lestat has never owned a clip-on? Give me a chance to get my money back?" After she graced him with only a raised eyebrow, he whined, "Come on, Raven. Where's your sense of fair play?"

Christian Delacorte would have stood out in any crowd, but amidst the tangle of street riffraff lining the hallway by the front desk, the man looked terribly out of place. Yet he didn't flaunt his difference. Hands in the pants pockets of an elegant charcoal-gray suit with black turtleneck sweater, he stared out a nearby window onto a harbor pier on Lake Michigan, lost in thought. The man looked good enough to eat with a very small spoon. But such a trivial analogy didn't fit Delacorte. He deserved *better*.

Alone in a crowd, he wasn't part of the world she knew. And as Raven stepped toward him, she caught the subtle fragrance of his cologne, another distinction from the smell of sweat and desperation in the waiting area.

"Guess after your shower, you're willing to accept a proper greeting." Extending her hand to force the issue, she kept her eyes on him. "Hi, I'm Detective Raven Mackenzie."

He turned and glanced down at her hand. She wasn't sure he'd reciprocate, but slowly he acquiesced. A firm grip.

"Can we get started?" The man was all business.

Tony raised his fingers in a wave. "Hey, how's it going? We got ourselves a room to talk. It's up on two. Raven will take you there. Can I get you some coffee? I'll brew a fresh pot."

Delacorte glared at them both, probably wondering if the coffee was laced with strychnine. Raven knew their brew didn't need poison to be considered downright lethal. But the man eventually accepted the offer.

"Yeah, make it black."

As Tony disappeared among the throng of people, Raven escorted Delacorte to the elevators. After she punched two on the elevator panel, they were hoisted to the second floor. Glancing to her right, she caught his reflection in the dull metal doors. *Those eyes*. She remembered her visit to St. Sebastian's cemetery, seeing the name *Delacorte* chiseled in stone. The man's past reflected in his eyes now. Then again, maybe she read too much into him.

When they reached their destination, the doors opened. Out of reflex, Raven touched his elbow to direct him to the interrogation room. An innocent gesture. But the intensity of his stare took her aback. Her reaction had been tangible—like an electrical shock to the heart. *Damn it all. Control yourself, Mackenzie.*

"This way." She swallowed hard. "We've got number four."

Delacorte held out his hand, indicating she take the lead. Still, he hadn't said a word since the first floor. His effortless sensuality unnerved her. *Only one way to combat that.*

"You know, if you've lost your voice, maybe we should stop off on three. File a report."

Her sarcasm earned her continued silence on his part, but for an instant, she thought she saw a spark of humor in his eyes. His expression softened for a second. It caught her by surprise.

Aha! Score one for the Raven lunatic. She basked in the glow of her small victory. More than likely, wishful thinking tainted her perception. She'd love to melt his icy veneer to see what lay beneath. Then again, maybe his true nature would leave her wishing she'd left well enough alone. The thought of him with his guard down sent shivers across her skin. She couldn't remember the last time she'd felt like this. *It scared the hell out of her!*

He allowed her to enter the room first, but his eyes were immediately drawn to the table strewn with photographic evidence. Raven was eager to see his reaction after they'd staged it for that purpose. And if he didn't recognize the church, she would ask him point-blank about the significance of the location. But his reaction had been anticlimactic. If Delacorte had been shocked by the graphic nature of the scenes, he never let on. His expression remained poised and unreadable as he sat in one of the chairs.

"The body was found in the small chapel at St. Sebastian's." She hesitated, allowing him time to react. Her eyes held firm, watching for a change in his body language. But the man looked unflappable as he thumbed through the photos.

"Was Mickey religious?" she finally asked.

A low chuckle escaped his chest, sounding more like he'd cleared his throat. "The only thing Mickey revered was the almighty dollar." Raising his gaze, he added, "And himself."

"Dunhill must pay pretty well. His apartment's nicely furnished and his clothes cost more than I'll make in a lifetime." She sat in the chair across from him. Her eyes never left his.

"That sounds like you're insinuating something, Detective." A thin smile appeared, then vanished. "Tomorrow morning, eight sharp at the Dunhill Tower on Michigan, ask for me. I trust you can detect your way there. I've got you set up with the Human Resources Department. They've been instructed to give you all that you need on Mickey Blair."

As if he'd heard a sound, he raised his head toward the large picture mirror along the far wall. Staring beyond his image reflected in the glass, Christian shifted his focus. Raven knew Tony stood in the next room, watching. Uncanny; the man seemed to sense her partner's presence.

"We'll want to see his office, too." Her voice rose a notch, echoing in the small room as she tried to distract him. "And any other place he might have personal effects."

"I'd anticipated that." He stood and stepped toward the glass, then turned abruptly to face her, leaning his back on the mirror with his arms folded across his chest. "You'll get what you need."

Raven believed in a strong offense when everything else failed. Time to be direct.

"St. Sebastian's. Are you acquainted with the church?" She stood and stepped toward the man, mimicking his stance, standing a safe distance from him. "It's quite charming, a historical area of Chicago."

A long moment passed. Silence. His face changed almost imperceptibly. Then a lazy smile curved his lips. She found her eyes drawn to those lips—like a damned moth to a proverbial flame.

"You're fishing, Detective, and without a license. I came here in the spirit of cooperation. You and your partner in there have turned this into an interrogation." Without a glance over his shoulder, he rapped on the mirror twice, a signal for Tony to quit playing games. "Am I a suspect?"

Before she answered, the door opened, with her partner holding a cup of coffee. "Took a little longer than I figured. Sorry."

Raven commended Tony's effort, but by the look on Delacorte's face, he wasn't buying any of it. Ignoring her partner's poor acting, the Dunhill Security man offered more.

"I was at the cemetery that night. But I think you know that. And I'm not in the mood to share anything more on the subject. So if you're gonna book me, then let's do it. I'd like time to call my attorney so I can make it out by dinnertime. Otherwise, I'm out of here."

His jaw clenched, and the look in his eyes dropped the temperature in the room. Christian pushed by her, but stopped when she placed her hand on his chest and raised her voice.

"Hold it."

She tried pushing him back to a comfortable distance, but he wouldn't budge. The man's chest felt as solid as a brick wall. And he wielded his gaze like a weapon. Reluctantly, she withdrew her hand.

"Okay then. You like cards on the table, let's do it."

She persisted as her blood churned. "What do you think about the message on the body? I didn't figure Mickey for a religious fanatic, not after seeing his criminal record. So my next leap was to assume the message had been intended *for* someone. And lo and behold, we meet you, Christian. Now that's what I call too much coincidence. *Seek the truth, Christian.* What does it mean?"

"I have no idea," he replied. "But I think you'll have to agree, it's not likely I'd kill the man, then sign my own work, directing the police to my door." He remained calm, staring at her and completely ignoring her partner. "Am I free to go?"

Closing her eyes, she filled her lungs, then let out a breath. *Calm down, Mackenzie.* He was right, of course. Still, she needed to make another point.

"We've granted you some privileges with regard to this investigation, in exchange for the complete cooperation of your employer. We could have subpoenaed the information we needed and left you out in the cold, yet we extended Mrs. Dunhill a special courtesy. Cooperation is a two-way street, Delacorte. I get the distinct impression you're holding out on me."

Raven knew she was posturing, having no intention of allowing him into the investigation completely. But what he didn't know would be no skin off her nose.

His eyes narrowed. She felt him harness his emotion, his hostility given away only by the slight stiffening of his jaw. In a move she hadn't anticipated, he stepped toward her, closing a gap already too awkward. Instinctively, she sucked in a breath and held it, filling her senses with the subtle cologne that tempered his act of intimidation.

"The police will get all the cooperation deserved, Detective." His voice low, he embellished his message. "I'll make sure of it."

Raven heard his underlying meaning clearly. A line had been drawn in the sand of mutual cooperation. Christian Delacorte had no intention of cooperating. She saw it in those captivating eyes. He'd conduct his own investigation, sharing only meaningless information under the guise of collaboration. He'd race ahead, outpacing her and Tony. And with the resources of Dunhill behind him, it would be an uphill battle to fight him.

Before she admitted defeat, her partner relieved the tension in the cramped room. "But don't you want your coffee? I brewed it myself." Tony held it out to Christian. "The city's finest."

"That's what I'm afraid of." Green eyes glared at Tony. "Some other time." Turning his attention back to her, he added, "Eight sharp, tomorrow. Coffee will be on me."

After Delacorte left, Tony closed the door, lowering his voice. "That's one cool hombre. If he's our guy, it's gonna be tough to nail him. But I admire your grit, girl."

"I don't know, Tony. I don't like him for this. He's not our guy. But my gut tells me he knows something. It's in his eyes."

"Yeah, maybe. And off the record, you may not like him for the murder, but you like him fine otherwise." He grinned.

"What the hell are you talking about? He's a suspect in a murder investigation. I'd have to be pretty hard up to—"

Seeing his insufferable enjoyment, Raven stopped her flimsy justification and thumped him on the shoulder with a finger.

"Next you'll accuse me of cruising the mug books."

"Hey, not a bad idea. For my sister-in-law, that'd be a step up." He chuckled. "Protest all you want, Mackenzie, but a partner knows such things. You just got this soft feminine thing going on, in between all the chest butting and bullying you tried on him. Personally, I found it charming. Would've worked on me, if I was single and into women with handcuffs."

Walking out the door at her heels, he poked fun at himself—a full-time job. "Now I'm just an old married guy into women with handcuffs. There's a big difference."

Damn it! Her partner was a perceptive son of a gun. An endearing yet lethal quality when directed her way.

"Yeah, well, enough of that. Come on. We've got a medical examiner waiting."

Something had indeed just happened between her and Delacorte. And she hadn't been prepared for it. Next time, she would be.

Christian's mind reeled as he rode down the elevator. It'd taken all his discipline to keep his reaction to a minimum. Who the hell had killed Blair, leaving a clear message to him?

Seek the truth about what?

Fiona had kept something from him. He felt it as sure as his heart beat in his chest. But he knew the woman. It wouldn't be easy to persuade his surrogate mother to reveal her secret.

And the point Detective Mackenzie had made about Blair's expensive taste hit home, too. He wondered about it himself, having special insight into the man's earnings as his boss. Walking out the front door of the police station, he welcomed the chill. The cold kept him on edge and sharp.

Heading for the parking garage, he made a decision. He would confront Fiona, throwing himself on her mercy. Giving her the benefit of the doubt, he felt certain she had no idea of the personal message directed at him, pinned to Blair's corpse.

Fiona had asked for his help in serving as the Dunhill liaison with the police, to be her eyes and ears in the investigation. He owed Fiona so much more than his loyalty. Perhaps it would make a difference if she knew he was nearly accused of the crime himself. That dark-haired detective with the fierce eyes looked like she'd rather lock him up and throw away the key.

One thing was certain. He'd conduct his own investigation. And he wasn't about to share anything with the damned police.

The naked body of Mickey Blair lay on a gurney pulled up to a sink, a sheet covering the lower extremity of the torso. No matter how many times Raven had observed an autopsy, she never got used to it. Medicinal odors mixed with the smell of death—a tang that triggered her worst memories. Long ago, she'd forced herself to get over the feeling that each victim's privacy had been invaded. Hell, in Blair's case, being sliced across the throat was the ultimate invasion.

Suited in surgical gowns, gloves, and masks with shields attached, Chief Medical Examiner Lucy Chapman and CSI Scott Farrell huddled over the corpse. A lab tech reviewed paperwork on a clipboard and labeled test tubes.

With a surgical gown draped loosely over her street clothes, Raven accompanied Tony into the room, slipping on latex gloves. Tony's voice echoed in the chamber. "We got a meeting with the chief in a half hour. Just wanted to see what you got so far. I know you've barely started."

"Actually, we found something interesting. It's not much, but it might give you a lead." Dr. Chapman spoke in monotone, with the composure of a CPA poring over a tedious tax return.

Raven admired her professionalism. Without any apparent emotion, the woman stood over Mickey with his gaping throat and shocked expression fixed at the time of his death. But under this light, Raven found it hard to dismiss the man's terror.

"When we removed his clothing, we found that pellet," the doctor explained. She pointed to a small plastic capsule bagged on a nearby counter. Raven bent to get a closer look at the evidence.

The medical examiner continued, "You'll need to confirm my suspicions, but one of my techs was familiar with that type of pellet. He says he's seen it used for paintball. Are you familiar with the game?"

Raven's stomach lurched. She knew what Tony would be thinking. She'd been trained to remain objective during an investigation, yet she found herself blinded to Delacorte's possible involvement. Blame it on her cop gut instinct—or had Christian tainted that, too? *Damn it!* With her eyes focused on the body, she fought to keep the emotion from her face.

"Yeah, just saw it played as a matter of fact." Her tone steady, she stepped back to the table, catching the eye of her partner. "But why wasn't the man plastered with paint? Wouldn't it have been on his clothes?"

"Good question, Detective. You're right, but not if the pellet had been filled with rubbing alcohol. It seems paintball pellets can be purchased separately. Filled by the buyer." The CSI man offered his opinion. "With rubbing alcohol, the sting of the pellet would be multiplied as it pummeled the body. It would explain the bruising."

Pointing to the man's temple and neck, Scott added, "He's got dark abrasions here from direct hits. See the breaks in the skin. His chest has only faint markings of impact, maybe lessened by his clothing. Still, it would have stung like hell, to be blasted with something like that. One of the pellets dropped into his shirt. We were lucky to find it."

"So we're looking for a sick bastard with a twisted game of paintball." Tony glanced at Raven with a grimace that spoke volumes. She knew Christian would be back at the top of her partner's suspect list. "Anything else?" he asked.

"Yeah. We've had a couple of other cases under a similar MO. Two homeless guys. Maybe a practice run using people that wouldn't be missed? The MO is too unique not to be connected. It's a theory." Scott offered his opinion with a clinical shrug. "And as you remember, his tie and coat were missing. Didn't find his tie stuck in a pocket, so those items are still gone. And buttons were torn from his shirt. You might get lucky and find them at the murder scene, if you find it."

"You still think he was killed elsewhere?" Tony confirmed.

"Given the blood evidence, I'd say yes. He was killed somewhere else." Scott pointed to the vic's pants. "And we found small flecks of some kind on his pant legs and hands. We've sent samples to trace, but it'll take time to process. You'll have to check back with me in a day or two. The lab's backed up."

"Speaking of his hands, anything on them or under his nails?" Raven asked.

"We scraped under his nails, no apparent DNA evidence. But we did find GSR on his hands. Looks like the guy tried to defend himself. With an empty holster, you'll be looking for a gun, too."

"We've got a check going for his permit to carry. Once we get that, we'll start the search for his missing weapon," Tony replied. "Anything on the wound? Time of death?" He glanced at the ME.

"From the angle of the cut, left to right, you'll be looking for a right-handed person. Not much help there. The slice was clean, no serrated edge to the blade. An incised wound transecting the left and right common carotid artery as well as both jugular veins, causing a fatal hemorrhage." The ME pointed a gloved hand to Blair's throat. "And as for time of death, the chill in the church distorted the time line, but my estimate would put TOD at approximately two hours prior to when the body was discovered and called in to nine-one-one. The absence of rigor at the church gave us that. I'll let you know if I change my estimate after the autopsy."

"I'll let you know what we find," Scott replied. "Oh,

and as for the trace evidence on his clothes and hands, I'll get the analysis bumped up. Put a rush on it."

"You giving us special treatment?" Tony teased, his dark eyes crimped with humor, putting Raven more at ease.

"Not for you, you ugly SOB. This one's for Mackenzie. I mean, it's not like I've never heard the word 'rush' before."

Tony grinned. "Well, thanks for the enlightenment. Call me when you have a report. I'll pick it up." Her partner stepped away from the gurney, tugging at his surgical gown.

Raven followed, yanking at her latex gloves. Catching a look from her partner, she asked, "What? Spit it out."

"I think I'm getting an allergy toward coincidences, Raven. And right now, I got hives in every nook and cranny of my body."

"That's an image I didn't need," she replied. "You talking about the paintball thing?" After he nodded, she heaved a sigh. "Yeah, I know. All my training tells me I should like him for this, but my gut says this is all wrong."

"Are you sure it's your gut?" He stopped and turned toward her. "Maybe your libido is doing all the talking." When she glared at him and opened her mouth to speak, he interrupted her. "Look, Mac, you're a good cop. I trust you with my life, but the coincidences are adding up. We gotta look hard at this guy. Can you do that?"

Without hesitation, she answered, "Yes, I can. I've built my life on the law, Tony. It was a gift from my father, the only thing that grounded me after his death. Central Station is my family, for crying out loud."

Fixing her gaze on him, she added, "But I gotta trust my instincts on this and speak my mind to my partner. Can you accept that?"

He searched her eyes for a long moment, then his expression softened. "Yeah, I can do that. I just had to check. Come on. The chief is waiting. And we gotta make nice for the media. Glad I wore my best clip-on tie."

"You mean you've got more than one?"

Raven followed Tony, but her mind dwelled on her reaction to Christian as a man. How could she explain something she didn't understand herself? And her partner had been right on another count. She had to keep her mind focused on the objective. If Delacorte was the killer, she wouldn't have the luxury to ponder her feelings. Tony might press for his arrest, and she'd have no choice but to do her job.

As Christian entered the Dunhill mansion through the kitchen, he found it spotless, without the normal activity. Fiona dined at this hour and usually invited him to join her. But they hadn't made such arrangements today with his late drive into town. The lights were dimmed. Peering around the stainless pots and pans hanging over the large butcher-block table, he spied the gas stove glistening in the pale light, cold as the room in which he stood.

A white envelope lay atop the butcher-block table, his name penned with Fiona's elegant script. Without opening the note, he knew what would be inside—the emptiness of the manor closed in on him, telling him all he needed to know.

He picked up the stationery and walked toward the night light, placing the page on the counter. As he suspected, Fiona had left for Paris, a sudden meeting with associates. He knew from experience that whenever she used the word "associates," she meant the side of the business she'd always kept hidden—to protect him. When he was younger, he'd hated the fact that she guarded her secrets. Now he understood her intentions, and loved her all the more for it.

Absentmindedly, he wandered through the darkened house toward her master suite upstairs. He flipped the light switch. Treading by her elaborately carved four-poster bed into the vast dressing area encircled by mirrors, he noticed her luggage gone. His heart sank.

She'd taken all of it. Fiona planned to be gone a long time.

"Damn it, Fie!" he cursed under his breath.

His voice sounded foreign even to his own ear. Reaching into his pocket, he retrieved his cell phone and pressed the direct dial he knew well. Maybe if he told her what he'd found out, she'd come home to help him make sense of it. But as Fiona's phone rang, a faint noise echoed in the master bedroom. His shoulder slumped. The sound came from atop her dresser.

Fiona had left her cell phone, severing another link between them. Set near the phone, another note had been placed on her bureau, meant for his eyes alone.

My Darling—

It pains me to leave you this way. I trust you completely, but the police are another matter. My phone would be a beacon for them to locate me. I hope you understand.

Be assured, this is not permanent. I need time to clear my head and figure out what to do. Un-

til then, I have key Dunhill personnel assigned to take care of my business affairs, legitimate and otherwise.

I will find you when it is safe. Know that I love you with all my heart, but my freedom and my life are at stake. My greatest wish is to see you happily married with children. I will not let my past sins tear apart my hopes for you, dearest.

All my love—
F

"What are you hiding?" he whispered.

She was protecting him from her own past. His heart wouldn't allow him to believe anything else. She probably didn't know the police were directing their investigation his way. For now, he'd keep that tidbit from her. She had enough on her mind if she was desperate enough to flee the country without him. Christian ripped the note in half, slipping it into his pocket to be burned downstairs. Fiona's note wouldn't become evidence against her.

Hitting another speed dial, he rang the hangar for the Dunhill jet. On the third ring, a man answered. "Dunhill hangar. Cooper here," the voice burdened with the boredom of night shift.

"Hey Coop. This is Christian. Just checking to see if Fiona got off okay."

"Yeah, before my shift." The man's voice was touched with concern. "Anything wrong?"

"No, everything's okay. Just checking on her flight plan." His effort at nonchalance made the call sound strained.

"Let me get it for you. Hold on a sec." The silence

dragged on, an eternity. If he knew where she was, he might be able to—

"Well, this is strange." Papers rustled in the background. Christian resisted the urge to ask what the man meant by strange. He already knew.

Cooper finally spoke. "The only flight plan is to Lanchester, a small private airstrip outside London. Looks like they touched down to refuel, then took off again, about an hour ago. No plan listed after that. Do you want me to make contact with the jet?"

"No. I'm sure everything is fine. Thanks for your help."

Christian switched off the phone before the man replied. If Fiona had gone to so much trouble to disappear, he'd honor her wishes. But he ached with the emptiness of her departure. She was his anchor, his only semblance of family.

Christian looked up. His eyes fixed upon the mirror. A stranger stared back. He'd grown used to the stark look of grief. Robbed of his innocence all those years ago, he'd never shaken the sense of loss. The tragedy cleaved to him like a malignancy, never letting him forget.

Yet the greatest cruelty was the things he'd never remember. He still kept his old baseball glove, but came up empty when he tried to recall his father giving it to him. An old photograph of a birthday party felt like the remembrance of a stranger. Joy lay buried in his brain, a casualty of violence. The intrusion of death into his young life had left him maimed beyond hope, leaving him to wonder why he'd been the one spared.

Then Fiona had rescued him from the institutionalized care of the state. She made sure he received the best treatment for post-traumatic stress, even taking him into her home. Never judging him, she was the only one who understood his rage—and his fear.

But now, he had never felt so alone. It reminded him of the first time he'd stared into a mirror, looking through a child's eyes yet no longer a child. Fiona had aligned herself beside him back then. Too numb to understand her reason for caring, he had resisted her tenacity at first, fighting her every move. Eventually, he drew from her strength, and accepted her nurturing.

But his demons had come for him at last, peering out of the shadows of his past. Now, they brazenly hovered like vultures, eager to strip him of what remained. The image made him weary. He'd grown so tired of hurting.

"Shake it off, Delacorte," he chastised. "Put an end to it."

Fiona needed him for a change. He owed her far more than he could repay. She'd gotten him to this point. The rest was up to him. His desire for revenge had become a weapon, an obsession to overcome his fear of the dark. It gave him purpose, a reason to crawl out of bed each and every day. His weakness flourished into strength, and darkness had become his ally—a link forged despite the countless nightmares he'd endured over the years.

Prepared to fight, he tensed his jaw. A stern resolve fired his eyes. He wouldn't let Fiona down.

The old clapboard house on Elm Street looked more like condemned property than the residence of Logan McBride and his men. Logan had always despised the accommodations. They were beneath him. The locale allowed him anonymity, decreeing the respect he earned. But fear had been the real driver. Anyone in the surrounding neighborhoods who knew of his reputation gave him a wide berth.

On the outskirts of the warehouse district, in a section of Chicago even the police feared to tread, the dilapidated, two-story structure was the property of Vinnie Buck, his number two man. Vinnie had earned his status after allowing Logan to leech off his good fortune, such as it was. And McBride's mercenaries soon followed, slowly rebuilding his followers after his stint in prison.

His quarters were extravagant compared to the others. Wall-to-wall cots dotted the interior of the house while he enjoyed the privacy of his well-appointed single room. *It was good to be king!*

Lying on his unmade bed with only a sheet over his bare body, Logan read the newspaper, his shoulders propped up against the old wooden headboard. A naked whore lay sprawled beside him, her dark hair splayed over his bed linens. For the entire afternoon, she'd taken his abusive and forceful behavior, whimpering in a tantalizing fashion when he got too rough. At one point, the pathetic wailing reminded him of a rabbit he'd set on fire when he was eight. This, of course, only spurred him on.

Now after reading about the dead body found at St. Sebastian's, a part of his anatomy grew rigid again as he relived the moment he'd robbed Mickey Blair of his future. Yanking the covers off the woman, he clutched her bare ass with his hand, squeezing it hard enough to earn him a yelp.

"Don't hurt me. I'm awake. What do you—" Before she finished, he'd grabbed a fistful of hair, forcing her head between his legs.

"I don't pay you to talk. Get to work," he demanded, closing his eyes and burrowing into the pillows at his back. The newspaper fell to the floor. Through his eyelashes, he watched her and grinned. The bob of her head and the feel of her warm, wet mouth really charged his blood, but her humiliation and willingness to take his abuse had been an even greater turn-on. A soft knock on his bedroom door disturbed his reverie.

"Go away!" he ordered impatiently.

The hooker's eyes sought his, looking for approval. Most probably, she prayed for his dismissal at the intrusion. With a cruel sneer, he gave her neither. Hope left her eyes. She continued with even greater determination to please him. He held back his contempt at her pathetic display to curry favor.

"It's Vinnie. I can come back." The muffled sound of the man's voice filtered through the closed door.

His smile broadened as he bellowed, "Come in, Vin." Then, under his breath, he added, "This should be interesting."

Barely opening his eyes, he glanced at the man's reaction as he waved him closer. Wide-eyed, Vinnie stared at the woman, in obvious admiration of her enthusiasm. Unable to ignore her, he licked his lips greedily, then eventually stammered, "You cut that pretty close last night. That little priest nearly got sent to his maker, paying a premature call to Peter at them pearly gates."

Vinnie's version of small talk amused him. And he appreciated the man's attempt at being cryptic in front of the whore. No need for that. If she talked about anything within these four walls, she'd be fish food by nightfall.

"I knew you could handle it. Nothing like the rush"—he gasped as he came, groaning his approval—"of almost getting caught." With a heavy sigh, Logan closed his eyes again. He shuddered at the woman's steadfast ministrations, then asked, "How did Krueger do? He have a sense of humor?"

His eyes on the hooker, Vin elaborated on their latest recruit, Danny Krueger. "He was cool. Took two of us, like you figured. Would've given anything to see the look on that priest's face. Bet he had to change his drawers."

A low chuckle rolled through Logan's chest. His hand brushed back the hair of the woman gazing up at him. An enticing mix of fear and adoration reflected in her eyes. As he glanced up at Vinnie, he noticed the man leered at the hooker once again. But his number two man kept up his end of the conversation, despite the lust filling his eyes.

"Yeah, Krueger's gonna work out. The bastard got a rush out of the hunt, wants to know when we can do that again. He's got a thing for killing animals. Guy's even more twisted about it than you."

Still stroking the woman's hair, Logan smiled. "I'll take that as a compliment. The hunt is more of a rush when it's up close and personal." His accomplice hadn't missed the insinuation to his work with the blade. He saw it in his eyes as he continued, "It's almost better than sex. Almost."

Directing his next comment to the woman lying across his lap, he ordered, "Go wash yourself in the bathroom. And shut the door. I wanna hear that water running."

She scurried away without question, not bothering to cover her bare body. He knew that by the look on Vin's face, the gesture titillated his depraved nature.

"You look like you got something else on your mind. What is it?" Logan demanded when they were alone and the water was running in the next room.

"Yeah."

Vinnie's teeth were stained yellow. And Logan smelled the man's breath from across the room, the stench only outdone by his body odor. He tolerated the man because of his interminable devotion. But there were days when Logan contemplated slitting his throat just for the fun of it. He watched the man's Adam's apple bob in place, fantasizing the feel of his blade across it.

"Thought you'd like to know. They had a female detective investigating at the church last night," Vin reported.

"Oh?" He crossed his arms over his chest after pulling the covers to his waist. Logan hated all cops, but by the look on Vin's face, this cop might have his interest. "Is she my type?" He grinned.

"Oh, yeah. I stuck around to check her out. Hung with the newspeople. I like the smell of that blond chick from Channel 4. I may need to get me some of that." The man laughed.

Vinnie's keen sense of denial always astonished Logan. The imbecile would never score with a woman he hadn't raped or bought.

"Not until the job is done. No more dead bodies until I say so. Those are my rules." Logan narrowed his eyes.

The last thing he wanted to do was piss off Blue Blood, the code name he'd given to his latest contractor. Only Logan would make the rules for his growing legion of followers, but the money on this job got his attention. He'd adapt to his new circumstances for the right price, until such time as his benefactor became a nuisance. Then all bets were off. It was his world. And no one would define it for him.

"Whatever you say." Vinnie never questioned him. One of the reasons the bastard still drew breath.

"Did you get a name for that detective? In case I get the urge to confess."

Vinnie snorted a laugh. "Yeah, the talking heads called her Detective Mackenzie, out of Central Station. But I didn't get a first name."

Glancing at the clock on his nightstand, Logan reached for his TV remote. "Maybe that arrogant police chief will have one of his many press conferences. The news at six is about to come on."

He turned on the TV with the volume low, keeping his eyes on the television set as he spoke, "Mackenzie?" When the other man shrugged, he grinned. "I must be the luckiest son of a— God, I just love it when a plan comes together."

Maybe his benefactor knew his history enough to throw him a bone. Blue Blood always arranged such tantalizing side benefits. One of the reasons he hadn't moved on, looking for his next gig. The man paid him well and provided protection to operate freely. He could express his true nature without some idiot passing judgment. Blue Blood needed wet work done, and he loved to kill. A match made in hell.

As the six o'clock news anchor announced the top stories, the water in the bathroom stopped, reminding him they weren't alone. "When she comes out of there, take her downstairs. Give her to the men with my compliments."

Vinnie grinned, flashing his stained teeth. "Can I do her first?" Hunger in his eyes, Vinnie looked like a wolf tracking the scent of blood.

"Do what you think is best, Vin. After all, you're my number two man. You've earned seconds."

Vinnie laughed like a crazed hyena, as if they shared an inside joke. Logan wanted the man gone. Craving his privacy, he added, "Get her out of here. She's had enough time in there."

Vin shoved the door to the bath open. The hooker, wet from her shower, wore only a towel. He didn't explain himself. Just grabbed her by the scruff of the neck and hauled her away, not giving her a chance to change. Where she was going, clothes would be needless. Her eyes pleaded with Logan from across the room, like staying with him would be a better choice. Knowing Vinnie and his men, perhaps she'd be right.

As the news started, all his attention centered on the TV screen. "We start our broadcast with breaking news. Chief Sanford Markham is holding a press conference at . . ." The reporter's voice droned on.

As predicted, Markham couldn't resist his face time. And standing behind him was a dark-haired beauty. The chief introduced Detectives Tony Rodriguez and Raven Mackenzie. Vinnie had been right. Mackenzie piqued his interest.

And now, seeing her for the first time, Logan would make sure their paths crossed. He would want his shot at both cops assigned to Blair's case. No one was beyond his reach. He threw off the sheet covering his naked body and walked across the room. Plans to orchestrate their first meeting festered in his mind. He hunched in front of the TV screen, touching the glass. His fingertips stroked the detective's face, along her ample mouth.

Surely, Blue Blood would understand his need. The hunt would soon be on. He wanted nothing more than to toy with his prey before the final confrontation.

"Raven Mackenzie." He spoke her name aloud. By defining his choice, he sealed her destiny. Seeing a new target for the first time always aroused him. "You and I have a rendezvous with fate."

*   *   *

After the press conference, Raven felt the tension from the long day in her neck and shoulders. The basement of the station house held the relief she needed. She spent more than an hour pushing her body to the limit with the usual workout, finishing by pounding her frustrations into a punching bag. She'd worked the muscles of her abs, arms, and legs until the strain poured from her like sweat.

Hair pulled into a ponytail and still damp from the shower, she left work in the spare CPD sweats she kept in her locker. She tucked a .38 into a fanny pack by sheer force of habit. Her navy suit and holstered Glock were unceremoniously stuffed into a gym bag. Dry cleaning would definitely be in order.

Tony had rushed home in hopes of spending some time with his kids before bedtime. His wife, Yolanda, had been a stickler for the family scene, but got her way on only few occasions. Such was the life of a homicide detective.

As Raven headed home, the details of Mickey Blair's growing file picked at her brain. Without deliberating much, she pulled a U-turn, feeling the need for another pass at the vic's upscale condominium near Lakeshore Drive. With any luck, she'd find a new lead to work.

Driving through the intersection onto Lakeshore, she followed the perimeter of Lake Michigan beside the trail system of the park. The volume on her radio turned low, classic rock played innocuously in the background. Private residences glowed warmly along the thoroughfare, welcoming beacons against the night. In contrast, the few lights on the other side of the avenue reflected onto the blackness of the churning water along a lighted trail system. On a sunny day, the waterfront property would be spectacular. But at this hour, with the remnants of winter in the air, the undulating black looked ominous. The scene prompted a lingering twinge—her fear of the dark. Her phobia had been exacerbated after the death of her father. But in time, she had overcome it.

Yeah, right. Lying to herself had to be a misdemeanor. She decided to let herself off with a warning.

She'd been an investigator on more than a few floaters hauled from the water's depths. Those cases always brought back gruesome memories. Another hazard of the job. Bodies grotesquely bloated in death were impossible to forget. Her detective's perspective of the world would be tainted with such images, offset by the greater satisfaction of bringing murderers to justice. If the reward didn't far outweigh the horror, she would've quit long ago.

Shaking loose the old cases, Raven cleared her mind as she pulled into the visitor parking for the Vista del Lago Condominiums. After locking the Crown Vic, she headed up the walkway to the secured front door.

The pristine grounds of the complex were strewn with fall leaves that swirled in the interior courtyard amidst potted evergreen shrubs. The front step tiled in textured clay lay beneath a stucco portico, accented with decorative mosaics, giving the building old-world charm. After hitting the buzzer, she prompted the resident manager to answer the intercom and let her into the lobby. She greeted the young man she'd met only the other day.

"Good evening, Mr. Walker. You remember me?" She showed her badge as he nodded. "I need into Mr. Blair's suite again."

"Yeah, no problem. And just call me Brian." Handing her the key, he added, "When'll you be done with your investigation? That yellow tape is bad for business," he said, but quickly realized his callousness on the subject of a dead resident. "Mickey was a class act. I'm gonna miss him."

"Yeah, well, not sure I can give you a time line. But we'll do our best." Hooking her finger into the key ring, she smiled and said, "Thanks. Not sure how long I'll be. If it's late, I'll keep the keys until tomorrow, give them back to you then."

Mickey's past had been questionable, given his frequent collisions with the law as a young man. Then all that stopped abruptly after Dunhill Corporation hired him nearly twenty-five years ago. Raven suspected the man was anything but a class act. Still, Brian didn't need to know his recently departed resident had a shady past. Innocent before proven guilty in a court of law, Mickey wouldn't have his reputation sullied now—one of the benefits of making the grand exit from this life before his past came back to bite him in the butt.

She stepped off the elevator on the eleventh floor and turned left. The elegant carpet runner covered the teakwood flooring along the corridor, deadening the sound of her footsteps. Mickey had been one lucky stiff, enjoying a corner suite with a spectacular panorama of the lake. Now yellow police tape crisscrossed the entrance to his abode. His luck had run its course.

But as she neared the door, her eyes caught a glimmer spilling into the hall at the base of the door. So faint, she thought she'd only imagined it. Reaching into her fanny pack, she retrieved her Smith & Wesson, glad she had her longtime companion from her training days. She listened at the door and heard a muffled sound.

Recalling Blair's floor plan, she knew the entry looked onto a posh living area with two large bedrooms to the left and a study and kitchen to the right. A balcony overlooked the lake, only blocked by a set of French doors and strategically placed custom windows along the far wall.

Where the sound originated, she had no idea. But given the layout, she assumed someone might be in the rear of the residence. Most probably the master bedroom or the study. The yellow police tape hadn't been disturbed. Whoever had slipped inside had done it with great care. Any other way into the condo would have been risky, but not out of the question.

After quietly peeling away the crime-scene tape, Raven stood to one side of the door, so her shadow wouldn't give her position away. She slid the key slowly into the lock and turned it to the right. At the sound of the dead bolt, the subtle noise from inside the room stopped. *Damn it!* She winced and waited. Her patience was rewarded when she finally heard a drawer slide open. Turning the knob and testing the door, she knew she'd have only a second to slip inside. The light from the corridor would telegraph her entrance.

As far as she could tell, the intruder still moved inside with lights out. Raven made her decision. Gripping the butt of her gun, she closed her eyes for an instant, hoping to get her night vision. She opened the door and crept inside. *Thank God for a well-oiled door hinge.*

Now she stood with her back against the wall. The entry shut behind her. Raven searched the darkness, holding her breath. Her ears strained for any subtle change.

Pitch-black. Only a dim glow from the windows shed a bluish haze into the gloom, backlighting eerie shadows. She stepped cautiously into the room, careful not to make a noise. Raven held her gun as adrenaline coursed through her veins, intensifying her wariness and prickling the hair at the nape of her neck. Her eyes darted across the suite. She conjured dark images that shifted in the murkiness—playing dangerous mind games.

And now, the room masked its secret—still as a crypt. Its hollowness aroused her worst fear. The prowler knew he wasn't alone.

CHAPTER 4

Gripping her gun in one hand, Raven splayed the fingers of her other along the wall and groped for the light switch. Eyes straining through the darkness, she hunted for any sign of movement. Her heart punished her rib cage, apprehension surging in her throat. She finally found the lights to the left of the front door, then paused. Once she flipped the switch, her eyes would take time to adjust, but she'd see more clearly. Unfortunately, so would the intruder. Her only advantage had been the element of surprise. With the room deathly quiet, she'd lost her edge.

She hesitated. Instinct signaled her to stop, to hold off on the lights. The emptiness of the room possessed its own sound. She sensed the trespasser's presence in the air, heavy like an oppressive fog. But something else lingered.

What was that smell? A scent washed over her, one she'd missed before. Her anxiety level morphed as the familiar tang touched her awareness. And the thrashing of her heart slowed—replacing fear with anger.

"You'd better have a real good reason for being here. You could've been shot." Her voice echoed in the darkness. She loosened the tension in her muscles but kept the gun ready in case she was wrong.

Silence. Her fingers tightened on her weapon. Had she been mistaken? Eventually, the faint rustle of material sounded from the study, followed by quiet footsteps on a wooden floor.

"How did you know I was here?" In the dark, the intimacy of the deep voice sent shivers across her skin.

Feeling along the bank of electrical switches, she turned the dimmer knob to slowly illuminate the room. The man walked carefully from the study to her right, hands raised shoulder-high. Dressed in jeans and a black sweater, Christian Delacorte still wore a brown leather bomber jacket and black gloves—a sign he hadn't been here long.

"Was I that loud?" he asked, his tone unfettered by contrition.

Raven had no intention of telling him her secret. Otherwise, he might stop wearing the cologne that teased her senses with a hint of his sensuality.

"Maybe you're not the only one that can see in the dark, Delacorte. A woman's got to have some element of mystery." Setting her jaw, she demanded, "How did you get in here?"

"That's my little mystery."

"Not good enough, Austin Powers." She didn't care whether he got the cheesy movie reference. Her tongue was on automatic pilot.

His eyes remained steadfast on hers until they dropped to the weapon she still aimed at his chest. To make a point, she continued the threatening gesture. By the expression on his face, Delacorte looked far too confident for a man in his position. Raven decided it was time for him to learn the error of his ways.

"Turn around. Hands on the wall, assume the position." Her voice stern, she jutted her chin and held firm to her .38, showing she meant business.

His jaw dropped. "You've got to be kidding." Delacorte stood his ground, hands still chest-high.

"I rarely kid with a gun in my hand. Now turn around. Up against the wall and spread 'em." She scowled. "Just be thankful I'm in a good mood."

Gloved hands placed head-high against the wall, he leaned and spread his legs. As she expected, the move had been well worth her time. Glancing down to admire the cut of his jeans, she wrestled with a smile.

He sighed and dropped his head. "Yeah. Counting my lucky stars. Now what are you—" He gasped when she answered his question with an abrupt move.

Stepping closer, she raised his sweater, sliding cold fingers across his bare chest, dawdling along the soft curls of hair spread along his pectorals and down his stomach. The warm skin of his taut belly sent a rush of heat to her face.

"Ah. Watch it." He jolted at her touch; his voice cracked faintly. "Your hands are cold."

"Just don't move. I'm not done." Raven fought to keep the mischief from her voice. She retrieved the Glock from his leather holster inside his jacket. Slipping his gun into a pocket of her sweats, she leaned nearer his ear. "Nice piece."

Rolling his head back, without turning around, he exercised his right to sarcasm. "You talking about the weapon?"

"Oh, yeah. That, too."

Sliding a hand down one thigh, then up his hamstring, she took her time with both legs, dawdling at the small of his back. He never voiced an objection, but fidgeted and huffed as she took liberties with the search.

At first, Raven had launched into the arrest procedure without thinking, hoping to impress her authority on him. It should've been an automatic motion. She'd done it countless times. Reaching under his sweater hadn't exactly been an approved search method. She'd improvised that twist to get his attention, keep him off-balance.

But with Delacorte, the act felt intimate and sensual, as if she'd exploited him and taken unfair advantage. Her intention to drag out his lesson in humility back-fired, hitting her squarely between the eyes. Now blood scurried to her face.

To his credit, he stood his ground, subjugating him-self to her abuse of authority until—

"I'm not well-versed in the arrest process, never having gone through it myself, but aren't you taking a little too much time for the pat down?" he asked.

"You complaining?" The flirtatious retort caught her by surprise.

With the men she worked with, a snappy comeback was a requirement of the job. But with Christian, the remark sounded brash. No doubt, dealing with the scum of Chicago had hardened her. Uncertain how to tap into her femininity, she desperately wished for a softer, feminine side to surface.

Reality check! Frisking a man at gunpoint would tend to inhibit her womanliness. Granted, the move got the guy's attention, breaking the ice of etiquette, but it lacked subtlety. She closed her eyes for an instant, won-dering about her sanity. Maybe she could blame Dela-corte. Ever since she'd met him, her world had taken a tumble.

Now her cheeks burned. She waited for his reaction to her reckless comeback. *You complaining?* Her taunt replayed fresh in her mind, making her cringe to think what he'd say.

It took him a moment to answer. Then he shook his head and stifled a grin. Looking over his shoulder, he found her eyes.

"No. No, I'm not."

His smile knocked the wind out of her. A sucker punch to the gut, followed by an uppercut inflicted by his dark green eyes. His usually serious expression warmed, softened with humor. *Hell, why did he have to smell so damned good?* Raven needed to regain control, shift it back to business as usual. Since she'd initiated the detour, it was up to her to get it done.

Stepping back, she wiped the grin from her face. "Now turn around. Slowly. Keep your hands where I can see them."

Tilting his head, he kept his hands raised. "Don't you think this is a little over the top? Even for you?"

Her gun leveled to his chest, she held her position, then slowly dropped her arms, gun at her side. "Is this what you call the spirit of cooperation? I could arrest you, except you'd probably get a perverse enjoyment from the handcuffs."

He lowered his hands. His expression held no remorse for the break-in. Quite the contrary. A hint of amusement spread across his face for an instant, then faded.

"You've caught me red-handed. Nothing to say in my defense. I'm throwing myself on your mercy." With audacity in his eyes, he added, "If you have any."

"Nice apology. You sound like a politician caught with his pants down," she quipped, glaring at him.

"I figure if it works for the Oval Office, no sense completely reinventing the spiel," he replied without hesitation. Leaning against the doorjamb of the study, he folded his arms over his chest in defiance. "What? Do I lack sincerity?"

"No, I'd say you're full of it." She stepped closer and raised an eyebrow. "You trying to charm me into forgetting about your little break-in?"

"No, just keeping up my end of the conversation." His interest in the debate waned, his somber expression reappearing. "We could banter all night. Even as entertaining as that might be, I have another idea."

"Oh, this I gotta hear. You know, this isn't the world of high finance with the Dunhill Corporation. You can't just negotiate your way out of—"

He interrupted her. "I'd like to propose a truce. Just for an hour or so. We can cover more ground if we work together. Since neither of us is big on sharing, let's ditch the spirit-of-cooperation bullshit. You're the one who wanted the cards on the table, so here's my compromise."

"You're in no position to negotiate anything, studly."

His eyes never wavered. He stepped toward her and closed the gap of her comfort zone.

"Come on. You came here for a reason. You don't want to hassle with my arrest. That'd just make for a very long evening for both of us." He stared at her, waiting for an acknowledgment she wasn't about to give so easily. So he forged ahead, "If we work together, and you drop the arrest talk, whatever we find tonight, we share. Deal?" Removing a glove, he extended his hand to seal the agreement.

Now he'd turned into Mr. Handshake! He'd turned the tables of getting caught in the act to one of mutual collaboration. *Well, no way, buster!* Yet after considering the words he'd chosen about "dropping the arrest talk," she wasn't exactly assuring him she wouldn't arrest him at all. It only meant she'd stop talking about it. If it came to snapping on the cuffs, she hoped he'd appreciate the subtle distinction.

"So where's the compromise, Delacorte? Sounds pretty one-sided to me."

"I had the displeasure of knowing Mickey. Can you say the same?" he challenged. When she found herself mute on the subject, he continued, "And I know computers. While you search the other rooms, I can—"

"Oh, no. I've got a specialized forensics team coming in here tomorrow to seize Blair's computer. You're not messing with my chain of custody report for any evidence found on his PC. If we come up with something of interest, I'll consider making a call to you." She glared at him, enjoying her advantage. "You haven't exactly given me a warm and fuzzy in the trust department."

Mr. Subtle let his guard down enough for her to see his resentment. His main purpose for the late-night home invasion had undoubtedly been centered on Blair's computer. Given his background, it was one of his specialties. With that not an option, she figured his "spirit of cooperation" would be in the dumper.

Raven was ready to slam the door shut on him, kicking him out on his delectable ear. But she saw this confrontation as an opportunity, one she couldn't pass up.

"Tell me why you came here. And not something I already know."

With his head down, Christian took a deep breath, deliberating her demand. Walking by her, he finally raised his chin and faced the living area with hands on his hips. She waited for his answer.

With barely a glance over his shoulder, he spoke. "I think your instincts on Mickey's lifestyle were dead-on. He subsidized his income. His closet is filled with designer duds—Armani, Versace, Dolce & Gabbana. And I can't explain it. As head of security, I know his salary. And by tomorrow, you will, too."

Turning to face her, he reluctantly continued, "We should be looking for a sniper rifle. Knowing Mickey and his field of expertise, that'd be my guess. It would be his style. But who hired him and for what purpose, I have no idea."

He hesitated for an instant, then added, "Neither does Fiona. She's in the dark about Mickey's time outside of work. I just spoke to her at home before I came here."

At first, his revelation pleased her. Christian admitted much more than she expected. Maybe this little chat had been worth the effort. She believed Mickey Blair to be a strong arm for the Dunhills, but a freelance assassin? Delacorte claimed to be unaware of Mickey's extracurricular activities—but was he? Doubt crept into her speculation. If Raven remained objective, she must consider that Christian had just tossed a red herring into the murder investigation. Even if she wanted to believe him, Fiona Dunhill herself may have kept secrets from Delacorte. *But why?*

His voice pulled her back. "Now you. Tell me something about this investigation I don't already know." His eyes were demanding yet skeptical.

Turnabout was fair play. But had he been honest with her? She'd expected full disclosure from him; now it was her turn for a sign of good faith. What would she offer? Once again, she trusted her gut instincts regarding the man standing before her. She looked him directly in the eye, to emphasize the risk she took.

"After your little stunt here tonight, I don't owe you anything." After she'd captured his full attention, she began. "But I will offer this. You already know Mickey's throat was cut. But there were bruises on his body. We suspect paintball pellets caused the marks." She let the theory register with him. His eyes fogged in reflection.

"Paintball? Why wasn't there any paint on his clothes? In the photos?" he questioned.

His surprise appeared genuine. But the man had been insufferably observant. A good quality, if Christian were a solid member of her team. Yet given his past, the man would not change sides so easily. She had to consider him the enemy, or at the very least, a hostile participant.

A part of her remained guarded, so she lied. "We don't know what the substance was inside the pellets. All we know is that it wasn't paint."

"Guess now I understand why I'm top of your hit parade," he grimaced, with a slight shake to his head.

"Let's not use the word 'hit' in this place. Shall we? Gives me the willies." She smiled, then gestured toward the door. "Come on. I've had enough entertainment for one night. Give a girl some privacy while she pilfers, will ya?"

Opening the front door, she made a sweeping gesture with her arm to show him the way out. Once he stepped across the threshold, he turned to ask, "My gun?"

With a sly look, she hesitated, making him wonder what she'd do. Then she reached into the pocket of her sweats and handed him the Glock.

"I shouldn't have to say this, but maybe you need things spelled out. Yellow tape across the door means stay out, police business. Am I making myself clear?" Before he shared his sarcastic wit, Raven beat him to the punch, "Wait for an invitation before you invite yourself to my party."

"I'll remember that." With an unchanging expression, he spoke quietly. "Maybe one day I can show you the same hospitality."

His words were like a double-edged sword. And his eyes didn't give any particular insight into his meaning. Delacorte clearly preferred ambiguity. So as he walked toward the elevators, she kept her eyes on him. Christian never looked back.

The way he moved intrigued her—fluid and commanding as a predator. Perhaps just as deadly. Yet with his guard down, when he allowed it to show, his eyes held the promise of kindness and good humor. He was certainly a puzzle. Hearing the elevator arrive, she slowly closed the door and let her mind wander.

Stepping into the room, she placed her hands on her hips and stared across the expanse. Finally, she settled on the study door. *What had he been doing?* Thinking back to when he walked into the foyer, she replayed the moment in her head.

"Well, I'll be damned!" Rushing into the study, she stepped behind the desk, her eyes searching for anything out of place. Nothing looked missing. "You had your gloves and jacket on, Delacorte. I thought you'd just gotten here, but what if you were just leaving. Damn it!" she fumed.

If he'd taken anything or been on Blair's computer, she might never know. But then again, she might have caught him in the act like she figured, before he'd done any real damage. Setting her jaw, she fought back her indignation. *Had she been played for a fool?* All the while she'd been posturing her authority, the guy might already have had a lead to follow.

Raven remembered the balcony looked onto the parking lot. If she hurried, she might catch him drive away. Yanking open the French doors, she stepped toward the balustrade, sticking to the shadows next to a wall. Snow swirled, casting a Norman Rockwell quality to a scene far from an image of Americana. As she expected, Christian stood by a black Navigator, the car door ajar casting a light on him. He stopped.

Turning slowly, he looked back toward the building, his eyes looking to the upper floors. Without thinking, she reflexively waved a hand. Raven shook her head, mentally chastising herself for the ridiculous display. Not possible he saw her from this distance and under these conditions—in the dark.

"You're acting like a schoolgirl, Mac. The man can't see squat," she mumbled.

Just as she spoke, Christian raised a hand and returned her wave. A simple gesture. It clutched her heart, caressing her like the tentative fingers of a first-time lover. For an instant, her breath caught in the back of her throat.

"How the hell do you do that, Christian?" she whispered.

Her words drifted into the frosty night, a moist vapor trail. Feathery snowflakes wafted to her cheeks and eyelashes, drawn to her warmth. After a long moment, well after he'd pulled from the parking lot, a faint smile curved her lips.

"And what were you up to?"

The serrated blade bloodied his plate as he carved into the meat. Slathering the fleshy wedge with steak sauce, he lifted the fork to his mouth. Logan dined alone.

His men would eat after him, feasting on a revolting concoction of spaghetti, when the dining room had been cleared of his setting. Anything better would be wasted on their crude tastes. He set the rules, including the one about not being interrupted while he dined.

Apparently, this rule was subject to interpretation by Vinnie Buck. The man stood at the entryway to the dining room staring expectantly at him, waiting for a gesture for him to enter. Glaring at his number two man, he continued with his meal, disregarding the rude intrusion.

Quietly, Logan chewed every morsel, ignoring the bastard. Only the sound of utensils scraping the plate filled the small room, punctuated by Logan's contentment at his full stomach. He sighed and wiped the corners of his mouth with a linen napkin. Still, Vinnie waited.

"This better be important, Vin." His tone was soft and even, yet clearly filled with contempt. "You've disturbed my meal."

"I'm sorry, Logan," he muttered, stepping into the room with his head lowered. "It's just that I thought you'd want to know."

Silence. The idiot expected his prompting.

"Know what, Vinnie?" His voice seethed. Fear showed in Vin's eyes, making them bug out of his head like a macabre carnival doll.

"I accompanied a team to follow both cops, like you ordered." The man squirmed, making Logan suspect he'd fucked something up. Such a simple assignment. Leave it to this asshole to mess it up.

The man's lower lip trembled as he continued, "The team I was on got the job done. We followed the Mexican cop home after the press conference. We know where he lives. But team two waited for Detective Mackenzie outside the police station for over an hour. They must've missed her."

"It was your assignment, Vinnie. There is no such thing as 'they missed her.' The failure is clearly yours." Logan stood and tossed the napkin to the table, keeping his eyes on Buck. Without looking down, his left hand found the serrated steak knife. By the look in Vin's eyes, he saw the move, too. "Say it. You lost her, right, Vinnie?"

He inched closer and clutched the knife. Before the man stammered his excuses, Logan quickly closed the gap between them. He launched a powerful backhand across the face of the repulsive sycophant. He dropped the man to the floor and knelt on his chest, stifling his breath. Shifting his weight, he dug his knee into fleshy ribs and yanked at the man's hair. Vin yelped.

"You know how I feel about failure, Vinnie. It's simply not an option."

The blade became an extension of his threat. He slid the blade tip through the skin of Buck's cheek, leaving a white line. Blanched skin soon filled with blood.

"Now, how are we going to rectify the situation?"

"Please, Logan. It won't happen again," he blubbered, his face turning purple. "I'll find her. I swear!" He gulped air. A tear rolled down his cheek.

"You failed me. And even after I gave you that hooker." Logan stood and turned his back, leaving Vin to pick himself off the floor. "I could've made you wait in line like the rest of my men. Rank has its privileges, Vin. It must. But only if you deserve it. You've taken advantage of my generosity."

On his knees, Buck wallowed in guilt as he lowered his head, avoiding his glare. His subservience pleased Logan immensely.

"I won't fail again," he mumbled, thin strands of blood racing down his cheek. "By tomorrow, you'll know where to find Raven Mackenzie."

Walking back toward his man, Logan towered over the kneeling Vinnie. Laying his hand on Vinnie's head, he glanced down, enjoying the feeling of superiority. "Tomorrow, then. Redeem yourself in my eyes and make me proud."

Vin dared to look up, his eyes paying tribute. "Yes, sir."

A flash of yellow teeth told Logan that all had been forgotten. His lieutenant would not falter.

After Vinnie left the dining room, Logan returned to his bedroom with a bottle of whiskey and the wife of his latest recruit, Krueger, in tow. The newcomer had made the gesture of offering his woman, hoping to secure favor. And without a doubt, the man had failed to inform *her* of his generous overture. She now stood in the far corner of his bedroom, trembling in the most delectable fashion. Krueger earned brownie points with every snivel.

Although the woman's hair and eyes were dark, that's where the similarities with Raven Mackenzie ended. The pathetic little mouse would never be the caliber of female he deserved. Krueger's woman would soon learn how he handled disappointment.

"Don't complain to me, woman. I'm not the one passing you around like a party favor." He sighed. "You should be grateful. I rarely lower my standards to this degree."

Perhaps he'd consider the woman an appetizer to the main course. His mouth watered for the stimulation of Raven Mackenzie. Taking a long pull from the bottle, he downed a slug of liquor, imagining the good detective on her knees before him.

Picturing it brought back his consuming rage for vengeance, despite the fact that the detective wasn't technically responsible. In his mind, there was a certain harmony to the idea that she would pay for the sin against him. A whimper drew him back.

"Come here, darlin'," he cajoled, not knowing her name. "Show Daddy how much you appreciate him giving you and your man a home."

She inched closer, her face pallid and frail. Strands of hair draped over her eyes as her chin lowered. When she'd gone as far as she dared, he closed the distance, insinuating himself next to her.

"Drink," he ordered, handing her the bottle. Purposefully, he kept his expression unreadable, although her eyes searched for indications of his humanity. Finding nothing, she tipped the bottle to her lips out of submissiveness, wincing as the liquor burned her throat. He chuckled as she gagged and offered him the bottle in return—when he wanted so much more.

He raised her chin, waiting for her to look up. A shy smile slowly gained momentum on her face. Alcohol raised her hopes. Logan brushed back her hair and stroked a cheek. When he saw the faint essence of adoration brimming in her eyes, he leaned closer.

"To your knees, woman. After tonight, you'll know exactly how to please me." She gasped, choking on her fear. He kissed her cheek, then whispered in her ear. "And I expect you to be an energetic pupil."

Large tufts of wet snow drifted aimlessly, measured only by the cadence of a clock that gave rhythm to it. Christian sat mesmerized by the constant descent, his low spirits magnified by the abundance of white in Mother Nature's assault. The steady barrage accumulated quickly and now started to stick to the windows of his cottage, encasing his world in a silent tomb.

The sight provoked his imagination. Cemeteries and crypts were silent, but death screamed its passage, forever seared on the intellect even beyond rational explanation. He'd learned that firsthand. Like a man diseased, he fought back the symptoms of his affliction, struggling to bury the grief so he might function.

In the library, a flickering glow from the fireplace bathed the room as he sat at his desk. His mind was only faintly aware of the sedate crackle of the flame, fighting its losing battle against the chill. He favored the dimly lit study with its deep cherrywood paneling and heady smell of books, its furnishings of black leather. It fit his sullen mood, a stark contrast to the cozy wintry scene beyond the draped windows.

Ice cubes shifted, falling against the glass as he drained the last of the liquor. A subtle burn of vintage Macallan scotch branded the back of his throat. The heat warmed his chest, but sapped his strength. It'd been one agonizing day. The weight of it played on his mind.

Absentmindedly, he held up his glass, staring through cubes of ice and cut crystal. The blaze refracted through rainbow prisms, distorting his gaze into the hearth.

Beep. His computer summoned his attention as it booted. The bright screens launched a kaleidoscope of color onto his face and sweater, barely capturing his fading concentration.

His world had been rocked today. Despite that, Raven Mackenzie had insinuated herself into his brain from the moment she'd held him at gunpoint. With all the turmoil plaguing him, he didn't need the added complication. Women always wanted more than he had to give.

Eventually, even no-strings lovers deluded themselves into thinking he should feel something in return. They'd all been wrong. He recognized it long ago. Being emotionally crippled, he accepted his lot in life. But a woman like Raven would never understand. She'd want more, and would deserve it. Yet beyond every other impossible rationalization, Raven Mackenzie was a cop. He couldn't allow himself to forget that.

"Get a grip, Delacorte," he scolded. "Keep focused."

His fingers moved across the keyboard, pulling up the county tax assessor's database off the Internet. Retrieving the only lead he'd taken from Blair's place, he pulled out the ragged-edged paper from his jeans pocket.

Before Detective Mackenzie discovered him in the study, Christian had spotted a spiral notepad by the faint glow of a small flashlight. Flipping the notebook cover, he'd run his fingers over the top page, noticing faint indentations. With a pencil from the desk, he'd gently rubbed the lead across the lined page. A numbered street address gradually leapt from the page, lifted in reverse like a photographic negative. Not having a crack at Mickey's computer, he had to be satisfied with the only clue to follow.

Maybe it meant nothing.

"3533 South Giles Avenue," he whispered, as he entered the address into the query page of the property database. His only familiarity with the area was that the Dan Ryan Expressway ran through it, in the general vicinity of Chinatown. Without delay, he'd gotten a hit on his query.

A second screen detailed the property description, map location, and ownership data. The name on the deed left him staring at the screen in disbelief.

"What the hell?" he muttered aloud. "Why would you have an interest in this place, Mick?"

Fiona's words played back in his memory—*I didn't have him killed, at least not in the way you might imagine.* From her note, he thought she had fled the country from the police, but maybe she had run from him? Had she been afraid of what he might find?

Slumping deeper into his chair, he rocked with his eyes closed. His mind played tug-of-war with his emotions. He loved Fiona like a mother, but if she had ordered Blair killed, would he cover up her crime? Could he walk away from the truth?

Too tired to dwell on Fiona's sins, he pushed his doubts aside. He'd have to obtain more information on the property before taking the next step. A visit was in order, but he needed more intel before he barged into a facility unannounced. More from instinct, his eyes fell to the weapon lying on his desk, lodged in its holster. He'd be armed in case he ran into trouble.

Hitting the print icon, he downloaded and printed the map. Glancing at a wall clock, his eyes blurred in fatigue. Already after midnight. Given his drive into the city at dawn, another long day loomed ahead. The police would be at Dunhill Tower by eight. But after they left, he would visit the Giles Avenue location. With any luck, he'd be ahead of Raven Mackenzie and her partner in his own investigation. It might be all the advantage he'd need to protect Fiona's secret.

CHAPTER 5

A terrifying blast jarred him from a dead sleep, echoing over and over. The deafening crack of wood shook the walls, threatening to collapse the room around him. Disoriented, he covered his face, unsure where he was until a loud rumble overloaded his senses. The menacing sound escalated, careening straight for him.

Like a haunting déjà vu, he'd been forced to witness the chronicle being played out.

"Chicago Police," a man shouted. "Come out with your hands up!"

Sitting bolt upright in bed, he clutched the layers of blankets to his chest. His eyes searched the darkness, finding nothing to give him comfort.

"What's happening?" he wanted to shriek, but words wouldn't come. He opened his mouth to cry out. Nothing. His heart cleaved to the effort, strangling his will to make any sound at all.

At the base of his bedroom door, eerie lights ebbed and flowed, amidst the screams and the ear-splitting eruption of macabre fireworks like the Fourth of July. Yet despite the utter chaos outside the room, he stayed rooted where he sat, unable to move. He fought his body, wanting to react to the threat. But he felt bound to a course of action as if he followed a script.

Then the voices came—the beginning of the end. His gut twisted with the sound.

"No, please. We're unarmed! *Stop!*" He'd never heard the man's voice so filled with fear. A loud crash made his heart leap. Something heavy hit the floor.

"Not my little girl!" A woman screamed. "Oh, my God—*no!*" This voice was familiar, too, but his brain resisted the recollection, in complete denial. Another thunderous pop and her wailing ended.

Outside his door, heavy footsteps stumbled toward him.

"Now I lay me down—" The steady mantra spewed from his lips, sounding foreign to his ear.

Like a marionette acting upon the commands of a puppeteer, he repeated lines he'd heard before. He stared into the murky void, not recognizing the voice of a child in prayer. The words resonating in his head should've been comforting. Instead, they triggered a deep-rooted warning—they were coming for him.

In desperation to discover more, he garnered all his strength. Then, as weightless as a feather, much to his surprise, he lifted himself to look down upon a small boy. Although the child was faintly recognizable, his face distorted in terror and challenged his recollection. ". . . pray the Lord . . . keep my soul," the boy muttered.

The words tumbled from the kid's mouth, the meaning distorting in his brain. Over and over the child repeated fragments of the prayer. "Now I pray . . . soul to keep."

A dark motion to his right caught his eye. The kid saw it, too. A shadow eclipsed a glimmer of light—someone was outside the room. To protect the boy, he once again infused himself into the small body without thinking, hoping to give the child a fighting chance to survive. Instead, the boy's horror assaulted him, strangling rational thought with sheer hysteria.

"If I should die—" The words came faster. His throat clenched with fear, cutting off his air. "Please, God!" he pleaded.

The small body rocked back and forth, his voice raspy. Tears spilled from his eyes. Still, he couldn't make the child move.

Another explosion ripped a hole through the door, jolting him from his stupor. A low, agonizing moan filled the darkness, sounding like a man who stood near the foot of the bed. It took his panicked brain a moment to realize he was still alone with the child until—

Someone leaned heavily on the door, scratching faintly to get in, rattling the doorknob. The child screamed.

Suddenly, the bedroom door flew open. A tall hulk of a man stood, then staggered toward the boy, the massive silhouette backlit by erratic flashes of light.

"The old man's got a gun," someone yelled from far away. "Where's the kid? We came for the boy. Find him."

Strangers' voices droned in the background, mixing with the shrill sound of a distant police siren. But like the child's, his complete attention had been drawn to the faceless shadow standing before him. A distinct smell swept into the room; a strange, sweet odor dominated his nostrils. The boy gasped, sucking in the metallic tang. Enveloped by the peculiar aroma, he felt his body and mind slow down, as if someone stalled the pace of a movie reel, clacking frame by frame. Shadow man seized the kid's arm in a viselike grip, grappling for him under the blankets. He fought his attacker armed only with the cooperation of the child—blindly flailing thin arms and kicking gangly legs.

"Noooo! Let me go!" he cried, his tone throaty and lethargic, every syllable distinct and drawn out. "Now I lay me down—"

The man spoke. He strained to understand the words. But like the boy, his mind felt numb with urgency. Only a garbled sound trickled through his awareness, drowned out by the prayer.

"Pray my soul to keep—" His body rocked violently, struggling for freedom, his chest on fire. Trapped in the defenseless body, he fought for freedom, if for no other reason than to defend the boy.

Helpless. Locked in frailty, he was paralyzed. He could only watch the tragedy occur over and over again—sinking in the quagmire of slow motion.

"If I should die before I wake—" Dizziness threatened to betray him. Bile rose hot from his belly. Tangled in his blankets, he shut his eyes and shrieked. His voice blended with that of the child, "God, help us. *Please!*"

"God help me!" he shouted. *"Please!"*

He no longer heard the boy. Only his voice remained. As the nightmare faded, the scene morphed into indistinct shapes.

Drenched in sweat, Christian threw a pillow across the room, knocking over a lamp. The crash only punctuated the terror he'd relived, embellishing the memory of a ten-year-old boy. His lungs burned with the exertion. Amidst dank sheets, he sat trembling in the dark—an adrenaline rush surging through his veins.

God hadn't heard him then, just as he'd turned a deaf ear to the adult Christian had become. "Oh, God," he whispered. "Make it stop." Still, the blind eye of God left his call for help unanswered.

With the pain so fresh, it wasn't much consolation that he lived on the Dunhill Estate now. His mind mercifully fast-forwarded to the present. The small house he'd lived in as a child had been demolished long ago, obliterating the last vestige of the heinous police action. So his memory, hazy at best, was all that remained.

Staring through the gloom, Christian found everything as it should be, except for one overturned light fixture. A single night light burned, a ritual from childhood. It'd been years since he'd been tortured by that nightmare. Having his past churned up had been the catalyst. Christian glanced over his shoulder to the clock on the nightstand. He'd been in bed only a few hours. He knew attempting sleep now would be futile.

In complete exhaustion, he fell back onto a pillow, wiping a hand across his damp brow. His bare skin prickled with the chill of realization. The remnants of the nightmare clutched at him as his lungs fought for air. Unyielding, the hellish images flashed like a strobe light through his mind. Dead eyes of familiar faces stared back, demanding answers that might never come. Their cries for justice penetrated the black body bags, seeking him out even now. He stared blindly at the ceiling. The lingering details of the dream faded despite his best effort to recall them.

Still, one thought remained. *Where's the kid? We came for the boy. Find him.*

The words leapt from his memory like a harsh slap in the face. It had been the first time he remembered hearing them—and the recollection stayed. Normally, such details would be wiped from the slate the moment he awakened from the nightmare. What did it mean? It must be significant. *Damn it! Why couldn't he remember?*

Christian struggled for every shattered image. Often in the silence, he strained to recall, all the while dreading the journey to relive it. More times than not, his memory was tainted with the terror of his family's final screams—abruptly ending his grisly pilgrimage. He blocked out so much.

Only after extensive therapy and hypnosis did he discover his deepest regret—the time he spent fighting the shadow man.

Ultimately, the man proved to be his savior.

CHAPTER 6

DUNHILL TOWER
DOWNTOWN CHICAGO

The Dunhill Corporation shadowed Michigan Avenue, a monolith in glass and granite acclaiming the amassed wealth of the family holdings. Raven had walked by it many times, never giving the notable family a thought. Standing at a crosswalk with her partner by her side, huddled with the masses, she burrowed into her overcoat. Her eyes fixed upon the gray morning sky, then trailed the height of the tower until it dissolved into the low-lying clouds.

Unlike her, Tony didn't appreciate the courtesy of being prompt. By her watch, it was five till eight and they were on foot, still a good five blocks away. Although, technically, they weren't late at this very minute, it would be inevitable nonetheless. In her mind, she imagined the unspoken judgment on Delacorte's face. The guy probably shot from his mother's womb precisely on time, right down to the split second.

"You're antsy this morning. What's up?" Tony asked. The light changed and they crossed the street.

"Nothing. We're gonna be late." She stuffed her hands into her pockets. "You know how much I hate that."

"Yeah. Kind of an endearing quality." He chuckled. "Just like I hope my procrastination is to you."

"Everything about you is endearing, partner. Now shut up and keep moving." She smiled. "I got my heart set on a big cup of joe. I bet Designer Boy has good taste in java."

The muffled sound of a cell phone summoned her. Reaching into a coat pocket, she answered the call, "Yeah. Mackenzie here." To listen, she plugged an ear with a finger, keeping pace with Tony.

"Hey Raven. Scott Farrell. We got an analysis off the GCMS, the trace evidence on the Blair case."

Raven was familiar with the acronym. The gas chromatograph mass spectrometer was a machine used to analyze material and trace evidence. She didn't have to understand how it worked, just that it did. True to his word, Farrell had promised a rush analysis and delivered. The man read through a litany of scientific particulars.

Interrupting him, Raven wanted to cut to the chase. "So, bottom line, what are we looking at, Scott?"

"Two main points. There was evidence of rust and paint on his hands, but what's interesting is the content of the paint. It was lead-based, indicating an older structure painted before 1978."

"An old building in Chicago? That should stand out, big time," she joked.

At the front entrance to the Dunhill Tower, Tony pushed through the revolving glass door, with her on his heels. Once inside, they stood amidst a lavish leather seating area, under the close scrutiny of the security staff at a circular kiosk.

"That's why they pay you the big bucks, Mac." Farrell laughed. "But remember I said there were two notable items. The second one may help make your job easier."

"I'm listening."

"The list of compounds I read off, we found them on his clothes and hands, but they boil down to one thing. Ammunition."

She took a moment to digest his assessment. "So we're looking for an older building perhaps used to store or make munitions?"

"That'd be my guess," he replied.

"Aren't some of those components considered controlled substances?" She asked, searching her memory. "Or some kind of hazardous waste?"

"Yeah, prior to a federal law enacted in the late seventies, treatment of ordnance waste wasn't tracked. Components used in explosives, as well as solvents and fuels, are reported more thoroughly now. But I know where you're headed. We have access to a property database that we could query on the munitions components, maybe get a hit on ownership of record. Since it's a fairly recent resource, I'm not sure we'll have luck on any buildings that old. It's gonna be a long shot."

"Well, you're talking to a Cubs fan. Long shots are what I do." She couldn't help but grin, thinking of her father. "Just give it your best. Maybe we'll get lucky. I'll check back with you."

"Give me an hour or two," he added. "Later, Mac."

"Thanks for pushing on this one." She ended the call and glanced at Tony, lowering her voice.

"Another coincidence just hit us broadside, my fine friend. Seems the trace evidence on Blair is related to munitions." She raised an eyebrow. "And with the Dun-hills rumored to be involved with illegal arms trading, I think Fiona Dunhill is neck-deep in this, up to her cultured pearl necklace."

"You think Christian Delacorte is running interference for her?" he asked, anticipating her thoughts precisely.

Raven had kept her midnight rendezvous with Dela-corte a secret from her partner. For what purpose, she didn't fully understand—not sure she really wanted to. But in light of this new information, she had to face facts.

Christian Delacorte was anything but an ally.

"Could be, partner," she speculated, shrugging out of her coat. "I think we should call on Mrs. Dunhill while we're here. And my gut tells me we should stick close to Delacorte. Whether he knows more than he's letting on, I don't know. But the man might be worth the effort." She stared across the room, her eyes not set-tling on anything in particular, lost in thought.

"Worth the effort?" Tony questioned, humor color-ing his expression.

Her partner had an annoying habit of *actually* listen-ing. Had she said he'd be worth the effort? Delacorte had definitely gotten under her skin. Would it take a radical surgical procedure to remove the two-hundred-pound growth? If only it were that simple.

Tony waited for an answer. To cover up her faux pas, she replied, "I think we should stick close to the guy. That's all I'm sayin'. And given the arrangements today, I've got an idea on how we can do that."

Christian discovered the Giles Avenue property be-longed to a division of Dunhill Corporation. By all accounts in the company files, the old armory was a historic site, abandoned long ago. So why did Mickey have the address written on a notepad at his home? Like playing a game of connect-the-dots, a link between Mickey and Fiona had been made with one easy stroke. The thought disturbed him, especially without Fiona here to explain the reason.

Now where would this lead him? All he could think about was checking out the old building. But one thing loomed on his horizon before he left on his personal errand—Detective Raven Mackenzie.

Swiveling his desk chair, he stood and walked toward the large picture window across his office. A console table had been set up with a coffee service and a modest serving of fruit and pastries for the visitors he expected. The thought of food turned his stomach, but the coffee was another story. Christian refilled his third cup of coffee since arriving at six. Slowly, he sipped the dark, pungent brew, letting the steam rise to his lips. A fog drifted off the lake, clouding the view. It tinged his somber mood with the blues. Adrift in the haze, his eyes probed the gloom as if he waited for an answer to emerge. No such luck.

His phone rang, pulling him from his funk. He glanced at his watch. Ten after eight. He suspected his guests from CPD had arrived, exhibiting their propensity for tardiness. Reaching his desk, he read the caller ID display—lobby security.

"Yes?" he answered.

"Mr. Delacorte. Burke here. You have two guests from the Chicago Police here to see you. They have an appointment?"

"Yes, send them to my office. Their appointment is with Human Resources, but I'll see them first. Give me ten minutes with them, then have someone from HR come to escort them."

After he hung up, a strange feeling gripped him. The dark eyes of Raven Mackenzie dominated his thoughts, along with the memory of her velvet touch against his belly. He found himself anxious to see her. With a slight shake of his head, he glared at the closed door to his office, chastising his foolishness.

"Damn it, Delacorte. You've got work to do."

The executive offices of the Dunhill Tower were beautifully appointed. Endless corridors were lined in plush rugs, adding texture and warmth to the lofty ornate ceilings, dripping with extravagant chandeliers. Framed in gold, massive canvases hung low on paneled walls, with subtle lighting to accentuate the vivid oils. The heady scent of fresh exotic flowers teased her senses, their elaborate arrangements surpassing the elegance of distinctive porcelain vases. Raven had never seen such fine decor.

She attempted to look nonchalant, but Tony gave them *both* away, openly gawking with his mouth open.

"*Ay, Dios mio*, Raven. Check this place out. If I worked here, I'd wanna bring in a mattress, stay awhile." Tony spun around, absorbing the ambience with all the finesse of a ball-peen hammer. "If Delacorte doesn't turn out to be a heartless, cold-blooded killer, you think he might hire me for his security team—that is, when I get ready to retire from the life?"

"And why would you be so picky as to exclude a murderer from your future employment prospects?" she joked.

"Excellent point, Mac. Maybe I shouldn't limit my potential."

Interrupting Tony's delusions, the receptionist greeted them. "Good morning, Detectives. May I take your coats?"

The young, petite brunette flashed a brilliant smile as they handed over their garments. "Mr. Delacorte is expecting you. Right this way." Stylishly dressed, the woman ushered them to a suite toward the right. "We have coffee and pastries inside, compliments of Dunhill. Have a nice day."

The sound of a delicate, high-pitched violin found its way to her ear, from speakers well-hidden. Classical music gave an air of serenity to the workplace. *All of it, so civil.*

The woman pushed open the massive door to Christian's office. As they entered, she announced, "Your guests are here. Anything else I can get you, Mr. Delacorte?"

"No, Denise. That's all. Thanks for indulging me this morning."

"My pleasure, Christian." The use of his first name, coupled with the inviting look in her eyes, told Raven that Christian had indeed been her pleasure.

Only another woman would recognize the coy move. Yet Delacorte appeared oblivious to her blatant flirtations. Raven knew his affairs were none of her business. Instead, she drank in the sight of him like she'd been wandering the desert for days without water.

Dressed in an elegant navy suit, pale blue shirt, and a tasteful tie in red silk print, Christian Delacorte stole her breath. *A constant habit.* Accentuating his tall, lean stature, the drape of his suit fit his body perfectly. The subtlety of his cologne embraced her. And as a welcome bonus, the feel of his skin teased her sense of touch, reminding her she'd taken liberties with him last night. She fought to hide a smile as she approached him.

Would he acknowledge his little escapade of breaking and entering into Mickey Blair's place last night in front of Tony? Raven didn't have to think about that for long. He'd be a fool to admit he'd broken the law. One thing was very certain—Christian Delacorte would never be mistaken for a fool.

Drawing closer, Raven noticed the pale blue of his shirt tinted his green eyes to a blend of deep azure. She'd always believed such perfection would be unattainable, featured only on exotic magazine covers using enhanced photographic techniques. Yet here stood living proof she'd been wrong.

Only the ever-present sadness in his expression reminded her his life was anything but perfect. Christian communicated all this in an instant. But perhaps she read too much into him again—a dangerous yet tantalizing addiction with a man like Delacorte.

He caught her eye and held her gaze long enough to communicate a special recognition. Then the flash was gone. Christian reverted to business as usual.

"Good morning, Detectives." He shook hands with them both, then offered, "I hope you like the coffee and feel free to enjoy the fruit and pastries. Someone from HR will be here shortly to escort you to your morning appointment."

Tony served himself a pastry and filled a china cup with coffee, looking back over his shoulder at his host. "Well, we appreciate your hospitality; the spread looks great. But before we head over to HR, we'd like to see Mrs. Dunhill, to thank her personally."

"Oh, no need for thanks, Detective Rodriguez. I assure you." Christian's face was unreadable.

"No, we insist." Raven asked. "Is she in today?"

His eyes fixed on her. "Actually, I'm not sure. I left the estate early, I didn't discuss her itinerary for the day."

"My, isn't that unusual, for the head of security to be out of the loop?"

If she hadn't been watching intently, she might've missed the subtle change in his expression. Playing cagey with Delacorte felt like challenging a grand chess master.

"That was more of a rhetorical question—just a general observation. I'm sure Fiona Dunhill is in very capable hands." She'd intended to make a point, but his sentiments shone on his face. Her insincere attempt to make amends fell flat.

"Are you always this obsessed with expressing your gratitude, Detective Mackenzie?" His eyes demanded an answer. "That question is not rhetorical. I'm quite interested in understanding the proper etiquette for coffee and cheese Danish."

Brick by brick, Christian erected a wall between them, using sarcasm for mortar. And she had only herself to thank for initiating the verbal tussle.

"We may have some questions to ask her." Loaded with nerve, she implied a skepticism for his version of the truth.

"You *may* have some questions? My, isn't that unusual for a detective to be so ambiguous. I haven't known you for very long, but aren't you a bit more direct?" Definitely on the assault, Delacorte found high ground and intended to hold it.

"Then how's this for direct. We want to talk to Mrs. Dunhill. How can we find her?" She folded her arms and stepped closer.

"Try her cell phone. I'm sure she'll be happy to make

arrangements with you when you speak to her." Walking to his desk, Christian pulled open a drawer. He wrote on the back of a small card. "My business card. Her private cell phone number is on the back." Rejoining her, he handed over the card, along with a heaping dose of cynicism. "Please be discreet with the use of it."

"Discreet? I can do discreet." She qualified, "Or a fair facsimile."

"'Subtlety' is not a word I would associate with you, Detective." Hearing a soft knock at the suite door, Christian excused himself. "I believe that is your next appointment. I'm sorry to cut short our visit. Pardon me."

The man was an odd mixture of absolute appeal and outright frustration, bundled up in a delectably dangerous package. A part of her felt hopping mad, but mostly, she enjoyed the challenge.

Raven watched Delacorte step away to greet the representative from HR. Her eye caught Tony in the midst of a chuckle. He'd found a comfortable seat on a nearby sofa and was wiping his mouth with a napkin. She hadn't even picked up a plate, having time only to sip her coffee. But his dish and cup were empty.

"This has definitely been entertaining, and I got a front row seat. It just don't get any better than this." Tony shook his head, still amused. "I sincerely hope Delacorte is not our guy. The way he pushes your buttons, it's worth the price of admission."

"Haven't you ever heard of bad cop, good cop?" she teased.

"Yeah, but not sure bad cop, hungry cop plays as well." He cleared his throat to stifle his laughter, then volunteered, "Let me give him the good news that he's stuck with you for a while longer. He's gonna love our divide-and-conquer tactic."

Divide and conquer. What had she been thinking? Her instincts told her to stick with him. The man was hiding something. It wouldn't be easy to extract it from him, especially not with Tony in plain sight. And with the secret they shared, her unexpected rendezvous with Christian at Blair's, Raven might have a chance to question him on the subject. So she'd proposed Tony take the HR appointment, leaving her alone with Delacorte.

Her partner agreed, reiterating his thoughts on her influence over Delacorte. "Influence" wouldn't be her first choice of words. Yet she had to admit, she consistently got a reaction from the guy. Now if only she could control her reaction to him.

Alone with Christian Delacorte. She didn't know what to make of her good fortune. One thought stuck in her brain. Every silver lining possessed a dark cloud. And without the stormy, unruly cloud, the silver lining wouldn't stand out as anything special. At least, that's what she told herself.

When had she become so philosophical—and so accepting of bullheaded storm clouds?

Christian thought he'd be rid of his guests so he could get on with his day. All they had to do was accompany the HR rep. He should have known Detective Mackenzie would find a way to spoil his plans. Now, he'd have to improvise. After all, the woman had ventured onto his turf at Dunhill. The advantage was his.

Or so he thought. Staring across the room at his tenacious visitor, he recalled the old adage about "best-laid plans." While her partner headed off to Human Resources, the willful Raven Mackenzie remained behind. Now, closing the door to his office, he was alone with her. Innocently smiling, she sat on his sofa, hands on her lap as if she awaited him to entertain her. Nothing could be further from the truth.

Dressed in dark gray slacks and an oversized ivory turtleneck sweater, she'd pulled her dark hair back into a ponytail, looking elegant in her simplicity. A small part of him wished they'd met under different circumstances, that his whole life had been different. But such maudlin thinking served no purpose.

He joined her in a chair near the sofa. Without fanfare, the detective spoke first. "You didn't sleep well."

It wasn't a question. He searched her eyes, surprised to discover concern. It stirred him. After their earlier verbal jousting, he hadn't expected such a personal remark.

Surprisingly, her presumption felt like comfort, that someone knew him well enough to confront him. So many people in his life left him alone, taking for granted his complete control. His pensive demeanor and aloofness sent a clear message by design. Yet with her boldness, Raven insinuated herself into his narrow circle of acquaintances. He should have resented her forwardness, but instead, he liked the way it felt.

With the precision of a laser, her dark eyes easily cut through the wall he'd erected, as if it were constructed of warm butter. Fearlessly and without effort, she debated him in her quiet way. The intimacy in her voice touched him.

"Sleep is overrated," he replied matter-of-factly, trying not to betray himself. "And it's for those who earn the right to it."

Avoiding her stare, he focused on the crumbs of pastry on the discarded plate of Detective Rodriguez. For most people, his response would've ended the subject, but not with Raven.

The woman calmly persisted. "Hardly. I've seen stone-cold killers sleep like babes." She reached across and touched his arm. He could no longer avoid the woman.

Her gaze held him as she spoke softly. "I believe a different kind of hell keeps you awake. And it's one I may know a little something about. If you ever want to talk—"

The woman had done her research. Now the look of concern made sense. He'd seen pity in her eyes. One of many reasons he avoided sharing himself with anyone. Pity was inevitable.

"Look, I appreciate your concern, but I don't need—" He stopped midsentence, hearing how he sounded. Her intentions were good, but most people had no idea of the living hell he'd endured. "Thanks. It's something I've lived with for a very long time. Not sure I'd know how to talk about it. But I appreciate the offer."

"My invitation still stands. I mean it." Once again, she squeezed his arm reassuringly, not backing down.

He nodded. His only reply to her invitation. He needed a change in subject.

"Mickey had an office on five and a gym locker in the basement. I'm sure you'd like to get on with your investigation. Shall we?"

As the detective stood and walked toward the door to his suite, Christian found himself wishing Raven met his expectation for a cop. It'd make resisting her so much easier.

And for what he had in mind to reclaim his day, he hoped she had a sense of humor.

"He ditched me, damn it." Raven grabbed Tony by the elbow as he exited the men's room on the twentieth floor, near the Dunhill human resources area. "I turned my back for only a second, and he pulled a fast one. Switched places with one of his security men."

"You mean he found a way to resist your feminine wiles? Amazing, Mac." He pulled away, facing her with a look of indignation. "Hey, did you follow me? How did you know I was in the men's room?"

"How long we been partners, Tony? I could set my watch by your morning constitutional." She smirked, temporarily setting aside her problems with Delacorte to tease her friend.

Without much discretion, he tucked the sports section of the paper under his arm. "Well, you know the expression—a man's gotta do what a man's gotta do." He grinned. "So you lost him, huh?"

Narrowing her eyes, she paced in front of him along the corridor. She gathered her thoughts, chewing the inside of her lip.

"As far as I can tell, he's not in the building. Believe me, I asked and searched a few floors." Leaning against the nearest wall, she crossed her arms over her chest. "And it seems Mrs. Dunhill is AWOL. I can't raise her on the cell phone Delacorte gave, and she's not in the building according to security. But they weren't exactly helpful, if you catch my meaning."

"That's because we don't sign their paychecks." He offered his explanation with a shrug. "I'm beginning to think this whole cooperation thing with the Dunhills has run its course. The chief won't want to hear that, but as I see it, we got an investigation to conduct. What say we grab our coats and blow this joint?"

"I'm with you, pal," she agreed, and accompanied him down the hall toward the elevators. "What did you find out?"

"Well, I got some general information on our vic, but nothing to shed any light on his extracurriculars, other than to make it painfully obvious the man was moonlighting. His salary didn't support the lifestyle he led, not enough jack to pay for all his bling. And what about you—find anything worth knowing?"

With her partner's question, Raven recalled the only high point of her search. Blair's office held few personal items, no photos or special mementos. The man had been a ghost at Dunhill, purposefully keeping his private life apart from his work. Considering Mickey had a more lucrative business venture outside Dunhill, this didn't surprise her. It looked as if she'd come up empty on any leads.

But catching a glint under his desk changed all that.

The waning sun had shone through Blair's former office window for only an instant, shedding some much-needed light. As she'd shoved a drawer closed and pushed back from the desk, a glimmer caught the fleeting rays of sunshine. Kneeling for a closer look, she'd crawled under for a better view and made a discovery. After punching the down button on the elevator panel, she turned toward Tony, holding her bonanza.

"I found a key, Tony." At eye level, she held up a plastic bag with a small silver key dropped inside. "It was on a ring along with the rest of his desk keys, inserted in a lock, just dangling there. It stood out from the rest 'cause it was a little longer."

"Longer gets noticed a lot. Trust me," he teased with an exaggerated roll of his eyes. "Even though most women won't say it to your face."

"Well, this woman notices things like that." She grinned, letting him infer what he wanted from her remark. "So I compared the lock number to the ID on the keys and found that the longer one didn't match the set."

"That Mickey was a sly dog, hiding it in plain sight like that. Did you happen to find a home for that key?" Tony asked. The elevator door opened, and they stepped inside.

"Not yet. It didn't fit anything in his office or his personal Dunhill locker. But I'm gonna ask around, see if anyone knows about a place outside of work that he could've had a locker or office."

Once on the ground floor, bundled in her coat, Raven stopped at the front security kiosk to check out of the building.

"Let's grab a bite to eat on our way back—" Raven's cell phone chimed, stopping her in midsentence. "Mackenzie here. Talk to me."

"Hey, Raven. It's Scott. Got something interesting on that property search. Looks like your long shot paid off in spades," the CSI man joked.

"Tell me something good, my friend."

"We got a download of properties, but there was one that stood out from the rest—an old armory belonging to the Dunhill Corporation. Any bells going off for you?"

"Loud and clear." She reached into her purse and pulled out a pad and pen to jot down the information. "Give me the address."

Tony's voice droned in the background as he grabbed the notepad from her hand. He was on his cell calling in the information so authorization would be granted to enter the vacant property. Thinking ahead, he wanted a jump on the paperwork while they made their way back to the station house.

"I owe you one, buddy. Thanks." Raven finished her

call, then turned to her partner. "Guess we can forget lunch for now, partner. We got places to be and things to do."

But her mood quickly changed. Stepping up her pace with Tony by her side, Raven tuned everything out, thinking only of Delacorte as she navigated the busy thoroughfare. She had a bad feeling that Christian was involved in Fiona's mess.

How much did he know?

He had deliberately ditched her earlier. She was sure of it. How far would he go to protect Fiona's interests, or worse, cover up a crime he committed? Her stomach twisted in a knot just examining the many questions in her mind. *Could she have been that wrong about him?* Even more disturbing—why did she care?

"Don't borrow trouble." Tony's voice brought her back to the steady hum of traffic.

"What?"

"My mother always used to say that, when she thought I was worrying over something I had no control over," he ventured. "Don't borrow trouble, Raven. Let's just see what we see, okay?"

She stopped for a moment to search his eyes, then smiled. "How did I get to be so lucky, having a partner like you?"

"He works in mysterious ways," Tony offered.

Surprised by the reference, Raven asked, "Who? God?"

"No, the chief. Same difference." Tony laughed.

It reminded her how much she loved her partner.

The limousine rolled quietly through the shabby neighborhood with the full-bodied sound of an orchestra playing faintly over the speakers nearest his ear. Music fortified his tolerance, but did nothing for his disdain at the squalor. He had no sympathy. There would always be poor.

"How else would civility stand out if not for the dregs of society?" His voice resounded off the glass pane. Boredom tainted his tone.

Gazing through the window, Nicholas Charboneau bore witness to the depth of disgrace as if it were a boorish documentary unfolding. He distanced himself from it. On the surface, a thin shield of bulletproof glass insulated him from the rest of humanity. Yet so much more distinguished him from the multitudes.

Slender pale fingers slid down his thigh, long red nails glistening. The scent of exotic spice wafted by him. Turning, he met her eyes. For as long as he'd known her, touch had been her preferred way of communicating. She quietly observed life when it suited her, but her sultry voice beckoned his complete attention.

"You forget yourself, Nicky. Remember, you thrive on the misfortune of others. Do not now condemn them."

Elegantly dressed, the petite woman at his side wore a silk dress of midnight blue, her coat tossed onto the seat. Her dark hair was pulled loosely from her face, accentuating her slender neck and delectable jawline. Because she was of Chinese descent, her serene dark eyes masterfully slanted, giving her a mysterious and intelligent quality. Flawless skin reminded him of creamery butter.

His young bodyguard was exquisite—and quite deadly.

"You know me well. And you are most correct, dear one. I can attribute my livelihood to the weaknesses of others. In theory, I should celebrate their adversity." Good-naturedly, he laughed at her bold observation.

Being the heir to a crime family, he often found himself surrounded by people who guarded their true opinion. They told him only what they thought he wanted to hear. Not Jasmine Lee. She always spoke her mind. He remembered how they'd met. And it always brought a smile to his lips.

Glancing down at her delicate hands, he remembered the time that he'd witnessed those graceful fingers taking a life, when she was barely out of her teen years. In a rough area of downtown Chicago, he'd accompanied a rather shady friend to some forgettable jazz club. Not much remained in his memory of that night, except for the vivid details of Jasmine. The man had been many times her size and looked as if he had instigated the confrontation. In actuality, she had quietly spurred him on and wielded a knife to make her point. For her part, and to witnesses, it would appear to be self-defense, but he recognized premeditation when he saw it. And he'd noticed with admiration that fear never once shadowed her face. The attack was over almost before it began, and she never hesitated to do what had to be done.

But it wasn't her efficiency that piqued his interest.

It was the essence behind her enigmatic eyes, vessels brimming with a lust for life—and death. She seemed to enjoy the kill, such a rare and valuable quality in an employee, much less one so beautiful. Yet she held her vulnerability restrained, not letting it show until later. She had killed the man for a sin he had committed against her family. It wasn't until later that she told him the whole story, and he admired her all the more.

The adrenaline rush compelled him to act, to take her into his life and eventually hire her. Yet a deeper desire to harness her savagery, for his own benefit, drew her into his inner circle—and into his bed. Her loyalty knew no bounds.

"We're almost there, Mantis."

His affectionate nickname for her brought a graceful curve to her lips, pleasing him immensely. The female praying mantis always devoured the head of the male in the throes of copulation. He often wondered if the male of the species believed such sacrifice to be worth the extra effort.

"I apologize for subjecting you to this unpleasant business. As soon as we conclude this distasteful interlude, I shall make it up to you over dinner."

"Just being in your company comforts me, Nicky."

Nicky. Prior to Jasmine, it had been many years since someone had called him by that name. His bodyguard and confidante had no idea that the nickname engendered many bittersweet memories in him. Only one other person called him Nicky. And he had already taken a course of action to destroy a woman he still loved. Memories flooded his mind, back to his early twenties—a lifetime ago.

Feeling like Romeo to her Juliet, Nicholas couldn't resist a young woman named Fiona Fitzgerald. In her late teens, she'd captivated his complete attention during an intermission in the opera *La Bohème*, her lithe form made even more beautiful by the white beaded gown she wore. Although their affair had been torrid from the start, it was all too brief, cut short by her arranged betrothal to Charles Dunhill, the heir apparent of a rival crime family to his own.

He never understood why she chose another. Especially since he felt so sure she loved him. Fortified by the invincibility of youth, he begged her to marry him instead, in total disregard of his own safety. For her love, he'd been willing to wage war against his rival. But in the end, she refused to see him, not giving him the satisfaction of an answer. His throat clenched with the memory.

But his Fiona gave him a precious gift, something her husband would never claim. Given such innocence, no gift ever touched him quite as much.

Despite his feelings for her, Nicholas had seen Fiona become his new rival after the unsolved murder of her husband. Conducting his own investigation of the assassination, he'd found the chink in the Dunhill armor, and discovered his lover had grown a spine— and a ruthless nature. To not take advantage of such an opportunity would have been foolish. And he no longer considered himself a foolish young man. Business was business.

Drawing him back to the present, the late-afternoon sun stabbed through the gray clouds and warmed his face through tinted windows. Even with dark glasses, he squinted against the light, catching his image in the glass when the sun cooperated.

His dark hair, infused with gray at the temples, glistened in the light. The deep blue of his eyes flashed in the warm rays, even under his designer frames. He had changed from the man Fiona knew. Time and cynicism had weathered him.

Yet in spite of being in his late fifties, he still garnered the attention of women, even before they discovered his identity. His reputation as a powerful and wealthy man drew them like bees to warm honey, augmented even more by his notoriety as an accomplished lover. He'd cultivated his celebrity over the years on all fronts. But he had never proposed marriage to any woman other than Fiona, preferring his solitude to anything second best.

"Perhaps some entertainment might distract you." Jasmine's soft voice kept him from falling victim to his memories. Her gaze directed him elsewhere. "I know how you are so easily bored."

A motion to his left snared his attention to a darkened corner of the vehicle. A drama played silently on a small television. A DVD looped images that served to inspire him. Scene after scene of death played out before his eyes. Even now, a pride of lions devoured a wildebeest, their muzzles red with blood from a successful hunt, their half-lidded eyes satiated with the kill.

The brutality made a mockery of the classical music lilting in the background. Yet, such was his paradoxical life—the exhilarating adrenaline rush of his criminal endeavors tempered by the civility he favored. He had been truly blessed, and cursed.

"Yes, you understand me indeed," he muttered under his breath, not taking his eyes off the screen.

No pretext of love existed between him and Jasmine. They filled a need in each other that no one else understood. And she knew merely what he allowed her to know. Only one woman understood his softer underbelly. It had been the last time he felt so vulnerable to another living soul. Love was a weakness. And it'd been a painful lesson indeed.

Dismissing his unsettling reflections, he watched the drama played out on the screen. A cheetah slowly stalked a herd of gazelle in search of the weakest—a fine example of Darwin's theory on survival. Terror in the eyes of prey infused him with a sense of power as menacing death pursued its next victim. *Truly an inspiration!* Yes, he'd never feel vulnerable again.

His driver slowed and turned onto another side street. He glanced at his watch. Just past three. If this had been a peer in his social circle, he would've been embarrassed by his own tardiness. But he planned to meet with one of his more depraved contractors—a necessary evil in his line of work.

Logan McBride could wait. The man was a bleak illustration of how much he'd changed over the years. Harnessing a beast like McBride reminded him of the power broker he'd become—one of the many reasons he minimized face-to-face meetings with the man.

The limo turned right and entered a cyclone-fenced parking lot near a warehouse. Standing by a loading dock, McBride waited, his hands stuffed into the pockets of a coat draped over a cheap suit. The driver pulled alongside the man. The vehicle stopped only long enough for him to grant entrance to the unwanted intrusion.

"Thanks for meeting me. I know this is a risk—" McBride spoke as he slid inside, his eyes cagily searching the interior. "Oh, my. I wasn't expecting company."

Charboneau kept his eyes on McBride, who was quite charmed by his Mantis. From experience, he knew that her expression would not change with the flattery. Her hand tightened on his thigh ever so slightly, communicating her dislike for the man. But McBride was obviously pleased at finding a beautiful woman so near. Charboneau had seen the look before. Taken by her beauty, many men underestimated her—another one of his distinct advantages.

"You said it was urgent. I trust your judgment," Charboneau interrupted. Of course, nothing could be further from the truth. But stroking the man's ego felt prudent.

A long, tedious moment passed before McBride shifted his eyes away from Mantis. Eventually, the man's gaze dropped to the decanter of Cognac, and with a nod, he gestured his intention. "May I?"

Motioning his permission, Charboneau made a mental note to fumigate the interior of the vehicle and toss what was left of a very fine family blend of liquor.

"What is so very important, Mr. McBride? I had hoped to keep our meetings to a minimum, for both our sakes."

Without an ounce of appreciation, the man tossed back the liquor as if it were cheap swill, wiping his mouth with the back of his hand.

"Yeah, I know, but something came up." Setting down his empty glass, McBride shifted his eyes to the woman, then back to him. "Can I speak freely?"

"Certainly," he replied, ignoring the usual social etiquette of an introduction to his female companion. Mantis slid closer to him, insinuating her intimacy without so much as a word.

"Before I get into it, I have to ask. Did you deliberately arrange for Detective Raven Mackenzie to be the homicide cop on this case?" The man smiled. Spikes of short blond hair stood at attention atop his head. Icy gray eyes awaited his reply.

A brooding Beethoven filled the void in conversation. Charboneau's eyes drifted toward the television screen once more, finding it more suitable viewing than the crass man sitting before him. The cheetah inched its way through the brush, then leapt from cover to launch an attack, its lean, muscular body poised for the kill. A smirk fought for freedom. He indulged it.

"It was kismet. I couldn't pass up such an opportunity on your behalf. And fringe benefits are plentiful with a job well done. Do you approve of my idea of job satisfaction, Mr. McBride?"

"I don't know how you arranged it, Blue Blood. I am truly in awe of your influence and abilities. But surely you must know how much I hate cops and that I have a long memory when it comes to settling an old score." McBride's eyes darted to the TV, clearly avoiding his.

He knew McBride had no appreciation for the raw power portrayed on the small screen. So for a brief moment, he allowed himself to indulge in his pleasure, but one thought nagged him.

Perhaps McBride had become a liability.

The music began a foreboding crescendo, rousing his blood. Yet despite the tension in the moment, he remained calm, unreadable. His gaze settled on the man.

"I knew you would want to tempt fate with a little retribution, but this mustn't interfere with my plan. What you do with her after our business arrangement is concluded, that is certainly up to you. Do we have an understanding, Mr. McBride?"

Silence. A long moment passed between them.

Logan finally replied, "I have no doubt we understand each other."

On the surface, the man's remark might appear conciliatory, but Charboneau suspected otherwise. McBride had indeed become a liability.

"For now, you have the ability to shape our future association, Mr. McBride. And I, for one, eagerly await your course of action. Whether you work with me or choose another direction, I assure you I am up for the challenge."

Without saying a word, Mantis tensed, her muscles preparing to attack if necessary. He felt her body stiffen, anticipating trouble.

"I'll consider your advice." Logan glanced out the window, then returned his stare. "Let me out here. I believe we've conveyed our intentions."

"I believe we have," he agreed, his expression rigid with contempt.

Signaling his driver to pull over, he watched in silence as McBride left the limo, but the man turned back for a final point.

"Sometimes an animal must remain true to his nature, don't you agree?"

"You will get no argument here, sir." A lazy smile crooked his lips. "I'm sure this goes without saying, but if you divulge our business arrangement to the authorities in any fashion, being torn apart and devoured by savage beasts will seem like the mythological Elysian fields. And as you've seen, my influence transcends many boundaries. Consider your future carefully, Mr. McBride."

As the door slammed shut, he watched the smug expression of the man standing at the curb, waving farewell as the limo pulled away. McBride would be too impetuous to heed his warning.

"It would be quite gratifying to kill that man, in a most painful manner."

"Yes, it would, Nicky." With a demure smile, Mantis slid her slender arm through his. "Would you like me to take care of that?"

"Eventually, my dear. But for now, Mr. McBride will determine his own fate. If he can postpone his revenge, then he might prove a useful ally, and live awhile longer."

"And if he cannot?"

"Then you and I may contrive a DVD of our own, featuring the vulgar Logan McBride."

Her soft, feminine laughter made him smile as his cell phone rang.

"Yes?" His greeting was cryptic; very few people had his personal cell phone number. The familiar voice on the other end needed no introduction.

"The package that you wanted traced? We've located it. When can I meet you to discuss the particulars?"

"Good work. Meet me in an hour at the usual location." Without a word more, he ended the call and turned to his lovely companion.

"Mantis, my dear, I'm afraid I must indulge in another diversion before we have dinner. I hope you don't mind."

Her only response was to softly touch his cheek with a velvet stroke of a finger. Shifting his gaze toward the window, he inhaled deeply, then slowly released it, in anticipation of his next meeting.

He'd paid a lot of money to locate Fiona Dunhill. In his heart of hearts, could he destroy her, or would he ultimately settle for something short of complete annihilation? Regardless, he steeled himself for the next step of his plan.

Only a face-to-face would determine her fate.

CHAPTER 7

The afternoon sun burned off the gray morning clouds, and glistening streams of melted snow held the promise of a break in the weather. None of it lightened Christian's mood as he drove his SUV down a deserted side street. His gut twisted over what he might find inside the old abandoned armory.

Would he be opening a Pandora's box of Fiona's creation?

After pulling a paper from his coat pocket, he confirmed the address. A gray cyclone fence, laden with rusted metal signs, declared the red brick armory to be the property of Dunhill Corporation. Set amidst other forsaken hulls of warehouses, the place looked like a disaster. In the fading gray of winter, even under the warming sun, it looked bleak and ominous.

"Why here, Mickey?" he muttered as he brought his vehicle to a stop. "This place is not exactly your style."

Christian parked next to the main gate, then walked toward the entrance. He reached for the padlock and metal links dangling from the fence. No need for the set of keys in his slacks pocket. The chain had been severed, leaving the gate open.

And just ahead, a discarded shell of a black Mercedes lay atop cinder blocks, stripped of anything valuable. Neon spray paint marred its once sleek finish. The local criminal element had marked their turf with cryptic taunts, thumbing their nose at law enforcement with bright paint. No attempt made to hide the metal remains. Through the vehicle identification number, the police would have identified it sooner or later. He had no need to check DMV records to know. It had once belonged to Mickey.

Hunching his shoulders against the cold, he shoved his hands deeper into his coat pockets. "You sure loved that car, Mick."

Shadowed by the old building, a metal door lay to the right of the elevated delivery bays. The door looked like it would've been Mickey's only option. With a tug, Christian found the entry locked. He tried his keys and gained access.

The sun poured in from the doorway, only dimly lighting the skeletal core of the old munitions factory. The gloom repelled the light as if the shapeless void were a sentient being, cowering from view and hoarding its secrets. Looking overhead, he noticed every window had been blackened, embellishing the sinister nature of the chamber. A faint smell of paint lingered in the air, making him believe the modification had been recent—and very deliberate.

He stepped farther into the darkness, but stopped short. Tiny feet skittered across the floor. With a frenzied screech, a rat darted to his right, shocked by the sudden exposure to daylight. The commotion caused a ripple effect. An army of unseen creatures slithered for more suitable places to hide, puckering the skin at the nape of his neck. *God, I hate rats!*

The old building gave him a bad case of the creeps.

The darkness came alive, seizing Christian with panic before he had mentally prepared for it. Despite years of therapy, he succumbed to the sensation, an unavoidable reaction. He kept the door open to reinforce his control over his phobia. If he shut it now, he'd be drawn into it, without footing. As if he were lying in a sensory deprivation tank, or had been set adrift in dead space, he sensed his equilibrium faltering. The oppressive silence weighed heavy, tightening his chest. He felt his breathing grow shallow.

An old, familiar affliction.

One thing was certain. The place could harbor his worst nightmare. No one needed to tell him Mickey had died here. Death loomed heavy in the putrid air. How he knew this, he couldn't quite grasp. Christian no longer questioned his bizarre link to the Grim Reaper. He just knew.

In an instant, he'd been transported back to his childhood terror, the wound made fresh with his early-morning nightmare.

"Deep breath." He found his center and searched for composure. The old terror was hard to quell. "Now let it go, slow." He uttered his reflexive mantra.

To avoid being swallowed by his habitual fear, he shut his eyes. He listened patiently for his heart to slow, until he no longer felt every single beat thrashing in his chest. Yet an odd sensation inched its way hot from his belly to his fingertips. An inexplicable aura warmed him, giving him immeasurable comfort. At first, he couldn't place the peculiar tingle. Soon it had a name.

Raven Mackenzie.

The delicate scent of her skin bathed in fragrant soap. The tentative touch of her fingers along his stomach.

The luster of her dark hair. Eyes that sucked you in, cradling you in safety.

Unlike his usual recovery method for anxiety, the thought of Raven spread rapidly throughout his body and mind. It filled him with serenity. Unnerving. A part of him would've preferred a merciful rap upside the head with a baseball bat. Another side of him longed for—

"Damn it!" he cursed. "Quit thinking from below your belt."

Finally losing the harsh rhythm to his heart, he opened his eyes again, letting Raven dissipate from his thoughts. Getting accustomed to the dark, he found the shapes making sense. Walls of wooden crates, rusted metal foundry equipment, and garbage lay piled in disarray, like his war room at the Dunhill Estate.

At least, that's what he told himself.

Venturing into the shadows to his right, he felt for the lights. His fingers found a panel pulled from the wall, wires exposed. If the damage had been done years ago, he would've expected the wires to be encrusted with dirt or cobwebs. These were free of such texture. Whoever cut the wires hadn't intended Mickey to find the light switch operable near the main entrance.

Closing his eyes again, he let his instincts take over, skills honed over the many years since the violent loss of his childhood.

Just like the war room, Delacorte!

He felt certain the old building maintained a minimal amount of electricity for security reasons. Allowing his mind to wander, he imagined how the electrical circuits might have been set up and began his systematic search for a backup light switch.

If Mickey had died here, surely there must be clues

to help him seek the truth. And he'd need light to do a thorough search.

Making his way farther into the darkness, he kept his eyes shut, heightening his other senses. When he neared a solid obstruction, the airflow around him changed with only a faint subtlety. The perception brushed his skin. Coupled with that, sound bounced from the mass and deadened as he drew closer, giving it dimension. He supposed his ability was similar to that possessed by a bat with its sonar. With skill and agility, he sidestepped the obstacles in his path, eventually discovering another light panel in a far corner. This one had juice. The lights crackled to life, flickering a meager battle against the darkness until they eventually won out. He squinted and raised his hand to shield his sensitive eyes from the welcome intrusion.

"Why the hell did you come here, Mick?" he asked again. The place looked like a war zone. From where he stood, light shed no greater understanding.

The obstacles he'd sensed earlier were arranged in a makeshift maze. Discarded machinery, heaps of trash, and rusted barrels were strewn in grand design. Barriers erected in a pattern created a funnel wider by the doorway, then narrowed as the path led farther away to an inner circle.

He wandered the main passage, feeling certain Mickey would've done the same, but he had the benefit of electricity. Mick would've been lost in the dark. Small breaks in the barricades allowed access between the passageways, but unless the man had known the layout, his escape route would've led into countless dead ends like a frustrating maze. Catwalks and metal stairways overhead gave high ground to his attackers, making Mickey an easy target.

When he neared the inner circle of the labyrinth, his jaw fell slack with shock.

A sense of what the man had endured submersed him in an emotional quagmire. He pictured Mickey being tormented, pummeled from above, then ritualistically murdered in the center ring like the main event to a circus. The twisted mind that orchestrated the macabre killing staggered him—a prime example of the cruelty mankind visited on its own. The same kind of deranged mind that could pull the trigger on his younger sister while she ran to her mother in fear.

Fueling his imagination, his senses dimmed the overhead lighting to black, setting the stage for savagery. Flashes of Mickey's terror darkened his eyes, infused by images of his own childhood trauma. Undistinguishable, visions lambasted him in rapid succession, embroiling him in a waking nightmare. Blinding him.

Now I lay me down to sleep— Please, God . . . Help me! The tortured screams of a child filled his brain. Powerless. Trapped. Happening all over again. But a familiar voice beckoned him to release his pain.

The voice cried out, "Stop where you are, Delacorte. We've got a warrant to search the place."

As if he had emerged from a thick haze, his mind slowly cleared. A figure eclipsed a bright light like a vaporous mirage. He raised his hand to shield his eyes. An image of a woman came into focus. Detective Mackenzie hurried toward him, armed with a document. Her partner was close behind. No doubt, he'd just lost his edge in the investigation.

"This is Dunhill property. What brings you here, Detectives?" His words sounded hollow. Jutting from his memory, cruel images still tortured him.

No amount of posturing or stalling would help. What lay in the inner circle would be incriminating enough. He had no hope of dissuading her from her duty. Whatever evidence remained of Mickey's murder would clearly imply a connection to Fiona. No way to stop it. Given his link to the family, he'd consider it a stroke of good fortune if the police allowed him to stay involved with the case at all. Now, he needed Raven on his side. How he would accomplish this feat, he had no idea.

Slapping the paper to his chest, the detective smirked, "Let's drop the charade, shall we? You ditched me earlier so you could come here alone and get a jump on your own investigation. Why are you here, Christian?" Raven questioned.

But the sound of her voice carried in the chamber. They'd have no privacy to talk about how he'd acquired the address. He didn't know how to answer without giving himself away. So he didn't.

Saving him from the wrath of Detective Mackenzie, her partner stepped past him, making his way to the inner circle. "You touch anything, Mr. Delacorte?" the man asked.

"No. Just got here. It took me a while to find lights that worked." His eyes shifted to the floor, taking in the disturbing scene. "What the hell—"

The cement floor was stained a deep brown, the stench of blood still in the air. Arterial spray tainted a wall, like a gruesome display of modern art. Dried blood told the story. Mickey had died here—in this desolate place. The man's coat and tie were carefully laid out on the floor, away from the heaviest concentration of blood. Shirt buttons had been gathered and set beside the high-priced coat in mockery, trivializing

Mick's lifestyle at the scene of his slaughter. Whoever killed him had no respect for the law. Everything had been laid out for the police in obvious contempt.

Most shocking were the copies of newspaper clippings placed upon a grouping of wooden crates. Some were unrecognizable, but the ones he knew well stole his breath like a punch to the gut.

FAMILY MASSACRED

GUNMEN KILL FAMILY

POLICE ACTION INVESTIGATED

The headlines and photos of his childhood terror filled his eyes and blurred them with tears. Disturbing as these articles were, those set alongside them made his mind reel with even more questions. A chill shivered through him and exposed his heart with the precision of a surgeon.

CHARLES DUNHILL MURDERED

SNIPER KILLS PROMINENT LOCAL

What connection did the murder of Charles Dunhill have to his family's horror? Whoever killed Mickey Blair knew the answers. Suddenly, the sign pinned to Mick's chest invaded his confusion. *Seek the truth, Christian.*

The truth about what? His eyes zeroed in on the newspaper clippings, blocking out the rest of the world—a world that had ceased to exist for him in that instant. He felt entrenched in his past. Sinking to one knee, he picked up one of the articles with trembling fingers. A tear lost its hold and trailed down his cheek.

Reality hit hard. His past had been nothing more than an illusion—devoid of substance. Fiona must have known. Yet she had chosen to leave him floundering in ignorance. The only person he trusted had left him behind, to discover the truth on his own. But why?

Who the hell was he? And why was he connected to so much death?

Christian slumped to the cement floor, stunned. Raven knew he shouldn't be touching the evidence, but she couldn't deny the man his shocking disbelief. He looked dazed. Her heart ached for him.

"Scott. We're gonna need a team here." Tony's voice droned in the background. Her partner served as a stark reminder of her duty. Despite her feelings to the contrary, she'd come to do a job. And Christian was not officially part of it. Kneeling by his side, she clasped his hand and squeezed it. She found defeat in his eyes.

"Christian, come with me."

She felt sure he hadn't heard her at first. Then he stood and let her lead him through the maze, toward the doorway. Although he stared straight ahead, he looked completely lost. Only a small part of him remained. With the sun low in the sky, a chill captured the intruding night air, hurling a gust at their feet. Standing by the entrance, she broke the silence.

"I'll make sure you get copies of the articles," she offered. In reply, he merely lowered his head. "What do you think they mean? Obviously, the killer staged it all."

By the pained expression on his face, she knew the question already had occurred to him. He just shook his head. For a long while, she wasn't sure he'd speak.

"*Seek the truth, Christian.* I wish I knew . . ." His thought trailed off, vanquished by his overwhelming ordeal. He didn't hide the emotion, nor had he wiped the drying path of a tear. Her attraction deepened. But she had a job to do.

"What do you know about the murder of Charles Dunhill?" The accusation was absent from her voice. He'd been only a boy when Dunhill had been murdered. "I want to help you find the truth, Christian. Please let me do that."

"I'm afraid of what I'm gonna find, Raven." The honesty caught in his throat. "I thought I knew who I was, but now—"

"You told me that Mickey might have supplemented his income with a sniper rifle. And Charles Dunhill was killed by a sniper."

Her words hung in the air like a malevolent cloud, judging by his reaction. She knew it wasn't directed at her. Yet his fierce green eyes absorbed her insinuation without a word, eventually softening to his shattered acceptance of her rationale.

"Do you think that's the connection to Mickey? Could he have killed Dunhill? Maybe that's the truth the killer wants you to find."

"I don't know. It was so long ago. But I think the killer assumes there's a link. Maybe the bigger question is why Dunhill was killed. That's the truth I need to find. That reason could shed some light on my past." He closed his eyes and lowered his chin. His shoulders slumped with the weight of his only reasonable course of action. "Look, I know I have no right to ask this, but can you locate the old police files for the Dunhill murder investigation? Maybe we can find a lead there."

"We?" she questioned. "Now we're a team?"

"I deserved that."

By the look of him, Christian knew how tenuous his status was in their investigation. But it didn't stop him from trying. She understood completely. If their roles had been reversed, it wouldn't have stopped her, either.

"I'm asking you. Please. You said you wanted to help. I need you, Raven. I can't do this on my own."

She searched his eyes. *God, how she wanted to trust him.* And as much as he needed help from the police, she and Tony could certainly benefit from his complete cooperation. Obviously, the case dealt with his past. Still, she had an active investigation to conduct—in the here and now. As if she were walking a tight wire, she balanced between personal desire and duty. No safety net.

"Let me talk it over with Tony. But if we share the old case file, I have to know you're completely with us. No more hidden agendas."

"I understand. And for me, there's more at stake here than just my past. Not sure I can make any promises until I talk to someone. Can you accept that?"

Raven had been willing to give him the benefit of the doubt. She expected a show of relief on his face. But instead, his usual somber expression returned, tinged with a seductive vulnerability. All he had to do was play ball, but he warned her that he couldn't make promises. Someone was in harm's way. And he'd forgo his own motives to protect whoever it was. Things just got complicated.

"You're stretching my patience, Delacorte." She furrowed her brow, unsure how to proceed. Another tack occurred to her. "Can you think of anyplace else that Mickey might have kept some kind of locker? I found a key in his desk that seemed out of place."

He thought for a moment. "Nothing comes to mind. But give me time to think on that."

"I need a show of good faith, Christian. You're not giving me anything to work with here."

"I know," he muttered. "But I will. It's just that there's something I have to do first."

An undercurrent of anxiety contradicted his usually stoic nature. Completely understandable. But it also looked like he struggled to confide in her—throwing her off-balance. How could she rely on him?

With a new resolve, he affirmed her notion. "I want you to trust me, but I haven't given you much reason to do that."

Somewhere in his words, she searched for honesty—needed to find it. Christian gazed upon her as if seeing her for the first time. He brushed back a strand of her hair. The act of tenderness implied an affection he hadn't communicated before now. It seduced the very breath from her lips. And by the restrained desire in his eyes, the move even caught him by surprise.

"Have dinner with me. Tonight." He pulled from her and threw out his invitation as he stepped through the door, safely distancing himself. "We need to talk."

"My house. Eight sharp. I'll cook." Her mouth promised what she couldn't deliver. For her, cooking was anything stuck in the microwave, ready in five minutes—or a heaping bowl of cereal. After giving him her address, she added, "You bring the wine." Despite a lack of competence in the kitchen, she promised a home-cooked meal, like they'd done this a thousand times.

A faint smile touched his lips, like he read her mind. It had been so subtle, she might have missed it altogether.

"Thanks," he replied. Picking up his pace, he headed for his car just as her team of CSI pulled onto the street.

What the hell had just happened?

Tony stepped beside her. "So you got a hot date tonight—and dinner, no less." He crossed his arms over his chest. "Is this a subtle interrogation technique, plying him with an overload of carbs and Pinot Noir?"

"He wants to talk."

"My wife, Yolie, will be the first one to tell you—I am a guy. And even if she didn't want to personally vouch for me, I got my *man card* to prove it. So I've got a pretty good idea what's on his mind. Not sure about you. Like the book says, women are from Pluto."

"And men are fresh from Uranus. What's your point, Tony?"

He turned toward her with a hesitant smile and placed his hand on her elbow, giving it a tug. "The guy's got more baggage than the airlines, Mac. And I should know; one of them still has my best Samsonite, a family heirloom lovingly bundled in duct tape. It might be you're setting up for a very big fall."

Despite his attempt at humor, concern shaped his expression when he spoke again. "And we haven't absolved him from any wrongdoing here. Keep that in mind. You're playing a very dangerous game with a guy who might've invented the word 'dangerous.' When you look up the word in the dictionary—"

"Yeah, I know. I'm gonna find his picture." She sighed, paraphrasing his long-standing joke. "And he'll be smiling."

"Still, if he does want to talk, you might be able to learn something useful about his past." Hooking a knuckle under her chin, he badgered her culinary skills.

"Why don't you stick around here for a while, then take off when you need to. Knowing you, your cupboards are bare of anything remotely edible by a man's standards. You'll need time to grocery shop and memorize a cookbook or two. I can take care of things here."

"Oh, God, you're right. Why did I promise to cook?" A jumble of expletives rolled from her mouth, easing a chuckle from Tony.

"You're gonna do fine," he lied, not very adept at the art. "Just take care of your heart, partner." His expression grew more solemn. "That part could use some Kevlar."

She smiled at Tony, giving his shoulder a soft punch. "Thanks for the tip, tough guy. Your Yolanda is one lucky woman."

"That's what I keep trying to tell her." He laughed.

Backing away, she let the CSI crew through the doorway, nodding a greeting. "Come on, Tony. We got a crime scene to process. The quicker we start, the sooner you'll be home with your beautiful wife and adorable kids."

"If I get home at a reasonable hour, Yolie will think I'm a burglar. She'd shoot me if she allowed a weapon in the house besides my service revolver."

"Maybe you're the one needing the Kevlar, my friend."

She loved getting the rare opportunity to make Tony laugh. Usually it was the other way around. Given their work, it tipped the scales to have a partner she had grown to love like a brother.

Within an hour, Raven rushed home via the neighborhood grocery store—a list of ingredients filling her brain. Before leaving, she heard Tony arrange to hitch a ride back to the station house with one of the crime-scene techs.

Beyond the normal anxiety surrounding her unsteadiness in the kitchen, her pulse raced at the thought of Christian in her home. She'd been trained to defend herself against larger opponents, scored well at the firing range, was proficient in multiple weapons. Yet the idea of this man crossing her threshold, being invited to share her personal space, unnerved her beyond reason. After all, she was no Martha Stewart.

What the hell had she been thinking?

"I made you a promise, Logan. I know where the pretty detective lives." Vinnie beamed as he spoke into his cell phone, pleased he'd finally satisfied McBride on the subject of Raven Mackenzie. "And you were right. It looks like she lives alone."

With the heater in his truck faltering, he recited the address, giving the man a general sense of the location. The small bungalow was situated northwest of Wrigley Field in a quiet neighborhood of neatly trimmed lawns, flower boxes, pruned hedges, and unattached garages set behind cyclone fences. He imagined the quiet suburb would be thrown off its axis when Logan McBride arrived.

"You think she'd be receptive to a male caller?" McBride asked. "On such short notice?"

Logan's soft laughter sent shivers down Vinnie's spine. He'd been on the receiving end of the man's idea of humor. A small part of him felt sorry for the woman. Fortunately, this weakness was short-lived, as he suspected the detective might soon be.

"She's just been grocery shopping. I'm sure she's up for some entertaining," he replied. If Logan hadn't been in the picture, Vinnie would have considered paying a social call himself. His blood churned south, giving rise to his show of bravado.

"Good job, Vin. Now get out of there before you draw flies." Logan ended the call with his usual lack of protocol.

Shifted into gear, his old truck rumbled a protest when it lurched forward. Vinnie grinned, content he'd done what he could to please McBride. He served up the good detective on a platter, ripe for the taking. After tonight, Detective Raven Mackenzie would understand what it felt like to have the Devil cross her path.

As for himself, he wasn't sure if he considered his involvement with Logan a curse or a questionable stroke of good fortune. But he was willing to share the experience.

Dusk resisted the impending darkness with the last-ditch effort of the sun, spewing tendrils of pale orange across a surging night sky. The sheer draperies of his bedroom window flushed in pastel. Yet in the dying light, his sense of urgency mounted. Christian rationalized that the tension stemmed from his habitual reaction to the coming darkness, understanding and accepting the daily occurrence. But his stress was exacerbated by his concern for Fiona. He stopped his pacing and pulled back the fabric, hoping the view of the lingering sunlight would calm him.

But two of his security personnel, dressed in black uniforms and carrying weapons, patrolled along a pathway outside his bedroom window. The reality of his predicament made painfully clear. Despite the beauty surrounding him, the threat of violence existed. It was his life. With a heavy sigh, he let the drape fall. Turning, he stared at the phone on his nightstand.

Christian dreaded what he had to do.

It went against years of trust, built by a bond forged

from a fragile and broken childhood. But he couldn't put it off any longer. He had to find Fiona, retrace her movements. Slowly, he moved toward his bed and sat on the edge of his mattress, imagining the sound of her voice. Still, he had no idea what she'd say.

How was she connected to Mickey? To him, she'd admitted a link to the man. If the police discovered that Mickey had killed Charles Dunhill, would the next logical leap be that Fiona had been involved in her husband's death? And what did all this have to do with his family's massacre?

Dread filled him, jarring bile in his stomach. Dialing the number to Dunhill Security, he waited for someone to answer.

"Security. Edwards speaking."

"Hey, Bill. This is Christian. Any luck on that special assignment I gave you?"

Christian had known Bill Edwards for a number of years. Trusting the man to be discreet, he had asked him to do a preliminary search on Fiona's whereabouts. The connection between Mickey and the Dunhill armory had instigated his initial concern. And after seeing the place, he felt glad he'd assigned the job to this man.

"Not yet, Christian. But something of interest just came up. I was getting ready to call you."

"Oh? What's up?" He wasn't sure he could handle another complication.

"Someone representing themselves as Dunhill Security has been asking about Mrs. Dunhill. Apparently, they're attempting to do the very thing you've asked from me—trying to find her." The grave tone of his voice only mirrored Christian's apprehension. "Whoever it is has contacted the hangar and some of her favorite haunts in Europe. I've determined they came up empty so far, but maybe their luck will turn. What do you want me to do?"

He shut his eyes and took a deep breath. Someone else searched for Fiona. It took him a moment to compose himself enough to speak.

"Keep looking for her. When she wants to hide, she's a damned ghost. I just wish she wasn't so good at it."

"I'll keep in touch, Christian. You'll know something the second I do."

"Thanks. And Bill, keep this assignment between you and me."

"I know, boss. Hang in there."

Without fanfare, the call ended. But he was more worried now than before. Why had Fiona run? And who trailed her now? The part that hurt the worst was her lack of faith in him to help her. He owed her his life. And she hadn't trusted him with her own.

Rising from the bed, he yanked the shirttail from his slacks and unbuttoned his shirt, heading for the bathroom and a long shower. He wanted to talk to Fiona before committing to help the police. But now, his surrogate mother would have to trust his judgment on the matter. The old police files on the assassination of Charles Dunhill might hold the key to this whole mystery—or be the last nail in Fiona's coffin. He had no choice. With someone after Fiona, his instincts told him to push ahead.

And after the way he'd treated the beautiful Raven Mackenzie, he'd have to coerce her into helping him. The thought of pressing her for help didn't entirely displease him.

Steam from the shower billowed in the small bathroom and blurred the mirror in a matter of minutes. Out of habit, Raven cracked the door an inch to let the moisture escape before she stepped in. Her old home had its bothersome idiosyncrasies, offset by the treasured memories crammed into every nook and cranny. Normally more frugal with her hot water, Raven made this concession to relax after a long day. Slipping her fluffy white terry-cloth robe from her shoulders, she hung it on a hook and slid open the opaque shower door. After stepping into the bathtub, she closed the door and breathed in thick steam.

A low gasp escaped her lips when the water doused her skin, reddening the surface. As she stuck her head directly under the hot blast, the water tingled her scalp and massaged her body with its scorching pressure. She closed her eyes and let the steady stream pummel her. Hot water poured down her face and shoulders. *God, it felt good*. It almost made her forget she had a guest coming.

Almost.

Spaghetti sauce was set to a low simmer on her stove. Bubbling pockets of tomato sauce infused fresh herbs all through the ingredients. A simple salad cooled in her refrigerator. All that remained was to cook the pasta and to pop garlic bread under the broiler.

Her father had taught her the sauce recipe, handed down from a mother who died when she was too young to cherish any real remembrances. It had been her father's way of sharing the woman he loved. So with every ingredient, her mother's devotion now filled her family home with a heady aroma.

Cooking for one had always been a challenge. It'd been a long time since she'd invited someone for a home-cooked meal. Too long. Her small dining table was set for two. And thus far, she had successfully resisted the urge to place candles as a centerpiece. This wasn't a date, she reminded herself. The last time she checked her manual on police procedures, candles were not a necessary formality for an interrogation. Under normal circumstances.

A smile touched her lips—a man like Christian was anything but routine.

Night had robbed the sky of light. Logan loved the anonymity of the dark. The modest neighborhood was now steeped in shadows. Only the occasional security light at a side door or the glow from a living room window would give him away if he were silhouetted by it. He parked on the next block over. Now on foot, he slowly crept closer to her bungalow, careful not to be noticed.

He had the tools he needed to break in. Now all he needed was a dark corner to work. He sneered when he found it. A tall evergreen shrub would give him cover, protection from any unwanted attention from a nosy neighbor. Carefully, he unscrewed an overhead light bulb by the carport, his hand insulated by a black leather glove. Cops were just as vulnerable to home invasion. Their egos probably made them feel invincible.

After carefully peering through a small window in the door, he made sure he wouldn't be walking into a gun and began his work on the lock. The entry gave way without so much as a creak to announce him. Sliding into the kitchen of Raven Mackenzie, he smelled the aroma of her dinner. By the amount of food, she expected company. The thought of getting caught only heightened his exhilaration. But if she walked in on him now, he'd have to kill her. That would spoil all his fun. After all, he had plans for her.

With his gloved hand, he grabbed a wooden spoon and sampled her spaghetti sauce. It tasted homemade, not just a lame facsimile out of a bottle like his men ate.

The flavor piqued his taste buds—and his interest in the woman. Good looks and she cooked. What a waste, considering what he had in mind.

The sound of the shower made his body react. He pictured the woman naked, her skin covered only sparingly by soapsuds. The thought aroused him. With even greater audacity, he skulked down the hallway toward the sound. Blood coursed through his veins at breakneck speed. Passing through a hallway of framed mementos, Logan felt powerful and bold, even in sight of her family's smiling faces. His intrusion made a mockery of it all. Then his eyes were drawn to an old photo of a cop in uniform.

"Fuck you, asshole," he whispered. "You're gonna regret messing up my life." Logan felt certain the man heard his curse, even from the depths of hell. "You and every cop that dares to screw with me."

Over his shoulder, he spied the bathroom door and opened it slightly. *So damned easy.* Lurking in the shadows, beyond the light, he peered inside. With a gray eye pressed near the opening, he caught the cloudy reflection of her body.

She moved seductively under the water. Dark strands of hair clung to her skin. Curves of flesh wafted in and out of focus with the billowing steam. The tantalizing image made him hard as a rock. Then, a devilish thought took hold.

He knew what he had to do.

Reaching for the shampoo in her shower caddy, she poured the creamy lotion into her hand, then lathered her hair. Tiny bubbles popped in her ears and tickled her skin, muffling the sounds from her bathroom. Suds trailed down her face. She loved the scent and didn't bother to wipe away the lather. Besides, with eyes closed, she could better imagine Christian.

The motion of her hands slowed to a crawl as she slathered frothy shampoo across her face and down her arms. The sensation magnified and focused her thoughts on the man.

She relived the instant she'd frisked him. Once again, her fingertips felt the muscled texture of his belly, entwined in the soft curls of body hair. His warm skin smelled so good. With him leaning against the wall, she had caught only a brief glimpse of the small of his back. But that part of the male anatomy always enticed her hands, beckoning them to play. Her imagination embellished the taut sinews of his back and broad shoulders. She found her breathing escalating. The man was an inspiration. The mental picture spurred her blood until—

An obscure shadow dimmed the bathroom light. Even though soapsuds covered her eyes, she still detected the movement. A dark shape eclipsed the light fixture. The sensation shocked her. This couldn't be happening—not in her home. Every instinct in her body screamed a warning. Her heart seized in panic. Had she only imagined it? Then, a rush of cold air brushed her skin.

Imagination be damned! This was real. Naked, Raven had never felt so vulnerable. She had her gun in the other room. And she couldn't shake the feeling that she wasn't alone. In a rush, she doused her head with water and cleared her eyes to a blur. She had to do something—*NOW.*

Not wanting to waste time rinsing off, she turned off the shower and let the soap creep down her skin. It felt like an unwanted touch, spiraling chills over her body. Squinting back the sting from her eyes, she pulled at the sliding door and fortified herself for a fight. Her cop instincts kicked in. But the steam in her small bathroom had parted like the Red Sea. To her shock, the bathroom door gaped open. *Oh, God!* She wasn't alone.

CHAPTER 8

An eerie silence mocked her. Maybe she'd imagined the whole thing. Her house was stone-still now. Even its usual creaks and groans were mute. Raven strained to hear anything out of the ordinary. Then the familiar sound of a simmering pot of spaghetti sauce on her stove reminded her. *What time was it?* For her, time ground to a halt. She found herself praying that Christian would forgo his usual promptness to be early for a change.

Alert to anything, she caught a motion at the corner of her eye. Her jaw dropped at the sight, sucking steamy air down her windpipe. A bloodless pallor—her own reflection stared back through streaks on the mirror. The bastard had left her a message.

You aren't safe—ANYWHERE!
Mickey learned the hard way.

Printed on the fogged glass, his warning ridiculed her. Mickey's killer was in her home, unimpressed with her authority. Naked as she was, she conceded his point. But she couldn't allow herself to be distracted now.

Easing out of the tub, Raven kept her eyes focused on the open door. Every muscle tensed. She waited for

a faceless attacker to make his move—prepared for the
intruder to rush her while she'd be most vulnerable.
Step by step, she inched toward the door. Fear massed
into staunch self-preservation. Holding her breath, she
listened. But in the pit of her stomach, reality gripped
her.

A killer stalked her, violating her home. She wasn't
safe. Not anymore.

Raven reached for the robe hanging on the bathroom
door. Her hair was soaked, strands stiffened from lingering soapsuds. Water dripped off her body, making
the floor slippery. Throwing the garment around her
shoulders, she didn't take the time to dry off. Adrenaline coursed through her veins. She felt the chill in the
air seep through the pores of her dank skin. If she was
attacked here, in her condition, only her training and
mental toughness would keep her alive. Her mind focused on the location of her weapon, willing it to her
hand. She prayed her intruder wasn't armed, or an even
worse scenario, that the coward might use her own
weapon against her.

With her back to the wall, she crept through the house,
dodging floorboards that would give her away. Her eyes
darted down the length of the hall as she made her way
to the bedroom—and her Glock nine-millimeter.

A faint sound, somewhere deeper within the house,
forced her to stop where she stood. Sweeping past her,
a draft of cold air made her teeth chatter, her body betraying the pretense of courage. *Why was it so cold?*

Peering over her shoulder, she used the mirror on her
bedroom dresser to improve her chances. No one was
behind the door. And with her closet open, just as she'd
left it, it would be impossible for someone to hide in her
small room.

Quickly, she stepped toward her nightstand and inched open the top drawer, not taking her eye off the doorway. Letting out a sigh of relief, she found her Glock still in its holster. Releasing the safety, she gripped the weapon, its heft steeling her for a confrontation. Now the odds were even.

Time to hunt in earnest.

"Junior? You better be brushing your teeth. I'm coming up for an inspection."

Yolanda Rodriguez raised her voice, calling upstairs. Even with her precocious child out of sight, she knew little Tony would still be playing his Game Boy. The ten-year-old had their nightly ritual down to a science, her warning part of the routine. By the time she got midstair, he'd shoot to the bathroom and conjure up a mouth full of froth for her benefit, practically rubbing the enamel off his teeth. It didn't matter that his little feet sounded like a herd of wild animals dashing down the upstairs hallway. A glint of satisfaction would shine in his dark eyes, like he'd fooled her once again. In those moments, he looked so much like his father.

That glint reminded her. Little Tony had been conceived on a night when she saw that exact look in her husband's eyes. Shaking her head, she continued her chore as a smile fought to break free.

Wiping down the kitchen counter, she made the room sparkle, a far cry from the condition it had been earlier. Make-your-own-chalupa night was a Thursday dinner ritual in the Rodriguez household. And as far as she knew, the first peanut butter and pineapple chalupa had been invented tonight, under her very roof.

"Celia? Time for bed, *mi hija*."

Even though her daughter slouched in one of the living room chairs watching a muted television, she still had to raise her voice to get above the music blasting on the young girl's headset. She supposed that flipping through TV channels fast enough produced some semblance of an MTV video. Not having cable, it was Celia's only option. According to her daughter, she was the only one in school not allowed to watch MTV—a social disaster.

"But Mom, Dad is still not home. Can't we wait up for him?"

She couldn't see Celia's face, but she pictured her brow furrowed with eyes rolled toward the ceiling, accompanied by a heavy sigh. Her twelve-year-old daughter was an admitted drama queen who still had a crush on her father. Yolanda understood completely. Even after two years of courtship and fourteen years of marriage, she still carried a torch for her husband.

"Dad's still not home? So what else is new," Yolanda muttered under her breath as she wiped her hands on a dish towel. Raising her voice once again, she answered, "No, honey. You've got school tomorrow. Your father will understand."

Walking over to her daughter, she gently raised the headphones from her ears, then cradled Celia's warm cheeks in her hands. Lowering her lips to the young girl's forehead, she kissed her, saying, "Time for bed, *cosa fina.*"

Leaning back, Celia turned and smiled. Between them, the nickname of "fine thing" in Spanish was just as good as saying—

"Love you, too, Mom."

Turning off the TV by remote, Celia walked toward the stairs. With a devilish grin, she turned and pointed upstairs, silently gesturing for Yolanda's cooperation. It took her only a moment to understand what her daughter wanted.

"You better be done with your teeth, Junior," she called her final warning upstairs.

With a silent chuckle, Celia raised the okay sign and stepped loudly up the flight of steps. A second later, a rumble down the hallway and running water in the sink told them both that Tony Junior was up to his old tricks. But tonight, she and her daughter had won the game. The twinkle would be in Celia's beautiful eyes.

Kids would be kids, she mused with a shake of her head. But then, what was her excuse?

Before she followed her daughter upstairs, she did her routine walk through the house. She'd lock the doors and turn off the lights with one last check of the thermostat. The laughter of her children kept a smile on her face. As usual, she left the front porch light on and a lamp near the front door so Tony would know he was loved—and missed.

But as she dimmed the light in the living room, a motion caught her attention. She'd seen something through the drapery sheers. Yolanda pulled aside the front window curtain and squinted into the night, blocking the dim lighting behind her with cupped hands to shield her eyes.

Again, to the left, near the street. A shadow darted for cover in the hedges of their property. *Their property!* She gasped. Backlit by a streetlamp, the movement had been abrupt.

On many occasions, the neighbor's cat yowled in the night, an eerie cry. Or the animal rooted around in the garbage, dropping a trash can lid to the ground from time to time. Her heart leapt every time. Over the years, she realized her mind sometimes played tricks whenever Tony wasn't home. Her first reaction was to chastise herself for being foolish, but tonight was different.

Quickly making the sign of the cross, she closed her eyes and prayed she'd been mistaken. But her only answer was the ugly truth. A red laser pierced the night and cut through the blackness like a knife. A hideous Cyclops with a bloody red eye glared directly at her, finding her peeking through the window.

Damn it all! This was no cat.

Racing to the phone near the kitchen counter, she grabbed the receiver to her ear. With trembling fingers, she punched the buttons, dialing 911. All she heard was her quickening breaths. She tried again. Nothing. No dial tone.

The phone was dead.

Her hand tightened on her gun as Raven stepped through her house. With every room she entered, her arms rigidly extended in a two-fisted grip, aiming the weapon into every corner in search of the intruder. Between rooms, she held her Glock with bent elbows as she made her way to the next room. She left the kitchen for last. A glimpse down the hallway revealed the source of the cold air. In the kitchen, the side door off her carport was flung open.

Still, it could be a trap.

The man might be clever enough to open the door, hoping she'd let her guard down. And the outside light was out, no doubt disabled on purpose. As she entered the room, her eyes peered anywhere someone might hide. So far, she was alone.

But more evidence of the intruder was plain to see. Her stovetop had been wrecked, spotted with sauce as if the pot had boiled over. Yet it was obvious what had happened. The man had made a contribution to her recipe.

A framed photo of her father in uniform poked out from the bubbling sauce. It'd been ripped from the wall and thrown into the saucepot, splattering a mess across her white stove. Maybe it had only been a diversion. *Stay alert, Mackenzie!*

Raven shifted her gaze to the opened doorway. She aimed her weapon into the void. For all she knew, the man stood just outside in the shadows. She wouldn't be able to see his silhouette.

"You'd better be long gone, you son of a bitch!" her voice was stern, so contrary to how she felt.

She slid out the door into the night. On the cement of the carport, her damp feet ached with the cold. In an instant, winter's chill seized her. She gasped, sucking icy air down her throat. Then a vapor steam billowed from her lungs. *Keep moving!*

In the distance, she heard a droning sound from a television. Her neighbor's house. The sights and sounds of her childhood suburb filled her senses. Even after someone had broken into her home, the rest of the world went on in blissful ignorance.

Damn it! Slowly, she let her guard down.

But just as she lowered her gun, a noise came from the front of her house. Her body tensed again. The sound had been faint. A scuff of a shoe? Racing around the corner, she brushed past an evergreen. Bounding up the step, she reeled her shoulders, trying to aim her gun. But her arms struck something immovable—the dark shape of a man.

A loud pop. Shattered glass.

Cold as she was, pain shot through her joints when

the man grabbed her in a viselike grip. He pulled her off the ground. She felt his warm breath against her neck. With elbows pinned to her chest, all she could do was flail her legs, kicking at her attacker.

She shrieked, not from fright, but from anger and frustration. A low, guttural sound. Writhing and twisting, she felt blood rush to her face. Her heels jabbed at the man's legs, striking without mercy. If she hurt him badly enough, he'd drop her. Only a matter of time before she found the sweet spot. With his grunt, she ramped up her assault.

"Damn it! Let me go, you bastard!"

The man had his hand on the barrel of her gun, trying to wrench it free.

"Hey, hey, stop it! Ow!" he protested. "Is this how you greet all your guests?"

Raven stopped. *Oh, my God!* She knew that voice. The man's hand pried the weapon from her grasp—only after she *let* him win.

"Christian? I thought—" She didn't bother to finish. Her heartbeat still hammered her eardrums.

He loosened his grip and stepped aside, setting her near the step to the front porch. "Be careful. I dropped the wine bottle. Glass is everywhere." Looking down at the robe and her feet, he asked, "Are you barefoot?"

Ignoring his question, she turned toward him. "Someone broke into my house."

A fleeting and cynical notion took hold, her cop instincts hard to deny. What if Christian had been the one in her house, then conveniently pretended to have just arrived? Her brow furrowed as she gave the idea shape, staring at him in the dark. Yet even with his face in shadow, she heard the concern in his voice.

"Are you okay? He didn't hurt you, did he?" After

brushing back her damp hair, he reached for her shoulders. "You're wet. You must be freezing."

God, how she wanted to believe in Christian. Being right about him meant her trust barometer was fully functional. But even now, she heard Tony's voice in her head, reminding her how dangerous this man was. Raven loved being a cop, but at times, she hated how it'd changed her over the years. Had she grown so jaded that she couldn't trust her own heart?

Before she delved deeper into that thought, he handed her the gun, then scooped her up in his arms, lifting her without effort. Stepping around the corner, he carried her through the kitchen door and slammed it shut with an elbow. With all his fussing, she felt ridiculous. But as she relaxed into his shoulder, smelling his subtle cologne mixed with the leather of his jacket, everything felt right. She'd been on her own for so long, it felt good to be taken care of for a change.

"Bedroom?" he asked.

Still stunned by his bold gesture, all she could do was point down the hall, eyes wide. Then her damned cop brain took charge.

"Christian. Please, I'm fine. You don't have to—"

Before she finished her objection, he'd yanked back the covers of her bed and set her down. She began to thaw the instant he pulled the quilt to her chin, more a reaction to him than the fine insulating capabilities of her comforter. But as he stared down at her, his confident expression melted like the chill from her skin.

Suddenly realizing where he was, he stood abruptly, then shoved his hands into his jeans pockets. Christian's sudden uneasiness surprised her. She fought back a smile. Before now, "cute" was not a word she would've ever associated with Christian Delacorte. But damned if he didn't have the word stamped across his forehead. *In blaze orange!*

He made her feel safe again. It felt good not to be alone. And by the way he avoided her gaze, she knew he felt awkward with the unexpected intimacy. *So, you're human after all, Delacorte!*

"I'm gonna look through the rest of the house, if you don't mind, make sure we're alone." He narrowed his eyes. "Can I make you some hot tea? Or something?"

"Please. The teapot is on the stove," she called down the hall after he'd slipped out. The cop in her added, "And be careful what you touch. I'm gonna call for a team to dust for prints."

Raven couldn't just sit, like some grand queen bee. Sliding from bed, she tightened her robe around her waist and gave the sash a tug. She picked up the phone from her nightstand and called the station house. A long shot, but maybe the bastard had left some fingerprints. Raven ended the call, knowing a team would be arriving soon. She had to get dressed.

"I'm just gonna rinse off, get the soap out of my hair," she called to him. The idea of a cold-water rinse gave her a shiver, but the message on the mirror had to be preserved. More steam would cover it up. Maybe a blast of ice water to her scalp would jump-start her brain.

Stepping back into the bath, she found Christian staring at her mirror, his jaw tense. He'd started his search of her house where the whole thing began.

"So this wasn't a random break-in. The bastard killed Mickey." He stared at Raven, trying to make a point. "And he tossed a photograph into your dinner plans. Any connection? The man in the photo was a cop in uniform."

"You're observant. A photograph of my father."

She crossed her arms, amazed how he'd noticed so much in his short walk through the kitchen. A wet strand of hair fell across her face. With a finger, she tucked it behind an ear.

"If this wealthy bachelor gig doesn't work out, maybe I can find an opening for you in law enforcement."

"Not exactly my thing, but thanks." With his green eyes fixed on her, he pressed, "Now answer my question."

"Not sure I can. Just give me use of my bathroom and fix me that hot tea you promised. It'll give me time to think." She led him by the arm and switched places in the cramped quarters.

Christian's stoic expression returned, as if she'd just given him the brush-off. But to his credit, he didn't interrogate her any longer. He turned toward the kitchen. A tinge of guilt gnawed at her, for what she'd thought about his intentions. Before he was out of eyesight, she called to him, peeking around the bathroom door.

"Christian?"

He looked over his shoulder, the concern for her safety still in his eyes. God, she hoped she wasn't imagining it.

"Thanks, for everything. I'm glad you're here." And she meant every word.

A faint light from her bedroom painted his handsome face with warmth. His expression softened. A lazy curve to his lips broadened into a seductive grin.

And time stopped. *Oh, that smile! Downright lethal.*

His eyes locked on to hers in knowing silence. Suddenly, she became aware just how naked she was beneath her robe. She clutched the collar of her garment and inched farther behind the door. Her cheeks flushed with need. Maybe he wouldn't notice.

In an awkward gesture, she cleared her throat to ward off the emotion. He seemed to read her mind. Without a word, his smile faded, and he quietly resumed his trek down the hall.

Just like that, the moment came and went between them. Slowly, she closed the door behind her, struggling with a grin of her own.

His smile. Just like she remembered. *Damn it!* She wanted to be right about him.

Pulling into his driveway, Tony knew Yolie would not be pleased with his late hour. He'd missed dinner and tucking the kids in bed. Admittedly, Celia and Junior would be mortified if their friends knew they were still getting tucked in for the night. But this was a family ritual that Tony wanted to keep sacred for as long as possible. A parent didn't get these years back.

As usual, his front porch light was on, as well as the living room lamp. Yolie always told him it represented her burning love for him. He liked that idea, very much.

His shoulders ached with tension from the long day, but the warm welcome home lifted his spirits. Parking the vehicle in the drive near the front of their house, he turned off the ignition and flung open the car door. The Latino radio station abruptly came to an end. Stepping out of the car, he fumbled with his key ring, looking for the one for the front door. Slipping from his grip, the keys hit the ground with a clink. His eyes followed the sound, then he stooped to pick them up.

In that instant, a shadow eclipsed the streetlight, casting its length along the driveway. He looked up, half expecting his Yolie to be standing there, something she did on occasion. But a darkened silhouette stood before him. A man.

He narrowed his eyes, ready to speak when a muffled scream jolted his attention. Looking over his shoulder, toward a second-story window, Yolie pounded the glass. Her face distorted in terror.

"Run! They have guns. *Run!*" she cried.

In his mind, the scene slowed as if he were mired in quicksand. Part of his brain knew it was already over. Too late. He reached for his service revolver, pulling it from his shoulder holster, instinctively releasing the safety.

The stranger didn't flinch. Calmly and without a word, the man raised his hand, then slowly pointed a finger.

A signal. A series of red lasers launched from the trees and hedges across the front of his house. A deadly light show. Five. There were five others. He was sorely outnumbered.

"What the hell—" It was all Tony got out.

Thud! Searing pain tore through his left shoulder, spinning him to the ground. As he fell, a ricochet sparked off the sidewalk. The bullet pierced his chest. *Oh, God!* This was bad.

Yolanda shrieked. "No! Tony, *noooo!*"

Suddenly, the side of his house erupted. Bullets came from all directions. Rounds shattered his front window and ripped apart the brick on impact. Careful with his aim, he fired two rounds, then rolled for cover behind a brick planter. Shards of stone nicked his face and hands. The man who'd given the order was long gone, becoming a part of the deepening shadows. He'd lost his best target.

Silenced gunfire? The precision of the attack, the hand signals, the stealth. It all pointed to one thing— mercenaries. *What the hell was happening?*

The front of his shirt grew wet and sticky. And he knew the tang of blood when he smelled it. He had to remain calm. For now, the shooting had stopped. But he still felt them out there, waiting for him to make a mistake. Keeping his head down, he shoved nearer his porch. His chest on fire.

None of this made sense. But it didn't matter. Now, he had only one thing on his mind—to protect his family. Ever the pragmatist, with his cop instincts he envisioned the worst. He pictured himself pinned down while others broke into his home from the rear. The imagined screams of his children overloaded his head like an insidious migraine. Only one thing left for him to do. Reaching into his pocket, he found his cell phone and dialed 911.

He recognized the dispatcher's voice. After giving his address, he added, "Officer d-down. I repeat, officer down. Proceed C-Code Three." He wanted sirens loud. Lights flashing.

"ETA five minutes. Tony, are you okay?" The female dispatcher broke protocol.

"No, Sara, I'm not. Just t-take care of my f-family, okay?" He ended the call.

Tony still heard Yolanda crying upstairs. He blocked out her agony, flashing on memories of his beautiful wife holding their firstborn child, Celia, in her arms, a tiny pink bundle. Tears filled his eyes. He was powerless to help her and the kids now. Their safety would be in the hands of others—and God.

He tasted blood in his mouth. The chest wound was nasty. A numbing sensation inched across his body. Before long, he'd lose consciousness. Picking a target, he carefully squeezed off another shot, and was rewarded by a grunt. Maybe that would give them something else to think about. The howling dogs in the neighbor-hood nearly masked the sound. Tony had never been so thankful for all the mangy mutts in his "hood." The more noise, the better.

His breaths came in short wheezes now. He was losing his fight. Choking up blood, he wiped his mouth with his sleeve.

"Please, God. H-hold my family s-safe—in your arms," he whispered his prayer.

Slowly, he slumped with his back to a brick wall, so near the front door of his home. The numbing cold began to claim him. Streetlights blurred, warping into a series of shimmering rings around the bright globes. In the distance, sirens teased his ears, becoming louder as the night was set on fire. Flashing beacons of red and blue circled the night sky, streaking their message. *The cavalry had arrived—Code 3.*

He wanted to smile, but couldn't muster the strength. His jaw went slack. He struggled for every breath. Tilting his head back, he turned his eyes toward the heavens. Beyond the lights, the stars dotted the sky and shimmered, until one by one they melted into inky black. He focused on the last star, but eventually, his eyelids fluttered closed. Still, one thought persisted.

He only hoped it wasn't too late for his family.

CHAPTER 9

Raven rushed from her home, leaving the CSI team to lock up after they'd processed her break-in. It couldn't be helped. Tony's wife, Yolanda, should not be alone at a time like this.

God, don't die on me, Tony! Please . . .

The call she'd received from dispatch still resonated in her head, triggering a painful memory from her past. Her partner had been attacked and mortally wounded outside his house. Early reports indicated six armed gunmen were to blame. Although barely conscious, Tony had told fellow officers on the scene that his assailants had been mercenaries. Except for his wife, no other witnesses corroborated his story. Too much of a coincidence that this attack had happened on the same night Blair's killer paid her a visit. Whoever was behind this had flagrantly thumbed his nose at the police—with deadly consequence.

On a deeply personal level, she grappled with the jumble of emotions in her mind. For the sake of Yolanda, Raven needed to dig deep for whatever strength lay buried under the despondency bubbling to the surface. Once again, violence had touched her life, jabbing at an unhealed wound.

With Christian offering to drive her, she sat in the passenger seat of his car, letting silence build between them. Overhead streetlights lolled in and out of the darkened interior of his SUV. The mind-numbing road noise and the interminable drive time worsened her anxiety. For all she knew, Tony was already dead.

Not Tony. Not her partner.

Nothing Christian could say would comfort her. Intuitively, he must have sensed this. He hadn't said a word since they started. Given his history, perhaps he was rapt in his own brand of hell. So Raven focused on her partner, struggling to pray for him as Christian drove. Eventually, she closed her eyes and quit, fearing her prayers might do more harm than good. She had no right to ask for divine intervention now, not when she had turned her back on her faith all those many years ago. Her throat clenched as tears blurred her vision.

With Christian by her side, she walked through the emergency doors at Mercy Hospital as they hissed open, numb to the possibility of her partner's death. Her memory flooded with images from another wintry night when she was seventeen.

This couldn't be happening—not again.

The waiting room hadn't changed, still colored in bland oatmeal and pale greens. With dour faces, the thick-skinned ER staff performed under pressure, handling desperation as if it were paperwork. Raven knew she filtered the scene through her own draining experience. She had blocked so much from her memory.

But one remembrance had been etched in her mind.

After being fatally shot, her father had never regained consciousness in the ICU. Thinking back to the day he died, she'd opted to sleep in, not getting up to make his breakfast on a Saturday morning. A part of her understood a father's absolution over the trivial incident. But as a daughter, she was less forgiving. She'd never gotten a chance to tell him how much she loved him or to kiss him good-bye.

As she spied Tony's wife down the corridor, she only hoped the woman would have at least that much.

The lustrous olive skin of Yolanda Rodriguez looked pale, tinged with gray. Her dark, shoulder-length hair fell across her face as she paced the waiting room, clutching a wad of tissues. Her eyes brimmed with tears and inconsolable heartache.

God, was she too late?

"Yolanda? Is he—?" She couldn't bring herself to say it. "How's he doing?"

"Oh, God!" Rushing to her, Yolanda collapsed in her arms, clinging to hope. "T-tell me this is all a bad dream, Raven. This c-can't be happening." Her sobs escalated into spasms, words choking in her throat. "I saw it all, and I c-couldn't help him. The phones were out. I couldn't help—"

The feeling of powerlessness overwhelmed her as she held Yolanda. She knew the feeling all too well.

"What's happening, Yolie? Where is he?"

"He's in surgery." Yolanda pulled from her arms. Her eyes barely met Raven's. "But I saw it on the doctor's face. It doesn't look good, Raven."

"Don't borrow trouble by reading into anything. Tony would hate it if you gave up on him. You know how stubborn he is." She searched her heart for any words of comfort. Her partner's own words about "borrowing trouble" seemed so right.

"Where are the kids? Are they—?" Raven didn't know what to say. She knew firsthand that the kids weren't okay. Tonight, Tony's children had lost their innocence and their sense of security. Nothing would ever be the same again.

"They're at a neighbor's house. I didn't know what else to do." New tears drained down Yolanda's cheeks. "I haven't called San Antonio, to let his parents know. What am I going to tell them?"

After leading Yolanda to a nearby sofa, Raven sat beside her and rubbed the back of the woman's neck. None of this would be easy. And it had only just begun.

Before she spoke, Christian interceded, handing them both a cup of coffee. "It's gonna be a long night. This might take the chill out of the room."

She'd nearly forgotten about Christian. Awkwardly, she made the introductions, knowing Tony's wife would be paralyzed with worry. "Yolanda Rodriguez, this is Christian Delacorte. He drove me." Any other explanation was far too complicated.

"I'm sorry to meet you under such terrible circumstances, Mrs. Rodriguez. If there's anything I can do . . ." Christian's voice faded. He extended his hand, gently taking the woman's trembling fingers.

Kneeling in front of her, Christian spoke to Yolanda in a hushed tone, meant for only her. But Raven was privileged to hear it all.

"I couldn't help but overhear. If you'll allow me, I'd like to offer the use of the Dunhill jet to transport Tony's parents to Chicago. Just give me the word and I can make it happen."

Yolanda turned her heartbreaking gaze to Christian, as if seeing him for the first time. Fresh tears welled in her eyes; her lower lip quivered. Without a word, she reached for his neck and pulled him to her. By his reaction, it was evident. The intimacy surprised him.

"May God bless and keep you, Christian," Yolanda whispered, clutching him to her embrace. "Thank you so much for your generosity."

Raven sipped her coffee to choke back the emotion, witnessing the exchange. In that moment, she felt certain. Christian Delacorte had been fighting his demons—and still was. And he might never trust her enough to confide in her. But her trust barometer had *not* been wrong. Christian *was* a good man who deeply understood the pain of losing someone.

The truth was as unmistakable as the tear rolling down his cheek.

CHÂTEAU DE BANVILLE
VERSAILLES, FRANCE

In the pale pink of dawn, the château reflected off the still lake, a pastel gem against the blue of a wakening sky. The image was crystal clear, like a photograph, in its perfection. Classic stone walls radiated a delicate pearled luster. Designed by François Mansart in the 1620s, the private residence was surrounded by exquisite gardens, accenting a spectacular fountain similar to the cascade at Louis XIV's Château de Marly.

But despite the beauty of the pristine and tranquil setting, Fiona was a prisoner of her own volition, no longer enamored with the breathtaking opulence. Her heart longed for something beyond price—*to be with Christian.*

In the chill of the early morning, she sat on the grass across the lake, gazing toward the grand château of a very dear old friend, her arms wrapped around her knees. Filling her lungs, she inhaled the earthy aroma of the water nuzzling the tall grasses. Even though her cheeks were still warm from her brisk walk through the wooded trails of the massive estate, she felt the cold creeping through the layering of her sweats and into her bones—the chill linked to troubling thoughts.

Christian had been on her mind since she'd left Chicago, leaving him to face his unsettling future—alone.

Late last night, it came to a head. She had a fit of conscience and placed a call to his Dunhill cottage. But when she heard his voice on the answering machine, emotion gripped her throat, and she lost her fleeting courage to speak. Perhaps it had been more from weakness that she made the call in the first place. She would gladly trade her wealth for his happiness. Yet for all her hollow wishes, she'd been the cause of his pain—all of it. And after her moment of frailty, she vowed that her past would not destroy his future. She must remain firm, for his sake.

Slowly, she stood and brushed off blades of grass from her clothing, her feet and legs numbed by the cold. From the start, desperation colored her world, robbing her of a normal life. How long did she have to pay for her past indiscretion? She knew unfinished business loomed heavy in her future. She would not escape it. Captive to her sins, the prisoner returned to her gilded cell, uncertain of most things—except one.

Her unbearable solitude could not go on forever. Like the bite of the crisp morning, she felt it in her bones.

The gray haze of daybreak arrived, migrating through small windows along the length of the room, at odds with the persistent nip in the air. Christian steadied his breathing to focus on anything but his discomfort, knowing his jacket had gone to a good cause. In the early-morning hours, the waiting room to the ICU had grown quiet, leaving him alone with a sleeping Raven Mackenzie. She had tried to stay alert, dosing herself with caffeine. But in the end, she had succumbed to exhaustion.

The stillness they now shared held a sensual quality, like the intimacy of watching a sleeping lover. Or perhaps that was just wishful thinking on his part.

Sitting in a chair, he stared at Raven from across the room, his elbows on the armrests with hands steepled under his chin. Curled up on an angular sofa not meant for the human body, she slept with her head propped against her balled-up coat. After she'd fallen asleep, he'd covered her in his leather jacket. In that instant, he discovered the innocence of a child in her serene face. Since he'd first met her, her expressions had ranged the gamut from fierce determination, to anger, annoyance, and teasing humor. And he'd instigated most of those emotions. But seeing such innocence had been a charming surprise.

Innocence. So rare in his world. With a quiet sigh, he let the stillness wash over him once again, a welcome respite from his life. Even though this lull felt like the eerie calm before the storm, the tragedy that had brought them together lingered heavy in the air. It stirred so much in him. The suffering and uncertainty in the eyes of Tony's wife were familiar.

But he would take what he could get, relishing the simplicity of early morning and the promise of hope. In this room, time mercifully stalled, giving Tony precious minutes to find his way back to the living. Time became an infinite chasm, one without a beginning or an end.

For the last several hours, he had watched Raven, dealing with the traumatic shooting of her partner, giving comfort to the man's wife, and making phone calls to the station house to keep the investigation into Tony's assault moving forward. A long line of police officers, including the chief himself, had come and gone through the ordeal. Seeing her with each of them, Christian sensed her connection. She was clearly part of a much larger family—a community that cared deeply for its own.

And despite her personal feelings to the contrary, she found the courage to push through the pain, something he understood and respected. Catching her in those fragile moments, he supposed she might have believed she was alone with her fear and outrage. But he had been with her, supporting her with his presence. A silent vigil. It had been a privilege to see her through the eyes and hearts of others.

No doubt, Detective Raven Mackenzie was a woman filled with compassion and courage. And this made it impossible for him to hate her as a cop. He felt the years of resentment in the pit of his stomach, embroiled amidst the violent images of his family tragedy. Enduring a lifetime of hate was exhausting. He'd grown bone-weary of the burden.

Barely able to keep his eyes open, Christian rested his mind, counting what few blessings they had. For now, Raven's partner and friend was alive but in critical condition. Every precious minute of life was a positive sign, but no guarantee he'd pull through. The man's wife sat with him in ICU, and Christian had arranged for the Dunhill jet to pick up Tony's parents from San Antonio. They'd be landing soon. And with their arrival, time would rush forward, drawing them into its undercurrent. Finally taking Raven's lead, he let his thoughts drift, relaxing their grip on him. As he did, the room dissolved to inky black when he shut his eyes, listening to the measured rhythm of Raven's breaths.

Only a minute lapsed before the hospital intercom system jolted him awake, a muffled voice through the waiting room doors. Opening his eyes, he found Raven staring back. Her puzzled look softened to a warm welcome.

"You didn't have to wait, Christian." Under protest from the crinkling sofa, she sat upright, stretching her arms and straightening her mussed hair with a quick finger comb. "But I'm glad you did. Good morning."

Her voice was husky with sleep. The sound of it stirred him.

"Good morning. Can I get you some coffee?" he offered. His voice barely above a whisper, he sat forward in his chair, elbows resting on his knees. "And you should eat something before things get too hectic."

"When are Tony's parents getting here?" She looked at her watch.

"They should be touching down any minute. The hangar will call when they've landed."

"Not sure I ever thanked you enough for that. His parents don't fly much. They would've gotten lost at a big airport like Midway or O'Hare on a normal day." She smiled, the emotion only fleeting. Her face darkened with the reminder of why they were sitting outside the ICU. "But today is anything but normal."

"Before they get here, we should talk."

He knew he had no right to express an opinion about police matters, but during the last few hours, he'd been plagued with worry for Raven's safety. She narrowed her eyes at him, opening her mouth to speak, but he interjected, "I overheard your conversation about Tony's assailants being mercenaries."

"This is police business, Christian. We're not sure if it's connected—"

Before she finished her thought, he called her on it. "Bullshit! It's connected, all right. The break-in at your place, Tony's attack, and maybe even something tied to your father. It's not just about my past. Whoever killed Mickey is gunning for you now. And if mercenaries are involved, you'd need a small army to defend yourself."

"When Chief Markham was here earlier, he authorized twenty-four-hour police protection for Tony and me. I'll be okay. All this comes with the territory of being a cop, Christian."

He stood abruptly, pacing the floor and pointing in her direction.

"Bullshit on that, too, Raven. According to the motto, your job is to protect and serve, not make yourself a target for some lunatic killer. I'll only buy that argument if they start issuing uniforms with bright red-and-white targets across the chest."

Hearing how he must sound, he wanted to stop from making an ass of himself. But it was too late. He'd gone way past that now. His voice raised, he continued his tirade.

"And for every cop pulled off duty to protect you, Tony, and his family, that's one less cop to find this SOB."

Rising from the sofa, she tossed aside his jacket and confronted him. With her brow furrowed, she stood her ground, hands on her hips. He knew the woman would not make this easy.

"And what do you propose I do about that? Believe me, I hate the fact that I've been assigned protection. I refused it, but the chief insisted, pulling rank on me." Her eyes bore the weight of her emotion, second only to her pale skin flushed with anger. Punctuating her outburst, she crossed her arms. "But the bastard that attacked Tony is gonna pay for what he did. I got plenty of cops willing to do whatever it takes to find this guy. There won't be a place he can hide. I'm gonna see to that."

"Let me help you," he insisted, aroused by her fire. The woman was fearless.

"Help me? You're not officially off the suspect list, for crying out loud. I'm not sure I can trust you. Are you forgetting about your own secret agenda?" With her chin jutting forward, she amassed the attitude, standing close enough for him to smell her warm skin. "Or must I remind you, Captain Cryptic?"

He watched her nostrils flare; her breast heaved in maddening swells. The heat from her skin seduced him. Raven orchestrated his body's reaction with the precision of a symphony conductor. Bellowing with the resonance of a bass drum, his heart pounded his rib cage, the sensation intoxicating.

For only an instant, she lowered her lids and gazed at his lips. With innocence gone, a desirable woman stood before him. Her eyes held him spellbound. She seemed to understand his intention even before he fully grasped it himself.

An impulse struck him like a blindsided sucker punch.

Without his usual deliberation, Christian merely reacted, following his instincts. Standing so close to Raven, he felt her pull like a force of gravity. His hands reached for her, taking on a life of their own. He had no will to stop. One arm found the small of her back, drawing her toward him. His right hand caressed her cheek, his fingertips stroking her velvet softness.

At first, her dark eyes brimmed with shock at his bold

move. Tension made her body taut. But just as suddenly, she collapsed into his arms, reeling with his impulsive intimacy. In his embrace, her body nestled warm against him, fitting into place as if he were made to hold her. With a faint tremble to her lips, she beckoned him with her surrender, her eyes enticing him once more. And the sweet fragrance of her skin filled him with the courage to take the next step.

"I want you . . ." His voice trailed off. Overwhelmed by his urge, he gave her every opportunity to stop before it was too late.

"Entirely too much dialogue, Delacorte." Her voice sultry, she closed the gap between them. "Kiss me, damn it!"

Slowly, he lowered his lips to hers. With a touch, the softness of her delicate skin sent shock waves firing through his body. He pressed for more. Gently parting her lips, his tongue took liberties, finding her just as eager. The sensual barrage jolted his senses, short-circuiting his brain with gratification. Skin flushed with heat, he grew rigid, his body straining against his pants. Fleeting control gave way to insatiable appetite as his hands eagerly explored soft mounds of flesh. And she responded in kind, equaling his growing desire. She tugged at his shirttail and slipped her hands next to his raging skin.

God! He never knew it could be like this!

He felt such a connection to this woman. Far more powerful than his physical hunger for her, he savored the deepening bond between them. Blocking out all other sensation, he wanted to focus on every inspired nuance of her, to give her pleasure. The room faded into nothingness. The sound of her throaty sighs and the arousing scent of her skin dominated him.

Only Raven mattered. Only she touched something within him—something he thought he'd lost. Only she made him forget.

And damn it!

Only he would get a phone call during a time like this.

The vibration of his cell phone nudged him back to reality. He would've ignored it, but with the phone hooked to his belt, its pulsating signal reached out and touched her too. She jumped. And with that, he'd been disappointed to learn that the tingling he felt in the pit of his stomach had not been entirely prompted by the alluring woman standing before him.

"Is that your cell phone, or are you just happy to see me?" Breathlessly, she teased him, hunger and frustration still vivid in her eyes. Her breasts swelled against his chest as she clung to him, nearly driving him crazy.

"Oh, I'm definitely happy to see you." His breathing rapid, Christian leaned his forehead against hers, his hands still cradling her body. "And I'd like to see much more of you, believe me."

"Forget the visual aids; I'm a tactile girl."

"Hold that thought." Reluctantly, he turned to one side, pulling from her embrace. Flipping the cell phone, he put the receiver to his ear. "Yeah, Delacorte here."

"I'd like to hold more than just a thought, Christian," she muttered.

As he talked on the phone, she nuzzled against his back. Raven wrapped her arms across his belly and burrowed her warm hands under his shirt. His taut muscles reacted to her touch, making the phone call a challenge.

He turned toward her, slipping the phone back to his belt. "It's the hangar. The jet has touched down. Tony's parents are gonna be here within the half hour." His finger brushed a strand of hair behind her ear.

Raven cupped a hand to his cheek, with a warm palm pressed against his chest. Even through his shirt, her touch aroused him beyond reason. And the suggestive timbre of her voice soothed him like warm honey in July.

"Look, I don't want you worrying about me." Her eyes softened to a rich mocha, a kaleidoscope of raw sensuality. Bathed in her light, he couldn't keep his hands from her. Every touch felt like redemption.

But reality struck home when she added, "The coward that attacked Tony and skulked into my house won't be able to get past the police protection. I'm gonna be okay." With a sly smile, she spoke softly. "Besides, I think the real danger is what just happened between us. They don't make an asbestos suit for that kind of combustion."

She ran her thumb across his lower lip, teasing his memory, attempting to distract him from worry. For a moment, he just stared at her, unsure if she was joking. Despite a clear sense of foreboding, he let a lazy smile tug at the corners of his mouth. Somehow, the woman found a way to yank him from the doldrums.

And once again, he let impulse rule the day.

"I want you to stay with me, at the Dunhill Estate. I've got the manpower to protect you. And your brothers in blue can focus on finding the man that hurt Tony. I'm sure whoever did this is behind Mickey Blair's murder, too."

"I think you're right, at least about a connection to the Blair case. But you've gotta let me do my job, Christian, on my terms. I can't just run and hide."

In his arms, she gazed up at him. He wanted nothing

more than to take her home with him, to make love to this beautiful woman. But Raven was a cop. And something in his past had drawn a killer to her door. Seeing the audacity of this cold-blooded butcher, he knew that twenty-four-hour police protection wouldn't be enough. For her sake, he had to get to the bottom of it all, without destroying Fiona in the process.

As if sensing his conflict, she grew somber. Compassion filled her eyes.

"I'm not sure you trust me enough to confide your role in all of this. I have no doubt that the case is linked to your past. Let me help you find the truth. I gotta believe that together we can do this, but you're gonna have to reach out to me. I won't betray your faith," she vowed. "Promise me you'll think about it."

If only it were that easy—to believe in Raven. She made that part effortless. But the life of someone else teetered on the brink, someone he loved as much as his own mother. Even though he didn't understand why she'd left the country, it didn't matter. Fiona was depending on him. And he wouldn't let her down. Not even if it meant keeping secrets from Raven.

"I promise," he whispered, kissing her cheek. The beautiful homicide detective had given him a great deal to think about.

She'd read the same line countless times. Once again, Fiona set down the book on her lap, a restless feeling burning just beneath the surface of her skin. Despite the comforter over her legs and the warmth from the heavily brocaded chair, she shuddered, her skin prickling with a distant anxiety. Her eyes drifted toward the large picture window, draped in muted gold. Sunlight filtered through the opaque sheers, daubing ribbons of light across the massive pastel rug at her feet. Even imagining the heat from the sun, she couldn't shake an uneasy feeling.

The fire in the hearth popped and hissed in warning, making her jump with its prompting. A faint gasp whispered through her lips. In this remote area of the world, far from her past life, she should have felt more secure. Despite her best efforts to ignore it, fear refused to be conquered.

Footsteps echoed down the corridor outside the library. Staring at the lavishly carved wooden doors at the entrance to the room, she waited and held her breath. And with certainty, she knew. Her time was up.

She stood and filled her lungs, resigning herself to the inevitable. Brushing off her dark gray slacks and straightening her black cashmere sweater, she raised her chin and pulled back her shoulders, swallowing the lump in her throat.

Armande stood by the door, softly clearing his throat. "Pardon me, madam, but you have a very insistent visitor." The manservant tightened his lips. "As I was instructed, I gave no indication you were staying here at the château, but the man insists upon seeing you. What would you have me do, Madam Dunhill?"

Clenching her jaw, Fiona turned and walked toward the window to pull back the sheer fabric. Her eyes lowered to the circular drive below.

As she expected, fate had come to Versailles.

CHAPTER 10

"You look lovely, Fiona. I'd nearly forgotten—"

His voice resonated through the formal parlor with its twenty-foot ceiling, the sound of his footsteps intruding upon his feigned cordiality. He'd entered the grand salon with a confident swagger, breezing toward her, dapper and dashing in his elegant navy suit. But as he neared, a reserve swept over him and now rested in his eyes of blue-violet. She hadn't seen eyes that color before or since. Truly, the man was one of a kind.

"Well, let's just say it's been a very long time." Nicholas Charboneau held out his hand, beckoning for hers. She lowered her eyes to the soft skin of his palm, resisting the memory of how that hand had once given her such pleasure.

"A lifetime, Nicky."

That name. She hadn't spoken his name aloud for decades.

Fiona hoped he hadn't seen the slight tremble as she gripped his hand. His eyes firmly entrenched in hers, Nicky held her fingers and brushed a thumb across the back of her hand. A suggestive move. To counter her weakness, a show of strength would be in order. She refused to dissolve under the pressure of his mesmerizing blue eyes.

"I thought I covered my tracks fairly well—no flight plans, a private airstrip at a friend's personal residence, paying off the French government to turn a blind eye. How did you find me, Nicky?"

Keeping her hand in his, she was determined not to give in to his obvious show of intimidation by pulling away. Fiona forced a smile. The best she could do.

"The first rule in the art of bribery, my dear. Never trust anyone who'd accept a bribe in the first place. A rather amazing paradox, really." He lowered his chin and tilted his head, unrelenting in his gaze. "Actually, I cheated. You'll find a tracking beacon on your plane, just inside one of the wheel wells."

With a haunting smile she knew well, he eventually released his grip on her. And in the wake of his touch, she didn't know which felt worse. The warmth of his skin lingered in contradiction, her fondest and worst memory.

"Otherwise, I'd say yours was a grand scheme. It would have worked on your standard fare of pursuers." His deep voice grew thick with intimacy.

He stood close enough for her skin to tingle at the sound of its familiarity. She turned her back on him, unable to steady her breathing. But as she stepped away, she caught a glimpse of him in the massive beveled mirror above the mantel of the marbled hearth. For a split second, a guileless younger man appeared in the reflection. Past and present stared her in the face. The image disturbed her. She flinched and shut her eyes for a moment. Fighting for control, she allowed sarcasm to imply a strength she did not possess.

"How utterly gracious of you, Nicky. Your charm

knows no bounds." She claimed an ornately carved and gilded armchair with vivid yellow brocade, set beside the fire. Fiona appreciated the symbolism. She'd always been the moth flitting too near the flame. "But it appears you didn't take the hint. I didn't want any visitors."

"I thought you'd make an exception for me, Fiona. Since we are such old and dear friends."

He stalled just long enough to make his point. Nicky never said anything without careful consideration and orchestration. Yet perhaps his ego far outweighed his discretion. As she thought back over what he had just revealed, a new question summoned her curiosity. For now, she would bide her time, watching him.

Following her toward the fire, he stood with his hand on the mantel, staring into its flames. A warm glow radiated upon him, outlining a handsome face ablaze in gold. His admirable good looks had seasoned well with age. She'd trailed her fingers along that strong jawline, known the softness of those full lips, and lost her soul to those eyes. That's why his offense provoked her, compounded by his deceit. It had been an act of betrayal to what remained in her memory of Nicky.

"Why are you here, Nicholas?" Fiona hoped the use of his formal first name would remind him. She only used it in anger. "And why would you plant the tracking device on my jet ahead of time, unless you knew I'd be taking a hasty trip abroad? Did you play some part in the abruptness of my departure?"

Seeing the slight flicker to his eyes, she knew she'd been right. He had arranged for the murder of a man. *But why? How had love twisted into such a vile thing?*

In disbelief, she waited for his response to her challenge. But as expected, his break in composure had been instantaneous, gone as quickly as it appeared. Slowly, his expression morphed into a sneer as his eyes shifted toward her.

"My, aren't you the clever one?" He smiled, with all the seductiveness of a snake coiled in high grass. "Are you insinuating I had anything to do with your most recent misfortune, my dear?"

"And what might that be, Nicky? Misfortune? I wouldn't exactly characterize my life as unfortunate." She stiffened, raising her chin in feigned arrogance and pride. "Quite the contrary."

His jaw tightened as he backed from the fire. Finding a chair opposite her, he sat and leaned an elbow onto an armrest. Resting his chin on his fist, he stared, unreadable. A faint pull at the corner of his mouth reminded her how much he enjoyed a good verbal joust—but not if his opponent held the upper hand.

"Perhaps you can live with your sins better than most." His hurtful words hung in the air for her to examine at length.

The simple observation gnarled her stomach, entangling it with the bitter truth. *What did he know? How could he—?* Uncertainty prickled the skin of her face, forcing an unsettling blink to her eyelids. She conceded his clever insight. Her lungs burned from lack of air. She reminded herself to breathe—just breathe.

At that instant, the bittersweet image of him as a lover invaded her mind without mercy. He'd been kind and generous once. Remorse over what might have been tugged at her heart. Though hardness tinged his eyes now, she still remembered love brimming in his gaze as they lay beneath white linens, his skin flush with satiation.

"Some things are not easily forgotten, Nicky."

A knot wedged in her throat. She didn't know what to add, to make him understand. Even if she told him everything, nothing would be gained by it. Too much had happened—far too many secrets. Despite the vast wealth between them, neither of them could turn back the clock and reclaim a life that could have been.

"It appears you've changed, Fie." The severity of his expression softened, reflecting the regret she felt. "You used to avoid unpleasantness. Now you indulge in it. Money and power have seduced you."

Oh, how he'd misread her. Her eyes blurred, drowning in tears. The sting of his accusation hit her hard, like an unexpected slap to the face. Futilely, she held back her emotion. But a tear betrayed her, exposing her weakness.

And Nicky witnessed her defeat.

A tear rolled down her face, its path glistening at the fire's edge. In his lifetime, her beauty had struck him many times. One of the more memorable being the day she'd willingly surrendered her virtue to him, a precious gift given only once. But none of these instances, grouped in aggregate, moved him as greatly as this moment. Such power reigned in the grace of a single tear.

He felt defeated before he'd even begun.

She wrung her hands, allowing her frailty to show for the first time since he'd entered the room. Many times, he'd rehearsed this conversation in his mind, yet none of it went as planned. He hadn't counted on his reaction at seeing her for the first time since she was nineteen years old. And if it were possible, she was more beautiful now than he remembered.

Dismissing such sentiment, he pressed with the cruelty he'd honed over the years, cultivated by her denial of his affections. He wanted desperately to regain control—at her expense.

"Is that regret I see in your eyes, Fiona, or pure, unadulterated guilt? How do you live with the harsh reality of having hired the assassination of your dearly departed husband, Charles? Was the money that important to you?"

Shock jarred her. Through the tears, resentment leached to the surface—all at his hand.

"I have no idea what you're talking about." Her words denied him, but the sternness and the staunch resolve in her tone spoke volumes. She knew exactly what he implied. "And why now? Why are you just now coming forward after all this time? It's been twenty-five years since Charles died."

"Was killed, Fiona. Charles was murdered. A sniper bullet, as I recall. I suppose you'd blame the hazards of the job. Being the head of a crime family has its disadvantages. For my part, let's just say I'm weary of the competition."

He was too clever to spell everything out for her. He'd tolerated their head-to-head arms-trading endeavors up till now. But when he'd used a freelancing Mickey Blair for another job, he'd learned the man had worked as Dunhill Security for more than twenty-five years, a curious fact for a hired assassin. The link to Fiona was too tantalizing to pass up. After a discreet background check, he put two and two together. Now, with the truth painfully obvious in her eyes, he knew he'd been right about Fiona's guilt. His gamble had paid off.

But to use Christian Delacorte, Fiona's charity case, as a pawn in their chess match—his part had been masterfully played. She'd given a life to Delacorte, keeping him apart from her criminal endeavors, perhaps buying the love of a troubled child to create some semblance of family. Irony of ironies. His rival would be imploded from within—at the hands of an innocent.

Checkmate, Fiona!

Defeat was manifest in her eyes. A culmination to his wicked scheme. The pinnacle of his success. *So why did he not feel victorious?*

"So this has all been about business, even after all these years?" She raised up, moving to the edge of her seat. His silence was her only reply. Then Fiona did something he hadn't expected.

She knelt at his feet.

Her hand softly touched his as she gazed at him, weariness etched in her face. The emerald-green of her eyes brimmed in misery. Her voice was only a whisper.

"I never stopped loving you, Nicky. You know how Charles was. He would have killed you if he'd found out about us. I couldn't let that happen." With fresh tears, she urged him to understand, clutching his hand. "It would have meant a war between the families—a vendetta. No one wins, and so many would have died needlessly. Charles wasn't a man to be trusted. If you only knew—"

"I know about trust broken, Fiona. We could have—" No use rehashing the past. He let the words flounder in his throat, replacing them with the question he truly wanted to ask. "If you still love me, why didn't you say anything before now?"

She pulled her hand from his and swallowed hard. Fiona couldn't look him in the eye. She was hiding something.

"You claim to love me, yet you keep your secrets. Why?" he pleaded, hearing the heartache in his voice, despising the weakness she provoked. "Why?"

"Some decisions are better left in the past, not dredged up for the world to see. It's not just about you and me anymore."

What did she mean?

For him, it had always been about her. He hadn't been the same since the first time he saw her all those many years ago. His successes, his competitiveness, all of it had been posturing for her. He'd never married, hoping she'd surrender to him. With her rejection even now, so much had been for naught. Yet the ultimate question still lay before him. *Would he knowingly destroy her now? Could he kill the last vestiges of the young, idealistic man he used to be when he was with her?*

"And some decisions are a result of the past, a past unwilling to stay buried," he contradicted.

Nicholas stood and gazed upon her, a lump rising in his throat. Crumpled at his feet, she looked broken. Her youthful innocence was gone, displaced by an agonizing love that had somehow endured. But he knew all about that.

In their youth, love had burned hot like a flame, wildly flickering and dancing for all to see. When she married another man, he believed that fire to be snuffed for good. Yet unexpectedly, today, he found the red glow of a fiery ember in her eyes, still raging against all odds. It caught him by complete surprise.

"And you're wrong, Fie. It has always been about you and me."

Stepping around her, he walked away, unable to look back. Instead, he focused on his hollow footsteps. The sound nearly drowned out the regret heard in her choking sobs. The splendor of the grand château drifted by in a blur. He felt numb.

He couldn't turn around. If he had, he might never want to leave.

"He's asking for you. ICU room eight." Yolanda smiled weakly. Raven could tell the woman was exhausted.

"He doesn't have the strength for a long visit, but I'm afraid you're going to have to be the judge of that. He's so stubborn."

Raven stood, rushing to Tony's wife with open arms. Closing her eyes, she held the woman firmly in her embrace, willing her strength. "How are you holding up?"

When they parted, Yolanda shrugged without complaint. "I'm gonna take his parents to the chapel, maybe get some coffee in the cafeteria." Unspoken emotion lay just beneath the surface of her words. "Come find me if—"

"I will." Quick to speak up, Raven didn't allow her to finish the thought.

Before leaving, Yolanda stepped toward Christian, who'd risen from the sofa when she entered the waiting room.

"He wants to see you, too, Christian." With a smile, she reached for his hand and kissed it.

"Me?" Delacorte questioned.

"Yes, you. I'm sure he'd like to thank you for bringing his parents to Chicago. I could tell your generosity surprised him."

"No doubt." Christian nodded, directing a sheepish look toward Raven. He looked unworthy, like an instigator of a prank that turned out to be mistaken for an act of kindness. But she knew better.

After Yolanda left the room, Raven turned toward Christian. "You heard the man. He wants to see us both." She swept her arm to the ICU room door, encouraging him.

Reluctantly, he stood his ground, stuffing his hands into his jeans pockets. "You go. He doesn't need to thank me for anything."

The aw-shucks routine was adorable, but Raven understood her partner. "Oh, believe me. I know that man in there. He has more to say than just thanks. Trust me on that one."

Christian narrowed his eyes at her, then slowly nodded again. She knew he was bracing himself for an audience with the ingratiating cop who'd attempted to serve him lousy coffee while setting him up for a subtle interrogation—all in the name of law and order.

"Lead the way." He sighed.

A flood of memories filled Raven's mind as she walked slowly down the sterile corridor of the ICU. Medical science blended its own pungent concoction of vague medicinal odors and pine cleaner, with a dash of human secretions laced in anxiety and hope. She avoided a curious glance into open doorways, not wanting to invade the privacy of the seriously ill who shared her partner's plight.

Room number 8 was the fourth door to the right, the only room with an attendant dressed in blue seated outside. Raven kept her eyes focused on the sympathetic gaze from a young police officer stationed at Tony's door, who stood as she neared. She acknowledged his service with a nod, the first shift of the twenty-four-hour police protection for the Rodriguez family. The assignment of the young officer meant her days of freedom were numbered. Soon, she'd be hampered with an entourage of her own. The thought saddened her, but nothing prepared her for what followed, seeing Tony for the first time after his assault.

Standing at the threshold of her partner's room, Raven shuddered, a faint gasp fresh from her lips. She'd never seen him so weak—and lost. Tubes and machinery sustained him. Tony looked so frail and thin, his skin pale from blood loss. It was as if the muscles of his body had atrophied overnight. With his eyes closed, he had the appearance of a corpse, except for the steady beep of his heart monitor.

Christian sensed her shock and grasped her shoulder, saying, "He's alive, and on the right side of the dirt. That counts for something."

At the sound of Christian's voice, Tony opened his eyes with a sluggish effort. In his condition, it took him a moment to place Raven's face. But once he had, a weak smile crossed his lips.

His lips moved to say her name, but opted for a simpler version. "Mac."

"The doctor said you were lucky. You're gonna be okay."

Pulling up a chair next to his bed, she gently squeezed his hand, knowing precious little of his medical condition. With effort, Tony filled his lungs with a shallow and unsteady pant. The man knew the difference between wishful thinking and the truth, possessing sure-fire radar to detect bullshit. But it didn't stop her from trying.

"They were m-mercs, Raven. Laser scopes." His voice nothing but raspy air, dry and faint. "Connected to Bl-Blair. Be careful."

She had kept the break-in at her house a secret from him and Yolanda. They both had enough to deal with. Tony's dark eyes already communicated his concern for her safety. Even with his life still at risk, he worried for her. *God, how she loved this man!*

"Listen to me, Tony Rodriguez. You've only got one job while you're here. And that is to stay alive. You hear me? Prove to that bastard that he can't keep a macho man like you down. A Tex-Mex is hard to kill." She smiled through the tears filling her eyes, choking back the lump in her throat. She tightened her grip on his cold fingers. "I love you, Tony."

Leaning closer, she kissed his cheek. One of her tears doused his skin, mingling with his own. She brushed it away with a thumb.

"*Te quiero, m-mi h-hermana.*" He returned the sentiment in Spanish, adding an endearment she'd come to recognize—*my sister.*

Tony was family now. And her family needed protection.

Wiping the tears from her face, she steeled herself for a fight. Under the cover of darkness, Blair's killer was a coward, resorting to an assault on an unsuspecting off-duty police officer in clear sight of his family. Unfortunately, in this quietly raging society, retribution against the police had become prevalent, and often for minor offenses such as traffic citations. *How screwed up do you have to be to kill over a parking ticket?*

Tony looked tired, barely able to keep his eyes open. But she knew he wasn't done.

"In case anything happens—" He swallowed and tightened his grip on her hand, fighting back a deepening shroud of pain in his eyes. "Please take c-care of m-my family. Yolie is strong, but—"

Raven opened her mouth to reject his withering hope, but now wasn't the time to deny him anything. Even though she refused to believe he might die, something as small as an errant blood clot could seal his fate, a familiar complication for gunshot wounds.

Clenching her jaw, she assured him, "You know I will."

A weak smile faded from his face. She knew her promise gave him comfort. Staring into his eyes, she let the contented silence build between them. Without words, Tony was preparing her for the worst.

"Oh, no, you don't." She nearly choked on the realization. "You're giving me that all-knowing Yoda stare, the one that says I shouldn't question my training officer." Despite the humor in her words and a crooked half smile, a tear contradicted her message. "You taught me everything, Tony. And I know you're just too damned ornery to die. I got my stubborn streak from you."

"Not so, Grasshopper. You c-came by that honestly—from your old m-man." The old Tony glimmered just beneath the surface of his pain, too frail to emerge. "Is Christian here? I'd like . . . to t-talk to him, alone."

Faced with reality, she discovered her partner was breakable after all. But leaving him to the care of others went against the woman she was, and her training. Tony released his grip from her fingers, letting go.

"He's here, Tony." Glancing over her shoulder, she nodded her encouragement for Delacorte to take her place. She ran fingers down Christian's arm as he stood by her side. Even in Tony's weakened condition, he hadn't missed Raven's subtle gesture of affection.

Her partner rarely missed a thing.

"This your idea of vacation time?" Once they were alone, Christian sat beside Tony's bed, lightly touching the man's arm to make a connection.

"Raven will tell you. I d-do anything for a little attention." Even in jest, Tony covered his pain, garnering his strength. "Thanks for m-my parents."

"You getting better is thanks enough. And your mom promised to make me some habanero hot sauce that'll rip my head off. That's all the gratitude I can handle." Christian stood to leave, but Tony grabbed his arm.

"The act of k-kindness toward my f-family, you seem like a good man." With his eyes, he beckoned for Christian to lean closer, the man's voice barely above a whisper. "She won't back down from this. I know how she is. These men are organized and d-dangerous. Please t-take care of her, of Raven."

Sitting down, Christian nodded. "I plan to do just that. At least until you're back on your feet." Christian tilted his head, patiently waiting for relief to show on Tony's face. "I agree with you. She needs someone to watch her back. Any bastard that would do what they did to you and your family deserves—" He stopped midsentence.

He struggled to control his anger. It was hard to let go of the past. But for Raven and Fiona's sake, he had to get beyond it. Self-pity wasn't an option.

"I was h-hoping y-you'd say that. Thank you." The wounded detective grimaced. "Now I gotta heal up. I'm gonna eat everything. Anything they put in fr-front of me, even if the f-food kills me. That's my plan."

"If that's the best you can come up with, you must be hurting." Christian reached for Tony's wrist, giving it a gentle shake. "Take care, man."

After leaving the ICU room, he quietly walked down the corridor toward the waiting room with Raven by his side. Numb to his surroundings, he was steeped in thought. He'd spent his whole life building a foundation of resentment toward the police. And in a matter of days, he had come to grips with the frailty of that cornerstone. Dread gnawed at his belly.

So hard to let go of the hatred. He'd nurtured it for so long, believing it fortified him. But perhaps his changed feelings toward the police and Raven Mackenzie would serve a purpose, to help him search for the truth alongside a very unexpected ally. Someone sinister had risked a great deal to stir up the past, killing a man to make a very public point. None of it made sense.

Who had passed judgment on Mickey? And why had they picked Christian to bring the truth to light? Time to find the answers.

The jet engine droned, making it easy to block out the world. He stared out the small window, his eyes not fixed on anything in particular. Night settled upon him as he left France, embracing him in black velvet, only a dress rehearsal for the real thing. With the time difference, he'd gain hours, landing on American soil to experience sunset in its finality, like opening night at the theater when little else remained but to raise the curtain. Feathery tufts drifted by, weightless. He felt lost in them.

The world had grown smaller—and he had been the cause.

Nicholas Charboneau replayed his long-awaited confrontation with Fiona in his mind. The woman held firm to her secrets. He knew when she was avoiding the truth. At least, he thought he could tell. So much time had been squandered between them, dulling his understanding of the only woman who'd made him vulnerable to love.

The steady vibration of his cell phone pulled him from his self-inflicted misery. He considered not answering the call, but his better judgment forced him to reach for his tether to the present.

"Speak."

"I thought you should know." Without greeting, the woman got down to business.

The sensual voice of Mantis prickled his ear. Normally, her lusty tone conjured up delightful images of his lethal flower. But only one woman plagued him now, lurking in the shadows of his memory.

"Yes, Jasmine, what is it?" His curt tone would be noticed. The young woman was most sensitive to his needs. The prolonged silence on the other end of the line confirmed it. Finally, she spoke.

"You should have let me come with you," she admonished tenderly. "Are you okay, Nicky?"

Rarely had he ever heard such doubt in her voice. The unexpected quiver of blame troubled him. He didn't like this sign of weakness in himself, nipping at his potency. It came much too naturally, and without warning. Was he suddenly developing a conscience? Briefly, he shut his eyes, dismissing the thought.

"I will be. Where are you?"

"Perilously lost in suburbia, counting my blessings that I met you. How do people live like this? I doubt I will ever understand the endearing qualities of the minivan." The disgust in her tone had returned. Jasmine was never sentimental for long. "You were right. Our ravenous predator is hunting. And as you predicted, he lacks subtlety and any semblance of discretion."

Under the surface of her sulking, childlike voice slithered the menace of death that he found most appealing. Sensuality and murderous intent wrapped in one tantalizing package. Nicholas had assigned his bodyguard to discreetly tail Logan McBride, suspecting the man would tempt fate by disregarding his not-so-subtle warning at their last rendezvous. Yet, he had to admit, the vulgar man had been right—an animal does remain true to its nature.

"He's marking his territory, pissing where he doesn't

belong," she warned, her femininity neatly disguised by her crude choice of words, a delicious paradox.

Even using a high-tech secured phone, Mantis always avoided any incriminating references. A gesture he appreciated. She cautioned that McBride had escalated his interest in the fair detective who was investigating Blair's murder. He had dangled the detective as incentive to McBride, for a job well done, not realizing the bonus would be more like tossing blood in shark-infested waters. Perhaps the man wasn't as predictable as he'd once imagined.

"And he paid a visit to the other. I believe we should send flowers to the hospital—or the mortuary," she added in a grim tone. "The outcome hasn't been decided."

Silence. His once useful contractor knew better than to lead police to his door. But the man had launched his own campaign of retribution, without regard to his warning. Anger surged deep inside his chest. To a point, McBride's vile nature had been custom-made for his little endeavor. Now, the man had outgrown his usefulness. Tension set his jaw, but his voice remained steady.

"I will be landing later this evening. Keep in contact if there are any further developments. By the time I arrive, I shall have a plan to remedy the situation."

"I look forward to it," she purred. "And Nicky, when I see you, I will have a remedy of my own concoction." Her purposeful diction and the intimacy of her voice pierced the distance between them. "Guaranteed to make you forget your troubles."

"Until then, Mantis."

He ended the call, turning his attention once more to the clouds spiraling by his window. On the horizon, the sea of soft texture held substance, backlit by the fire of a waning sun. Light gained its fleeting stronghold, spearing its tendrils through holes in the sky. The constant struggle between light and dark was a battle doomed to failure from both sides. A winner would never be declared. Considering himself a poet with an appreciation for bloodlust, he appreciated the analogy.

"If only it were that simple, my dear. If only—" he whispered.

She thought the day would never end. Her eyes felt thick with exhaustion; an ache overwhelmed her muscles.

As Raven drove up to her house, accompanied by the two squad cars assigned to her, darkness settled. A trace chill of violation still lingered in her memory. Her safe haven had been forever tainted by the break-in. Turning the key to the side entrance off the carport, she glanced overhead, remembering her intruder had pulled the bulb from her security light. It would have to be replaced.

Uncharacteristically, she drew her weapon to walk into her dark kitchen, Lieutenant Sam Winters at her side. Though pitch-black, the room echoed its emptiness. She knew they were alone. As she flipped on the lights, the aftermath of her ruined dinner with Christian doused her with melancholy. The tainted aroma of spaghetti sauce hung in the air, its remains still splattered on the stovetop. The image forged its imprint on her mind.

Backing up Lieutenant Winters, she conducted a search of her home before lowering her Glock. Her fellow officer and family friend had volunteered to oversee the night shift. Close to retirement, he had partnered with Raven's father and visited her house on many occasions. Her first night under police protection would be strained enough, but she felt reassured having Sam watch over her.

"We'll be setting up in front and back. You know the drill. The last of the cowboys went out with John Wayne. You're no gunslinger. So call us if you hear anything."

Sam's face had been shaped by his years. Deeply furrowed laugh lines branded him a character. Red hair infused with gray stood on end, defying gravity. She had seen his stern grimace whenever he glowered at a suspect, but that expression melted away completely when he relaxed amidst friends. Like a stubborn cowlick unwilling to behave, his face sprang routinely into a crooked smirk. She knew firsthand that his scowl took much more effort. Sam's warm smile comforted her now, reminding her how much the man made her father laugh.

"I've got a thermos or two. How about I make some coffee for you and the troops." She grinned, not wanting to be alone so soon. "You can keep me company while it's brewing. We can talk while I clean up this mess."

"Whoa, what happened to your old man's photo?" He reached for the framed memento ruined by dried tomato sauce. "You trying a new recipe?"

"Not me. The bastard that broke in here added his own special ingredient." Working around the mess, Raven busied herself with the coffee prep as she spoke, filling the pot with water from the sink.

"But I'm glad we can talk about this, Sam. When you and Dad partnered, were there any hard cases that come to mind that could do such a thing?"

After prying open the lid to the coffee, she scooped

out the dark, rich-smelling granules. Raven restrained a smile. Ever since associating Christian Delacorte with the pungent aroma of freshly brewed coffee, she couldn't think of java without conjuring sensual images of him. Truth be told, everything reminded her of Delacorte these days. She had it bad.

"From the message on my bathroom mirror, the guy's connected to the Blair murder, too. My gut tells me the SOB knew my dad."

"Give me some time to think about that, baby girl. I can dig through some old case files, too." The man ridged his brow in irritation. "I hate it that this psycho has singled you out. The world sure has gotten twisted."

He pulled back a chair from the breakfast table and flipped it around, straddling the seat and resting his meaty forearms across the back. Shoving his glasses down the bridge of his ample nose, he lowered his chin to gaze over the top of the frames, his mustache animating his upper lip.

"You know, back when your daddy and I rode together, we didn't have all these high-tech laptops in our patrol cars and GPS for the dispatchers to know where we were every friggin' pee break."

With coffee gurgling, Raven sprayed down her countertops and waged war on the tomato splatter. She'd heard this commentary from Sam many times before. And if she closed her eyes, her father's memory rang clear. It felt good to remember him.

"Hell, these days, every cop has got a video cam in the dash, and a triple-encrypted communication system more like the CIA. We even got our own TV show and theme song." He shook his head and grinned, a twinkle of mischief in his eyes.

"And don't you dare start singing it, LT." She pointed a threatening finger in his direction, like it was loaded. "It sounds like you miss the good old days."

"I'm not complainin', mind you. We need all that shit just to keep up. And the world keeps churning out sick bastards for us to clean up after. Talk about job security. And your guy is no exception. What he did to Tony really chaps my hairy butt. Pardon my French."

Raven stopped working with the mention of her partner's name, remembering how much Tony enjoyed the man's company. He'd often egg him on, trying to bait him for a rowdy discussion on the "good old days." But Sam was the most politically incorrect person she knew, from his chauvinistic terms of endearment to his colorfully inventive curses. It tickled her to think he was now asking her forgiveness for his "French." After being a cop for so long, she'd heard it all. Most probably, he only wanted permission to embellish.

"I find it ironic that we got ourselves a war on drugs funded in part by seized drug money. Which comes first, the whoppin' big golden egg or the tight-ass chicken? All I know is, that's gotta hurt. You know what I mean?"

She'd been right. He saved the best for last, mixing fables and old sayings in typical Sam fashion. Staring him straight in the eye, she nodded her head as if she agreed, then said, "No. Have no clue. And it scares me to think you do. But I love you anyway."

Fighting a grin, she poured hot coffee into two thermoses. As he stood, she shoved the containers in a crook of his arm.

"Draw the drapes and stay away from the windows." He smirked, drumming a knuckle on her forehead with affection to make his point. "And start leaving a light on inside."

"Why? I'm not afraid of the dark." Reacting too quickly, Raven lied about her fear of the dark, afraid to show her sign of weakness.

"Oh, it's not for you, darlin'. I call it target acquisition. If I have to come in here, gun drawn, I wanna see what I'm aimin' at."

"Okay, I'll concede the point."

"And just in case you hear any noises outside, I'm gonna have our guys take regular walks around the perimeter. It'll keep 'em sharp. You know what they say— the brains can only take what the tail end can stand." With a wink, he cheered her with a grin. "Thanks for the coffee, sweetness. And I'll get back to you on those old case files."

Before he walked out the door, he turned back, a serious expression on his face. "I probably don't say this enough, Raven, but your old man would have been proud."

She rubbed his shoulder, squeezing it gently.

"Thanks, Sam. For everything."

Down the block, well out of sight, Logan sat behind the wheel in the dark, clenching his jaw until it ached. The damned police thought a couple of cruisers would deter him. Nothing could be further from the truth. His men were well-trained and loyal to his command. To get at Raven Mackenzie, he was certain—nothing could stop him. And bloodying a few more blue uniforms held no significance. Retrieving his cell phone, he punched a speed-dial number. A man answered on the second ring.

"Yeah, Vinnie. Call the party off for tonight. She's got visitors," Logan ordered. Earlier, he'd thought about sending someone else to do reconnaissance, but after seeing the young detective in the shower, he decided to do the job himself. He wouldn't share her with anyone.

"Krueger's gonna be disappointed. What now?" Vinnie asked.

Logan took a deep breath, then smirked to himself.

"I'm stickin' 'round here for a while longer, get a look at their setup. When I come home, I'll lay out a plan."

Short of formality, he ended the call. With the help of night-vision binoculars, he scoped out the area. Logan knew police protocols. He welcomed the challenge and thrived on the adrenaline rush. It wasn't just a question of making the hit, then finding a safe egress. It was all about the thrill of the hunt, the fear of his prey. And given his recent canvassing of the neighborhood, he'd already begun to formulate a game plan.

Taking Raven Mackenzie out of play was only a matter of time.

Raven's eyes had grown accustomed to the dark. Even though her bedroom was nearly pitch-black, the night light from the living room poured beneath her door, giving her comfort. A dim glow from an outside streetlight outlined the curtains, casting shadows into corners. All she had to do was close her eyes, but frustration got the better of her, manifesting in a heavy sigh.

Throwing the comforter off, she got out of bed and made her way toward the large window in her bedroom. Clad only in a large CPD tee, she pulled back the drapery and stared into the void. Immediately, her eyes trailed to the heavens, their attention stolen by the brilliant moon. Nearer the horizon, the lights of the city robbed the sky of its own brilliance, their beauty obscured by man's cheap imitation.

Outside her window, the hiss of brittle winter grass crunched under foot. Her body reacted to the implied threat. Raven peered though the darkness, careful not to jostle the drapes. Her eyes darted across the back-yard. She held her breath, ruling out every familiar sound from in and around her old house, listening for the exception. Just then, a shadow moved to her right.

She remembered what Sam had told her earlier. *Just in case you hear any noises outside, I'm gonna have our guys take regular walks around the perimeter.* She breathed a sigh of relief when the shape became clearer. The shadow was one of her watchdogs. Leaning against the window frame, she rolled her eyes and shook her head.

Heaving a breath, she expelled tension from her lungs. The earlier home invasion had spooked her more than she realized. She closed her eyes, calming her heart. She was a prisoner in her own home. Resentment colored her attitude—until her thoughts turned to Christian.

She wondered what he was doing this very second. Outside the city, at the Dunhill Estate, the night sky would be glorious. Perhaps one day, when the nightmare of this ordeal was over, they'd share its beauty. The hope of that moment soothed her beyond measure.

Christian spent the afternoon digging through Fiona's life. Her delicate perfume still in the air, it reminded him of her absence. He'd grown melancholy with the futility of his effort. Searching the study and her bed-room took longer than he'd expected. Tomorrow, he'd tackle the attic, not knowing what he'd find there.

Hours ago, darkness had crept across the bedroom in lengthening shadows, forcing him to flip on several of the lamps nearby. He'd become so engrossed, he hadn't been affected by the gloom closing in. Any other day, the impending darkness would have captured his atten-tion, like holding a snarling beast at bay. But today, he was on a mission.

Letters faded with age and old photographs lay cluttered across the carpet of Fiona's bedroom. Sitting
cross-legged in the midst of it all, Christian realized he
knew so little about her. Many of the mementos he'd
never seen before. But then again, he'd been so defined
by the violence in his life, he hadn't reached out to Fiona
except to eventually take the lifeline she offered. Her
life was more of a mystery than he cared to admit.

And something peculiar troubled him. No newborn
baby pictures. Gaps existed in his early life. Some of that
could be explained away. His childhood had not been
normal. For the most part, his mind was a blank slate.
Post-traumatic stress had destroyed much of his memory.

The one constant in his life, since that tragic day, had
been Fiona. And now, he felt like such a voyeur, delving
into her past. But he was certain the answers would be
there, if he only knew where to look. Or, perhaps, *how*
to look—

Slowly, he reached for a photo of Fiona and Charles,
flipping it over. One word was written across the back,
along with a date. *Honeymoon.* He recognized Fiona's
script. Something in the photo gnawed at him. His eyes
had been drawn to the image several times during the
course of his search. Yet he couldn't put his finger on
the reason for this. Dressed in summer attire, the hon-
eymooners squinted into the bright sun, standing at a
harbor dock. Charles was beaming, his arm around
the beautiful woman he'd married. And a young Fiona
graced the scene, barely out of her teens. On the surface, an idyllic moment captured by the photographer.

Then, it struck him.

Fiona wasn't smiling. And her body language showed
tension. It was etched in her face. In contrast to her
young husband, who clung to her like a prize, she

showed no such affection. The single-word description on the back was purposefully written, without embellishment. Not even the location had been given, so contrary to what a newlywed might have done.

Sifting through other photos, he began to see a pattern. *Why hadn't he noticed it before?* Christian knew the woman well enough to grasp it.

Fiona hadn't loved Charles. And the years hadn't improved their relationship, chronicled in the many pictures spread before him. A discernible pattern.

"Why, Fiona? Why did you marry a guy you didn't love?" he muttered. It didn't make any sense, given the strength of the woman he'd grown to love. He couldn't imagine her being coerced into a loveless bond.

As he picked up the honeymoon photo once again, another thought roused him from out of the blue—something Raven had asked him at the armory.

Can you think of anyplace else that Mickey might have kept some kind of locker? I found a key— Raven's voice teased his memory.

An image popped into his mind.

Now, Christian knew where to look for the answer.

But tomorrow would be soon enough. The tension and stress of the day invaded every sinew. Standing, he stretched the muscles of his back. His stomach growled in emptiness, but he was too restless to indulge it. He wandered to the French doors and onto the balcony off Fiona's bedroom.

After sucking in the chilly night air, he exhaled a warm breath in a vapor trail. In no time, the cold absorbed into his shirt, chilling his skin with every brush of the fabric. The sensation invigorated him, clearing the fog from his brain. With only the dim radiance from Fiona's room shining through white window sheers, the grounds of the estate were cast in a bluish haze, charged by the moon's energy. Shining brightly, the moon loomed overhead, growing larger by his estimation. The night sky cloudless, it proudly displayed its dazzle. He felt small and insignificant.

Yet despite the beauty above, his thoughts of Raven moved him far more. The woman had burrowed deep under his skin, never allowing him to forget her. Her beguiling infiltration had been subtle, with a rare sensuality. But the self-inflicted wound, named Raven Mackenzie, had not been without pain. With every remembrance, Christian felt just how lonely he'd allowed his life to become. And the thought that he could lose her made his stomach churn.

Given the firepower of the attack launched against her partner, Christian feared for her safety. By all reports, her partner's home had been annihilated. By turning down his offer of protection, Raven was in denial about her ability to defend against such an assault. Her modest home would be indefensible. Yet if he was being truthful, he'd have to confess his attraction to her stirred him more than he cared to admit.

Damn it! Why had everything gotten so . . . complicated?

Her dark eyes haunted him. Still, he contemplated betraying Raven's trust, for Fiona's sake. Tomorrow, he'd investigate on his own, looking for the secret that Mickey might have kept under lock and key. But depending upon what he found, he'd have a decision to make.

Would he share it with Raven?

CHAPTER 11

The details of the Blair file blurred on the page as she searched for anything she might've missed. Her ability to focus had waned, and it was only midmorning. She hadn't slept well. Raven pinched the bridge of her nose and shut her eyes. When she opened them again, she caught sight of Tony's clip-on tie tossed on his desk. The image left her hollow. Now, her eyes trailed to his empty chair, her misery complete.

A distinct chill lingered in the room. She couldn't shake it. Despite being dressed in jeans with layers under a black cable-knit sweater, she still found her skin prickled in goose bumps. No amount of layering or rounds of hot coffee fended off the cold.

"Did one of you guys turn down the thermostat again?" Normally, the question would've generated profuse finger pointing and offers on ways to stay warm, but not today. All she got was polite smiles and a few shrugs.

And the clock on the wall ticked away at an interminably slow pace. The world hadn't stopped altogether. Tony's absence loomed like a dark cloud in the bullpen. Out of respect, her fellow officers were uncharacteristically quiet. Their sideways glances and sympathetic expressions reflected their concern. Every time her phone rang, their eyes shifted nervously her way. She knew they wondered if the call meant news from the hospital. The calm made her anxious. Even her Cubs cap, turned around rally style, hadn't provided any comfort.

Feeling like a fleshy chunk of her had been carved out, she ached for her missing partner. Her early-morning visit with Yolanda at the hospital hadn't remedied her concern. He'd had a bad night. Tony still wasn't out of the woods. But a familiar face drew her back into focus, warming her soul.

"Hey, honey, got any coffee for the old man? I could use a whole pot in a very large syringe." Lieutenant Sam Winters held a cardboard box in his arms, grinning ear to ear.

"Hey, LT. Thought you'd be sleeping?" she teased, glad for the distraction.

"Got to thinking about your daddy's old cases. Been searching through the archives after I got off shift." He set down his burden on Tony's desk. "Care for a temporary partner for today, while yours is on the mend?"

Sam spoke as if Tony had a bad case of the flu. Somehow, his denial reassured her, like everything would be all right.

"I'll get you that coffee. But the preferred method of dosing around here is Styrofoam. The syringe is up to you."

By the time she returned from the break room, he had settled into Tony's desk, laying manila folders in piles.

"Figured I'd go through these, set aside any that stick in my brain as possibles. I got your old man's case notes. You ever looked at 'em?" he asked. He handed her a black spiral notebook. Her father had kept them by year. "Your daddy was the best cop I ever worked with. I still miss him."

"Good partners are like that." She fought the lump in her throat. Her hands reverently brushed the top of a bound notepad.

She knew looking into his old cases would take time. But the malicious act of the bastard who'd invaded her home and destroyed her father's photo provided insight into the man's egotistical nature. And she was determined to capitalize on his mistake.

"This is gonna be a long shot, Sam."

"Yeah, but when you're a Cubs fan—" he replied with a crooked grin, setting her up. In unison, she joined him in one of her father's old sayings, "—long shots are what we do."

The waterfront off Lakeshore Drive glistened in the sun like a jeweler's case. The dazzle caught Christian's eye as he neared the Chicago Yacht Club. Boat masts normally speared the sky, but were noticeably absent. The vessels had been pulled from the lake and dry-docked for winter. Set near the Chicago Loop amidst a myriad of cultural offerings, the yacht club was a focal point to many sporting activities and home to Lake Michigan's finest regattas. Even with the change in season, the dock drew people to the waterfront and its adjacent trail system. Nature's tranquillity was a magnet. Compared to the hustle of downtown, the harbor reflected serenity, an oasis from a more hectic pace.

Christian turned his SUV into the Monroe Street parking garage, then walked across Lakeshore Drive toward the two-story Monroe Harbor Clubhouse and the sign indicating the marina office.

Seeing the harbor in the photo of Fiona's honeymoon

had jogged his memory. At one time, he had heard that Mickey owned a boat and kept it in a slip at the yacht club. Perhaps the man still had a connection to the posh facility. As Christian neared the water's edge, a breeze humbled him, coming through his khaki cargo pants. The bright sun held little warmth. Winter heralded its arrival with the wind off the lake. He zipped the front of his leather bomber jacket, covering his ivory cardigan. His hiking boots echoed his approach along the wooden pier.

Just as he remembered, a set of glass doors revealed the location of lockers, near the guest shower facility. Although the area was open now, instructions printed on the door laid out the hours for the secured card key access. Then his eyes found one security camera, and another, his training made him a creature of habit. The upscale facility would have suited Mickey's taste.

Raven's mystery key might have a home after all. Still, he hadn't decided if he would share whatever news he might find with her. The thought sent a pang of guilt jabbing at his conscience.

He followed the walkway past the office, his eyes drawn beyond the shoreline. Without the narrow building to break the sporadic gusts, the chilly breeze stole his breath as he rounded the corner, tousling his hair. And the untainted smell of the lake carried on the wind, beckoning like a haunting siren's call.

The irresistible view drew him to the railing, his hands stuffed into his jacket. Even under dark glasses, his eyes watered with the cold. The expanse of water churned, mesmerizing him with its swells. Thoughts of Raven crept into his mind. Surely, such beauty was meant for two.

"She's like a mistress you can never forget." A man's voice interrupted his thought.

"Excuse me?" Christian turned to see an older man standing farther down the wooden pier. It took him a moment to realize the stranger had been talking about the appeal of Lake Michigan.

The man was dressed in layers. His gray hair peeked out from under a navy wool hat pulled over his ears, his bulbous nose red with the cold. The sparkle of the lake had been captured in his engaging eyes, despite the man's age.

"The lake. She's kept me coming here like an addiction." The old man's voice fit him, raspy and gnarled like his weathered skin. "You visiting? I haven't seen you here before."

Christian didn't offer a reply. A faint smile curved a corner of his mouth. He treasured his anonymity far too much to reveal anything to this stranger.

"Have a good one, mister. Enjoy your day." Turning, he walked back toward the office and left the old gent. Time to move on.

Down from the lockers, another set of glass doors under an awning led to the small marina office. Once inside, he slipped off his sunglasses, his eyes adjusting to the darker interior. An unrecognizable melody wafted from overhead speakers. The walls were covered with dark wood veneer and cork message boards. Sitting between a sofa and armchairs, an evergreen shrub had seen better days. Beyond the vacant counter, a small office with metal filing cabinets was abandoned. No one manned the desk.

Just then, the door behind him opened. And the old man from the wharf entered, sporting a grin on his face.

"What can I do for ya, young man? Folks consider me Father Confessor 'round here. Talk to me. You'll find I'm a good listener."

Christian returned his smile, sharing his subtle brand of humor. "Yes, sir. And I just bet they'd be right. Was wondering if you could tell me if Mickey Blair still leases a boat slip here? Or maybe has a locker?" He hoped no other information would be asked of him.

The man stepped behind the counter. The humor faded from his lined face. "That information is generally considered private, mister. Did you know him?"

"Not well," he cautiously replied. Christian narrowed his eyes and cocked his head to one side. "Couldn't help but notice you used the past tense. You hear what happened to Mick?" Christian followed his instincts. As long as he kept him talking, the man might eventually cooperate. The trick was to get more information than he had to shell out.

"Man's gotta keep up with things, right?" Aged eyes held Christian's stare. "Guy's dead anyways. Couldn't hurt, just talking. He used to keep a boat here. *The Freelancer.* But he gave that up earlier this year. Said he was going someplace warmer."

"No doubt." If there was a hell, Christian suspected Mick felt plenty of heat now. Mickey would have been as secretive about himself as Christian was, but somehow, this man had kept an eye on him—and had gotten him to talk. Interesting.

And the guy continued to amaze him.

"And as for a locker, he still has it until the end of the year. Membership has its privilege. But I guess you could say Mr. Blair expired before his locker did." The man's abrupt chuckle filled the room. "Anyway, I saw him down at the docks from time to time, carryin' a duffel bag like he still had business here."

"Have you told the police about his locker?"

"Nope. Figured I'd get around to it sooner or later.

What're they gonna find in a locker anyway, some old sneakers and a snorkel? Besides, I'm not the kind of guy that'd stick his nose in other people's business."

Christian fought to keep a smile from his face.

"I don't know. You look like a man that keeps up with the goings-on around here. Don't suppose you could tell me which of these lockers is his." Christian reached into his jacket pocket, pulling out his wallet. Thumbing through his bills, he waited for—

"Yeah, I've always been real good with numbers." The man smiled and gave a wink, hand outstretched. "And mister, a man could always use a new friend. What did you say your name was?"

"Ulysses S. Grant." Christian smiled, handing over a fifty-dollar bill.

"You don't say. What's the *S* stand for?"

"You get me into that locker—and *S* will stand for satisfied."

The old man's laughter sealed their arrangement. But the image of Raven's dark eyes kept Christian from enjoying his small victory.

With a bite missing, a chili cheese dog loaded with onions sat atop Raven's desk, alongside a mound of untouched fries. The smell hovered in the air like a living, breathing thing. Sam's choice of lunch had no appeal. In contrast, the man was finishing the last bite of his foot-long like he'd never get another.

"You gonna eat the rest?" He raised both eyebrows, waiting for her answer. Once again, Raven looked up from her father's case notes, smiling when Sam's face reminded her of a big yellow Lab she had as a kid.

"With your schedule, you better keep up your strength. Go ahead, LT."

"Thanks, baby girl." After taking a mouthful, he kept talking. "I got a handful of cases here we can talk about—everything from a scumbag that killed his pregnant wife with a hunting knife to a DUI that got nasty. Where do you wanna start?"

His voice buzzed her ear, not fully sinking in. A note in one of her father's cases unexpectedly caught her eye. "What, Sam? Sorry, I was just reading—"

"You got something?"

"I don't really know." Her voice trailed off into a whisper, her eyes engrossed in her father's handwriting. "Just a car theft. Some teenager. But Dad sure seemed agitated by the guy. He even makes a personal note here."

"What did he write?"

"Just three words, printed and underlined in the margin—*Gray dead eyes*. Most of his work deals in the facts of each case. But this is different. Do you remember this one, Sam?" Raven handed over the black notebook, opened to an entry dated two years before the death of her father.

With one glance at the name of the car thief, he focused his attention to the stack of manila folders to his left.

"Hadn't gotten to that pile yet." With a grin, he found what he was looking for. "Yep, here it is. Logan McBride."

Quietly, he read through the material, narrowing his eyes with concern. "I remember this loser. A young punk with heaps of attitude." He looked up, tossing her the file.

Raven knew what her father had seen in the man. His black-and-white booking photo was chilling. Defiantly, gray dead eyes stared back at her, without an ounce of contrition—or fear.

"Logan McBride," she whispered to herself, trying to imagine the confrontation between her father and this man. She committed the face to memory.

Sam spoke, bringing her back to the present. "Looks like we got plenty of possibles. Let me give you the rundown so far, then we can make our top-ten hit parade. Sound like a plan?"

Before she could answer, her phone rang. Raising an index finger to Sam, she picked up her line. "Mackenzie."

"Raven? It's Christian. We've gotta talk."

"You sure this is gonna be okay? Maybe we can find someplace else." Given the look of concern on Christian's face, Raven had only one option for a reply. She lied.

"Yeah, this is fine. I love hot dogs."

Having a serious case of déjà vu, she didn't have the heart to refuse his choice of pseudocuisine. It was the only food readily available this late in the afternoon. By the time she'd finished with Sam's case run-down, the lunch hour was long gone.

Just her luck. Hunger had come back with a vengeance. After Christian heard her stomach growl at the station house, she lied about not having eaten, hoping he'd pick a quiet bistro. His only suggestion, a deliberate one, was a walk toward the yacht club.

Now, she held a mystery-meat Popsicle in her hand, minus the stick and wrapped in foil. No amount of yellow mustard and relish could hide it. The only thing that made it palatable was the view and the man walking by her side.

Lake Michigan looked breathtaking, glistening in the afternoon sun. As they meandered back toward the waterfront, she filled her lungs with fresh air and nibbled at her slice of Americana in a bun. But she did a double-take when she glanced over to Christian. He was suspiciously eyeing his hot dog, avoiding his first bite. No doubt he'd chosen the red-and-white-striped hot dog stand more for expediency than for the culinary wizardry of the vendor.

"Why'd you bring me here, Delacorte?" She raised an eyebrow. "You on a first-name basis with the maître d'?"

She found humor in her own remark, but he appeared distracted, avoiding her stare. Instead, he dodged her question by taking a bite of his dog. By the look on his face, it'd been a bad choice.

Forcing it down with a swig of bottled water, he finally replied, "Was just wondering if you had a chance to dig up the old Dunhill files? I've come up against a brick wall on my end, got nothing so far."

This close to the dock, Raven got the distinct impression he was fishing. She wasn't about to take the bait so easily.

"Those old files are archived, Christian. But I'm getting them delivered this afternoon, as soon as they've been located." She eyed him surreptitiously, observing every nuance of the man. He was even more difficult to read under dark glasses. "Not sure I've decided to share them yet. I haven't seen much in the way of good faith from you."

She let the implication hang in the air. An ordinary person would have filled the void in conversation, unable to leave silence be. Christian was anything but ordinary. He reversed her ploy, being content with utter stillness. A chess match with the man would be quite the challenge.

Fighting a smile, she found a quiet spot with a wooden bench and a beautiful view of the waterfront. He joined her, without a word. After tossing his half-eaten meal in a nearby trash receptacle, he sipped at his water and waited. The standoff might've been comical, except Christian was so preoccupied.

"Something's wrong. What is it?" she asked, setting aside her lunch.

He deliberated a moment, then pulled off his sunglasses, tucking them into a jacket pocket. Without the buffer, his eyes commanded her attention, softening his doleful expression.

"I can't help worrying about you. Whoever killed Mickey has no regard for the authority of the police. And gunning your partner down in front of his whole neighborhood just emphasizes that point." Turning, he fixed his eyes on her and brushed back a strand of hair that had blown across her cheek. "The Dunhill Estate is a fortress. I want you to stay with me."

Those eyes had the power to make her say yes to just about anything, but so much more was at stake than her personal feelings.

"I've got a job to do. You know that."

"Nothing's worth your life, Raven." Staring out across the water, he shared his tainted view of her career choice. "What you do. It's all about dealing with destruction and loss."

"No, Christian, you don't understand. For me, this job is about putting things right. It's about justice." She leaned toward him, touching a finger to his jawline. Eventually, she drew him back.

Yet by the look in his eyes, he still searched for an understanding. "After all the savagery that you see day after day, doesn't it chip away from who you are? The effects must be permanent. How do you deal with that?"

She felt certain his thoughts no longer reflected his view of her job. The emotion in his words ran much deeper, centered on his own grief. She could identify with his sentiments. The death of her father had robbed her of the innocence of her teenage years. In many respects, they had so much in common. Her connection to him was undeniable.

"But the effects don't have to be terminal. At some point, you gotta let go. Move on. The loss of my father pales in comparison to your tragedy, but I do understand some of what you've gone through."

"Then understand this." He reached for her hand, enfolding it in his. "You putting your life on the line, it's painful for me to watch. Please. I'm asking you to reconsider."

She ached hearing his heartfelt plea. With anyone else, she might've dismissed the concern. But gazing into Christian's eyes, it was nearly impossible. Nearly.

"You and I both have to remain strong. Don't you want to know who's doing this?" She squeezed his hand. Focusing on the facts of the case, maybe she could distract him from his apprehension for her personal safety. "Somehow this is all connected to your past. We just gotta find the key, that's all."

She caught a flicker in his eye. Something she said must have hit the mark.

"You wanted a sign of good faith?" With a pained expression, he jutted his chin down the pier, back toward the clubhouse. "That key you found in Mick's office. It probably belongs to a locker in there. Ask the old man at the marina office."

His words left her stunned. Then he stood, leaving her with her mouth open and squinting toward his silhouette, shielding her eyes with a hand.

"Wait. Where are you going?"

He didn't answer. But his next comment shook her.

"Just let me know what ballistics has to say."

As Christian turned his back, her mind grappled with her heart. The cop in her wondered how he knew what would be in the locker, suspecting he'd tampered with evidence. But the woman in her wanted to blindly trust him. He must have sensed her inner turmoil. He stopped, and with barely a glance over his shoulder, he spoke in a hushed tone.

"The old man was with me. He can tell you that I did nothing more than look in the bag."

For once, she was thankful not to be under the scrutiny of his eyes. It gave her the courage to ask the question she'd had on her mind.

"She's gone, isn't she?" Standing, her arms clutched across her chest, Raven held firm to her link with him. "I've tried her cell number countless times. Fiona's left you to deal with this, hasn't she?"

No words were necessary. The betrayal in his eyes told her everything she needed to know. Lowering his head, he put on his dark glasses and walked away. She found herself hoping he'd stop and turn around.

But that never happened.

Christian had given her more than just a sign of good faith. He'd made himself vulnerable to her investigation.

"Well, I'll be damned," she whispered.

By the time Raven got home, it was after dark. She flipped the light switch and elbowed her way through the kitchen door, carrying a large cardboard box. With a toe, she kicked the door closed behind her, then traipsed into the living room. After setting her burden on a coffee table, she shrugged out of her holster, placing her Glock beside the box. The weight of it lingered on her shoulder. Dim light from her kitchen bled into the small living room as she collapsed onto her sofa, feeling her exhaustion.

A long night lay ahead. She planned to keep working, focusing on the archived box about the Dunhill assassination and a selection of her father's old case files. With so much at stake, her curiosity far outweighed fatigue. The shadows and the comfort of the sofa enticed her to close her eyes, taking a short mental holiday. It had been quite a day.

Just as she nodded off, in that space between reality and dreams, a soft knock at her kitchen door woke her. Sluggishly, she rose off the couch and went to the door, taking a peek through the small window. With a grin, she tugged on the doorknob and gazed upon her partner for a day, still sporting his signature grin.

"Hey, Sam. Come on in." Stepping aside, she let her family friend through the door. "On duty again? You gotta be one tired hombre."

"No, baby girl, not tonight. This old man is wrung out. Just came by to make sure you're settled in for the night." He stood near her kitchen table. His body language told her he wasn't going to stay long. By his changed expression, he was all business. "Any word on that rifle you found?"

"I don't expect to hear anything from ballistics until tomorrow. With any luck, the striations from that H & K will match the bullet retrieved from the body of Charles Dunhill."

"What? You don't have enough to do, you gotta reopen the old Dunhill case? That was a very splashy headliner some twenty-plus years ago," he teased. "If you can pin this on Blair as the shooter, then you got a fresh lead. You might be able to trace who gave the order on the hit."

Normally, the cop in her would have been thrilled by the discovery. Solving such a high-profile case wouldn't hurt her career, but she knew the implications. As with any murder, the investigation would start with the person having the most to gain from his death. That person was obvious. Fiona Dunhill had gained a great deal. Even if she had nothing to do with her husband's killing, the woman's public reputation would be sullied by the new inquiry, dredging up the ugly innuendos. A nightmare revisited.

On the other hand, if she were guilty . . . The thought wrenched Raven's heart. Her duty would obligate her to build a case and arrest the woman. The courts would do the rest. If she and Christian had any hopes of a relationship, surely they'd be dashed now. How would they weather such a devastating storm—no matter what the outcome? She felt certain that Christian had been protecting Fiona, making his show of good faith in turning over the contents of the locker all the more astonishing. Why the sudden change of heart? So many questions bubbled to the surface.

"What's the matter, honey? I thought you'd be more excited."

"Oh, nothing, Sam. Guess I'm just tired, that's all." She rubbed her forehead, feeling a stress headache coming on.

"Well, that's my cue to leave. You got a big day tomorrow. Get some rest, honey girl." He yanked the door open, standing near the threshold. "The troops are positioned outside, like last night. As soon as I get some rest, I'll be back at it tomorrow. Maybe we can finish our talk about your daddy's old case files."

"Yeah, sounds good, LT." Standing on her toes, she gave him a quick peck on the cheek. His face reddened to the color of his hair. "Thanks."

"Good night, darlin'. Don't spend the whole night readin'. Getting your rest is important, too." He gently tapped a knuckle to her chin, then walked toward the street. From the shadows, she heard him say, "I'll tell your watchdogs that you'll be up late."

Locking the door behind him, she leaned against it, folding her arms across her chest. Her eyes found the cardboard boxes in her living room. Feelings of exhilaration and dread skirmished in her brain. No matter what she discovered, the foundation of Christian's life would be undermined. In that moment, she understood the courage it took for him to open his past to her. But the responsibility weighed heavy.

"I just hope you're not gonna hate me when this is all over," she prayed, her voice a whisper.

The beam of the flashlight strafed his position. He held his breath, willing himself not to react. At one point, the cop stared right at him. With nerves of steel, he remained calm, confident he wouldn't get caught. He melded into the shadows like a ghost. In such a quiet, unsuspecting neighborhood, the dark side of his nature took control, a predator among sheep.

The cop finished his patrol, securing the perimeter of the small bungalow. He understood their routine, counted on it. They had no idea what to expect. He'd parked several blocks away and stuck to the shadows that deepened after two in the morning. He had a clear plan in his head with only one objective—to find Raven Mackenzie.

Taking a risk, he left the cover of an evergreen shrub

and prowled around the corner of the house, brazenly following the cop on patrol at a safe distance. Carefully tracking the beam of light, he waited until the uniform swept the far corner, then counted to five. Patience would be key. Now crouching by a brick wall at the back of the house, he held his breath. His eyes peered through the gloom. He forced his body to remain still, fused to the darkness. The wind bounced sounds through the night, playing tricks on his ears.

But adrenaline galvanized him, tensing his body. He listened for any sound out of the ordinary, relying on his training. Even dressed in black, he knew part of him would be exposed to a stippling of pale light from a streetlamp filtered through tree limbs. He had to make it quick. He lowered his body to the ground, flat on his belly, crawling toward the narrow basement window. Along the frame, no wiring connected to an alarm. One less thing to contend with. Propped on a shoulder, he clutched the handle of the suction clamp he'd brought with him. A gloved hand secured it to the glass.

A faint hiss. Now the glass cutter scratched along the smooth surface, a high-pitched, grating sound.

Seconds. He had only seconds to make the cut and slip inside if he wanted to remain undetected. Getting this close to the house spurred him on. The police protection had been no match for his skill.

With a tug, the glass broke free, still connected to the metal clamp. He tossed the tools behind a bush. Sliding his hand inside, he released the window latch. In one fluid motion, he rolled through the opening and lowered his boots quietly to the floor. The basement smelled musty and dank, the chill of the night leaching through the cinder-block walls.

His eyes adjusted to the dark, then located the stairs.

He was close now. Soon, he would have her in his sights. The thought churned his blood, fueling his excitement. With each step deliberate, he moved through the clutter of boxes and unused furniture, the obstacles only dimly lit from the narrow windows at his back. Arms outstretched, he felt his way up the wooden staircase, careful not to give his position away.

If he was discovered now, he might lose his life to a bullet. But failure was not an option.

At the top step, he turned the doorknob, then gingerly pushed it open. Slipping through the door, he placed his back to the wall, reconnoitering and assessing his plan. Down the hallway, a lamp burned. He listened intently, then crept forward. Using a mirror on the wall across from him, he peered into the small living room, careful to keep his face in the shadows. In the reflection, he found her.

Raven Mackenzie lay on the sofa, a file folder spread across her chest. A Glock lay in its holster on a nearby table. Her head was turned away from him. Strands of hair had fallen away, exposing the pale skin of her neck. He waited to make sure she was sleeping. With mesmerizing steadiness, her breasts heaved, gently moving the papers in the manila folder. The intimacy of the act electrified him.

Even though the front drapes were drawn, he didn't want to take the risk of moving in clear view with the lights on. From the front of the house, his large silhouette backlit by a living room lamp would be like sending up a flare. Before he went any further, he slid his gloved hand along the wall and doused the lights. From the street, it would look as if she'd gone to bed. The cops outside would have no reason to suspect anything out of the ordinary.

The room plunged into darkness. It took his eyes a moment to adjust. Her silhouette was tinged in a faint glow from the window. Measured breaths told him she still slept. One careless mistake now would draw the posse in blue. But an even greater concern was the gun on the living room table. She could shoot him without a court in the world condemning her for the action. Careful not to wake her, he crept closer.

All of his effort would come down to the next few seconds. And he wasn't about to back down now. Not in his nature.

Slowly, his hand reached for the gun, but his instincts stopped him. His eyes darted through the room, unsure what had triggered his reaction. Then he realized—her breathing had changed.

Too late. He'd lost his edge. A shrill alarm jarred his brain.

Grab the gun!

CHAPTER 12

Her eyes opened. At least, she thought they were. Darkness deceived her, toyed with her perception. Black-and-white images of Charles Dunhill, with part of his skull missing, reminded her she had fallen asleep reading the old case file—a hazard of the trade. Now, her warm breath touched her cheeks, deflecting off the back of the sofa. Her face burrowed against a pillow.

Exhausted as she was, she couldn't force her body to move. Her limbs felt like lead. She lay there in the dark, content to waver in and out of sleep. But something jolted her out of a stupor. The room was dark. *Who had turned out the lights?*

Shutting down her body's natural recoil, she listened intently, hoping she'd only overreacted.

A faint sound . . . A presence weighed heavy in the room, just behind her—

Tensing her jaw, she resisted the urge to turn around. She assessed the situation, relying on her memory for the layout of the room. The chances of getting to her gun in time weren't good. *One chance!* She'd have one chance to get this right. And only one option remained. Without hesitation, she made her move.

Raven was determined to kick some ass.

Lunging off the sofa, she used its leverage to shove her body into the shadow of a man. Her shoulder lowered like a linebacker's. She hit her target with all her strength. The intruder let out a painful groan and fell back against the wall, hitting hard. A gasp of air resounded as he sank to the floor. She'd knocked the wind from his lungs. But she prepared to do some real damage. Set on knocking him into next week, she escalated her assault.

Propped against the wall, the man lay panting, trying to recover. With her legs straddling his, she pummeled his face with her fists—first the right, then the left. She'd have only a short time to get her licks in before he'd launch his counterattack. Every strike felt like hitting a brick wall. Her knuckles were raw and ached with pain, compounded by a burning tingle in her shoulder. Adrenaline kept her arms pumping, inflicting as much damage as she could. Her face burned in outrage.

Taking a moment to glance over her shoulder, she glimpsed the dark shape of her holster. The butt of her weapon was near the edge of the table. With no time to waste, she crawled toward it, slowed by the damage to her shoulder and hands.

But she'd made a fatal miscalculation.

The man had shaken off her beating and lunged, rolling her to one side, away from the gun. With all his weight, he pinned her to the floor, bracing his hands to her wrists. The lower half of his body fortified his dominance over her. Darkness closed in. She bucked and rocked to free herself. Bright flashes streaked across her eyes with the exertion. Think, she had to think. His face was too far away for a head butt. Her only recourse now was to scream.

"Arrggghh." A guttural sound escaped from deep inside her lungs, fueling her rage.

"Hey, don't! Stop it," he pleaded. "I'm not gonna hurt you."

Had she heard right? As soon as she stopped thrashing, the man eased his grip of her hands. The darkness obscured his face. But the voice was—

"Damn, you pack a punch. I think you busted my lip." His voice. "Are you okay?"

A part of her had been relieved, but an even larger part was mad as hell.

"Get off me, damn it! What the hell were you thinking?"

Christian didn't budge, his full weight upon her.

"I didn't want to read about you in the paper, knowing I could've done something. I had to make my point. And showing you was the only way to do that. You're not safe here."

Those eyes. Even in the dark, they found hers. And the deep baritone of his voice and the feel of his body, rock-hard against her, sent chills along her flesh. His chest heaved with every breath, his skin radiating heat to match her own. The blood rushed to her cheeks, then pulsated to other parts of her. The sensation was intoxicating.

She knew he felt the pull of attraction. The hunger in his eyes was undeniable. Yet the awkwardness of the moment left few options.

"If I let you up, are you gonna behave?"

It was the last thing she wanted, so she milked the moment.

"You bust into my house, in the dead of night, and you're worried about *my* behavior?" She challenged those eyes, then set her jaw. "You let me up, and I might have to kick your ass all over again."

"Feeling a little cocky, are we?" He shifted his weight, nearly driving her insane.

"As a matter of fact"—she snickered—"nothing little about it, if my memory of the male anatomy serves."

The low rumble of his laughter coerced a broad grin to her lips. She closed her eyes and enjoyed the sound.

Slowly, he released his grip, letting her go. Sitting back on his haunches, then rising, he held out his hand to help her up. She gripped his strong fingers, feeling weightless as he lifted her from the floor. In the dark, she groped for the light switch, then flipped it on. Turning back, she tilted her chin and furrowed her brow, assessing the damage.

"I think I did bust your lip."

Dressed in black military garb, Christian dominated her small living room with his athletic build. He towered over her, broad shoulders narrowing to slender hips and long legs. Only good timing and her surprise attack had brought him down, and then for only a brief moment. Still, she'd connected her blows. Blood from the cut on his lip painted his chin. She'd left her mark. With her reminder, he dabbed at his wound with a finger, drawing his tongue over the spot.

"You realize this was a very dumb idea. You could've gotten yourself killed." She crossed her arms, standing defiantly.

"I had to take the chance." His eyes held no apology. "I didn't bring a weapon. If I had, you would've been dead."

Her smile quickly faded. The truth of his words chilled her.

"And the men out there? I would've taken them out first. No one would have been able to help you, Raven."

He was dead right. And he had been only one man. Tony had seen a small band of mercenaries with state-of-the-art weapons. The conspicuous squad cars and the police patrolling the grounds outside her house would have deterred the common criminal. But there was nothing common about this situation. Using her quiet neighborhood to stand her ground suddenly seemed foolish. So many innocent people were at risk. Reality hit her square in the face.

"But this is not your fight, Christian. Why should you take this on?"

"Whoever this guy is, he's sent a very clear message for me to seek the truth, and punctuated it with a dead body. And for whatever reason, he's drawn you into it, and Tony." He stepped closer, the intimacy of his voice commanding her senses. "I am involved, even more than you. This is my fight. I've made it mine."

"And what about Fiona? I'm not so sure she'd want you aligning yourself with the police on this one." Her eyes drifted to the Dunhill files strewn on the floor. The autopsy photos and other evidence carelessly spread over her rug.

At first, he met her eyes, a stern resolve in his tone.

"I have to trust my instincts. I honestly don't know anything about this. But I want to believe her." Then his voice wavered and he couldn't hold her stare. Christian had his doubts.

Maybe together they could sort through this mess. She had the old case file here. Pooling their resources, they might make some headway. Raven considered the option he offered. But with a glance down at her knuckles and a roll of her aching shoulder, she had things to do. She had to trust her instincts, too.

"I'm gonna accept your offer, for now. How could I

refuse such a persuasive invitation?" she teased, wincing as she lightly touched a finger to his bruised lower lip. "The Dunhill Estate is so fortified, the bastard would have to be a fool to launch an attack against it."

In response to her sympathetic touch, Christian torqued his jaw, making sure it worked. If he had a bruised ego, it wasn't showing.

"Let's get cleaned up. I gotta pack a few things, call off my police protection, and talk to some folks." With a sly glance over her shoulder, she smirked. "You always go to so much trouble to get a woman to come home with you?"

Christian's smile broadened to a devilish grin. "It's usually not this difficult . . . No."

With a shake of her head, she laughed and tugged at his arm, leading him to her bathroom. "I don't doubt it, Delacorte. I don't doubt that at all."

In the hours before dawn, the Dunhill Estate glowed on the horizon, its security lights serving as a beacon. Before her, the ribbon of asphalt emerged from the darkness only as far as her headlights reached, winding through the shadowy terrain. Raven gripped her steering wheel and followed the red taillights ahead. She knew Christian's plan made sense. Yet the idea of spending so much one-on-one time with him sent her stomach reeling. The thrill of expectancy and the uncertainty of cold feet vied for position. It would have been more comforting if she'd ridden with him, so they could talk. But she'd been determined to have her independence and drive her own car.

The massive stone wall with its wrought-iron gate loomed ahead. Several men in uniform bounded from the shadows, weapons drawn, surrounding both vehicles. In the lead, Christian spoke to a guard, then waved a hand back to her. The other men peered through the headlights into her vehicle, without a change in their stern expressions. With a curt nod, the guard standing closest to Christian's SUV waved her onto the property. He commanded the others to stand down and resume their duties.

Part of her felt secure behind these gates, yet another part felt trapped and alone. She wondered if Christian ever felt that way.

The old oaks lining the drive stood like sentinels, more ominous under the sweeping headlights than she remembered from her first visit. The imposing presence of the Dunhill mansion intimidated her, emerging even larger as she approached. Its size alone made her feel small and unimportant. With eyes on the grand front entry up ahead, she reminded herself to breathe. On her first visit, she'd been a cop with a job to do. It had been a distraction. But this time, she'd have her Cubs cap in hand, staying for a while.

"I hope they give out maps at the door. 'Cause I can guarantee I'm gonna get lost in there," she whispered, the blue dash lights casting shadows on her hands and clothing. "And what the hell am I going to do with a butler or a maid? How do you live like this, Delacorte?"

Humor didn't ease her worry. It only reminded her just how different her life was from Christian's. He'd practically grown up here, accustomed to such wealth and self-indulgence.

"Tony was right. I must come from a long line of Raven lunatics."

She chalked it up to raw nerves, being a fish out of water. She wasn't sure what to expect from a man who'd been a total stranger just a short time ago. Correct that—a suspect. *For cryin' out loud, the man had been a suspect.* She rolled her eyes, chastising herself again. Doubts played serious havoc with her judgment.

As Christian approached the circular drive leading to the front steps, he didn't slow his speed. It threw her. He bypassed the main house and drove around a bend. His taillights disappeared. Where was he going? She knitted her brow and blindly followed his lead. As she made the turn to the right, a quaint cottage lay just ahead. Subtle landscape lighting gave it a gentle radiance, illuminating the encircling trees. Its charm reminded her of a Disney flick.

She pulled in behind him and turned off the ignition to her car. "So this is where you hang your hat, Delacorte. Very nice." She nodded her approval, craning her neck toward the windshield for a better view.

Then it hit her.

The pretentious mansion with its many, many rooms was one thing. *But this?*

"I'm going to be staying here with you, in this small, intimate cottage. Oh, my Gawd!"

The minute he opened his car door and turned to see her face, he realized something had changed in her resolve. For the first time since he'd met her, Raven looked unsettled, off her game.

But then again, he knew exactly how she felt.

His home had always been his oasis. A refuge. Despite his joking with her about bringing women home, he'd never brought one here. Tensing his jaw, he wondered why his mind drifted to something so personal. *This is business, Delacorte!* Yet with Raven, it felt like anything but—

The evidence box hoisted to his shoulder, he turned

the key to the front entry, then quickly entered a pass code into the security system to his right. With a sideways glance, he watched her walk past him and stop, setting her overnight bag beside her feet.

"I called ahead, had the housekeeper change the sheets and stock the kitchen. You take the bedroom." He set the evidence box in the study, then took a deep breath before heading back to her. Stepping back into the living room, he found her still standing near the entry. Her eyes absorbed every detail of her limited accommodations, without uttering a word since she'd crossed his threshold. He hadn't known her for very long. Even so, he knew Raven being speechless would be highly improbable.

He took a risk, hoping to break the ice.

"I assure you I can control my manly urges. You're safe here." Hand to his chest, he waited for a smile from her.

None came.

Instead, she slowly stepped into the living room. Her eyes darted to the room just beyond. His bedroom. Its double doors were open, its lamps lit and welcoming. And from what she could tell, the housekeeper had even left a chocolate mint on the pillow. Still, she avoided the bedroom with a vengeance. Tension dominated the space between them. He felt the need to defend his decision.

"An outsider's assumption is that you'd be staying in the mansion. And the smaller place makes it easier to defend. Is this arrangement a problem?"

She hesitated for only an instant. "No, not at all. It's just that I don't want to take your bedroom. Let me— I'll sleep on the couch."

It wasn't what he wanted to hear, but at least she was talking.

"No way. If it'll make you feel any better, I can barricade the doors once you're inside, block it with this console table . . . maybe that chair."

She crossed her arms and eyed him suspiciously, her defiance back. "The barricade would only work from the *inside*, Delacorte."

"Yeah, well. Just seeing if you were paying attention."

Her expression finally softened. He'd even coerced a soft chuckle from her. It gave him the courage to speak freely.

"Look. If it makes you feel any better, this is as awkward for me as it is for you. Contrary to what you might believe, I've never brought a woman here. Not here. This is my home. And I want to welcome you to it. Please relax. I want you to feel safe, especially from me."

Raven smiled. And as she stepped slowly toward him, he found himself holding his breath.

"On occasion, truth has come from those lips. And I do trust you, Christian. I keep asking myself why, but I do trust you," she teased, placing her hands on his chest, a finger circling a button.

He swallowed, hard. Already, his body reacted to her familiarity. With her standing so close, he wanted nothing more than to kiss her again, to feel her body next to his. But this was all about building trust between them. If anything more were to follow, it had to start on a foundation of trust. She'd have to make the first move. Having her here would be the combination punch of ecstasy and pure torture that only a woman inflicted upon a man. And he had the bruises to prove it.

With his past in question and his future an even bigger mystery, his truce with her would be difficult enough. He wasn't sure he had the strength to endure the sweet torment of Raven Mackenzie.

*   *   *

She cleared out of his bedroom long enough for him to move some toiletries to the guest bath, retrieve a change of clothes for the morning, and take a quick shower. As she wandered into the library, she heard the shower start. Perusing his book collection would not keep her from imagining his firm body under a hot stream of water, but it would have to do.

From the little she knew of him, his life focused on violence. He trained like a warrior, a result of his traumatic childhood. And armed men surrounded his home. All of it had comprised violence or his fear of it.

Yet in this library, in his home, his struggle for serenity was so apparent. Classical music and literature, books of poetry abounded, leaving her all the more confused by this enigmatic man. Her fingers lightly trailed along the book spines, maintained with great care, on polished cherrywood bookshelves. This had to be his favorite room. It was hers, too. She pictured him reading by a crackling fire or working at the computer on his desk. And yes, he'd fight the urge to gaze out the window at the picturesque grounds with only the measured beat of a clock to keep him company. The image was so vivid, lonely and comforting at the same time.

Christian was definitely a man of contradictions.

"I left towels for you on the bed." His low voice melded into her mind like an afterthought. "Sleep in tomorrow morning if you'd like."

She turned to find him standing barefoot by the study door. His dark waves still damp from the shower, he was dressed in a black T-shirt and jeans. A pale blue towel draped his neck. As she stepped closer, the faint scent of herbs mixed with the unique essence of his skin, teasing her senses. The color of the towel tinted his green eyes to a familiar deep azure, making it nearly impossible for her to walk by him.

But the cop in her took over, reminding her she was here for a reason. A killer was free. The bastard had nearly killed Tony and had invaded her home, forcing her from it. *Damn! Reality bites.*

"Good night, Christian."

"Sleep well."

She resisted the urge to touch him as she walked by, clenching her fingers into a fist. But one urge she couldn't fight was the impulse to fill her lungs with his scent. Why did he have to smell so good?

It was a very long walk across the living room. Before she closed the bedroom doors, she looked for him one last time. He stood at the threshold of the library, his arms folded across his ample chest. And those eyes held her just as sure as if she were in his arms. Her breath wavered, catching in her throat.

Normally, a polite smile from her would have severed the connection between them, allowing her to carry on. But her attraction for him had been undeniable from the start. Now, the hunger was impossible to ignore. After shutting the doors behind her, she leaned against them and closed her eyes to capture the memory. Her whisper broke the spell.

"You've crossed the line, woman. You've leapt over it and thumbed your nose. There's no going back now."

CHAPTER 13

Nicholas disapproved of the music selection off his home stereo system. This morning, the classical piece felt far too grim for his mood. But it was better than the alternative. Dead silence gave him too much time to think.

His fork scraped the gold-trimmed china as he cut into his last bite of pastry. The noise resounded hollowly across the formal dining room, competing with the crackle of a small fire in the hearth and the faint strains of an orchestra. The emptiness reminded him of the solitary nature of his life. His gaze dropped to the newsprint, scanning the morning headlines for any distraction. Nothing piqued his interest.

He poured himself another cup of coffee and sat back in his chair. His gaze drifted to the crystal chandelier overhead. He found the rainbow prisms quite mesmerizing in this light. Then the crass noise of his cell phone drew him from his self-pity. He recognized the number.

"Good morning, sweet Mantis." He welcomed the intrusion. "Where are you, my dear?"

"I find myself a mere three blocks from the gates of

hell. But rest assured, Nicky, I'm never so far from civilization that I cannot find a Starbucks."

A smile spread over his face as he pictured his bodyguard. Her propensity for understatement and dry wit was always a source of amusement. He had ordered her to follow Logan McBride, keeping track of his whereabouts. As he read the morning paper, catching up on the news of the world, Jasmine had called to bid him tidings from its seedy underbelly.

"Leave it to you to find the light at the end of the tunnel to be a mocha frappuccino. What word from our little zoo menagerie?"

"Our vicious hyena is curled in his lair, but as you expected, he did make another reconnaissance run early this morning . . . and he wasn't alone this time. I think he had planned an unexpected party. Needless to say, he was not pleased to find the nest of the Raven abandoned."

"Abandoned? How so?"

"My resources were divided at the time. The uniforms were noticeably absent. But I will find out where the bird has flown if you order it."

He sipped his coffee, pondering his next move. "Yes, I'm curious. See what you can find out. But first, locate a suitable replacement and get some rest. I have a feeling our beast will soon be more frenzied in his hunt. What is your opinion, Mantis?"

"A very astute observation. I would agree. Should I put him out of his misery? You only have to give the command."

"This is developing into an interesting standoff. The timing could prove to be most . . . entertaining."

He stood, brushing off his dark gray suit with his linen napkin. Walking to a window, he gazed upon the drab day, a true reflection of his disposition.

"My contacts abroad have informed me that my recent trip to Paris had some effect. And if I had to guess, I'd say guilt will soon be winging her home."

Silence. It took Jasmine a moment to respond.

"Are you okay, Nicky?" The beautiful woman was most perceptive. "I can end it now; just give the word."

He considered her words, then responded, failing miserably to keep the melancholy from his voice.

"There is still time, Mantis. I'm not ready for such finality. As you've said before, it shall not be difficult to lay the blame at the feet of the dearly departed hyena."

"Not so dearly departed from my perspective. But I shall respect your wishes. I will see you shortly."

"And I will be waiting." He ended the call.

He knew Jasmine perceived a change in him whenever he talked about Paris. She allowed him to keep his distance on the subject of Fiona, even though he suspected his bodyguard knew more than she let on. He confided so much in her, but not about this. His pride and his disdain for vulnerability would not allow it.

After a quick breakfast, Raven set up a work area in the study, spreading the case files over a table near the fireplace. A steady flame burned atop a bed of white ash with orange embers glowing through the pyre. Finally looking up from her work, she gazed toward the windows. Through the sheers, the gray morning must have dispersed, leaving a sunny day, without much notice from her. The work had been tedious.

Burrowed into the corner of an oversized black leather sofa, she tucked the edge of a comforter under her legs, an ankle resting on Christian's thigh. Earlier, she had ventured the bold move, forgetting herself. Once she realized what she had done, the intimacy of the act sent chills across her skin. But he took it all in stride, only sharing a faint smile and a steamy glance from those bedroom eyes. Now he intently studied a file as he sipped from a coffee mug. She winced when she spotted the bruise on his lip, then fought to hide her smile at the memory of last night.

After a while, he broke the comfortable silence between them.

"So, if I'm reading this report correctly, the investigation on Fiona came to an end without any link found to the murder of her husband. According to this, her phone and bank records were clean." He thumbed through the last pages of a detective's findings, his eyes searching the details. "No indictment."

"At the time, yes. But I've started a new search on Mickey's past. We've already instigated a look into his phone records and banking information. We'll be looking for any frequently dialed phone numbers or deposits of any significant size. If there's a connection to Fiona, or anyone who might've given the order, it may still turn up."

She saw defeat in his eyes. "It's standard operating procedure for an investigator to look at the person who had the most to gain by the victim's death. I'm exploring all my options, that's all."

"I know. But Mickey could have worked for someone else, even if he was the shooter, right?"

"Yes. But keep in mind that he got his security job at Dunhill shortly *after* the killing. That's too much coincidence, Christian." She knew he would be grasping at straws, looking out for Fiona's interests. "I know this is difficult for you. We're gonna be opening up some very old wounds. Can you handle it?"

His eyes fixed upon her, letting the silence fill the void. Then in a soft voice, he began. "Fiona gave me a home when I had no one. I would have been a ward of the state if she hadn't intervened. To this day, I don't know why she did it."

"You were a young boy needing help, and she had the resources. Still, it was very generous of her. But why you, Christian? Did you have any other connection to her?"

"No. She said she took pity on me from reading the story in the newspaper." He shook his head, a sad smile on his face. "I was a real basket case. The fear, the anger—I fought her every step of the way, like it was all her fault. But she never backed away. She waited for me to reach out to her."

Raven's cell phone vibrated on her belt. The timing couldn't have been worse. "Mackenzie."

The voice of CSI Scott Farrell recited his findings on the ballistics test conducted on the sniper rifle found at the marina locker. It looked as if Christian were holding his breath until she finished the call.

"The ballistics report came back positive. The striations matched the bullet retrieved from the body of Charles Dunhill. And Blair's prints were the only ones found on the rifle. Pretty good indication that Mickey was the shooter."

He swallowed hard as he digested the new information, clutching the file on his lap. "I just want you to understand that I owe her everything. And she's not the kind of woman that would kill her own husband. Don't get me wrong, she's one of the strongest women I know. But to kill for money? It's not possible."

"But she might kill for another reason?"

At first, her suggestion that Fiona could kill for any

motive looked like it surprised him. The shock of it registered in his eyes. Yet his silence told her all she needed to know. Fiona Dunhill was indeed a strong woman. But what would force her to condone murder as a necessary evil? And the cop in her was plagued by another piece of the puzzle.

"It still bothers me that the killer staged the old armory, suggesting there's a tie to the death of your family and the murder of Dunhill. Have you thought about the link?"

He shook his head, pulling a hand through his dark waves in frustration. "That's been bugging me, too. I was always told police had a hand in the killings, some kind of botched police raid on the wrong house. But no charges were ever filed. Any way for you to check that out? I've blocked so much from my memory."

"I've got an old family friend checking on that one. He was a partner to my father. Sam's got a pretty long memory. Maybe something will turn up."

Christian's sad gaze drifted toward the crackling fire, his mind clearly rooted in his past. With his chin resting on the back of his hand, his expression grew more solemn.

"What's the matter? Did you think of something?" she prodded.

After a long moment of silence, he finally confided in her. "You were right about Fiona being gone. And it's not like her to run from a fight." The fire flickered in his eyes. "I just found out how little I know about her. I've been so wrapped up in my own misery, I forgot how much she's done for me."

Coaxed by his words, she turned her thoughts to the memory of her father. He had made parenting look effortless. At least, that's how she chose to remember him.

As a bulletproof teen, she believed he would be with her forever. Now all that remained was the foundation of love he'd built for her.

"No matter how all this turns out, Christian, it's important that you always remember that." It was all she could say to comfort him.

Vinnie stepped quietly up the stairs, then knocked on Logan's bedroom door. The heavy tray in his hands carried the man's dinner. If everything wasn't perfect, Logan would unleash on him. These days, it didn't take much to set him off.

"Come in." The muffled directive finally came.

"I thought you might like some dinner." Vinnie walked across the room to set the tray down on a table.

The smell of sex mingled with another scent he knew well. Blood stained the sheets, confirming his suspicions that Krueger's woman had borne the brunt of Logan's hostility. Hoping she'd weather the storm, he had sent her to the master suite to appease Logan after the disappointing trip to the pretty detective's house.

Now her clothes were strewn about the room, stripped from her in his apparent frenzy. She lay naked beneath the stained sheets of the man's bed, bruised and bloodied. Her tears signaled her complete surrender.

"If you're done, I can feed her downstairs, let you have your privacy," he offered. Logan stared at him, his expression unreadable. Vinnie swallowed hard, finding it difficult to suppress his ragged breath. "Or can I interest you in another diversion? Whatever you like, sir."

"There's only one sport that interests me, Vin." Rage surged, coloring the man's skin. "Nothing pisses me off more than a botched mission! You know that."

Vinnie saw his fury as clearly as if the man were a kettle on a stovetop, on the brink of boiling over. He'd seen it before, at the detective's house. Logan tore the place apart after he'd found the woman packed and gone, the police cruisers nowhere in sight.

But just as quickly as the anger swelled, it subsided with Logan's insane laughter. The man's mood swings were getting worse. His amusement only twitched Vinnie's flesh. And the woman at Logan's side clutched the bedsheet to her bare breasts, cowering from his twisted brand of humor.

"I think I know just how to jump-start this hunt. And that bitch won't be able to refuse. She's gonna give herself to me, Vinnie. Just like all women do, eventually."

He stroked the head of the woman lying next to him. Cruelty dominated his eyes. With the tip of his tongue, he licked the blood from the corner of her mouth, savoring its taste. "I think a little divine intervention is in order."

With a relieved smirk, Vinnie waited for his orders.

During their simple dinner of sandwiches, Christian found himself telling Raven about an area of the mansion that he'd yet to explore. He had nearly forgotten about it until she prompted his memory, delving into Fiona's past. Now he shoved the east wing attic door open, getting his bearings with a flashlight.

The air felt thick with the smell of dust. He flipped the light switch. Only on rare occasions had he been in this particular storage space, and only when accompanied by Fiona herself. Without her, he felt like such an interloper into her past. Cardboard boxes, a rack of old clothes wrapped in plastic, and a couple of wooden trunks marginally filled the space.

"I hope you're not allergic to dust. The air is a little stale," he warned. Once he determined the layout, he lowered his hand to his guest, steadying her as she took the last step up the ladder.

"This place is larger than my whole house." Raven stood beside him. Her eyes peered through the pale light. "But considering some of the things I've got in my attic, she's not much of a packrat."

"She told me once that these were the things she couldn't part with, too many memories."

Raven wandered to the clothes rack. "Hey, put that flashlight to good use. Shed some light on these clothes." She slid the hangers apart for a better view once he directed the beam of light. "God, she was a tiny little thing. Check out the size of this dress."

Holding up a white beaded evening gown, she wedged the wooden hangar under her chin. "The only time I could've fit into this was when I was a teenager."

"I bet you'd look amazing in an evening gown." He smiled. Even in this light, he knew she blushed. Normally, the dark space would have raised his blood pressure, but with Raven along, he felt comfortable.

"Do you think they make a thigh holster for my Glock, one that wouldn't break the line of this gown? Just another makeover challenge, I suppose."

She opened the clasp of the beaded bag that had been stored with the gown.

"Oh, look. This evening bag still has a ticket stub for— Can I have the light, please." She grasped the flashlight he handed her, then squinted to read the small print. "*La Bohème*. And judging by the date on this, she'd been a teenager. Wow. Must've been some performance. The attic is like one big album of memories."

Once again, Christian realized how little he knew the

woman who'd saved his life from the ruin it might have become. Raven helped him sift through the boxes and trunks, opening one after the other. With every revelation, he became more reticent, letting her fill the gap in conversation.

"Hey, Christian. This one is locked. You have a key? Maybe it's just stuck." She tugged at the lid without success.

"Here. Let me try this." In his hand, he held an old metal shoehorn that he'd found.

Raven directed the light over his shoulder as he wedged the piece of metal between the trunk and its lock. After a couple of attempts, he eventually pried it open. Propping the lid against the wall, he gazed inside. His hands leafed through old papers and photographs until . . .

"Oh, my God," he exclaimed. "What the hell is this?"

Father Antonio neared the end of his time in the confessional. It had passed quickly, considering this was his first day back after administrative leave. The archdiocese had offered him relief from his regular duties, but the idle time only made him remember. It felt good to be a contributing member of this community once again.

Between parishioners partaking of his service, he distracted himself with the rosary in his hand. To ensure the anonymity of his congregation, only a small night light lit the inside of his compartment. Accustomed to the dark, he relied on his sense of touch, rolling the smooth black beads between his fingers. His whispered prayers kept the deathly grimace of Mickey Blair at bay. It gave him strength to know that in the small space of the confessional, God kept him company.

Pulling him back to his duties, the confessional door opened. He heard the creak of wood as the member of his flock genuflected. After putting the rosary beads in the pocket of his vestments, he slid the screen open, allowing him to see only a man's faint silhouette kneeling in the booth next to him.

The man didn't speak. His face was a blur, covered in shadow. He waited, permitting the man time to gather his thoughts.

Still, nothing.

"Can I help you? Is there something you'd like to confess?" He turned his head and focused on the blackened image.

In the pale light, he made out the side of the man's face. To his surprise, he was grinning. Giving him the benefit of the doubt, he made an assumption about the man's reaction.

"There is no need to be ashamed. In the eyes of God, you are his child. Don't be afraid to ask his forgiveness."

"God would never claim me as his own, trust me." The voice was a raspy whisper. A low, guttural sound. "And I don't need or want his forgiveness, Father Antonio."

"Then why are you here?" The priest stiffened his back and pulled away. Something wasn't right. "And how do you know my name?"

"I came here looking for you, Father. You see, I'm in need of a little divine intervention. And only you can help. So I made it a point to find out who you are from one of your parishioners."

The man's voice was chilling. How had he missed it before?

"If you aren't here to confess, then I'm afraid my time here is done." He stood and reached for the door.

It wouldn't budge. He turned the knob, but it wouldn't open. He shoved, putting his shoulder into it this time. It jarred open an inch, then shut again with a slam. Someone rammed it back, pinning him inside. What was going on?

"Please. I don't understand," he begged.

"You're right, Father. I'm not here to confess. And your time here is done." The man laughed softly. "Come with us quietly or we'll start shooting. I don't think God would care for more dead bodies in his house of worship. Do you?"

"No, please. Don't. I'll come with you." He swallowed hard. His words caught in his throat. "Just don't hurt anyone else."

"Now that's the spirit."

His confessional door finally opened. Pale gray eyes stared back. *Cruel eyes.* The large man dressed in dark clothing and a long coat yanked him from the booth. The stranger's hand dug fingers into his neck. Two other men stood at his shoulder. Their footsteps resounded on the tile floor as they headed down the aisle toward the entrance.

His eyes darted across the small chapel, desperately trying to make eye contact. Several parishioners had their backs turned, heads lowered in prayer. No one would notice him leave. He considered running or fighting his way free, but these men meant business. Someone would die.

Then his eyes found those of a small Asian woman covered in a dark shawl. He'd never seen her before. Her dark eyes followed his gaze, but he couldn't read her expression. She did nothing to help, or give any indication she was aware of the danger he was in. In an instant, he'd been pulled past her. His last hope gone.

His captors shoved open the front door to the church and hauled him outside. Cold night air shocked his system. The harsh reality of his predicament hit home. He looked over his shoulder one last time. Father Antonio feared he would never see St. Sebastian's again.

She stood and sidestepped toward the aisle of the church, genuflecting as she exited the pew. Jasmine waved a hand in the sign of the cross, having seen the gesture before. She didn't wish to stand out. As she neared the back of the chapel, she lowered the shawl from her head, then gripped the butt of the gun in her coat pocket. With caution, she peered out the heavy wooden door at the side entrance, not wanting to draw attention to herself. Logan and two of his men escorted the holy man to a car they had parked along the street. The little priest did not look pleased by their intrusion. After they drove away, she reached for her cell phone.

"You were right, Nicky. Things just got more interesting."

"How so, my dear?" His seductive voice teased her ear and brought a smile to her lips.

"Logan has called upon a higher power in his search." Before he asked any more questions, she added, "And it doesn't matter where the Raven has flown. Soon I will know where she will be. The hyena offers bait she won't be able to refuse."

"I trust you implicitly, Mantis. You know my wishes."

"Yes, I do." She smiled, picturing his handsome face. "And I will not fail you."

Jasmine ended the call and walked to her car parked on a nearby side street. No need to hurry. The tracking beacon would make her job easy. And she had a suspicion where Logan might be headed.

Her mind went over the inventory of the equipment in the trunk of her car as a plan took shape. Nicky always made sure she had the best of everything. The trick would be in not calling attention to her employer. But one thing was absolute.

She would not deprive Nicky of his victory.

Raven stood beside the sofa, hands on her hips. Anxiety and frustration colored her words.

"Talk to me, Christian. I helped you lug that thing across the grounds and into your living room. What did you see? We're a team. Remember?"

Brooding silence.

Sitting on the area rug, his back against the sofa, he crossed his arms over his chest and stared intently at the old trunk. With jaw clenched, he glared at it as if it were a living, breathing thing, ready to lash out at him. His dark green eyes swirled with anger and . . . confusion. She'd never seen him so lost. Clearly, he felt disturbed by the contents he'd discovered hidden away in Fiona's attic. But he hadn't spoken a word since he pried open the lid.

"Please, Christian." She lowered her voice and knelt beside him, a hand on his shoulder. "Say something."

After a long silence, his expression softened. "Raven, you have to trust me. I know I haven't given you much reason to do that, but I need some time to myself."

He reached for her hand, holding it in his. Then he took a deep breath, fixing his eyes on her.

"In that locker are . . ." He paused and shut his eyes, letting the emotion wash over him. She watched him struggle to find his way. "My past is there. But I gotta do this alone. Do you understand?"

She swallowed the lump in her throat, moved by compassion for his personal journey. Whatever he'd found had stirred up a past already embroiled in mystery. She couldn't imagine the demons lying in wait for him now. Raven understood his need for privacy, but it broke her heart that he wanted to do it alone.

"I can be a good listener if you want to talk." She squeezed his hand. "I wish you'd let me help."

"I just can't. Not with this." Letting go of her hand, he kissed her cheek, then whispered, "Good night."

"If you need me, for anything . . ." She returned his affection, then slowly stood.

"I will," he assured her. But as she neared the bedroom doors, he called out to her. "And Raven? Thanks."

It pained her to leave him sitting on the floor under the pale light of a lamp—all his attention focused on the locker across from him. She left the bedroom doors open a crack. If he called out to her in the middle of the night, she wanted to hear it.

Even when the morning came, would he share what he'd found? Share his pain? It would be a very long night.

A muffled groan woke her. The room was pitch-black. It took a moment to orient herself. Then a cry jarred her and raised the hair at the nape of her neck. Sitting upright, she listened for the sound, unsure what had happened.

"God help us, *PLEASE!*" he shrieked, fear bellowing deep. "Let me go. Shadow man . . . *PLEASE!* You're hurting me."

She thrust the covers off her legs and ran to the living room, throwing the bedroom door open.

"I'm here, Christian. You're okay."

The lamp was still on. Tossing his boots and folded jeans to one side, she knelt on the floor near him, running her fingers over his fevered brow. But he solidly resisted the gesture, still snarled in his ordeal.

"Now I lay me . . . down to sleep," he muttered, eyes closed tight. He thrashed at his sheets as he lay on the couch. The bare skin of his chest glistened with sweat. "If I should die before—"

She touched his arm, not knowing how to awaken him without causing more damage.

"Make them go away. Don't touch me!" The panic in his voice ranged from childlike to threatening within seconds, as if he were possessed.

"Christian, you're safe. It's me, Raven."

With a swing of his arm, he knocked her over, his frenzy escalating. She had to take charge—*now!* She stood quickly, then waited for the right moment to gain control of his arms. She pressed hard, practically sitting on his chest to make him stop.

"Christian, wake up! Now!" she shouted. His eyes popped open at the sound of his name, but the fog hadn't cleared. She had to get his attention. "Talk to me. Can you hear me?"

He finally released the tension in his muscles and gasped. With a low moan, he shifted his gaze as if seeing her for the first time.

"Raven?" he whispered. His eyes darted around the room. He looked so lost. "What are you doing here?"

"You were having a nightmare." She lowered her body to the floor. Kneeling by the sofa, she stroked his brow. "Are you okay?"

"Damn! That was so—" Christian stared at the ceiling, looking exhausted by his effort to recall. "It was happening all over again."

"I'm gonna get you some water." She raced to the kitchen and filled a glass, keeping her attention on him as she dampened a washcloth. "All these old memories must have stirred it up. Can you remember any of it?"

Raven hurried back to his side. After raising up on one elbow, he gulped at the water, letting it dribble down his chin. She ran the wet cloth down his arms and over his forehead, cooling his skin.

"I've had this one before. When I was younger"—he coughed, then took another gulp of water—"it used to happen all the time."

"Who is shadow man?"

"What?" By his expression, he was shocked by her words. "How did you know about—?"

"You cried out the name, like he hurt you. Don't you remember?"

"Oh, God." He rubbed fingers hard across his forehead, then sat upright, pulling the sheet over his boxers. "Shadow man. That's what I called him . . . when I didn't understand."

Raven sat beside him on the couch, waiting for him to remember. With his breathing more stable, he stared ahead, rapt in his memory.

"The shadow man. He was my . . . father." The word "father" stuck in his throat. In a daze, he continued, "It took years of therapy for me to understand that. In the dark, all I saw was . . . his shadow. And with the confusion that night, I thought he was there to kill me."

"With such trauma, it's understandable. You were just a child." She dabbed the cool rag to his temple. But she had the feeling he wasn't aware of her touch. Not anymore.

"After they shot my sister . . . and mother"—a tear rolled down his cheek, his eyes suspended in a blank stare—"he came to my room. He'd been shot, but he fought them off to get to me. The smell of blood was everywhere."

His face blurred through the tears welling in her eyes. She saw the child he'd been as he struggled to relive his past.

"It wasn't until he hugged me that I recognized his voice. He calmed me down. Then helped me out the window." He began to rock, back and forth, on the sofa where he sat. His eyes were still clouded by his nightmare. "I fell to the ground, my ankle on fire. I crawled away, but the darkness seemed to squeeze my chest. It smothered me. I couldn't breathe. I felt so . . . helpless."

She suddenly understood his obsession to train and fight in the dark. He had to overcome his phobia, regain control of his life. A frightened young boy had found his own road to recovery.

"Then they shot him again . . . and again. I couldn't take my eyes away. His body convulsed until he fell against the window. I knew he was dead. Even in the dark, I pictured his face." He stopped his rocking, furrowing his brow as if he were confused. "Then the night sky filled with spiraling lights, red and blue, shrieking and high-pitched sounds."

She'd read about his past in the newspaper clippings from Father Antonio. His family tragedy was blamed on a bungled police raid. Yet something in his story bothered her; the timing was off.

"But Christian, if the night sky filled with lights of red and blue *after* your family was already dead, how could the police be responsible?"

For a moment, he fell silent, using the time to replay his own words back. She saw him fight to remember every last detail.

"But Fiona told me—" His breathing became more rapid and shallow. Closing his eyes tightly, he grappled with his memory. It pained her to watch him go through it. She felt powerless to help.

"If the police weren't responsible, then who killed them?" He raised his voice, pleading for an answer. "Who killed my family?"

His expression changed, his eyes widening with a realization. As if he'd been struck in the face, he dropped to the floor on his knees. He yanked open the old trunk, throwing its contents on the rug. A child's schoolwork and crayon drawings were strewn at her feet. She joined him, picking up the pieces and taking a closer look. A small curl of dark hair was wrapped in plastic, tied in a pale blue ribbon. She had a similar one from when she was a baby. None of this made sense.

"These are your things, Christian—when you were a child? How did Fiona get a hold of these? I thought she took you in after your family was killed. Did she get these things from the Delacortes?"

He didn't answer. He found an old photograph and stared at it, totally consumed. After a moment, he muttered, "Look at this. Something bothered me about this old photo."

He thrust the faded picture into her hand. Christian, as a young boy, stood beside his father in front of a car. Their faces were beaming. He was dressed in a Little League uniform, his hand still in a baseball glove. His father stood behind him, hands on Christian's narrow shoulders. A nice picture, but she couldn't see the significance of it.

"What? I don't see—"

Christian never let her finish. He pointed to the image, his finger directing her to the car behind them.

"See? In the reflection on the windshield? Check out who's taking the picture."

It took her only a moment to recognize the face behind the camera.

"Fiona," she whispered. The pieces to his puzzle were falling into place, but things were still cloudy for her.

"When I first went through this, I kept coming back to this photo. I just now realized why." He reached again into the locker and retrieved a bundle of old letters. "And earlier I found these."

All the letters were addressed to Fiona—sent to a post office box. But the return address caught her attention.

"These letters are from the Delacortes. And they go back for years before they were killed. How can that be?" she questioned. "What connection did they have to Fiona?"

"All the letters are progress reports—*on me*." He handed her a folded piece of paper, yellowed with age. Christian stared at it as if it were vile. "And this is the reason why."

Raven carefully unfolded the stiff paper. The elaborate blue border registered in her brain. "Your birth certificate? Christian Evan Fitzgerald, born to Fiona Fitzgerald. No father listed."

He clenched his jaw. "All these years, she lied to me. Fiona is my mother. The Delacortes weren't—" He couldn't bring himself to say it aloud. "How could she watch me go through all that pain and not tell me? Why did she give me away in the first place?"

"And she kept up with you all those years. Only a mother would— It doesn't make any sense, Christian." Setting the certificate aside, she pulled him to her, closing her eyes as she hugged him.

"And the worst part—" He burrowed his face into her neck. She barely heard the words. "I remembered something from the dream, the last time I had it. Whoever killed my . . . the Delacortes . . . was after me. I was the reason they broke into the house. I remembered them saying they were after the boy—*find the boy.*"

Eyes wide with her shock, Raven pushed back. Her mind searched for the words to console him. "How do you know? You can't know that for sure. You were too young."

"I blocked out so much. I thought it was the trauma I'd gone through, but now, it's all beginning to make a twisted kind of sense."

"But why? Why would someone want to kill a little boy?"

Slowly, he shook his head. His exhaustion showed. She felt certain he hadn't even heard the question she posed.

"All I know is that it was my fault." He avoided her eyes and stared into the locker. "They died because of me."

She understood survivor's guilt, had seen it before. Nothing she could say would raise him from the depths of his unfounded blame. Raven felt the magnitude of his loss. The death of the Delacortes had forever robbed him of his childhood, his sense of well-being. Just as the death of her father had done to her—magnified tenfold.

Raven pulled him to her, kissing him until he responded. He collapsed in her arms, worn out by his emotional roller coaster. Her comfort didn't last long. He let her go and looked over his shoulder.

"Raven, I need to understand . . ." His voice trailed off as he bowed his head, his eyes drawn once again to the memories strewn along the floor. "Why is my life so surrounded by death?"

The old trunk embodied Fiona's betrayal and the violent death of the only family he had ever known. Raven just wanted it gone—out of his sight.

"Don't do this to yourself. Someone else is responsible. You were only a . . . a scared little boy." She swallowed the lump in her throat. A tear slid down her cheek.

He avoided her eyes. It pained her to see him like this. She stroked his cheek with her fingertips, then caressed his face in her hands, lowering her lips to his. An impulse. The kiss started as a gentle and nurturing connection. The warmth and smell of his skin made her lose herself to the sensation.

But as a shudder ran through his body, she felt his need take over. Christian pulled her into his arms, his body hard against her. A low moan exposed his urgency.

She couldn't stop it, even if she wanted to.

Her velvet softness jolted every fiber of his being. The scent of her warm skin drilled his senses. Christian picked her up and carried her to his bedroom. His mind grappled with his desire for romance with this woman, to take his time making love to her. But he knew this was all about one thing—NEED. No turning back now. His body stiffened with the curves of her flesh pressed hard against him. With all the reminders of death around him, he desperately wanted to feel alive, to replace the pain.

"I want you. I need—"

She smothered his words with a passionate kiss. And as he set her down by the bed, he replenished his spirit with the longing in her eyes. Backlit by the pale light from a lamp on the nightstand, she looked like an angel—with devilish intentions. Her eyes probed his body, devouring him like he was food.

"No more talking—" With a wicked smile, she raised her arms above her head, inviting him to explore with a whisper. "I surrender."

She wore a large navy tee with *Police Academy* emblazoned on the front in bold white letters. Without taking his eyes from hers, he trailed his fingers to her thighs. Slowly, he caressed her warm skin, raising the thin cotton inch by agonizing inch. Pulling the tee over her head, he watched her hair cascade to her shoulders, her pale skin made more perfect by the dark strands.

Adrenaline and anticipation surged through his muscles when she returned the gesture, sliding his black boxers down his thighs to the floor. Her hands lingered in all the right spots. Completely unencumbered, the sensation of skin on skin drove him insane. Kneeling at her feet, he stroked her with the tip of his tongue. The sound of her pleasure filled the air. His lips explored her body, eager to learn every nuance of her sensuality. She collapsed to the mattress and pulled him with her.

As her mouth nuzzled him, every movement of her tongue, every touch of her teeth made him shudder. The sound of her moans reverberated against his skin, sending quivers through his belly. Not being able to control himself any longer, he rolled onto one elbow pulling her to him, plunging his tongue into her warm mouth. He could no longer resist what she offered. He pleasured her with his fingers, then rolled his hips against hers, wedging himself between her legs.

"Oh, please . . . YES," she cried out as he pressed into her for the first time. "Don't stop."

Tears streaked her face as he filled her, her velvety tightness claiming him. With her outcry, he thought he'd hurt her and almost stopped, but she encouraged him with her throaty moans and urgent kisses. Aroused by her hunger, he plunged deeper, his sense of urgency swelling.

Cradling her hips with his hands, he thrust until she clutched his back. Her orgasm rippled through her in forceful waves. Raven's cries of pleasure taunted him until he couldn't control himself any longer. Arching his back, he exploded with his own powerful release. He filled her, time and time again, then shuddered in exhaustion. Depleted of his strength, he was seized by the faint tremors of complete gratification. He'd never felt so . . . *alive.*

Christian rolled onto his back, pulling her with him. She fell limp against his chest. Kissing the top of her head, he nuzzled closer, never wanting to let her go. As he stroked her hair, she raised her chin, finding his eyes in the dim light. Her pale skin glimmered with beads of sweat and the enticing blush of sex.

"God, you're beautiful." The words were out of his mouth before he even realized he'd spoken.

"That's funny. I was just thinking the same thing of you." Her shy smile disarmed him. Then her expression grew more solemn. "Let's switch places. I want to hold you, Christian . . . until you fall asleep."

Her offer touched him—compassion brimming in her eyes. He fondled a strand of her hair, then kissed her with all the tenderness he felt in his heart.

Violence had stilted his life, robbed him of innocence. His repeated visits to the cemetery fed his obsession for penance as a sole survivor like an addict on a fix, but the pain and emptiness never went away. Over the years, he'd become the master at erecting barriers to keep people at a distance. Hiding his emotional scars had become second nature, a draining effort. Now, someone else knew his pain—all of it. And he'd let it happen. Somehow it felt right. With her, it had been effortless.

Making love to Raven forged a deep bond between them. She touched him in a place he thought had died long ago. Nothing he'd experienced before matched how he felt, just holding her.

Drawing the comforter and sheets over their bodies, he nestled into her embrace, welcoming her comfort. He fit to her body like it was always meant to be—listening to the beat of her heart in the stillness of the early morning.

In her arms, he'd never felt so connected to another human being. The intimacy of the gesture seduced him. He drifted to sleep, completely letting go, reliving his pleasure with the woman who held him in her arms.

Only Raven mattered—

CHAPTER 14

The gray haze of winter's morning shone through the draperies of Christian's bedroom as he opened his eyes. It took his mind a moment to remember the trunk filled with the awful truth. His world had come to a grinding halt. An uneasy sadness dampened his spirit. The foundation of what he had believed lay crumbled in the wake of Fiona's lie.

Seek the truth, Christian. The message pinned to the body of Mickey Blair taunted him. Who could have engineered such a thing? And for what purpose? He still felt no closer to that answer.

Just when the venom of bitterness threatened to contaminate his day, the warm body next to him stirred. He gazed upon Raven as she nestled into his shoulder, strands of dark hair lying across her pale cheek. Asleep, she looked like an innocent child. How had a guy like him gotten so lucky? He smiled as he gently pulled back the hair from her face with a finger. A sweet moan reminded him of his change in fortune. He didn't feel alone anymore.

With her skin next to his, his body reacted, stiffening with the memories of last night still fresh in his mind.

Gently, he kissed the top of her head, then rolled to his side. He cradled her in his arms, his lips in search of his favorite places.

"Hmmm . . . so good." Her voice sounded throaty and suggestive as he nuzzled her ear. "You an early riser?" A smile graced her lips, warming his heart. She kept her eyes closed as her hand reached for him.

"Always," he answered, her velvet touch inspiring him. "I believe in rigid discipline." A faint gasp escaped his mouth as her hand came to rest. "Oh, yeah."

"I see that," she purred. "Let me put you through your paces. Nothing like an early-morning workout."

This time, it would be about Raven. Christian would learn the subtleties of her body, giving her the pleasure she deserved. And with Raven, he forgot the ugliness of his past, no longer dwelling on the crippling pain of it.

For the first time, he felt whole, brimming with hope for his future.

With the shower still going. Christian grinned, remembering how Raven had joined him earlier. She taught him the lost art of "sudsing," as she called it. Her "workout" routine left him drained, but completely relaxed. Laughing aloud had never felt so good.

Wearing only his thick navy bathrobe, he headed for the kitchen to start the coffee, a grin still on his face. But when he stepped through the door of the master suite, all that changed. Reality hit hard.

The contents of the old trunk lay strewn on the floor of his living room. His discovery harsh in the morning light. To punctuate the blow, the abrasive sound of his cell phone reminded him that life went on. Retrieving his phone from the coffee table, where he'd left it the night before, he answered the call.

"Delacorte."

"Yeah, boss. Bill Edwards here." He recognized the voice of his trusted security man at Dunhill. "I just heard from the hangar. You wanted me to keep you informed on the whereabouts of Mrs. Dunhill."

"Yeah. Something new?" Christian kept his tone steady, but his heart was another matter.

"The pilot has got a flight plan returning to the Dunhill hangar. She's heading back to Chicago. Her ETA is four this afternoon. She's asked for a pickup." Bill cleared his throat, broaching an opinion. "I figured if she called for a ride from security, she hadn't contacted you. What do you want me to do?"

He closed his eyes. *And so it began.* Fiona was coming home.

A part of him felt relieved to finally know her whereabouts. But an even bigger part was angry as hell at her gall. She'd left him to deal with the murder, intentionally holding back her secrets. Why come back now? Since she hadn't called him, did she have any intention of contacting him at all?

"No pickup, Bill. I'll do it myself. Thanks for the heads-up." He ended the call and tossed the phone onto the sofa, then pulled a hand through his damp hair. "Damn," he muttered.

"Something wrong? You look upset." Raven's voice came from behind him. Dressed in his white bathrobe, she towel-dried her hair.

"No, just something at Dunhill Tower. I'm gonna have to drive to the city this afternoon." He busied himself with the coffee and hoped she hadn't seen his uneasiness.

His meeting with Fiona had to be one-on-one. Even though he had a personal connection to Raven, she still

worked for the police. His instincts told him to honor
the loyalty to his . . . to Fiona. The word "mother"
stuck in his craw. At this point, he wasn't sure he could
ever bring himself to call her that. Yet before all this, he
would have been honored by the privilege.

"You'll be safe here while I'm gone. I'll leave instructions with my men before I take off. It'll only take a few
hours."

"Oh no, you don't. You're not gonna ditch me again,"
she teased with a smirk. "If you're going into Chicago,
I'd like to hitch a ride. Can you drop me off at the station house?"

Her suggestion was not unreasonable. Unreasonable
would have been her insisting that she drive her own car
in total disregard for her own personal safety. But her
compromise took him by surprise. His mind raced with
how this scenario might play out. He finally thought of
a way to keep Raven off his scent and meet with Fiona
alone. The execution of his plan would be tricky.

"I've got a better idea. You drop me off at the tower,
then you can have my SUV. But I need to know where
you'll be. No deviations. If you're at work, I figure you
can't be any safer than that. But promise me you won't
deviate from the plan." Stepping closer, he trailed a
finger down her cheek and stared into those dark eyes.
"And I want your cell phone number, so I can find you
when I'm ready to leave."

His smile felt forced. Christian hoped she wouldn't
notice. He hated lying to her.

"Okay. I understand. But I can take care of myself,
you know." Raven crooked an eyebrow and lowered her
eyes to his chin.

He stared at her for a moment, then chuckled, rubbing his jaw. "Yeah, I found that out the hard way."

"That was just a little love tap." She raised up on tiptoe and kissed his bruised lip. "Something I learned from the WWE."

"I should have figured you for a girl into wrestling." He kissed her cheek, then whispered in her ear. "When we hook up later, I'll show you some of my patented moves. No spandex required."

"My, you are a man of many talents. Hunk Hogan move over."

"I believe that's Hulk Hogan," he murmured.

"Whatever."

Wedging herself between him and the counter, she undid the tie to his robe, sliding her fingers to his bare skin. He slipped his hands under her robe, allowing them to stray. He closed his eyes and nuzzled her neck, drinking in the smell of her skin.

The woman made it damned hard for him to ignore her. Yep, Raven made it damned hard, always.

By midafternoon, the sun speared through the dark clouds only sparingly, dashing Christian's hope for a better day. He followed Raven out the front door of his cottage, setting the alarm and locking it behind him. The air smelled heavy with moisture. Today's forecast called for thunderstorms later in the afternoon. On his front step, he turned up the collar to his long black overcoat and heaved a sigh. His eyes fixed on the gathering clouds overhead. Even Mother Nature had conspired against him.

With his mind being so troubled, he wondered how he'd ever hide it from his beautiful passenger.

He should have enjoyed the ride into Chicago. Raven did her best to distract him. Somehow, even with a ruthless killer stalking her, with murder and mayhem blowing his life to smithereens, the intriguing woman at his side made their time together feel normal. Idle conversation should have been a welcome respite from the scenarios jumbling in his brain. Yet all he thought about was Fiona. He had no idea how this would play out. The uncertainty wrenched his gut.

As the traffic picked up and they neared downtown Chicago, Raven yanked him from his brooding.

"You've been putting up a pretty good front, but I can tell. Something's bothering you. Can you talk about it?" She looked up from keying her cell phone number as a speed dial entry into his phone. Her dark eyes filled with concern for him. *He felt like such a jerk!*

His rendezvous with Fiona loomed heavy between them, a barrier he couldn't deny. But he wasn't prepared to talk about it. At least, not yet. A part of him wanted to tear down that wall of lies. For so many years, that obstacle had amassed deep within him, like a cancer. It kept him a prisoner to his past. He wondered what it would feel like to shed light on all his dark secrets. The burden finally lifted. And he imagined doing exactly that with Raven.

But he took the path of least resistance.

"I can't. Not yet." He stared out the windshield, gripping the steering wheel a little tighter. He made the turn down Michigan Avenue, heading for Dunhill Tower, then broke the strained silence between them. "But I want to. Just have a little more patience with me. I gotta sort through some stuff first."

He pulled to the curb in front of the tower and left the SUV running. Reaching over, he touched a finger to her cheek, then leaned toward her. With fingers laced in her hair, he kissed her, drawing from her humanity to fortify him. As his lips touched hers, his mind flooded with images of Raven, his heart unwilling to leave her behind. But he had to. With his past so much of a hindrance, he had to find a way to set himself free from it. And it was a journey he had to make alone.

"Remember, no deviations. And I'll call you when I'm done so we can set up a time for the ride home." He forced a smile, tapping an index finger to the tip of her nose.

"You got my number. Maybe we can swing by the hospital to see Tony later."

"Yeah, no problem." He yanked open the door to the car and waited for her to come around to slip into the driver's seat.

After a final kiss and a wave good-bye, Christian stood at the curb, watching her drive away. Under his overcoat, he reached for the cell phone clipped to the belt of his jeans. He hit a speed dial, then headed for the front entrance of the building, his face hardened by determination.

The man answered on the second ring. "Edwards, here."

"Yeah, Bill. This is Christian. I've got a favor to ask."

"Anything. What do you need?"

"Get me a pool car. I'm heading out to the hangar to pick up Fiona."

"Sure thing. Anything else?"

"Yeah. Just one more thing. I want you to start tracking the GPS on my SUV. I'll fill you in when I see you upstairs."

"You loaned out your high-tech baby?" the man teased. "Who is she?"

"What makes you think—" With a grin, Christian shook his head. "Never mind. Just tell me if it deviates from the South State Street area of downtown."

He ended the call and pushed through the revolving door, waving an acknowledgment to the guards at the front security kiosk. With the change in logistics, he knew the timing would be tight now. His face taut, he shifted focus. Soon, he'd be seeing Fiona again—and in a whole different light. And he still had no idea what would come out of his mouth.

"It'll be one of life's little mysteries," he muttered under his breath as he hit the elevator button, riding up alone. He jammed his hands into the pockets of his coat, clenching his fists.

Cynicism gripped him hard, coupled with a mounting resentment. Christian felt certain that seeing Fiona again would only reinforce his callous attitude. His mind reeled with all the questions he would demand her to answer.

"Welcome home, Fie." He furrowed his brow. "It's a whole new world."

Raven spent the first hour reviewing the case files Sam had laid on her desk, the ones from her father's past. Sam had placed a note on the top file, telling her he'd already conducted a background check on the "Top Scumbag" list. He'd narrowed the prospects considerably. She set down her pen after making the final entry into her casebook. The connection to her father was a slender thread. And she knew it.

"It's gonna be a crapshoot." She sighed, then dosed herself up with the caffeine from stale coffee. Her eyes trailed over to her partner's desk as she repeated a line from the movie *Top Gun*. "Talk to me, Goose."

Tony always used the old line whenever he felt the need for her sage advice. Now the tables were turned. She picked up the phone and placed a call to the hospital, needing to hear the voice of her wingman. But first she would speak to the guardian at the gate to get the truth.

"How is he, Yolanda?" She tightened her grip on the phone, holding her breath as she waited to hear.

"He's in stable condition. Thank God. And the doctor says his prognosis looks good." She heard a smile in Yolie's voice. The woman was practically giddy. "He's eating up a storm. Can you imagine him eating hospital food, without loading it down with hot sauce? I couldn't be happier."

Raven pictured her smiling face. Her euphoria was contagious.

"Oh, that's so good to hear. Call me if there's anything I can do for you or his parents." Her eyes welled with tears, happy to hear the good news. "Can I speak to him?"

"Oh, sure. Just a minute."

She heard Yolanda's voice in the background and a rustle of fabric. In a moment, she heard Tony on the line.

"Hey, Mac." His voice sounded weak, nowhere near his old self. But he still sounded damned good to her. "How's the case?"

"Hey, Tony. I've made some headway, but I miss my partner." Raven worried about telling him too much. She imagined how she'd feel if their situations were reversed and she was the one flat on her back, unable to help.

"I hear from the guys that Sam is helping you with some old case files. How's that going?"

She closed her eyes and shook her head. Tony was one tough guy. Still working the case even from the hospital. And the constant flood of visitors in blue uniforms would have kept him plugged in. No use shielding him from anything.

"I'm staring at a stack of old case folders right now. Thanks to Sam's help, we started with eleven cases, but are now down to four." She flipped open her case notes and reviewed the summary. "Two are dead, three in prison, one deported, and one moved out of state. That leaves four still living in the greater Chicago area."

She read the rap sheets of the final four to him.

"Real maggots, huh?" His breathing sounded labored. "What does your gut say?"

It took her a moment to retrieve one file. Flipping over the cover, she held up the mug shot inside.

"Dad made a personal note in one of his casebooks. He wrote 'gray dead eyes' like it really was supposed to mean something. My money is on Dad and old gray eyes, Logan McBride. But unfortunately, we've got no address on him."

Staring at the old black-and-white photo, she knew her father had been dead-on. The man made her skin crawl, even in 2–D. The old rap sheet was a long one, and her father had arrested the bastard on a grand theft auto when he'd been a teen. But even at that age, McBride had all the makings of a hard case.

"Follow your instincts, Raven. My money's on you." Tony cleared his throat. "How are things going with Delacorte?"

Images of Christian flashed in her mind, his handsome face, the feel and smell of his skin. She had it bad. The time she'd spent with him now felt like a surreal dream. And a hollow sensation plagued her with the mention of his name. Raven craved him like a junkie off a bender.

"Too good. I just feel like pinching myself, like I'll

wake up and he would be a figment of my sex-starved imagination."

"Oh, Lord. I think that falls under TMI—too much information." His attempt at laughter turned into a coughing jag. She knew it was time to cut the conversation short.

"Yeah, guess so. I forgot you're such a lightweight." She grinned. "Hey, Tony? I miss you. And I'm glad you're okay. I've been praying for you, you know."

It was true. She found herself talking to no one, in her own head, confiding the desperation and fear for her partner's safety. It took her a moment to finally recognize that she was praying. Out of practice as she was, it felt like the closest she'd come to believing again. And with Tony taking a turn for the better, who was she to argue with the process?

"Will wonders never cease?" he replied. "Take care, Mac. Let me know how those hard cases turn out."

"I will, partner. I miss you. Did I mention that?"

"Yeah, a time or three."

She hung up the phone, struggling to control a grin. Maybe things would turn out after all.

A menacing rumble called her attention to the window. The sky had turned nearly black with the onset of dusk and a brewing storm. The thunder bumper had been expected, but its timing for the five o'clock rush hour was just plain cruel.

The ominous rumble made her skin crawl. Maybe her optimism was a bit premature.

A crack of thunder made her jump. Her pulse quickened. Fiona felt thankful the jet had landed before the weather had gotten this bad. She clutched at her coat collar and drew it tighter around her throat. Her eyes peered over her shoulder into the gloom. The rain poured down like the heavens were angry. And she understood why.

With luggage near her feet, she paced the small waiting room of the Dunhill hangar, glancing at her watch once again. She'd asked for a ride to meet her. The service was late. Rush-hour traffic and the bad weather no doubt contributed to the problem. But the delay didn't entirely displease her. It gave her time to think about what she would say to Christian when she saw him.

Her son.

A lump formed and wedged in her throat. *Her beautiful son.*

She stopped and closed her eyes, clenching a fist to her lips and pressing hard to stanch the onset of tears. What would she say to him? She had come home to face Christian, to tell him everything. With the reality of that confrontation so near at hand, she wasn't sure she had the courage. But she owed him the truth—*and so much more.*

The glass door opened behind her. Fiona turned, expecting to see a security driver with her limousine service. She flinched, a gasp punctuating her surprise.

"Christian?" Her voice quivered.

He stood at the door, raindrops clinging to his dark hair, his face slick from the downpour. Those brooding green eyes told her all she needed to know. It had taken years of therapy to find even a semblance of joy buried deep in them. And even those moments were few. But something else lurked beneath the surface of his eyes. Resentment. It was undeniable.

"Surprised to see me?" Cynicism colored his voice. "No more of a shocker than when I came home to find you gone, leaving me in the lurch, neck-deep in a murder investigation."

He hit dead center. Christian never minced words. She wasn't sure she could take the strain of his hostility. And when he bridged the gap between them, stepping closer, her throat tightened. How could she justify what she'd done?

"If I stayed, it would have been worse." She wanted to explain, find the words to make it all right. But everything she said came out wrong. Christian was an intelligent, sensitive man. He would see through her stonewalling.

"Worse for whom? For me . . . or for you? I guess you want me to believe you left to protect me." His face grew cold with skepticism. "Nice try. Pardon me if I sound cynical these days."

This was not how she'd envisioned their conversation, but she deserved the full force of his bitterness. Now Christian moved even closer. Her arms ached to hold him, finally as his mother. But she knew he'd never allow it.

Clenching his jaw, he took another tack. "I found out someone else was very interested in your whereabouts, besides me. Did your past catch up with you, Fie?"

Nicky. What did he know about Nicholas? A sinister growl of thunder mirrored her fear. The rain continued its assault, crying the tears she held back.

She had never known Christian to be cruel, but it was clear in his taunt. He had been hurt by her betrayal. The use of his nickname for her twisted his words like a knife to her heart. She merited every ounce of his animosity.

"Yes, I suppose it did." She should have known she could never flee the reality of her base nature. Nicky had stirred the pot, but it was a black kettle of her own creation. She had no one else to blame. "I should have known I would never outrun it. I just wish—"

Regret choked her, but the pain in his eyes tightened the noose.

"Were you ever planning to tell me the truth?" he asked.

His words struck her. Eyes wide, she couldn't hide her reaction. The truth? What did he know exactly? Once this all began, she had wanted to ease him into the reality of his past. But everything had happened too fast. Her instincts forced her to stall, to find out precisely what he knew before she blundered with a reply.

"I wanted to." Her response sounded cagey, even to her. "You deserve to know everything."

And by the look of him, Christian wasn't buying her trite justification.

"Good intentions aren't gonna cut it. When I needed some answers and you weren't around, I searched your personal things." He broke his accusing stare for the first time. His admission apparently shamed him. But he soon recovered. Sarcasm returned to his tone. "I hope you'll forgive the intrusion, and the breach of faith. Trust is so rare. It should be cherished, don't you think? At least, that's what I believed when I was more gullible."

He no longer looked at her. Folding his arms across his chest, he turned aside and shut his eyes with the strain. After a long moment of silence, he looked over his shoulder. It disturbed her to see him so hurt.

"I thought I knew you . . . and myself. Guess I was wrong on both counts." He spoke in such a hushed tone that she nearly didn't hear him over the storm. Yet even through the low timbre of his voice, she heard the wounded child. That child had been burned into her memory, branded forever by the condemnation of her actions. She raised a hand to touch his shoulder, but stopped short.

"Tell me what you know, Christian. Please."

Rain pelted the window, blowing sideways with erratic winds. Her concentration waned as the blustering storm elevated her uneasiness. It was after five when Raven glanced to the clock on the bullpen wall. She had expected to hear from Christian by now. Playing over their last conversations in her head, she wondered what had happened at work that would keep him so late. Didn't he have enough on his plate without the added stress? And with his employer being Fiona Dunhill, the woman who'd kept such damaging secrets from her own son, her anxiety mounted.

"What's up with you, Christian?" she muttered.

"Hey, Mackenzie." The desk sergeant poked his head through the doorway. "I got a message to deliver. From Father Antonio." He handed her a note.

"Why didn't you just direct the call back to me?" Her eyes were drawn to the pink slip of paper. "Did he want me to call him back?" She glanced up.

"No. He just wanted to leave the message." The officer slouched against the door frame. "Seemed in a hurry."

"How did he know I was here?" It seemed odd that the priest only left his message, not waiting to speak to her directly. She narrowed her eyes at the note, finding it hard to decipher the message. But the sergeant elaborated.

"Oh, he asked about you and I told him you were here. Then he asked if he could just leave a message."

The man shrugged. "He wants you to meet him at the rectory in a half hour, by the side parking lot. Says he may have a witness for the Blair case."

"Oh, yeah? Well, what do ya know? What's this about flashing something? I can't read your writing, Sarge."

The man chuckled. "Yeah, well, I can think of a couple things a man would like you to flash, Mackenzie. But this man is a priest, for cryin' out loud. Show some respect."

She rolled her eyes, then arched an eyebrow, waiting for him to answer.

"The note says that when you pull up, flash your lights and he'll join you. Guess he wants you to drive somewhere. With rush-hour traffic, you might want to leave now," he added.

"Yeah, thanks. Good idea."

She suddenly remembered what Christian had told her. *Promise me you won't deviate from the plan.*

A trip to St. Sebastian's definitely constituted a departure from their game plan. But surely he would understand. She was only meeting a priest at a church rectory. How dangerous could that be? A loud crack of thunder nearly jolted her from her seat. Both she and the sergeant looked out the window, catching a violent flash of light streaking across the sky.

"Rush hour is gonna be a bear. My workload's gonna triple." He scowled. "You better get going. Drive safe."

"Yeah, later, Sarge. I gotta see a priest."

"I've always thought that'd be a good thing for you, Mackenzie. God works in mysterious ways."

"So I've heard." She shook her head and grinned at the man.

After grabbing her coat, she put a hand on her Glock in its holster, an old habit when she was on the move. She glanced at her cell phone, checking the battery. It had plenty of juice. The plan could still work. He'd call her and she'd answer the phone.

What could be simpler?

Christian wondered the same thing. What did he know . . . exactly? Good question, Fie—and a clever stall tactic. So much was supposition on his part. Only she knew all the answers.

Lightning streaked across the night sky, hurling its wrath into the void. And with it, his anxiety multiplied. Yet Christian persisted in this verbal joust with Fiona. The vaguer his responses, the more he might get her to admit. It was a gamble. But she was an intelligent woman, smart enough to outwit his lame attempt at a subtle interrogation. And the pained expression on her face made him feel heartless.

"Let's just say that I'm gonna have mixed feelings when it comes to celebrating Mother's Day." He wanted to bite back his cynicism, but it swept through his words like an infection. He couldn't look at her any longer. Even with everything she'd done, she was still his mother. Nothing justified his cruelty to her, not without first hearing her side of it.

"Oh, God. You don't know how many times I wanted to tell you the truth, especially after—"

"There's a lot I don't know, Mother dearest."

He walked toward the glass door to the hangar waiting room, his eyes boring through the darkness beyond the lights of the small parking lot. Pulling back his coat, he jammed his hands into the pockets of his jeans. He caught her in the reflection of the glass. A shimmer of tears influenced the lines of her face. She looked older than her years.

But there was still so much he needed to know. He couldn't spare her. Not now. With her propensity to disappear, he had to know the truth before it was too late. He let his mind delve into the depths of his pain.

"And you just watched me go through that hell and didn't say a word. How could you? Why?"

Quietly, when she thought he hadn't noticed, Fiona clutched at her stomach as if she were nauseated. He knew the feeling. Slowly, she regained her composure and joined him at the door. She stood by his side and stared into the heavy rain.

"I know you're not going to believe this, but I did it for your own good."

Closing his eyes, he tilted his head back, not sure he wanted to hear her crafty dodges.

"You owe me an explanation." Glaring forward, he kept his tone even. "Let's start with something simple. Who were the Delacortes? If I was your son, how did I end up being raised by them?"

Flashes of his family's faces blew through his mind, like a reel of film played out of context, remembrances he thought he'd buried. Memories long forgotten suddenly sprang from the darkness. Strange images mirrored in the glass of the waiting room.

Glimpses of a happier life. Loving smiles. Laughter. Childish games with his precocious younger sister. Replaced by the screams he knew well—and all that blood.

Then, just as suddenly, the throng of memories faded. Yet one image remained. Bathed in light, shadow man now had a face, a memory he would keep.

"John Delacorte." Fiona spoke the man's name as if she read his mind.

"Yes." His trance slowly cleared with the sound of his own voice. Christian gazed at Fiona. Odd, she had a smile on her face.

"I met him when I was pregnant with you, Christian. Back in those days, there was such a stigma to an out-of-wedlock pregnancy. My family made excuses for me, sent me away."

Pulling her coat around her, Fiona folded her arms. She stepped to the chairs across the room and collapsed into one.

Her voice sounded very far away. "He was a groundskeeper at the facility, Serenity Clinic in upstate New York—very private, very discreet. John and I became friends. He was such a compassionate young man."

She patted the seat next to her. Defeat showed on her face. He couldn't refuse her. Moving the chair from the wall, he squared off, facing her knee to knee.

"I couldn't give you up, especially not after seeing your eyes. Green, like mine." She smiled. Tears pooled, then drained down her cheek. "I was betrothed to Charles Dunhill. A very dangerous man. If he knew—" It took her a moment to continue. "I paid John to adopt you. Once I got married, I had access to more funds. It got easier to support you, to keep you hidden. I subsidized John and his growing family for years. He was such a good man."

"But you gave me up. Why? And why keep me hidden? Were you that . . . ashamed?"

"God, no. I loved you, so much." A sob caught in her throat. She clutched at his hand. The unexpected touch made him flinch, but she held firm. It was her way. "It broke my heart when I wasn't there to see your first steps, to hear you call someone else Mother." With a frail hand, she wiped tears from her face. "It was the best I could do, Christian."

He narrowed his eyes. She still hadn't answered his question. Why did she keep him hidden? She caught his look of skepticism.

"Besides, John loved you like a son. After the years went by, I saw how much it meant for you to be a part of his family. He couldn't have loved you more if you were his own. I saw that, too."

Her diversion worked, for an instant. Christian swallowed hard, choking back the emotion.

"What?" She squeezed his hand, encouraging him. "Say it."

The connection he felt for Fiona now reminded him of the many conversations they had when he was a kid, so messed up. She had a gift. She could draw things from him that he didn't know were inside.

"Lately, I've been having that same recurring nightmare. The one I had when I was a kid. But this time, I remembered more of it." His eyes found hers. "My father . . . John saved my life. He died because of me. They *all* did."

"No, Christian. If anyone takes the blame, it should be me. I was too weak to deny my family and stand up to Charles. Don't do this to yourself."

"It wasn't the police that killed the Delacortes, was it? Why did you lie about that?" His accusation came from nowhere. But he saw by her reaction that he'd stumbled onto the truth.

She refused to answer. Fiona's jaw dropped, her eyes wide with his abruptness.

He yanked his hand from hers and stared in disbelief. "Damn it! You owe me the truth. Don't hold back now."

She wasn't going to answer him, but he couldn't let it go. Standing, he thrust the chair out from under him and stalked toward the door. "Those men were after me. I remembered that too. Who killed the Delacortes, Fiona?"

"I just can't—" She pleaded for his mercy with her eyes and in the pitiable quiver of her voice. "Saying it aloud . . . the truth is so ugly. I'm not ready for it. Not yet. Please. Can we go home? I need to go home."

She looked lost. He had come so close to hearing it all. But her refusal now was like waving a red flag in front of a bull. Fiona had to know the ramifications of her actions. Surely, if she knew, she would tell him everything. It was the only way.

"Charles Dunhill, the Delacortes, Mickey Blair . . . how many have to die for you to tell the truth? After you fled the country, one of the detectives on the case was gunned down on his front lawn, in front of his family. The ICU is gonna be his home for a while. The police believe it's the same man that killed Mickey."

The shock on her face was undeniable. But he couldn't stop.

"And Detective Raven Mackenzie is under my protection, because the same bastard is stalking her."

"I didn't know. You have to believe me, if I had known—"

"If you'd have known, would you have come back at all?" His words were brutal. They found voice through his pain and his betrayed trust. He glared, unwilling to mask his anger. "What are you not telling me, Fiona? Who is my biological father? And did you have anything to do with the death of your own husband?"

As he gazed out the window, he heard the creak of a chair as she stood. In the reflection of the glass, he saw her walk toward him. Christian felt her presence by his side. Any other time in his life, the act would have given him comfort. But now, he knew pain would follow. He was about to learn the truth. Only the rhythm of the rain filled the emptiness until—

"My husband, Charles, killed the Delacortes. He made it look like a police raid gone bad, but it was all him." She cried, her arms clutched around her waist. Her shoulders shook with every sob. "I despised him for what he did."

"But why did he—? What did they do to deserve that?"

"He wanted you, Christian. He was after my son." Her eyes glazed over. She was in another world. "We were so careful, John and I. But Charles must have found out. I never discovered how." She turned and reached for his arm. "By the grace of God you survived. Maybe John had more to do with that. I don't know. But I had to do it. Don't you see? Charles wouldn't have stopped trying to find you . . . to kill you. You were only a boy—"

She collapsed in his arms. He held her, supporting her weight until he walked her to a chair.

"I had to do it. I had no choice," she muttered, staring out the window as if he weren't there. "I hired Mickey to kill my husband. It was the only way to keep you safe. Charles was such a jealous and vengeful man. And with his money, he had a long reach."

He gripped her hand as he knelt in front of her. The pieces to the puzzle had fallen into place. Only one question remained.

"Who's my father, Fie?"

Her eyes widened. She clenched her jaw. Suddenly, her cooperation ceased. Christian saw it in her face. She would keep her secret. And despite his complete devastation over her betrayal, he still loved her enough—to let her go.

"You have a choice, Fie. You can get back on that plane. I won't tell them where you are. Bury yourself deeper this time." He lightly touched his fingers to the back of her hand, not taking his eyes from her. "Or you can stay, help me sort this out. But I'm not sure it's in your best interest to do that. Whatever you decide, I'll try to understand."

He wanted to take her in his arms and protect her from her demons, as she had done for him all those years ago. But whatever would have happened, he'd never know. The harsh sound of his cell phone called for attention. In denial, he waited for the second ring to answer it.

"Yeah."

"She's on the move." The gruff voice of Bill Edwards yanked him from his misery. He stood and left Fiona sitting in the chair, confused by the look of concern on his face.

"You have the coordinates?" He listened intently and shut his eyes tight, trying to regain his focus. "I'm heading out now. Get someone over here to take Fiona anywhere she wants to go. When I get on the road, I'll call you again, to feed me the information. Don't lose my SUV, Bill."

He ended the call, his heart racing. Raven was on the move, even after promising she'd stay put.

"What's going on, Christian? Is it the case?"

"I've gotta go."

"Please don't shut me out now," she pleaded.

"What you did . . . hurt me, Fiona. You lied to me all those years. Every time you comforted me after one of my nightmares, every time I raged against the police, blaming them for what happened, you perpetuated the lie. I'm not sure I can live with that. I'm not sure I want to." He stood and walked toward the door, leaving her behind. "You severed the tie between us—not me. Having an attachment to you? It may come at too high a price." He swallowed hard, knowing his cruelty hit a new low. But he had no time to ease her burden. Raven needed him.

"I gotta go."

"Christian . . . *please*."

Ignoring her, he ran into the pouring rain. The weight of it soaked his hair and clothes. He dashed to his car, hitting the keyless remote and fumbling for the cell phone on his belt. Turning the ignition, he pulled from the parking space and hit the new speed dial for Raven.

As it rang, he took a final look at Fiona alone in the waiting room, her face blanched by fluorescent lighting. She looked so small and frail. That image would haunt him, along with all the rest. And he deserved every ounce of guilt. Finally, he turned away.

"Come on. Pick up," he urged.

Raven didn't answer. When his call rolled into voice mail, he left a quick message, trying to hide the concern in his voice. But something wasn't right.

His headlights caught the heavy drops bouncing off the pavement, his windshield wipers drumming a rhythm to match the cadence of his heart. Something felt terribly wrong.

Taking a deep breath, he steadied his mind, employing the techniques he'd learned long ago to calm himself. With only a brief glance, he punched a second number on his cell. Staring into the night, his eyes on full alert, he steeled his senses for the hunt.

"Talk to me, Bill."

*   *   *

The streets were congested with slow-moving traffic. Rolling along at twenty miles per hour, Raven knew she'd be delayed in meeting Father Antonio, and being late always made her anxious. It couldn't be helped.

The storm robbed what precious little light remained of the day, and the pounding rain made visibility non-existent. For a moment, she considered pulling over to let the storm pass, but opted against it. At least she was moving.

With the windshield wipers beating on high, she squinted through the downpour, tightening her grip on the steering wheel. The colorful lights of the city bled through the streaks of rain. Large drops pelted the SUV, making it hard to think.

She saw St. Sebastian's Church on the left and almost missed her turn. As she pulled into the side parking lot nearest the rectory, she parked the SUV, but kept the engine running. Father Antonio would not recognize the vehicle as hers, so she followed his instruction and flashed the headlights.

Nothing. She peered through the darkness, looking for any sign of life from the modest living quarters.

From the corner of her eye, she saw a man in the shadows, waving a hand and jogging up to her car from the right side. Although the hood of the man's coat covered his face, she thought he might be the priest judging by his build and stature. She narrowed her eyes and craned her neck for a better view. But as he drew closer, she saw the cross hanging from his neck and she unlocked the doors.

Suddenly, a dark shadow eclipsed the streetlamp behind her. A motion caught her eye, reflected in the side mirror. A man crept toward her car, too damned sneaky to be harmless. On pure instinct, she reacted without hesitation. Laying her shoulder into it, she shoved at her door, jamming the heavy hunk of steel into the man like a weapon. With the first strike, he doubled over in pain, his arms attempting to shield his knees. To make her point again, she pulled the door back for a second assault. This time, she used her leg to thrust into him.

As he fell to the ground, the man cried out, "Shit! Stop that bitch."

Grappling with her seat belt, she had only an instant to make her next move as the man writhed on the ground. Blindly, she pressed the clasp of her safety belt, then felt for the butt of her gun. But the passenger side door flew open and another man accosted her from the right, knocking the Glock from her hand into the shadows of the floorboard.

"What the hell?" she cried. Raven kicked and punched, fighting the man in close quarters. "Chicago Police. Back off." Her voice was loud and forceful, but her warning went unheeded.

A shrill ring broke her concentration. Her cell phone. Christian. It had to be him. Like a cruel taunt, his words of reason repeated in her head. *Don't deviate from the plan.* The image of Christian spurred her on. She couldn't let up now.

But as she fought the second man, the delay allowed her first assailant to recover. He lunged through the driver's side door, gripping her neck with a beefy forearm, choking off her air. The distraction didn't daunt her. Still fighting the other guy, she drove a heel into his head as he came in from the passenger side. Connecting with the kick, she caught a glimpse of him falling to the ground with a grunt. But she had a bigger problem.

Caught in a headlock, her airway squeezed tight, she wheezed her next breath, quickly losing control. The bastard yanked her from the driver's seat, not letting up on the pressure. Rain pummeled her face, making it hard to see.

With very little effort, her assailant could snap her neck. She felt her arms and legs tingling, the numbness spreading. Shooting pinpoints of light played havoc with her eyes. Dizziness fogged her senses. Soon, she'd lose consciousness. If that happened, she knew it would be over.

With all her strength, Raven clenched her fist and stiffened her forearm, ramming her elbow hard into the solar plexus of the man behind her, just as she'd been trained. The first shot barely got the man's attention. The second time, he cursed with the damage she inflicted. His body felt like a brick wall. Her elbow quivered, deadened by pain. On the third punch, he loosened his grip around her neck and stumbled backward.

It was all the break she needed.

Raven spun and quickly shifted her hip behind him, then yanked his shoulders back with her right arm. His weight and momentum propelled him to the ground. As he lay stunned, she gripped his collar with her left fist to steady her target. Drawing back the heel of her right hand, she prepared to shatter his nose, driving bone splinters deep into his brain, dealing a deathblow. But a hard metal object shoved against the back of her skull.

It could be only one thing. She stopped cold.

A menacing voice captured her attention through the driving rain. His rock-steadiness told her he was in charge.

"You connect with that next shot and the last thing you'll see is your brains all over Krueger's chest. Personally, I could care less one way or the other. So you take your pick."

The man named Krueger blinked twice, clearly unsure whether the man with the gun meant what he said. She, on the other hand, knew the ruthless scumbag meant every word. Deliberating her choices, she held firm to Krueger, a stubborn streak influencing her bravado. Raven knew she had little to think about. Attempting to recover, she drew cold air into her lungs. Her chest heaved with the effort, her throat raw. The chilling rain seeped under her open coat and through to her skin. Strands of hair stuck to her face.

It was over.

Raven loosened her grip and raised her hands high. Still kneeling, she waited for the next instruction, hoping the man holding her at gunpoint wouldn't shoot her dead on the spot. As long as she was alive, she had hope.

"Stay on your knees." The man standing behind her laughed—a low, threatening sound. "After all, you're practically at a church. Try saying a prayer if you think it'll help."

Cupping his hand under her chin, he yanked her head back and stroked her neck with his icy, wet fingers. With the gun still to her ear, he whispered, "Seeing you so submissive, it's a real turn-on. Every woman should know her place."

And to Krueger lying on the wet asphalt, he changed his tone and ordered, "Get up, before she kicks your ass again."

Krueger raised up on his elbows and drew the back of his hand over his mouth—the look in his eyes downright lethal. In a slow and deliberate manner, he stood, never taking his eyes off her.

"I think you really pissed him off." His vulgar laugh grated her nerves.

Raven's eyes darted to the left then right, looking for her next opportunity to strike back. But the man didn't give her a chance.

"Tie her up."

Her hands were yanked behind her. She felt her wrists being bound, the sound of duct tape tearing off the roll.

And to make matters worse, her phone erupted a second time, calling attention to her only lifeline. It must be Christian again. An arm reached from behind her and tugged at the phone on her belt. The man's hand palmed her in a vile manner, retrieving her badge.

"She's got an empty holster. Where's her gun?"

Another voice yelled, "Check the car, the floorboard on the passenger side. I seen it fall."

She shut her eyes tight for an instant, then asked, "What's this all about?" No answer. She tried again. "You have my badge. You know I'm a police officer with the Chicago PD."

"Oh, believe me, I know exactly who you are, Detective Mackenzie."

A hand shoved her to the ground, and her feet were restrained in duct tape. She was going nowhere, trussed like a pig going to slaughter. Unceremoniously, she was jerked to her feet by the collar of her coat. Strong hands grasped both of her elbows. She teetered on her feet, unable to move. The man whose voice she'd come to recognize stepped around to face her.

Gray dead eyes.

"You." She couldn't hide her reaction. "Logan McBride."

"At your service." He looked surprised but eventually smiled, touching a finger to his forehead in a mock salute. His looks didn't improve with the gesture. "Now, let's not keep Father Antonio waiting."

"If you've hurt him—" Her threat fell hollow.

And by the look on McBride's face, he wasn't intimidated in the slightest. A grimace twisted his expression.

"I've heard enough from you, Mackenzie. You've got a big mouth, just like your daddy."

He cut a piece of duct tape from the roll with a sharp knife. She watched him make the slice and wondered if this blade had slit Mickey Blair's throat. Jerking her head back, he stuck the tape across her mouth, shutting her up for good.

"Take her SUV and follow us to the location we talked about. Get going." In an instant, she heard Christian's car start up and screech away. "Let's get out of here," he ordered.

Hoisted from the ground, she was thrown over a man's shoulder. Bile rose hot from her belly. She dangled helplessly, her arms and legs useless. But she still had her mind. She could think.

Where was Father Antonio? Since McBride had his cross, she assumed the priest was being held or already dead. The injustice toward the innocent cleric enraged her. And another thing twisted her gut, ever since the break-in at her home. McBride had more to do with her father's past than Christian's. What was McBride's connection to Mickey Blair? Instinct told her McBride had killed the man, but for what reason? None of this made sense.

Thrown into the back of a dark-colored and windowless utility van, she heard the doors slam shut. Cocooned in darkness. As the engine rumbled and the vehicle lurched forward, a sense of foreboding seized her heart.

Something else was very wrong.

None of these men had made an effort to hide his face. Hell, McBride downright flaunted his ugly mug, not caring much how she recognized him. He even used Krueger's name without regard for secrecy. Raven felt certain they had no intention of letting her go. No doubt in her mind.

She'd have to use her brain and fight like hell if she hoped to make it out alive.

CHAPTER 15

The van finally came to a stop. In the dark, Raven listened for sounds of her captors as she wrestled with the duct tape binding her wrists. The damned tape hadn't budged the whole trip. She wrenched her jaw again, hoping to open her mouth, but nothing.

The intensity of the rain dwindled to a faint tapping on the outside of the vehicle. Tensing her muscles, she rolled to face the door, prepared to kick it open. With her legs bound, she had no idea what she'd do next. But by the sound of things, more of McBride's men had gathered outside. She wouldn't stand a chance.

As the van door opened, she stared into the grim faces of three men, then heaved a sigh. She had to be patient, pick her spot.

"Look what Logan gift-wrapped for us." One man laughed, his bristly face twisted to a sneer. "Prime hunting stock."

She wanted to respond, but her instincts warned her to play it smart. A hand gripped her ankle and tugged her effortlessly to the rear of the van. As she cleared the darkened interior, a man grabbed the edge of the tape covering her mouth and jerked it free, with no regard for her skin underneath.

"Hey, watch it." *So much for playing it smart.* She moved her jaw and lips, making sure everything still worked before she mouthed off again. "Aren't you afraid I'll scream?"

"Counting on it." His offhand remark sent chills along her skin.

To regain control of her emotions, she focused on her surroundings, ignoring the manhandling of her body. Hoisted over a man's shoulder, she hung upside down. Strands of hair blocked her view. She craned her neck to see anything that would help. And adding insult to injury, the bastard carrying her stroked her ass like he'd discovered Aladdin's magic lamp.

"You cut me out of this duct tape, and I'll show you my idea of foreplay."

The man laughed and gave her one final squeeze from his meaty hand. "Not on your life, sweetheart."

As far as she could see, shabby red brick buildings extended into the darkness, with only a small section of them illuminated by the headlights of the van and Christian's SUV. One of the delivery bays was open. Voices echoed inside. From the belly of the largest structure, several flashlights cut through the darkness. They cast an eerie glow, elongating the shadows of McBride's men. No electricity told her the buildings had been abandoned long ago.

None of this place looked familiar. The only signs of life were the vehicles parked in front. And she had a suspicion they'd be pulled into the old building, out of sight. When that happened, not a trace of her would be left behind. The decayed warehouse would swallow her whole.

Now she would know firsthand what Mickey had experienced.

Once inside, the stale smell of mildew stifled her breath. It was difficult enough to breathe upside down. Sparingly, she sampled the air as if it were toxic. But the sound of McBride's voice made her stomach lurch.

"Fresh meat for the slaughter." He grabbed her hair and gave it a tug, straining the muscles of her neck. "But first, I propose a little reunion."

Enlisting the aid of one of the hangar crew, Fiona found a phone in the office. Behind a closed door, she gripped the receiver and stared at the buttons. Her chair creaked as she shifted her weight, her nerves getting the better of her.

Months had turned into years and the years spun into decades—and still she'd resisted making contact with Nicholas Charboneau. Now her pulse raced in anticipation of hearing his voice again, so soon after she'd seen him in Versailles. He had instigated that encounter, a complete surprise. This time, she would be reaching out to him, asking for a favor.

Her focus drifted in and out as her trembling fingers hovered near the numbers. But she must swallow her pride. Much more was at stake. Slowly, she punched in the number she had committed to memory long ago. She'd locked it away in her heart.

Nicholas answered on the third ring. "Yes?"

Fiona felt certain he had caller ID and would screen his calls. But the number would only show Dunhill Aviation—and that might pique his interest. For an instant, she weighed the consequences of her actions and considered the risk. Once she spoke, he'd know she was

Stateside. What other torturous games would he launch against her?

"Nicky. It's Fiona."

Dead silence—as cold as the stern glare from his violet eyes.

"You've come home." A long moment ticked by. "Why have you called?"

No games. No feigned cordiality. His tone scared her. He held the advantage. All she could do was—

"I need your help," she pleaded.

A low rumble of laughter ridiculed her. He wasn't going to make this easy. Fighting back tears, she tightened her lips and choked down a sob. Her Nicky had grown so cold.

"After all these years, Fiona? You know any help from me comes with a price. Are you willing to pay it?"

By his tone, she knew he flaunted his superior position, presuming she'd never yield to him.

"For God's sake, haven't we both paid that price?" Her question rhetorical, she didn't wait for his sarcasm. "What do you want, Nicky? I'll do whatever you ask. Just stop this vendetta of yours."

Silence. Only the sound of his breathing filled the emptiness.

She needed him to understand. "You've won. But this killing must stop. You don't know what you're doing." She regretted her poor choice of words the instant she'd said it. And desperation seeped into her voice. It couldn't be helped.

The face of her son flashed in Fiona's mind. She knew Christian. If Detective Mackenzie was in danger, he'd protect her, without regard for his own safety. *Damn it!* All those years ago, her cowardly actions and poor judgment had come full circle. And it might cost the life of her only child. She'd have gladly taken the retribution upon herself, being the guilty one. But Christian deserved none of it. He'd already suffered too much for her sins.

"Oh? Then enlighten me, my dear," he taunted, still the cagey player. "What exactly am I doing?"

Even now, her instincts stopped her from blurting out the truth. Nicholas would never find out from her that Christian was his son. She'd have to find another way to get him to listen to reason.

"If death is all that will appease you, then I am offering myself." Closing her eyes, she filled her lungs and let her breath out slowly, allowing fear to wash over her. She swallowed hard, then spelled it out for him. "Kill me. It's what you really want, isn't it? Tell me where I can meet you."

Once again, he fell silent. Startled for a moment, she thought he'd hung up the phone. Fiona tightened her grip on the receiver and listened for any sound at all. As she opened her mouth to speak, he broke the stalemate.

"It's out of my hands, Fie. We'll both have to live with the aftermath."

His words stabbed her heart. *No! It couldn't be over.* Her mind wouldn't accept such finality.

"Nicky, *please*—"

A dial tone mocked her. He ended the call, bitterness in his voice.

It was too late.

Nicholas stared blankly into the crackling fire, his eyes mesmerized by the only light in the room. The flames cast eerie shadows along the stone hearth and into the cavernous study. Sitting amidst his fine collection of books and artifacts and rare paintings, he'd come to the realization that none of it meant a thing. Echoing in his mind, Fiona's frightened voice bedeviled his dubious sense of morality.

His gaze drifted toward the crystal snifter in his hand, its contents a fine family blend of Cognac. Slowly, he swirled the amber liquid along the inside of the glass and watched it coat the rainbow prisms with its ambrosia.

If he placed a call to Jasmine now, he might endanger her, placing his bodyguard at risk with the sound of a cell phone that might give her position away. Most probably, her phone would be switched off altogether.

Trust. It all came down to trust.

His soft chuckle invaded the silence. *Trust?* Irony was a self-inflicted wound, its own brand of torment. Was he truly trying to convince himself that he trusted Jasmine—trusted anyone at all?

"You arrogant fool," he chastised himself. The sound of his voice echoed in the hollow space of his heart. He tossed back the fine Cognac. His throat burned with its honey.

His grand scheme had lost its luster. Nicholas had seen Mickey Blair as a loose end, one that needed his attention. Fiona would never have taken care of the man on her own. Even now, Nicholas wasn't sure why he had stepped in the middle. Was he protecting her, or in his arrogance, did he want to be the only one who knew her secret?

None of that mattered now. He had set this whole fiasco in motion. Now he would live or die with the aftermath.

It looked like a dead end. *Bad choice of words.*

The beam from a flashlight was her only guide

through the long, dark corridor. One man carried her and another walked beside Logan McBride. Three savage men. Raven would soon find out what McBride meant about a *reunion*. Her stomach twisted into a knot of fear, her mind filling with the horror of rape or some other brand of torture. She steeled herself for any outcome. No matter what they did to her body, she vowed to come out of this alive. She had to believe that. Giving up wasn't in her nature.

She closed her eyes for an instant, garnering her strength. But her mind grappled with one thought. For her to walk away from this, she would have to take lives. Like her father, most cops went through their whole career never actually faced with that dilemma. No such luck for her. She would have to decide. Would she kill to stay alive?

Her answer? A resounding *YES!*

Through the murkiness, her eyes spied a door ahead. With the beam of light focusing on it, she felt certain it would be their destination. But what the hell was behind it? All too soon, she would know.

The door creaked open, rusted at its hinges. Before she got a good look, she was thrown roughly to the ground, her spine and shoulders punished by the concrete floor even through her coat. A beam of light blinded her. Squinting, she turned her head, her only defense. With hands tied behind her back, she couldn't shield her eyes. Catching only glimpses of motion, she counted boots, trying to decipher where her captors stood.

But a sound coming from the far corner of the dark room jarred her. Shoes scuffed the cement floor. A low moan. Who else was in the room? *Damn!* Were there more of them? Before she allowed her instincts to cloud with fear, she had to know.

"Detective? You remember Father Antonio."

She peered through the dark and caught a motion on the fringes of the light. The priest cowered in the corner. His hands covered his face. By the looks of him, he'd been beaten. Raven wanted to comfort the man, but McBride wasn't through with him.

"Father, don't be so uncharitable. If this woman beats the odds, she might just save your pathetic ass. Would that buy her a ticket into heaven?"

The priest gave no response. But that didn't stop McBride from dishing out more of his abrasive charm. He knelt by her side, amusement in his voice. "Got a challenge for you, Mackenzie. Just think of it like a game of Monopoly. If you get past Go, you win."

"I don't like games." She rolled to one side, her eyes searching the dark. The small room had only one door.

"All women like games, Detective. Besides, declining is not an option. Quite frankly, your life depends on it. And to up the ante, Father Antonio's life hangs in the balance, too."

"What's the objective?" she asked, stalling to better assess her options. The priest's hands and feet were unbound. If they were going to play a game, would she be cut loose?

"Oh, it's very simple. The objective is to stay alive."

McBride enjoyed his role as the demented master of ceremonies. And the men in the room laughed. The low rumble ridiculed her predicament and told her what these men thought of her chances. With these odds, even she wouldn't take the bet.

"You see, there is only one way out of this building. If you get by my men, and find your way to freedom, you live."

Backlit, his face was in the shadows. But she visualized his pompous grin as he shrugged and gestured his decree.

The bastard needed killing—bad!

But McBride wasn't done spouting his rules for survival. "I'm presuming, of course, that you'll take the good Father with you, not just leave him to my wolves. But that's your choice. Tell you what—extra bonus points if you escape with your guardian angel in tow. How's that?"

"And what do I get for taking you out?" She narrowed her eyes and searched for his in the murkiness.

"Oh, I want you to find me, darlin'. That's endgame— the center of the maze." His words raised the hair on her neck. "In the end, it's just gonna be you and me. I'm gonna be the last thing you hear."

His voice echoed through the room like the hiss of a snake. He slid a finger down the length of her cheek, his fingernail nearly breaking the skin.

"And my hands will take liberties with your body. But you won't care. 'Cause you'll be sucking down your own blood, drowning in it. Makes me hard just thinking about it."

The SOB had just dropped the temp in the room by twenty degrees. Her body trembled with the chill, her back against the cement.

McBride stood, staring down at her. "See you on the other side of this door. I'm sure Father Antonio can help remove your restraints. Once you cross the threshold, the game begins. There's no going back."

His men headed for the doorway. But McBride turned once more, finding her in the gloom. "Don't keep me waiting."

"McBride," she called out. As he turned, the flashlight cast an eerie glow onto his stern face. "Riddle me this, Batman. Why did you kill Mickey Blair? That was your handiwork, wasn't it?" The cop in her ignored the danger, wanting only his confession.

He laughed, the sound echoing through the room. "You are one stubborn bitch, Mackenzie. What the hell . . . Yes. I killed that arrogant SOB Blair. Was rather proud of that job. And as for the reason? Let's just call it professional courtesy."

She tensed her jaw, not fully understanding his cryptic comeback. But she wouldn't get another crack at him.

As the door creaked closed, she and Father Antonio were thrown into darkness. Her eyes fought for any image to define the space. *Nothing.* The emptiness overwhelmed her. Raven closed her eyes, then opened them again. *Still nothing.* Her equilibrium thrown off-balance, she imagined herself floating weightless and free.

Sound was another matter. The shallow breathing of Father Antonio alerted her. But under his breath, she heard something else. The muffled sound of the priest's voice came from dead ahead. With the dank air sucking into her lungs, Raven crawled along the gritty floor. Drawing closer, she realized the man was praying.

"Father? Talk to me," she whispered.

"I'm . . . here." The priest's voice cracked with fear. "But I can't d-do this." He'd already given up.

Raven pulled and scrambled her way to a sitting position, shoulder to shoulder with her fellow captive. Despite the nip in the room, sweat trickled down her spine.

"Listen to me, Father. You keep praying to God. Lord

knows we could use his help," she urged. "But until he comes through, you gotta get this tape off me. You and I have some planning to do."

He stopped his prayer, but the man didn't move. She had to find another way to sway him. "I'm not gonna leave you, Father. You understand me?"

Silence.

Eventually, he reached for her, struggling to set her free. Unable to see his face, she had no way to read him. It would be difficult enough to get herself out of this mess. In a fight, the reluctant priest would be an albatross around her neck. But she didn't have a choice. The life of another human being was in her hands. She had to try.

Yet despite being in the company of a holy man, she vowed one thing. If this was her time to die, she'd take Logan McBride with her!

CHAPTER 16

Christian crept along the brick wall of the deserted warehouse, eyes alert. He hadn't found his SUV yet, but Bill Edwards and the GPS readings had led him to this place. And with his latest discovery, he followed a thin trail—*as thin as a wisp of smoke.*

The cleansing storm had left the air crisp in its wake, but in the dying breeze, a scent lingered. And like a predator, he followed. Although deep shadows deceived his eyes, he relied more on his other senses to guide him.

Christian had mastered the technique, the sensation arousing him. He never felt so alive as when he hunted. And his skill held another side benefit. Putting all his efforts into the chase, he forgot his fear of the dark, the weakness that defined him.

But in his war room skirmishes at the Dunhill Estate, no one died. Tonight would be different.

Up ahead, a faint red glow drew his attention, fading in and out at irregular intervals. He crouched low and breathed in the scent, listening for what he knew would follow—the crunch of gravel on asphalt, the scuff of a shoe. Cigarette smoke provided the trail, tinged by the stench imbedded in the clothes of the target. The guard had been careless.

He peered through the darkness, then allowed an inner peace to take root. Eyes closed, he slowed his heart rate to heighten his awareness, feeling the oppressive weight of the stranger displacing air with his pacing. He tasted the man's proximity with the whole of his senses.

Slowly, Christian advanced, his muscles tensed in anticipation. Soon, he'd be close enough to—

A shadow moved to his left.

He dropped to the ground on instinct, flat on his belly. The wet, cold ground seized his skin.

What the hell—? Alert to any noise, he waited. A dark silhouette prowled, unaware of his presence. He listened for the man to make his move, unsure what that might be. But he soon got his answer.

In one fluid motion, the guard was taken out, his body dropped to the ground with only his dying breath to mark his passing. The execution flawless; only the glint of a knife revealed the weapon used in the stealthy kill, caught in the pale light from the moon. The assassin melded into the shadows, as if he were never there.

Who else hunted with him? Did he have an ally or a new enemy?

So intent on his prey, he nearly missed the movement himself. A humbling experience. Now, if he wanted to make contact, how would he do it without getting himself killed? Only one way came to mind. He evaluated his options, the opportunity for cover being minimal. Yet it might work.

Christian tensed his jaw, fortifying his determination. The odds of getting inside and saving Raven worsened with the added wrinkle. He'd have to confront this new adversary. And given the man's skill, his abilities in the dark would be put to the test.

Even inside gloves, her hands felt sticky. The blood soaked through. The kill had its merits, but cleanliness was not one of them. Jasmine cleared the outside perimeter, the last of the guards dispatched without challenge. Now, she would burrow into the darkened warehouse through the passageway she'd found on an earlier scouting trip. Nicholas had released her to hunt McBride.

Relishing the thought, she smiled. Nicky always did know how to please a woman.

But as she inched her way along the wall, toward the rear of the building, she heard a faint sound. Almost undetectable.

A single beep, loud enough to spoil her plan. The sound carried on the cool night air. Unsure of its origin, she peered through the dark, searching the shadows for any sign of movement. As she neared a corner, Jasmine squared her back to the wall, cautiously moving forward. With a turn of her head, she edged close enough for a sideways glance. The space had once been some kind of storage unit. Its door hung lopsided, off one of its hinges. Adjacent to the main building, it did not give access to McBride's stronghold, so she considered it useless. Oddly enough, the noise came from within. Perhaps she'd dismissed the importance of the room too hastily after all.

She looked inside.

The place conjured up an old memory. *Broker of Death.* Nicky had called her that once. Being a death dealer, Jasmine believed it far better to give than to receive. But with the interior of the bunker completely black, it possessed all the qualities of a crypt. It felt more like an omen of her mortality, leaving her edgy. Yet with the door wide open and busted, a bluish haze cast into the space, reassuring her. She would be in and out quickly.

In the far corner, an object lay on the cement floor. It reflected a pale light onto a brick wall, partially hidden under refuse. It looked as if someone had dropped a cell phone. As she stepped within earshot, the beeping sound took on a rhythm, a steady chirp. It wasn't intimidating in the least, but its power-driven nature sent a clear message.

Someone had been there.

Crouching low, she checked her surroundings one final time. Trusting her instincts, she sensed no one and slipped closer to the object, eyes focused on the glow. She removed debris, making the light more conspicuous. *A phone?* By the time she laid her hands on it, she realized her fatal mistake. Impaired by the light, her night vision was temporarily useless.

Then she heard it.

The door of the bunker wedged shut, throwing her into total darkness, except for the dim glow of the phone's display. She shut it down, not wanting to draw attention to her location. Fortified for the kill, she moved left, relying on her senses to guide her.

The air felt thick with a presence, the sensation elusive and indefinable. *Most remarkable!*

Even the faintest sound reverberated inside the compact structure. She held her breath, not giving any advantage to her new adversary. Although cornered, she prepared to fight. Her hand reached for the gun in her thigh holster. A voice emerged from the void, deflecting off the walls.

"No need for the gun. I'm just here to talk." The man whispered, moving as he spoke, making it impossible to pinpoint his location.

Her eyes followed the sound as it rebounded off the walls. But even more disturbing—the voice sounded familiar. Normally, she prided herself on composure under fire. Yet this completely baffled her.

And how did he see her movements? Surely the darkness encumbered him in the same manner. The man moved too quietly to be laden with night-vision gear. *Very intriguing!*

She must know more.

"Why do you hide in the shadows? I am only a defenseless woman, more afraid of you than you should be of me." Using her femininity to bait the trap, she would draw him out, a practiced maneuver. She knew from experience that his ego would do the rest. But to her surprise, the man stifled a laugh, a low, sensual sound with a familiar ring of intimacy.

"Lady, you scare the hell out of me, but I'd still like to talk."

"The cell phone. Is it yours?" she asked.

"Yes. Just my way to reach out and touch someone."

As he replied, she powered up the cell and hit the function menu to find his name in the registry, allowing her body to be edged in light. But the only name on the display caused her to rethink killing him.

Dunhill Corporation. With keen interest, she searched for the man, eager for a glimpse.

"You move well." She tempted him with flattery. "Come closer so we may talk."

"As appealing as that sounds, this is not a game for me." The man changed his tone, forgoing the subterfuge of his whisper. He stepped forward, risking a show of good faith. She admired strength, a quality so few possessed.

"I have someone inside who needs my help," he admitted. "So I have one thing to say."

"This promises to be interesting." She resorted to her usual sarcasm.

But as the man drew near, curiosity won out. She took a risk of her own, powering up the cell phone to shine its light. As his face emerged from the shadows, she nearly forgot to breathe. The uncanny resemblance stunned her—the strong jawline, the full lips, and those most expressive eyes. She swallowed, hard. It took great discipline to hide her reaction. Still, there remained no doubt in her mind.

Nicholas Charboneau had a son.

Softening her voice, Jasmine encouraged him. "Please, enlighten me."

"You either help me or get out of my way. I don't have time for a debate."

His confidence fascinated her. And his underlying message held much more than an idle threat. She saw it in his eyes. A smile curved her lips. Suddenly, things had gotten much more interesting.

A woman. She wouldn't give her name. And he returned the favor, keeping his anonymity. This wasn't a social occasion.

With a watchful eye, Christian followed her to a rusted Dumpster. Behind it, she stashed her gear and knelt beside it, rummaging through the contents.

By the light of the moon, he observed the woman. Dressed in black with a Kevlar vest for added protection, she wore a thigh-holstered Glock and a knife in her belt. If Christian didn't know better, he'd swear she looked like part of a police tactical team. But something in her manner told him she wouldn't play by anyone's rules, especially on the side of law enforcement.

And what connection did she have to the men inside? He didn't have time to find out.

"I'd like my phone back."

"I do not believe it would be in my best interest to comply. You might call the authorities," she reasoned.

"With or without your cooperation, that's done. If I don't make a call saying my friend inside is safe and sound, my man has been instructed to call the cops"— he glanced at his watch, illuminating the dial with the push of a button—"in thirty minutes. But I can't wait for the cavalry, not knowing what's happening inside."

The woman quit rifling through her belongings and stiffened at the mention of police.

"I can't be a part of this if the police come. Once I see flashing red cherry, I don't care what's going on. I'm out."

"Not a part of this?" He found her eyes in the dark. "Then why are you here?"

"I have my reasons." Her voice low, she focused on her bag once again.

"Not good enough, lady." He didn't appreciate her evasive response. And time had run out. The urgency of his predicament tested his tolerance.

"You don't have a say in what I do." She narrowed her eyes in defiance. "I scouted this location, and I know another way in. It will take longer to get into position, but you will like the advantage. As I see it, you need me."

"Need you for what exactly?" He didn't wait for an answer. "I'm gonna ask you again. Why are you here?"

For a moment, he thought she would refuse to answer. But eventually, she explained. "I am only after one man. Once I have acquired my target, you are on your own. I have no interest in the woman or the little priest."

"Priest? What priest?"

Part of him wanted to understand her involvement, another part wanted to leave her behind, bound and gagged. He resisted the latter. She might prove to be useful. But who was this man she wanted to kill? He realized he made an assumption she would kill him. From what he'd seen, the woman didn't come to chat. And who the hell was this priest?

Damn it! He had to remain focused. Raven needed his help.

"They took a priest from St. Sebastian's, used him as bait to lure the pretty detective. Who knows? Maybe the men inside felt the need for confession."

Her smile lacked any real humor, no doubt spawned more from a perverse nature.

"How do you know the woman is a detective? And that the priest was abducted from St. Sebastian's?"

He remembered Bill giving him the coordinates for the church. He'd recognized the address from his frequent visits to the cemetery. But according to his security man, the SUV didn't stay long. Now, things were beginning to make sense.

"I know a lot of things." Her only reply.

"Just do what you came to do, then get out. I can take care of the rest." He knelt by her, gazing down at the canvas bag. "And I don't want any casualties from friendly fire. What kind of firepower did you bring?"

Friendly? The more he knew about this woman, the more the word "friendly" failed to apply. She wasn't the warm and fuzzy type. Far from it. He watched as she powered up a small flashlight. She held it in her teeth to free up her hands, shining the small beam into the black rucksack. To his astonishment, the light reflected onto a small arsenal.

"Flash bangs, grenades— Who the hell were you intending to fight? A small third-world country?" He touched her shoulder to get her attention. "They've got hostages. You can't use the grenades in such tight quarters."

She took the flashlight from her teeth, switching it off. "I will admit the hostages do pose a complication. Just think of my preparedness as . . . overkill. Besides, I had no intention of being a hero. I only want the one."

If Christian thought she would help, that hope crumbled into a thousand pieces. With the woman's only goal being her mission, he'd be on his own.

Detecting his reaction, she liberally dosed him with sarcasm. "Butch and Sundance. Good movie, but I work alone. Now what can you use? We're running out of time."

"I'll take the knife . . . and a flash bang." His hand retrieved what he needed, then he stood. "That's it."

Mentally preparing for the next step, he held the flash bang in his hand. More of a diversionary device used by police tactical teams, the weapon would be useful to render night vision useless for a time. A fuel-air explosive, the device ignited particles of aluminum powder through small holes in the bottom of the canister, reacting with oxygen to produce an acoustic pulse and a brilliant flash of light. Once it was activated, detonation would occur within two seconds. The device would set off a deafening explosion of blinding light, leaving anyone within range of the blast dazed and seeing stars for up to six seconds, his hearing temporarily out of commission. Perfect for what he had in mind. But he'd have to pick his spot to use it. The effects of the blast would be temporary.

Diversion. His plan centered on it. He would stall until the police arrived.

"I've got night-vision binoculars with a built-in boom mic. You sure you don't want something more high-tech?" She pocketed what she needed in her tactical vest and gazed up at him. After zipping the bag, she stood and hoisted it over her shoulder.

"That'll only slow me down." He shook his head, slipping the canister in the pocket of his coat. "In the dark, muzzle flash will blind you, so be careful. If you have to shoot, no ricochets. Make damned sure of your target. I don't want anything to happen to the hostages . . . or me."

"Your skill in the dark is truly a gift," she observed. Standing by his side, she smiled again. This time, the humor reached her eyes. "If we both get out of this alive, perhaps you can show me more."

His mind already distracted by the hunt, he ignored the sexual innuendo in her voice.

"Just show me what you got, lady. Lead the way."

"Now remember, Father, stick close to me and keep your hand on my shoulder so I know where you are. It's going to be as dark out there as it is in here. I don't want to lose you."

"I'll remember, yes." His nerves were fraying. She heard it in his voice. For his sake, she fortified her own.

"If we get separated, just find a hole and hide until I find you." Raven held the man's shoulders, giving them a firm squeeze. Unable to see his face, she relied on her hands to convey the message. "Once we get out of this room, no talking. It'll only make us a target."

"I understand, Detective." The priest's voice quivered.

She spoke with authority, more for his benefit. In reality, she knew the odds weren't good. *A sucker's bet.*

"And keep praying, Father. Silently. We're gonna need it."

The creak of the door heralded the start of the *game* for McBride. But for her and Father Antonio, it would be a fight for their lives.

Once she got into the corridor, she stopped to reconnoiter, waving a hand in front of her face. She couldn't see a thing. The staleness of the air stifled her breath. But any chance for freedom lay ahead. She had no choice but to move.

One hand along the wall, she felt for direction, then extended her other arm in front like a buffer. It would be slow going. She tried to visually recall the length of the corridor, to give it substance in her mind. Without a notion of up or down, vertigo played havoc with her senses, her equilibrium short-circuiting.

And with every step, the grip of the priest tightened. The man expected to be attacked at any time. And she couldn't argue the point. Being a sadistic bastard, McBride wouldn't play by any rules, so why not have a man stationed in the dark hallway, ready to pounce. To some degree, the priest's hand comforted her. She wasn't alone. But his grasp also served as a reminder that she held his life in her hands.

Cautious with each step, she moved forward. The grit on the wall caked her fingertips. She listened for any sound, but the priest's breathing would mask much of it. She prayed his fear wouldn't get them both killed.

Halfway. She believed half the corridor lay behind them. The real fight would soon begin.

Despite the chill, sweat trickled from her temples and trailed down her spine under her clothes. The sensation played on her nerves, feeling more like the uninvited touch of McBride's finger. His despicable sneer haunted her memory. And in the dark, that image loomed larger than she cared to admit.

As she neared the end of the corridor, she crouched low, pulling Father Antonio with her. Her mind tried to recall the layout of the place. She never got a good look. McBride said there was only one way out, but had that been a lie, too? Her gut wrenched with the weight of her decision. Once beyond the cover of the hallway, if she turned the wrong direction, she might seal their fate with the mistake. Her fingers found the edge of the wall as it crooked into the cavernous warehouse.

Time to fight or die. Her instincts would have to take charge. She didn't have the luxury of deliberating her actions. She tensed her muscles, ready to make her first move. But in that instant, her thoughts turned to Christian and his unique sensory gifts.

Slowly, she closed her eyes and trusted her inner voice—knowing that voice would be his.

Deep within the center of the labyrinth, in a spot especially made for him, Logan crouched with his night-vision headgear activated. A creak of a door warned that the hunt had begun. And from his vantage point, he would watch his prey move along the corridor, then into the maze, bodies edged in a kaleidoscope of pale greens and reds. The barricade construction only allowed his quarry to come toward him, tricking them into believing escape was possible.

But nothing could be further from the truth. Raven and the priest would be served up, warm and breathing, delivered center stage, with him as the star of the engagement. *Perfect!*

His fingers reached for the knife attached to his belt. His thumb stroked the handle, with the motion gaining momentum, matching his adrenaline rush. He loved the advantage night-vision gear gave him, but it deprived him of one very essential element of the hunt. He lived to see fear in their eyes and smell defeat oozing from the pores of their skin after they accepted their fate, giving their bodies to him. Every fiber in his being cried out for that sensation. It empowered him.

Even now, blood churned in his groin. His body hardened with his imaginings. His need to experience the intimacy of death up close compelled him to use a knife for the kill. He had no choice. It was an aspect of his nature he refused to ignore.

His thoughts fixed on Raven. The smell of her blood already teased his fertile imagination. He pictured her body writhing in death, thrashing against his grip. The flesh of his cheeks grew warm. Without the ability to control his impulse, he quit stroking his knife, a poor substitute. He shoved his hand into his pants, unable to wait for the release that only the kill delivered.

He focused on his need, his breathing urgent and shallow. Then she appeared. Raven being the smaller figure in front, she led the priest to the end of the corridor, then stopped. He would take her first, making the priest an easy target. Two kills nearly sent him over the edge. His efforts grew more frenzied until—

A motion to his right deprived him of gratification.

"Shit!" he cursed under his breath.

Someone else had joined the party—unannounced.

Who the hell came without an invitation? And how had they gained access from that location? The intrusion fueled a slow, burning rage. Reluctantly, he pulled his hand free. A sneer warped his face. Whoever it was, they'd have to wait their turn to die.

He heard the paintball rounds slamming below, his men already launching an assault. But given the location of the intruders, the pellets would do no good. The meddlers had too much of an advantage. And to complicate matters, Raven and the priest had moved into the maze, with two of his men focused on them.

Switching to predator mode, he moved out of his bunker, howling like an animal into the void, his unique signal. The eyes of his men were on him. With a motion of his right hand, he gave the signal. Time to play in earnest. Time for Plan B.

Raven heard the paint gun blasts erupting from above, the sound reverberating through the hollow cavern.

What the hell were they shooting at?

Father Antonio gripped her shoulder, giving it a tug. Adhering to her rules about not talking, the man gave her the only sign possible. He wanted to know what was happening. And so did she. To reassure him, she fumbled for his hand. The token gesture would have to do, for now.

A barrage of paintball pellets hurled to the floor, McBride's men obviously targeting a spot across the room. That meant only one thing. Someone else had joined the fray, maybe providing a diversion for her and the priest to escape. Hands out in front of her, she left the security of the wall. She crouched low and moved right with the priest in tow, away from the altercation.

Thud! Smack! Two rounds struck her in the arm and

back, splattering liquid over her face and clothes. And by the way her companion reacted, he'd been hit, too. The smell familiar, she remembered her investigation at the church and her meeting with the ME. The odor of isopropyl alcohol choked her. Its vapor stung her eyes. She wiped her face, trying to relieve the burn.

Keep moving! Don't make an easy target.

As she picked up her pace, the toe of her boot clipped something heavy. She fell to the floor, dragging Father Antonio with her. The weight of his body knocked the wind out of her. Her throat raw, she heaved to fill her lungs, taking a moment to recover.

Thwack! She shielded her head with an arm, then rolled to her knees. Inching her way forward, she crawled on all fours, feeling along the cement with Father Antonio right behind her. Eventually, she found cover against some kind of barricade. She extended her arm across the priest to protect and reassure him.

Zing! Splat! Dodging pellets, she kept her head down, shoving a shoulder into a wall of damp burlap, judging by the smell and the coarse weave. The moldy odor was tainted by the toxic vapor of the chemical.

From her investigation of the Blair murder site, she knew this point started the death maze. A cold reality hit. In his ordeal, Mickey Blair had no way out of his trap. McBride made sure of that. Why would her chances be any better? He dangled the carrot of hope, telling her a way out existed.

Raven knew now—*the bastard lied.*

Not knowing what was happening on the other side of the room, she took a chance. To find another way out, she'd have to risk exposure. Do the unexpected. And with the diversion across the room, this might be the only time to do it.

"You stay here," she whispered to the priest, her voice raspy. "But when I call, you follow my voice. I'm gonna try to crawl over the top. Give you a hand up."

She stood and drew fire. Pellets whizzed by her head and pummeled her back. She ignored the painful bruising of the attack and held her breath from the fumes. One foot wedged into a niche in the burlap sacks. She raised her hand above her head and dug into the barricade for a grip. The structure felt sturdy enough to support her weight, but situated at an odd slant, the wall made it difficult to hoist herself up.

Finally, she took a step up, clinging to the burlap. Her arm wedged into it. But as she reached to pull herself over, her hand recoiled in pain.

"Aarrrggh!"

A chill shot across her skin. In her shock, stars spiraled through the darkness, assaulting her eyes. Something sharp had pierced her hand, shredding flesh as she slid away. Blood drained warm down her arm, the cuts deep.

Thud! Another round struck the back of her neck, dousing her. She fell to the cement floor, hard. Her hand stung as the alcohol mixed with blood, the wound swollen and throbbing.

"Damn it!" She groaned, tucking her hand against her waist, applying pressure to the cut with her other arm. "Oh. God. Won't do that again."

"What happened?" The priest knelt by her side.

"Nails, glass, something up top. It'll cut us to pieces if we try to scramble over."

"Are you hurt?"

"Not much, Father," she lied. "Come on. We gotta move." She gestured for the priest to follow.

Now, no other choice remained. She had to pool her

resources with whoever else was involved in the fight. By sheer numbers, they might muscle their way through the labyrinth. But she knew the risk. In the heat of battle, would the other target of McBride's men allow her to get close enough to explain—or would they kill her on the spot as the enemy?

In her mind, there was only one way to find out.

Another pellet whizzed by Christian's head as he ducked against a small barricade. Without having a clear shot, the men above had curtailed their steady barrage, for now. He and his strange companion had already taken out two men. They lay unconscious at their feet. He felt the obstacle of their body mass, even in the dark.

"The advantage I spoke of earlier?" The mysterious Asian woman whispered and tugged at his sleeve, pulling him toward a more massive obstruction. She placed his hand onto it. "We are on the back side of the barricade. We shall have full access to the scaffolding above . . . and to his men." With another gesture, she indicated the stairway to the left. "I will take the other side. Do not keep track of me; I will stay clear of you."

She drew a hand to his cheek. He hadn't expected it. Never saw it coming. Christian flinched at her familiarity. Apparently, his reticence amused her.

"May we both live to fight another day." After a soft chuckle, she added, "And I do hope we meet again. I believe you will find we have much more in common."

What the hell did that mean? The woman had a fondness for being cryptic. Christian said nothing in return. He suspected sentimentality would appear trite to this woman. She left his side to hunt on her own. He preferred it that way, too.

From the sound of it, she drew fire. The pellets pummeled the floor to his left. But soon after, he became a target again, hearing the chemical-loaded ammo zip by his head. He evaded much of it. But the alcohol vapors grew stronger, screwing with his sense of smell. Much more of this, and he wouldn't be able to trust his perceptions.

From their sniper positions above, the men could hold out for a long time, bombarding pellets from their aerial perches. As the woman advised, he would take his fight to them, eliminating them one at a time. Closing his eyes, he listened for a consistent blast from above and a soft creak in the metal grating, acquiring his next target. Imagining the staircase configuration, he would move to where he believed steps to be. But first, he prepared himself.

Deep breath. Shutting his eyes, he found his center and searched for his quiet inner voice. *Now let it go . . . slow.* The familiar mantra calmed him. His heart slowed.

Just like the war room, he reminded himself. It helped to believe that. Then a new image replaced the old and familiar.

Raven Mackenzie. Ever since he'd met her, she'd never strayed far from his heart. Now would be no different.

Scanning through her night-vision binoculars, Jasmine located her targets, eavesdropping on their candid whispers with a boom mic. Two men stood near the railing of the catwalk, their paintball guns aimed below, carrying handguns in thigh holsters. No doubt smug with their lofty advantage, they didn't hear her come up behind them. These men were isolated from the rest. Easy pickings.

Jasmine reached into her vest pocket and withdrew

the flash bang canister. She formulated her attack and visualized every detail in preparation. She would have only seconds to take them out before they reached for their guns.

She initiated the canister and tossed it at the first man's feet, then ducked for cover. She kept her eyes on the target until the very last second. It bounced twice, clacking to a stop inches from the man. By design, the sound drew the attention of both men.

One second. She covered her ears and hunched against a nearby wall, waiting for the blast. *Two seconds.*

BOOM! Blinding white light seared the dark. A glowing ball of fire radiated like a shock wave in all directions, followed by a billowing stench. Being in closer proximity to the detonation, the men were shoved to the walkway with its thunderous force. The blast resonated along the walkway, making the steel hum in vibration.

She knew from experience that the fierce image would leave its imprint on the eyes of the men. The white light would hang suspended in darkness, then splinter into spangles, blurring the vision of anyone looking directly at it. In a daze, the men would have minimal hearing, registering only muffled sounds. She had only seconds to gain advantage.

Jasmine leapt from cover and grabbed the collar of the first man as he sprawled on his back, yanking him off the scaffold. In a practiced maneuver, she thrust the knife across his throat, severing cartilage. Warm blood doused her clothing. The sound of it pattered her vest like rain. The man screamed, but the sound warped into a moist gurgle.

Then silence.

The second man rolled to one side, reaching for her. Jasmine sprang to her feet and kicked his elbow, hyperextending it. She heard it crack with the force of her foot. As he writhed in pain, she rolled him onto his belly. Yanking a clump of hair, she flexed his head back to expose his neck. Within seconds, it was over.

Two down.

Jasmine tore off the headgear of the dead men, shining a dim light onto slack faces. McBride was not among them. She cleaned off the blade of her knife, wiping it across the chest of one of the dead men. A commotion caused her to look up. She heard the rumble along the scaffolding. Others were coming. Jasmine scrambled for cover down the grated steps, wedging her small frame inside a crate she had modified at the base of the stairs behind the stockade. Even if Logan's men strafed her location with night vision, she would appear invisible. As long as the room lay in darkness, she would snipe their positions without detection. It was a good plan. But what of Nicky's son?

No! She had only one target, and taking on someone else's fight could get her killed. Besides, the police would soon overrun the place. This was not her fight.

The police. She grimaced at the thought of their intrusion. She needed a shortcut to ID McBride.

Jasmine reached for her binoculars and stuck the earpiece to the microphone into her ear. Rising from her hiding place, she scanned the remaining men. Across the floor of the warehouse, within the confines of the stockade, one man stood out from the rest. He directed the others with sweeping gestures rather than verbal commands. It had to be McBride.

Then she heard the roar of another flash bang from above. Its piercing light cast elongated shadows on the brick walls for an instant, then it was gone. Taken off guard by the explosion, she felt a jolt of pain slice through her brain as the bright light blinded her. But the echo of the blast lingered long after the light faded, resounding off the brick walls.

When her vision cleared, she swept her binoculars across the room and into the rafters, looking for her comrade in arms. Curiosity or concern? She made no distinction. Locating her target, she marveled at his sensory skill . . . then smiled.

Jasmine loved a man who understood the finesse of a kill.

But soon, her attention shifted back to McBride. He moved out from cover. And so did she. Yet from the direction Logan headed, Nicky's son would not be pleased.

Christian plugged his ears against the blast, tightly closing his eyes to retain his night vision. The metal scaffolding vibrated under his boots. After the smoke blew past him, its smell dissipated in the chilly air. He listened for any sound of the men taken out by the detonation.

A moan. The rustle of fabric. A hand gripped the tail of his coat. He had to move quickly.

The sound of heavy breathing drew him in, giving him a target nearly waist-high. He reached for the man's collar and tugged him forward, ripping the night-vision gear from his head. Disoriented, the mercenary swayed as he tried to stand. Christian balled his fist and punched, connecting with the man's jaw. He felt it give way on the second blow, then finished with an uppercut. As his target lost consciousness, he released his grip and let the body tumble to the grating in a heap.

But too much time had elapsed. The disorienting effects of the flash bang had worn off.

A second man grabbed his shoulder and spun him around. A fist buried deep into his ribs, lifted him from the catwalk. Another blow nearly took his head off. He stumbled back, shaking his head to clear the fog. It didn't take long for him to recover.

Both fists up in defense, Christian lowered his chin and launched his attack, pummeling the man with combination punches to the body. He stepped toward the aggressor, beating him senseless. His opponent teetered back on his heels. Focusing his intensity, he spun to his right, ramming a kick to the man's gut. The mercenary fell against the metal railing, the air forced from his lungs. But to his surprise, the man remained standing.

No time for fair play. Without mercy, Christian lowered his center of gravity and hoisted the man up, shoving him across the railing.

Christian suspected the hurdle would do damage, but little else. The top of the barricade below would break his fall. His objective had always been Raven's safety, not to kill. But when the body dropped to the burlap barrier, he heard a bloodcurdling scream. The pitiable cry echoed through the emptiness until the body toppled to the cement floor with a heavy thud. Then utter stillness.

What the hell happened? Why did he scream like he was being ripped in two? Christian dropped to a knee, peering through the darkness as if sight were possible. He sensed death below, smelled the blood. And another thought gripped his heart.

Raven was in greater danger. He just knew it.

She had no idea what was going on.

A battle raged above. Without knowing the players, Raven avoided the crossfire. Seeking shelter for her and

Father Antonio, she hunkered next to a stockade wall. She recognized the flash bang detonations from her training with tactical.

Even through all the chaos, a tinge of hope survived. The men of Logan McBride were falling one at a time. It *had* to be good news.

Father Antonio gripped her hand, his palms damp. An occasional whisper escaped his lips, but despite her rules about not talking, she let him be. His prayers were welcome.

Raven cursed the never-ending emptiness. She closed her eyes, resting her head against the barricade. Her thoughts turned to the rhythm of the priest's prayers, finding comfort in the act. And she joined him, a tear of acceptance rolling down her cheek.

But the quiet didn't last.

A faint scratching to her right. The sound gripped her, conjuring a revolting image in her mind.

A frenzied screech. The irregular patter of small feet scurried toward her. With all the commotion, the rat population had been disturbed. She heard it coming. More than one hairy rodent headed by her. Raven gasped, unable to avoid a reaction. Not wanting to make a sound, she closed her eyes tight. She hugged her arms around herself and drew her knees to her chest.

"Holy mother of—" Apparently, Father Antonio had no great fondness for God's lowly creature. Slowly, Raven forced herself to move, raising a hand to the lips of the priest to silently warn him to be quiet.

Repulsed by the filthy vermin, Raven trembled. Beads of sweat layered her body and dampened her clothes, a contradiction to the chill in the air. Her stomach wrenched with nausea. A rat bumped her hip. The nails of its feet scraped her pant leg as it started to climb.

Her skin prickled, an unforgettable chill. She jabbed an elbow and shoved the damned thing, its weight branding her memory.

But as the creature slithered away, she instinctively turned the other way. A new presence fueled her panic, looming overhead. And without the benefit of her eyesight, fear overwhelmed her. She scooted against the wall. Her arm clutched Father Antonio.

Someone stood above them. She felt it.

Gritting her teeth, she steadied herself for a fight. She pictured Logan McBride—gray dead eyes. The feel of his fingernail skimmed the surface of her skin, sending the chill of revulsion down her spine.

She'd been in the dark far too long. The deprivation and the strain played tricks on her mind. Cruel images jutted from memory like a drug-induced hallucination, a torturous strobe effect. Gruesome images of past murder cases flickered before her. The glazed eyes of the dead hurled out of the shadows until—

Mickey Blair's death grimace.

In her mind, she pictured him still hanging on the cross. His head slanted in grisly detail, exposing a gash so deep it nearly severed his head. The image spawned a waking nightmare. The dead man's face warped into her own reflection, her throat slashed. The smell of blood threatened to smother her. Dazed and numb, she blocked out the horror until a hand grabbed her, hoisting her up by the hair. Her scalp throbbed in pain. From the sound of it, Father Antonio fought alongside her.

In shock, she cried out. "Damn it! Let go."

Even with the blackness around her, she knew who held her firm, yanking her up with little effort. Only one man possessed hatred that ran so deep.

"In the end, I promised it would be you and me, sweet meat." His raspy whisper taunted her. "I told you my voice would be the last thing you hear. I just hope your daddy is watching."

The man yanked her to his chest. His stench filled her nostrils. She knew it was only a matter of time. Who would investigate her murder—stare into her glazed eyes? Despite the hopelessness of her situation, Raven would not give in to death. She pitched and rocked her body, straining to free her arms.

Then the weight of cold steel pressed against her temple—killing any hope for escape. She would die at the hand of Logan McBride. It had come to this.

CHAPTER 17

Once again, McBride had her bound and gagged with duct tape. She and the priest were hauled to the center of the maze by two of his men. Their deaths would be made a spectacle. She wanted to scream at the injustice.

But why had they restrained her again? Raven thought back to the Blair case. The man had no evidence of tape on his body. This didn't make sense.

She heard McBride's voice through the dark, a fleeting sound, giving instructions to his two mercenaries. ". . . stay hidden . . . gonna draw him out."

She could make out only fragments of his words. She tried to eavesdrop on the huddled men, their voices too low to hear. Then his demented disciples scurried off into the darkest crevices, like roaches running for cover. But from the sounds of it, his men didn't stray far. Whatever was about to happen would take place center stage.

It was obvious. A trap had been set.

With the men gone, Logan knelt by her side, pulling up the night-vision gear to rest on his forehead. The intimacy of his cruel whisper sent a shiver across her skin.

"Let's put out a little cheese for our rat, give him the proper motivation."

Whom were they going to ambush? Raven didn't like the sound of this conspiracy. She held her breath, gathering courage for what would follow. Suddenly, a beam of light flickered into her eyes, blinding her. After she'd been in the dark for so long, the brightness shot through her brain like needles. She squinted and turned to shield her eyes. McBride yanked her head back and held his gun to her temple. The loudness of his voice took her by surprise.

"You wanted to play. I got a game for you," he shouted into the void. His insanity pierced her eardrums. "Show yourself. Or I splatter gray matter dead center. Your choice."

Whom was he talking to? Raven wondered. The man had finally lost it. With a sideways glance, she shot a questioning look to the priest. Father Antonio stared into the darkness, his eyes a mix of fear and hope. She followed his lead, searching the gloom.

One voice broke the stalemate. A man lingered beyond the narrow circle of light. McBride strafed the emptiness with his flashlight.

"Let her and the priest go and I'll stay. Just you and me."

The breath caught in her throat. She swallowed hard. It was Christian.

How did he—? It didn't matter. The sound of his voice filled her with expectation for only an instant. Then reality hit. Christian would walk into McBride's trap, putting himself at risk. And she could do nothing to stop it. Now they'd all die together.

She couldn't contain her raw emotion. Raven screamed through the gag, shaking her head, trying to warn him.

Logan laughed at her feeble attempt, an insulting cackle. "You got nothing to bargain with, my friend. I'm holding a royal flush, ace high. All you got is a pair of twos." Logan set his flashlight onto a burlap sack, shining the beam into the shadows. He jerked her head back hard. Sweat trailed down her cheek as he jammed the gun under her chin. "Come out so I can see you. No weapons, hands up."

Slowly, Christian stood, squinting into the light with his hands raised. He carefully shrugged out of his coat, then held out his knife in surrender.

"Toss the knife over the wall. Then turn around, real slow."

The knife clattered on the cement floor outside the labyrinth wall. And with a slow turn, to show he carried no other weapons, Christian kept his eyes on McBride. Yet as he stepped closer, Raven detected something else—a fierce determination. She'd seen it the first day they met when he surfaced from the war room.

The predator had emerged.

Given McBride's ego, she suspected the man believed he had everything under control. And she conceded the odds were stacked in his favor. But Raven wouldn't count Delacorte out. If she were a betting girl, her money would be on Christian.

And she hoped Logan McBride would soon find out why.

The Asian woman was nowhere in sight. He expected as much. She'd never take on his fight. Still, he could have used her help.

The meager glow of the flashlight left much of the warehouse in shadow, but it was enough to bring his plan to a screeching halt. As he stepped into the light, he knew one thing. He'd lost his edge. And now he had no weapon. Yet his eyes remained focused on the man holding Raven. Her life would depend upon his instincts—and his ability to manipulate a sociopath.

"What's your name?" Christian kept his hands raised, his tone even. "I gotta know who would wage war on a priest."

The smug look on the man's face faded, twisting into something more sinister. "Logan McBride. And while we're on the subject, care to share?"

"Delacorte, Christian Delacorte."

"Ahhh. Seek the truth, Christian." The man laughed. "So we finally meet. Blue Blood will be ticked off when he finds out what I'm gonna do to you."

"Don't know a man named Blue Blood, but maybe I can help you with your dilemma." His voice low, threatening. "Dead men don't have to answer to anyone."

"You're a cocky son of a bitch." The stare of McBride wavered, his irritation showing. "I see you don't carry a gun."

"The bigger the gun, the smaller the— Well, you know the old saying." A lazy smile spread across Christian's face. His gaze drifted to the Glock in McBride's thigh holster. "Let's just say I have nothing to prove."

Silence.

Christian knew the man would have something to prove to the men standing in the rafters. He taunted him with his insolence, daring the man to take up his challenge. McBride would figure that only one alpha male would leave the maze. All he had to do was stall long enough for the police to arrive. Whether he had to kill or not, Christian was determined—Raven would make it out alive.

He knew McBride had had enough. The man glared; his jaw tightened. His hands clutched Raven's hair. Her eyes filled with pain.

It hurt Christian to see her suffer. Yet he kept his face unreadable, for her sake. Maybe he went too far with the taunts, but McBride would smell weakness and take it out on her. So he decided to push it even further by using the man's ego as a weapon against him, redirecting his hostility.

He lowered his hands and crossed his arms over his chest in open defiance, mirroring the mercenary's arrogant expression. By the look in his eye, McBride couldn't resist the pissing match.

"You look like a guy who enjoys dangerous games. How about we play one?" A menacing sneer twisted McBride's face. "Just you and me."

"And you look like a coward, the kind of guy who'd prefer to tip the odds in his favor. Your men won't interfere?"

"Not if I give the order." Turning his head, he yelled over his shoulder. "You men on the catwalk, stay put. That's an order." He shrugged, then lowered his voice. "Good enough?"

Christian didn't answer.

As McBride reached for his flashlight, he slid his night-vision gear back in place. "And since you like the dark so much, let's make things more interesting. Lights out."

Christian caught a motion to his left. Raven shook her head, screaming under the gag. Her eyes brimming with terror.

The last thing he saw before the lights went out.

*   *   *

The darkness came. And with it, Christian felt serenity for only an instant, anonymity a welcome change.

"You're mine now." A raspy voice jabbed his awareness like a sucker punch.

"You talk too damned much," he taunted, and braced for the man's rage. "And bring on your dogs, coward. I prefer a challenge."

McBride's anger might force a blunder, giving him an edge. It was a theory. For Raven's sake, he hoped the gamble would pay off.

By the sounds, three men surrounded him. He crouched, hands held waist-high, ready to move. Slowing his breathing, he shut his eyes, his weight poised on the balls of his feet. His muscles grew taut, ready for the first attack. He didn't have long to wait.

A hand grabbed his right elbow, slinging him into the barricade. The sandbags felt rock-hard. It knocked the wind from his lungs. The coarse burlap scraped his chin. A fist punished his back, battering a kidney. Wedged against the stockade, he couldn't move. His arm wrenched by a firm grasp from his first attacker, his shoulder nearly yanked from its socket.

The abuse continued.

"Is this the kind of challenge you wanted, smart ass?" the man whispered at his back.

But a familiar sound drew his attention, catching the breath deep in his throat. A knife unsheathed, slipping from leather. The lethal whisper of a blade.

He listened, trusting his instincts. Shoving hard off the wall, he hurled his body into two men. Full force, he rammed his boot into a knee. The crack echoed through the dark, followed by a tortured scream. A man fell hard to the floor. The sound of a low, guttural moan lingered after he crawled deeper into the maze.

Christian launched into the man to his left. Ripping off the man's night-vision gear, he pitched it over the wall. His fist connected with the mercenary's face, knocking him off-balance. Blow after blow, he punished the man's ribs until he doubled over, recoiling from the abuse. Gripping the man's tactical vest at the shoulders, Christian thrust him hard into the barricade. He collapsed to the cement in a heap, unable to get up.

But while he focused on the second man, he had lost McBride. With all the sounds of men overhead and the mix of scents in the air, his sensory radar betrayed him. He strained to hear the sound of breathing. Where was McBride? Raising his chin, he sniffed the air. *Still nothing.*

As Christian turned, he felt the knife. A gasp burst from his lips, the thrust stealing his breath.

He felt searing heat from the blade as it punctured his belly. His eyes watered with the agony. McBride held him close, stepping in for the kill. The man twisted the blade upward, his breath warm on Christian's face.

"Arrgghhh," Christian cried out. "Oh, God."

Even through intense pain, he heard Raven's muffled cry, thankful she couldn't see. A bead of sweat trickled down Christian's cheek. It stung his eye as it mingled with a tear.

"That's gotta hurt." McBride wedged an elbow into his throat, propping him against the wall. The man pulled out the knife, forcing another choked gasp from his lips.

"You're mine." The whisper mocked him. "Don't fight me."

Christian smelled the sickening sweet odor of his own blood. His legs grew numb. Only the weight of McBride held him in place. The chill of shock skittered across his shoulders as he sucked air into his lungs. His belly churned hot, slick with blood. He shoved against the man, trying to fight free. But his arms felt heavy and sluggish. Blood loss had taken its toll.

All he could think about was Raven.

"Shhh. Just let go. I'll make sure—" McBride never finished. The words hung in his throat.

The mercenary howled, a long, wailing cry, then dropped to the floor. The haunted cry echoed, its sound pulsing through the emptiness. A low murmur of voices, too far away to hear.

Without McBride to hold him up, Christian slid to the cement, his body deadened. Taunting his senses, he heard the lethal efficiency of a knife thrusting into flesh again and again. He fought for consciousness.

What the hell was happening?

So focused on the kill, the man never saw it coming. And Jasmine took her time, indulging in the moment.

She only wished she'd entered the maze sooner, to save Nicky's son from getting stabbed. Not knowing how bad the wound was, she took it out on McBride.

The man held her comrade in arms, pinning him to the barricade with a meaty forearm. She crept up behind him, knife poised. The bastard held an advantage with his height and bulk, but Jasmine knew how to remedy that.

With a thrusting jab and a powerful slice across, she tore into his hamstring muscles, crippling him. McBride dropped like a rock, shrieking in pain. His terror fueled her with adrenaline. As he rolled onto his back, she kicked the knife from his grip, hearing it clatter across the floor.

With conviction, she rammed a knee into his chest, clutching a fistful of his hair. The man quieted long enough for her to speak.

"Blue Blood sends his regards."

"Go to hell, bitch!"

"You first."

She slid the knife across his throat, bearing her weight into it. A warm spray baptized her, sticky sweet. The man's body rocked under the pressure, then surrendered to the blade. She committed every detail to memory.

Nicky would want to hear it all.

A stillness bathed the empty space. Even Raven had stopped thrashing. Christian felt death heavy in the stale air. Then a presence knelt by his side. Soft fingers touched his cheek. A woman's voice whispered.

"You better not die on me. At least, not until we've been formally introduced."

In spite of the pain, a smile shaped his lips. "My name is—"

The beautiful Asian woman touched a finger to his lips. "Save your strength. I am a patient woman who loves a good mystery. I will find you, when the time is right."

Her hand traveled down his chest, trailing to his wound. The metallic tang of blood lingered in the air.

"Hold this in place. Help is on the way." She braced a cloth to his belly, applying pressure to stanch the bleeding. The muffled sound of police sirens filtered through the haze. The cavalry had arrived.

He closed his eyes in relief, comforted by her gentle ministrations and soft voice. Then, she surprised him. Her lips touched his, stifling his gasp at the intimacy. He resisted, but she held firm, ignoring his objection.

When she released him, he asked, "Why did you—?"

"I possess the soul of an ancient warrior and the skill of a thief. I take what I want." She chuckled, a soft, feminine sound. "I had better leave before your woman discovers me."

His woman. He liked the sound of that. The dark eyes of Raven filtered through the shadows, warming him with her light.

"Not to mention the army of blue outside. The law and I do not always see eye to eye." She fumbled for his hand, placing it on top of the cloth to replace her own.

"I can't imagine why." Even in his condition, he felt obliged to dole out the sarcasm. "You intervened, saved Raven and the priest. I owe you."

From a distance away, her voice found his ear. She had started her prudent retreat.

"And I will not forget that, my love. There may come a time when I collect on that promise, if you survive."

A high-pitched ringing filled his ears, muffling the sound of her voice. As he slumped against the stockade wall, his heartbeat slowed, faintly thrumming in his head. With the blood loss, his sensory skills faltered to nothing. He never heard his mystery woman leave.

The police tactical unit rammed the side door. Flashlights strobed the shadows. A dim haze flickered over the stockade wall like a surreal hallucination, the twilight end to a nightmare. The flurry of activity slowed to a crawl before his eyes.

Still, Christian caught sight of Raven, tears shimmering on her skin. Or had he imagined her beautiful face? He pictured her dark eyes reflecting the luster from a single candle. Then darkness edged her radiant face, despite his attempt to stop it. Without the strength to pressure his wound, he felt his arm grow numb. His hand collapsed to the floor.

He struggled to keep watch over Raven, but failed in the effort. His head too heavy to hold up any longer, he lowered his chin to his chest. With his release, pain ebbed from his body, fading with the rhythm of his shallow breaths.

Finally, blackness won.

CHAPTER 18

For an instant, her gaze focused on the light up ahead. Emergency crews hustled to treat the wounded and haul off the dead, their faces bleak with the daunting task. And her fellow officers were busy rounding up the rest of McBride's men. The warehouse parking lot was a lesson in controlled chaos.

Raven emerged from the darkened belly of the old warehouse, her body racked with pain. Drawing in a deep breath, she remembered how she'd felt just hours before, convinced she'd never make it back from Logan's hell.

But Christian hadn't been so lucky.

She squinted into the floodlights, holding up her bloodied hand to shield her eyes. With the other, she held Christian, his cold, lifeless fingers clutched in hers. She only hoped he would know she was with him.

Strapped to a gurney, he wavered in and out of consciousness as the EMTs transported him to the ambulance. A plastic oxygen mask covered part of his face. Under the spiraling emergency beacons, his skin blanched in the light. A sickly pallor radiated over his skin, spreading like a disease.

Seeing him like this, Raven felt a slow panic grip her heart.

"Don't leave me, Christian. Not now," she whispered for his ears alone, squeezing his hand. As they neared the ambulance, his eyelids opened. The technicians loaded the gurney. Christian's gaze followed her as she stepped into the vehicle and knelt by his side.

"Are you a-all right?" His voice weak and muffled under the plastic mask, he swallowed hard. "He didn't—"

It pained her to see him striving to be heard through the breathing apparatus.

"Can I?" She gestured to one of the EMTs, asking if she could remove his mask.

"Just for a minute. Then I'm gonna need some room to recheck his vitals once we get under way." The man pulled back the blanket covering Christian's bare chest, monitoring his breathing through a stethoscope. He spoke into a radio clamped to his shoulder. "Lungs still clear. Will draw some blood for type and cross match. We're heading home."

The engine to the emergency vehicle rumbled. As they pulled away from the warehouse parking lot, the sirens wailed. The motion of the vehicle jostled Christian. She bent over him, lifting the breathing device. She felt the warmth of his breath on her skin.

"I'm fine. Thanks to you." She touched a finger to his cheek, tears welling in her eyes. "You risked everything . . . for me."

"Seemed like a good idea at the time." Hurt colored his eyes. "How's the priest?"

"Father Antonio is okay, just really shaken. While they were stabilizing you, they took him to the hospital to get checked out. I just wish this never—" She choked on her regret.

"This was all McBride. Don't take responsibility for what that sick bastard—"

He coughed; pain surged across his eyes. "Oh, God," he gasped.

"Christian . . . I can't lose you. Please—" A sob lodged in her throat.

"Don't worry. I'm pr-pretty st-stubborn. And you owe me . . . dinner, remember?"

Every word was a struggle, his weakness more pronounced. But even with pain etched on his face, she saw through his attempt at humor, for her benefit. And she loved him all the more for it.

"How could I forget?" Her fingertips longed for the feel of his skin. She gently pressed her lips to his, caressing his face with a hand. Then she gazed into his eyes, laying a palm to his chest to feel the soft, steady beat of his heart. "I love you, Christian."

"What t-took you so long? You had me . . . when you ordered m-me to assume the position." He grimaced, his eyelids drooping. "Spread 'em, scumbag."

She pressed a knuckle to her lips, suppressing nervous laughter.

"I never called you that." She shrugged. "I thought it, maybe—"

She wanted to keep him talking, fearing she might not hear his voice again. Every moment with Christian felt precious—a gift.

"Raven?" He squeezed her hand, straining to stay alert. But he was fading fast.

"I'm here, Christian." She touched his cheek. "I'm not going anywhere."

He stared blankly ahead, as if he couldn't see her.

"Want you to know, if s-something should h-happen. I'd do it again. No regrets. I love—" Slowly, his eyes fluttered closed, his head leaned to one side.

Raven held her breath, letting his sweet words wash over her like a cleansing rain. She ran a finger across his lips, then repositioned the oxygen mask.

With Christian passed out, she turned to the grim-faced ambulance attendant, trying to hide her fear. "What's our ETA?"

LAKEFRONT MEMORIAL
DOWNTOWN CHICAGO

Raven paced the waiting room, bleary-eyed with the late hour. The surgery was taking longer than expected. Christian had been out of her sight more than four hours with no word on his condition. As ominous as that sounded, at least he was still alive. In her mind, no news was good news. Yet for her, time became a boundless chasm, one without a beginning or an end. Images came and went, her perception clouded by a suffocating fear.

Would she ever see Christian again?

Her thoughts turned to Fiona. In the ER, a nurse took what little patient history she knew of him, then asked a very simple question. "Is there anyone we can call? Now would be a good time to contact next of kin."

Closing her eyes briefly, Raven filled her lungs to garner strength. "No. He has no one—not anymore."

The nurse left after a curt nod, the door hissing as it closed behind her. Now, the empty waiting room echoed Fiona's betrayal. Alone to endure the vigil,

Raven slumped into a chair. She had no idea how to contact the woman. Did Fiona love her son enough to come forward, risking possible arrest for the murder of her husband? Her involvement in the death of Charles Dunhill might never be discovered, but Raven vowed to uncover the truth, especially if Christian—

She pushed the thought from her brain.

Her mind waged war against the thought of living her future without him. *Hell! Who was she kidding?* Her life began the day they first met. He awakened something in her, something she had never felt before. As she leaned her head back against the wall, tears filled her eyes. She gazed up at the clock as it squandered precious minutes, struggling to keep her eyes open. Shutting them only reminded her of the ordeal she'd barely survived.

A motion to her right caught her attention. The waiting room door opened. As Raven turned, a friendly face greeted her.

"How is he, Detective?"

"Father Antonio, please sit." She laid her bandaged hand on the chair next to her, forcing a weary smile. "He's still in surgery. Are you okay?"

"Yes, thanks to Mr. Delacorte. I owe him my life."

"Yes. I just hope—" She closed her eyes, demanding her brain to focus on the positive. He was still alive, still in surgery.

"God does work in mysterious ways." The priest reached for her uninjured hand, tugging at it affectionately.

"Yes, I've heard that said a lot lately." She smiled.

"I know it's a cliché, but so true. God had brought your friend to my door on many occasions. I used to be afraid, perhaps intimidated by your Mr. Delacorte.

Something in his eyes scared me, like death found
refuge in him. But after what he did for us both, I can
no longer believe that. I owe him everything. I just hope
I get a chance to tell him how I feel."

"He knows, Father."

"No, you don't understand, most likely because I'm
rambling." The priest glanced down at her hand as he
held it, closing his eyes for a moment. He took another
breath, then spoke softly. "In that room, in the dark,
when I was by myself—I could do nothing but think.
And I have to admit, I wasn't ready to die. I have never
been so scared."

He looked up and found her eyes. "But when you
came, I found the courage to hope. You could have left
me behind, but you didn't. I will always be grateful to
you for that."

"Father, you don't have to—"

Father Antonio raised his hand to stop her. "Please
let me finish. I need to say this, to fully grasp it myself."
With a blank stare, he gathered his thoughts. "When
your friend offered his life in place of ours, I have never
seen such sacrifice—except in the Bible, of course. It
gave me courage to face my own fear. In that moment,
I felt a deeper connection to Christ. And I wasn't afraid
anymore. I was ready to die."

Raven understood the man's epiphany, and she had
one of her own. "And when I saw what Christian had
been willing to sacrifice, it had the opposite effect on
me. I just wanted to live." She patted the back of his
hand and crooked her lips in a smile. "I love him so
much, Father."

An odd sensation came over her. Just a short time ago,
Christian had been a complete stranger. Yet now, she
felt like she'd known him for a lifetime. He had risked

everything to save her. Raven knew all she needed to know about the man she loved beyond all reason.

The priest's voice drew her back. "I think after all we've been through together, you can call me Antonio." A shy grin warmed his face.

"And you can call me Raven. I hope this is the start of a beautiful friendship, Antonio."

"With such an auspicious beginning, how can it not?" His smile was fleeting. "Do you mind if I pray for your friend?"

His simple request took a moment to sink in. Tears brimmed in her eyes as she nodded. She had no words for how she felt. Praying for Christian felt more like last rites. The finality of it scared her. Yet having Antonio by her side gave comfort all the same, a strange contradiction.

Raven watched the priest mouth the words. The meaning clouded her mind. His familiar mantra soothed her, but an unsettling feeling of dread lurked beneath the surface of his kindness. A tear lost its grip and dropped to her cheek.

She closed her eyes to shake the feeling, but a noise drew her attention. Raven turned her head toward the sound. As if in slow motion, the waiting room door opened once more. A man dressed in faded green stepped into the room.

Raven swallowed hard. Expectation took its toll. Her heart punished her eardrums. A rapid incessant beat. She gazed upon the doleful expression of a surgeon, his eyes depleted and unreadable.

"Oh, please—*NO*," she cried, her voice drained of faith. She gripped the hand of the priest. "Antonio, I can't do this. I just can't—"

Chapter 19

Raven pulled the coat tighter around her neck as she walked, fending off the lingering chill in the morning air. The ground gave way with each step, still saturated from the runoff of melting snow. As blades of brown grass poked through, she noticed they were infused with tender green sprouts, a hint of the coming spring. She pushed open the wrought-iron gate that encircled the cemetery at St. Sebastian's. It creaked in protest and clanged when she shoved it closed behind her.

This early on a Sunday morning, the cemetery was empty except for a tall, dark-haired man and a petite woman wearing a black hat, a veil covering her face. Dressed in long, dark coats, they stood with heads bowed, their backs to her. The image of grief left a memorable impression. She lowered her head, her gaze focused.

In reverence, she neared the headstone marked *Delacorte*, then crouched in front of his. Raven ran a gloved finger along each letter, giving thanks to the man for his selfless act of courage. He had changed her life and touched so many others. Looking at the date on the marker, she commemorated his birthday with a dozen long-stemmed white roses, removing one for herself. As she stood, the fragrance of a single white rose filled her nostrils. Its velvety softness touched the tip of her nose.

But she hadn't been the first to pay respects. A colorful batch of fresh flowers had already been placed on the grave, along with a new doll, replacing a worn, tattered one. The tiny cloth toy looked so lost in this place of death, a sad reminder of Christian's tragedy. It broke her heart.

Closing her eyes, she lowered her head to say a prayer.

"I'm glad you could make it." His rich baritone brought a smile to her lips. Before she turned, Raven drank in the familiar honey of his voice, committing the sound to memory. "It means a lot to me that you're here, Raven."

Christian stepped closer, pulling her into his embrace. His hand cradled the back of her head as he nuzzled her neck, the tip of his nose cold to the touch.

"Thanks for celebrating my father's birthday with me."

"I wouldn't miss it, honey," she whispered into his ear, then kissed his cheek. "If it weren't for your father's courage and sacrifice, I wouldn't have you."

Releasing her, he gazed into her eyes as if he were absorbing every detail of her face. No words were necessary. He trailed a finger down her cheek, then brushed back a strand of hair. For her, the chill in the air disappeared and the cemetery faded into nothingness. Only her connection to Christian lingered. She had come close to losing him. Raven had so much to be thankful for.

"The chief officially made me close the Blair case."

"Well, you said yourself, McBride confessed to killing Mick."

"Yeah, but my gut is in a knot over this one. Logan was more connected to my father than to anything dealing with your past. It just doesn't make any sense. Something feels—wrong. And when I asked the reason why he killed Blair, McBride said *professional courtesy*. What's that all about?"

"The man enjoyed his head games. Maybe that's all it was. I mean, he and Mickey were both hired guns, right? Maybe it was a case of doing away with the competition."

"But why tie this to you, and to Fiona?"

"Yeah, that's been bugging me too. And McBride mentioned the name Blue Blood, like I would know the reference. I'd never heard it before that day." He narrowed his eyes in thought, then heaved a sigh. "*Seek the truth, Christian.* Guess the truth doesn't always set you free."

"And that's another thing. The phrase about seeking the truth? It's way too sophisticated for a scumbag like McBride. The man was a pig. The subtlety of that message would have been lost on the goon." Raven laid a gloved hand to his coat sleeve and squeezed his arm. "How is Fiona these days? You haven't talked about her in a while."

"She's putting up a good front, but I know better. Fie's got a court date in three weeks." His eyes filled with pain as he reached for her hand. "With all her financial resources, I figured she would've contested the charges. But after she confessed, all she wanted was an opportunity to get her affairs in order before—" He shook his head. "I don't know how she's gonna do the prison time."

"And how are you doing, with her, I mean?"

He grimaced, then stared off toward the church.

"She still refuses to tell me who my biological father is. It's like she's protecting me from something. I just don't get it." Frustration tinged his voice. "She's admitted so much; why hold back on this?"

"Give her time, honey. She's got a lot on her mind. It took courage to admit what she'd done. And without any real evidence against her, she could've skated on the charges. Yet she chose to do the right thing. That took guts."

Christian looked deep in thought as he put his arm around her. He led her toward the church, walking at an unhurried pace.

"Yeah, that it did. But knowing what she did still hurts too much. Maybe I'm the one needing a little time."

She stepped in front of him, bracing her hands on his elbows. Standing before him, Raven gazed into his expressive eyes, cherishing the miracle of his existence.

"And I'm so glad you have it, that *we* have time. I thought for sure that I'd lost you. Now every minute we have together, it's a gift, Christian."

"You make it sound like I'm living on borrowed time." A lazy smile graced his handsome face for an instant, then faded. "My life had been balanced on a single point in time. I couldn't move forward and I couldn't go back and change it. I'd been held hostage to that one dark moment. But now, I feel more alive than I ever thought I could be. And I have you to thank for that."

He pulled her to his chest, wrapping his arms around her. The subtle fragrance of his cologne fused with the irresistible scent of his skin, filling her senses. He lowered his lips to hers. Raven shut her eyes, wanting to feel every nuance of his kiss. Slowly, his lips explored hers with an unrivaled sweetness. But his tender show of affection soon gave way to hungry need, matching her own. She belonged to Christian as surely as he carried the mark of her love.

Raven had never felt so loved.

Father Antonio walked briskly through the breezeway with only the soft rustle of his cassock and the sound of his footsteps to keep him company. Morning rays of sunlight filtered through the arched windows along the corridor, suspending dust particles in the warm light. A change of season from winter to spring always lifted his spirits.

Movement from the cemetery below caught his eye. He stopped for a look. Squinting into the light, the priest grinned at the sight of Christian and Raven in each other's arms. The moment of déjà vu gave him a feeling of contentment. Everything had come full circle.

He was pleased to see Christian standing in the light of day. The significance of this was not missed on him. Death no longer haunted his new friend. A woman's love reflected in his eyes now.

"You've awakened the voice of your heart, Christian. Perhaps in her eyes, you'll find the peace you've been looking for. I hope so, my friend."

Eager to share the significance of this day with his friends, he turned to leave. But the sight of two strangers compelled him to stop. An elegantly dressed man in a long, dark coat stood in the tree line along the wrought-iron fence. A stunning young Asian woman stood by his side. Her face looked familiar, but he couldn't quite place it. A feeling of dread slowly crept into his mind, tainting his optimism.

After his unfounded misgivings about Christian, he should have dismissed the silly notion about these strangers. But the man and woman held his attention with their peculiar behavior. Intent on only one thing, they stood along the periphery of the cemetery, with eyes fixed on Christian and Raven. They had no interest in any of the headstones, nor did they hold any tokens of remembrance in their hands. And their eyes had not wavered. They continued to stare at the lovers. He furrowed his brow, then breathed a sigh.

"Not very charitable, Antonio." He shook his head, chastising himself as he turned from the window. *Had he not learned a thing about standing in judgment of another human being?*

Jasmine's gaze drifted toward the man by her side. Staring beyond the shadows, Nicholas stood with his hands in the pocket of his overcoat. His jaw flinched in controlled anger.

"And how did you know he would be here today?" His voice lacked emotion, but Jasmine knew otherwise.

"The birth date on the tombstone for John Delacorte. I suspected Christian might pay his respects to the man who—" She cut herself short, unsure how he would take her presumption. "Today is the man's birthday."

"You know I am not pleased that you kept this little bit of information from me—the fact that I have a son."

Slowly, his eyes found hers. Normally, his expression disclosed nothing of his true nature, but today, he allowed an unbridled contempt to rise to the surface. His look of disdain shot through her like a deadly jolt of electricity.

She swallowed, fighting against the lump in her throat. In all the years she had known him, Jasmine had denied her affection and dependence on a man as ruthless as her Nicky. But perhaps deep in her mind she knew this day would come—when she could no longer deny the love she felt for him. Love meant vulnerability, a weakness she could not afford.

"I was concerned for you, actually," she postured.

Her bold move captured his complete focus.

"Oh?" His glare was tinged with curiosity. "How so?"

"Such sentimentality is beneath you, Nicky." She hoped her curt remark would be enough explanation. Jasmine stared straight ahead, avoiding his eyes.

Slowly, he raised his chin and returned his attention to the sight of Christian leaving the cemetery with the police detective, heading for the chapel.

"You may be right," he agreed. Jasmine ventured a look, catching the subtleties of his smile. But Nicky was not done. "I would never be suitable father material, but I resent the implication that Fiona concurred. She never allowed me to come to my own conclusions on the subject. And that, my dear, is inexcusable."

Jasmine's worst fear was realized; Nicholas would not let this go.

Calmly, she slid her arm into his. Ever the gentleman, he allowed the gesture. He escorted her back to his limousine parked on the street.

"What will you do, Nicky?" She found herself holding her breath.

"Revenge is an act of passion, Mantis." A haunting laughter rolled from his chest. "And as you know, I am a very passionate man."

Jasmine knew exactly what he meant.

The following is an excerpt from

NO ONE LIVES FOREVER

Available June 2008

Gripping his nine-millimeter Beretta, Nicholas Charboneau peered through the peephole of the penthouse suite, responding to a soft knock. The red-and-black uniforms of hotel personnel should not have given him any cause for alarm. And yet, the hair at the nape of his neck reacted to a rush of adrenaline. Two men stood by a rolling cart of white linen, covered with food platters and a bottle of Brazilian Merlot with a distinctive label.

Compliments of the house . . . or a Trojan Horse? The bottle of wine told the tale.

A lazy smile curved his lips. At his age, he relied more on wit and cunning, leaving the chest-thumping to younger men. He had no intention of answering the door, making himself vulnerable.

"No way," he scoffed, muttering under his breath. "Nice try, but never would've happened."

"Who is at the door?" The voice of his young bodyguard, Jasmine Lee, drew his attention. Towel drying her black hair, she stood near the wet bar dressed only in the white robe of the hotel. "Did you order room service, Nicky?"

He raised his hand and shook his head, silently mouthing the word, "No."

Her body tensed, dark eyes flared in alert.

The sound of shattered glass from across the room

broke his concentration. Jasmine darted from his sight, heading toward the noise.

As he rounded the foyer corner, three men dressed in black paramilitary uniforms burst into the room from the balcony, guns raised. Without hesitation, Jasmine tossed her towel toward the nearest man, a distraction. She punched a fist to his solar plexus, doubling the man over. To finish her attacker, she elbowed the back of his head, toppling him to the carpet. Now, she faced another, chin down and fists raised in defiance.

One down. White queen takes black knight's pawn, threatening the rook.

Nicholas's body reacted on pure instinct as chess maneuvers ran through his head, a practice in discipline and control. Adrenaline fueled his anger. He raced across the room, Beretta leveled. Unarmed, she wouldn't stand a chance if they started to shoot. He chose a spot to her far right, forcing the men to split their attack. A tactical maneuver.

Nicholas squared off with the man he'd coerced into turning his back on Jasmine. His assailant flinched, fear in his eyes as he faced the Beretta. Not wanting to start any gunplay, he backhanded the man across the jaw, knocking him down.

"Arrgh." Wincing in pain, the man writhed on the floor, holding his jaw. Blood dripped through his fingers.

Two down. White knight to king four, checkmate in two moves.

He smelled victory. With Jasmine at his side, he tilted his head and glared at the final man. His gun aimed dead center between the stranger's eyes. "Who sent you? And you better pray I believe you."

"*Mãos ao alto.*" A stern voice came from behind.

Clenching his jaw, Nicholas wavered for an instant. He gripped the Beretta, maintaining what little tactical leverage remained. But he had a feeling all that was about to change. Unwilling to lower his weapon until he knew for certain, he shifted his gaze to catch a reflection in the mirror behind the wet bar.

The seductive country of Brazil had beckoned Nicholas to its borders, the fertile ground of corruption awaiting his influence. Now, the reality of that summons had a face. The room service attendant narrowed his eyes in challenge, matching his stare in the mirror.

Despite the night air coming from the open doors to the balcony, he noticed the man had a bead of sweat at his temple. The droplet lingered on the brink of a sun-weathered crease, one of many lines marking his face.

Nicholas did not speak Portuguese. But since the uniformed man held a Kalashnikov assault rifle aimed at his head, understanding the native tongue became a moot point. The universal language of the AK–47 made his meaning perfectly clear. Nicholas lowered his weapon, allowing one of the men to take it, then raised his hands in compliance.

He had no option. Given the odds against a semiautomatic rifle in tight quarters, they were severely outnumbered. And one of the men held a gun on Jasmine. *Check. The black bishop had taken his queen out of play.* As in the game of chess, he would voluntarily topple his king to concede, not wanting to risk her life.

Checkmate. Game over. In an instant, everything changed.

Glancing toward Jasmine, Nicholas noticed her dark eyes communicating a clear message. He knew from experience she would fight if he gave her the slightest encouragement. The beautiful woman's unspoken connection to him made words unnecessary. With a subtle shake of his head, Nicholas gave his order.

You and I shall live to fight another day, my love. He would not challenge the inevitable. Whatever the purpose of these intruders, he would soon find out.

"I'm sure there's been some kind of mistake." He glared at the menacing faces of the five men. The two who entered through the front door via a passkey had wheeled in a large portable table. Aroma from the food wafted in the air, making his stomach grind. "The hotel knows never to send me wine made in Brazil."

Insulting the local wine was his calculated attempt to determine whether these men spoke English. The leader's expression remained deadly focused on him. The man held the rifle tight to his shoulder, clenching the weapon in a taut grip. With no reaction to his first offense, he ventured a second for good measure.

"I hope you realize"—Nicholas raised an eyebrow—"there will be no gratuity."

The head honcho had no sense of humor, nor did he apparently speak any English. Nicholas would not be dissuading him with his keen negotiating skills. Without the use of his quick wit, his best weapon would be gone from his arsenal, along with his gun. Nicholas churned his brain, considering his limited options.

The intruder spoke again.

"*Você quer tirar sarro de mim, porco americano? Respeite quem aponta a arma na sua cabeça. Você vai saber logo quem esta engarregado ou vai morrer.*"

The comment had been directed at him. With so few visits to this country, he had picked up very little Portuguese, but he did recognize the term *American Pig,* and the word *morrer* had something to do with death.

All things considered—this was not a good sign.

The man standing before him clearly had Indian blood coursing through his veins with his mocha brown skin, pitch-black hair, flat nose, and high, angular cheekbones. The hotel uniform did little to disguise his raw, primitive intensity. An ancient lineage reflected in his dark eyes. The man looked out of place in this urban setting.

So why was he here—and holding a rifle with deadly determination? Desperation forced men to take chances. Unlike the men in this room, Nicholas was not desperate. At least, not yet. Greed was a familiar vice in his area of the world, but Brazil had refined it to an art.

"I'm sure we can come to some . . . arrangement. If you would allow me to get my wallet, I'll reconsider your gratuity." Carefully, he gestured with his hands, making the universal sign of *payola*.

Encouraged, he watched the headman give a nod, directing one of his followers to act. Nicholas heard a sound behind his back. Maintaining eye contact with the leader, he resisted turning around until . . . He gasped when something pierced his neck, a sharp sting. Pain forced him to wince and shrug a shoulder.

Too late. The damage had been done.

"What have you—?"

Within seconds, the skin at his neck burned. Muscles in his legs tingled. His equilibrium challenged, he felt weightless, and the room swayed. Walls drained their color.

Gravity pulled at him, forcing him to submit to its will. Nicholas dropped to his knees, his arms falling limp by his sides. He no longer had the strength to lift them. From the corner of his eye, he caught a motion.

Jasmine fought for her freedom, a blur of white. Sounds of a struggle distorted in his head, as if filtered through mounds of cotton. Noise deadened to a dull throb—an erratic and faint pulse. A dark shadow eclipsed his line of sight and an arm flung in retaliation. He sensed Jasmine's loss. It spurred him to stay conscious. His concern for her overwhelmed his body's surrender to the drugs injected into his system—drugs flooding him with an unmerciful indifference.

Falling face-first to the carpet, he held one eye open, searching for her. The muffled sound of his breaths came in shallow pants, slowing with each passing second. With his eyesight failing, he sensed Jasmine's dark hair near his face. Her familiar scent penetrated the veil of his stupor. The coppery smell of blood tainted the memory.

Was she—?

The possibility of her lying dead by his side made his heart ache. Dulled outrage compounded his torment. If anything happened to his beloved and loyal bodyguard, the eternal damnation of hell would appear like a day at the spa for the bastard committing the deed.

He vowed this with his last moment of consciousness, before he drifted through a threshold to his own brand of hell.

The foreign woman lay at the feet of Mario Araujo. Blood trailed from her mouth. Drops of deep red marred the luxurious white robe. It had not been necessary.

But time was of the essence if his plan worked at all. With a quick gesture, he ordered his men to move into action.

"Esta na hora de sair da cidade com a nosso premio, camaradas. Vamos sequir conforme a plano. Rapido."

They hoisted the American's body, jamming him into the hidden compartment of the room service cart. Tomorrow, he'd feel the pain of his unceremonious departure from the city. For now, the drugs in his body made him a compliant guest.

As leader of his people, Mario had taken the job of scout. He would not order his men to undertake such a risky job if he wouldn't make the same sacrifice. After all, the idea of kidnapping for profit had been his from the start. So for two years, he worked at the menial job of bellhop under the name of Rodrigo Santo. He'd taken the name and identification of a young boy who had died years ago in his village.

The dead rarely took offense to fraud and were good at keeping secrets.

Mario studied his usual prey at the deluxe hotel and suffered the indignities of the *civilized* world. Normally, he resorted to luring his targets from the hotel by way of an official-looking document from the Interior Ministry of Brazil or a memo from the Prosecutor General's Office. And business had been fruitful.

Then, nearly a year ago, a man made contact with him over the phone.

He remembered the conversation as if it were yesterday. Mario had gotten the call at the hotel, during work hours. The voice on the phone specifically asked for him and threatened to expose his little enterprise. The man claimed to have proof of his involvement, even had times and dates and known accomplices. Mario had listened, sure the police would burst in and make an arrest that instant, hauling him from the hotel in handcuffs. But when that didn't happen, he regained his composure and assessed his situation in a different light.

"What do you want in return?" he had asked.

"In return?"

"Yes. You'd have me arrested if that were your purpose." Mario persisted, hoping he'd guessed right. "What do you want?"

After a long silence, the man began to laugh, an abrasive sound.

"You see? I knew I picked the right man. You and I are going to get along."

To this day, Mario hadn't told anyone of the secret alliance he had made, not wanting to put any of his people at risk. And with his new partner, Mario had no complaints. His enterprise thrived more than before.

So when the man had called about a rich American, Mario listened again. The kidnapping had been ordered and planned in haste, without Mario's usual care. His *associate* had told him the foreigner wouldn't stay long and would be far too cagey to be lured from the hotel, as the others had been. Normally, Mario's instincts would have cautioned him against moving forward with the plan, but two things swayed him.

First, everything had fallen into place without effort, making it too good to pass up. The rich foreigner had been delivered into his hands, yet another generous gift from his anonymous benefactor. But more importantly, his *associate* had shared vital information on the American and his purpose in this country. For Mario, this carried far more weight than any ransom.

Regardless of whether he trusted the man, Mario couldn't ignore the compelling intel. Although it would take time, he'd verify what he could, but shortly it wouldn't matter.

His mysterious comrade made a big show of this being their last venture together, even giving him a special encrypted phone to take with him, for emergency contact only. The phone would work where they were going. And the man had made it worth his while with the American, too. Mario would soon return a hero to his beloved home and provide well for his people. Nothing would make him more proud.

Far enough away from the lowland heat, his childhood village had been located at the base of the rocky outcrop known as the Chapada dos Guimarães. Now a distant memory. It had overlooked the flat plain of the Paraguay River and the marshlands of the Pantanal. Mario longed for the misty cool of those folding hills, still vivid in his dreams. Its pillared rock formations were dotted with the ancient caves of his ancestors. And only the hand of God could have graced such stunning waterfalls.

But too many tourists and the far reach of his own government left him torn apart from his memories. Years ago, he had relocated his tribe to a spot deeper in the jungle, far from civilization and its corrupt influence. Yet there were days, resentment swelled in his belly like a virulent cancer. He would compromise no more. After today, maybe he wouldn't have to.

"*Até o nosso próximo encontro,*" Mario said in a hushed tone. He watched three of his men escape from the balcony, leaving as they had come.

He'd depart with his accomplice, similarly dressed in a hotel uniform. They'd brazenly haul the American to a service elevator. Once in the parking garage, an inconspicuous van awaited the rendezvous with his men. Soon, he would be on his turf, among his own people.

But before Mario left the extravagant hotel suite, he knelt by the side of the Asian-looking woman who had fought so bravely.

"*Para o bem do seu amigo, você tem que obedecer as nossas ordens.*"

He tossed an envelope of the hotel stationery on her chest and lightly tapped the side of her cheek. By the time the beautiful woman warrior awoke, they'd be long gone. And she would know what to do.

He only hoped she also knew how to follow orders.

* * *

Searing light blinded her. Jasmine squinted and the effort sent electrified shards of glass into her brain. She felt the left side of her face throb, swollen and hot. Yet the night air in the room prickled her skin. The sensation made her aware of a metallic tang in her mouth. With a brush of her tongue, she found the source of the blood.

Unwilling to move, she lay perfectly still, waiting for the pain to subside. It only dulled and spread through her body like venom. Soon, her eyes concentrated on the elaborate chandelier overhead. Its iridescent prisms swirled rainbow luster . . . until the shimmer stopped dead center, coming into focus.

Oh, God . . . she had been so careless.

"Nicky? What—?"

As she raised up from the carpet, her head nearly exploded. She planted an elbow beneath her weight to keep from collapsing. Nausea churned her stomach. She held back a strand of dark hair and heaved, spitting up pale yellow foam. Her vision dotted with pinpoints of light from the exertion. Signs of a concussion.

Yet Jasmine knew she deserved far worse for her failure.

A dismal ache centered deep within her chest, spreading its heat to her face. She had failed Nicky, allowed him to be taken. For all she knew, he was already dead. She envisioned his handsome face, strangely passive in death. His violet-blue eyes glazed in milky white. The image would be forever branded in memory for her sin of failure.

Love blinded her, made her weak and neglectful. And Nicholas had paid the price. Splaying a hand against the carpet, she lifted her body to a sitting position. Her fingers touched a different texture.

An envelope.

The note inside the hotel envelope provided little information given the many questions looming in her mind.

The instructions were brief and to the point. She had ten days to comply. The ransom wired to a Swiss bank account listed in the note—or Nicky would be killed.

Yet with the instructions in English, it left her wondering who was in charge. Did the uniformed man know exactly what Nicky had said in English and only pretended his ignorance? Or had someone else pulled the strings? For these men to kidnap Nicholas Charboneau, ignorance would be the least of their problems. They obviously had no idea the extent of their offense.

Once more, she stared at the note. No organization laid claim to the abduction. And the ransom was far more money than she had access to. She held no special authority over Nicky's affairs. By outward appearance, he was her employer. End of story. Yet her heart could claim so much more. If only she had disclosed her feelings to him. Now she might never get the chance.

For the first time in her life, she felt completely powerless. That was inexcusable.

Her mind began to formulate a strategy. Because of Nicky's reputation, she was not sure how her demand for help would be received. She would direct the attention of the local law enforcement, overseeing the efforts herself. The nearest American Consulate would be contacted tonight. The US State Department tomorrow. Time was of the essence.

Surely she could garner support, even in this uncivilized corner of the world. And if money was required, she knew how to get it.

Christian Delacorte owed her a very big favor. Despite Nicky's orders to the contrary, perhaps it was time for Christian to learn about his rightful connection to Nicholas Charboneau.